The Old Man, His Dog & Their Longest Journey

The Old Man, His Dog & Their Longest Journey

IAIN MAITLAND

PEACOCK

First Published in the UK in 2023 by Peacock Paperbacks, an imprint of
Vellum Publishing
PEACOCK edition 2023

Published by Vellum Publishing,'
Turing House, 5 Archway, Manchester M15 5RL, UK

ISBN 978-1-915608-07-9 Paperback
ISBN 978-1-915608-09-3 Ebook

Cover design by www.team-design.co.uk

Cataloging-in-publication record for this book
is availiable from the British Library.

Printed and bound in the UK

www.vellumpublishing.co.uk

PRAISE FOR IAIN MAITLAND

THE OLD MAN, HIS DOG & THEIR LONGEST JOURNEY

'An utterly compelling and intriguing story of a man, in late middle age, confronting his personal demons by walking out of his home one day without word, warning or explanation. Very funny in some places, unspeakably poignant and sad in others. A philosophical and moving tale for our times.' Charlie Mortimer, *Dear Lupin.*

'A tender and thoughtful novel exploring the bond between man and man's best friend… sincere and evocative…' Michael Simkins, Actor & Author.

DEAR MICHAEL, LOVE DAD

'This is a wonderfully entertaining and moving book, with lessons for every parent.' *Daily Mail*

'Wonderful, moving, humorous… extremely poignant.' Charlie Mortimer, *Dear Lupin*

'… by turns acidly funny, exasperating and poignant, painting a moving portrait both of mental illness and of a father in denial. But paternal love… shines through.' Caroline Sanderson, *Sunday Express*

'A moving read – honest, funny and sad.' *Woman and Home*

OUT OF THE MADHOUSE

'I love this book; profoundly moving, beautifully written

and above all incredibly important. I read it in one sitting, often nodding, often crying and ultimately I was left feeling wonderfully hopeful.' James Withey, founder of The Recovery Letters project, editor of *The Recovery Letters*

'The Maitlands provide a brave, retrospective recount of a socially sensitive topic, where its strength lies in the powerful nature of the book's dual perspective. An honest and touching approach with advice grounded in invaluable, personal experience. *Out of The Madhouse* is an excellent exploration of the phenomenology of mental illness and its wider impact.' Joshua Fletcher, Psychotherapist & Author of *Anxiety: Panicking about Panic*

'*Out of the Madhouse* confronts the shocking bleakness of mental illness head on. Michael's diary of his battle to equip himself with both the tools and the will required to re-join something approaching mainstream existence is sobering… and Iain's tips and explanations are a big positive.' Charlie Mortimer, *Dear Lupin*

'This reflective book presents Michael's recovery from the multiple clinical effects emanating from abject low self-worth and loneliness. Whilst both traditional treatment as well as self-help and lifestyle strategies have helped him, the overriding ingredients that stand out in making positive change and enhancing resilience are the warmth of his connections, both family and friends, and the power of communication – spoken, written and art.' Dr Nihara Krause, Consultant Clinical Psychologist, Founder & CEO Stem4

SWEET WILLIAM

'A compassionate novel imbued with a deep knowledge of mental health issues… tense and insightful… a heart stopping thriller with a powerful denouement.' Paul Burke, *Nudge Books*

'Extremely well written and very frightening.' Barbara Nadel

'Tense... astounding... dark and chilling... and shockingly realistic. Gripping and immersive... an intelligently written thriller that deals with the intricacies of the human brain, mixed up with the emotional ties of the family.' Anne Cater, *Random Things Through my Letterbox*

'A dark, rocket-paced thriller that will give you plenty to think about.' Jon Wise, *Sunday Sport*

'A story of danger, delirium and devastation... an absolutely electrifying read that gripped me from start to finish.' Alix Long, *Delightful Book Reviews*

'An edgy and ultimately terrifying read... Iain Maitland pulls off and captures the whole thing through Raymond's flippant reasoning. It makes petrifying reading... this is an edge of your seat, nail-biting read that will haunt you way after you finish reading.' *Books From Dusk Till Dawn*

MR TODD'S RECKONING

'Splendidly creepy.' Geoffrey Wansell, *Daily Mail*

'Superbly crafted... spellbinding and gripping... brilliantly observed... and the setting of an ordinary two-bedroomed bungalow in suburbia is genius. Iain Maitland makes sublime use of the concept that none of us knows quite what goes on behind other people's closed front doors, so that the possibilities presented in *Mr Todd's Reckoning* are quite terrifying... sparkling, mesmerising... absolutely magnificent.' Linda Hill, *Linda's Book Blog*

'Just great. Truly scary, a fabulous dive into the mind of a classic, self-justifying psychopath… a fantastic book.' Barbara Nadel

'From page one, Iain Maitland hurls you through the secret underground tunnels of an insane mind bent on destruction. Cleverly conceived, what begins as quite touching drives relentlessly onwards into furious criminality. *Mr Todd's Reckoning* is phenomenally dark and utterly compelling.' Chris Dolan

'The characters are brought to life so vividly I could see and smell them… genius… you can't stop turning the pages… a jaw dropping, atmospheric, creepy and uncomfortable read.' Tracy Fenton, *Compulsive Readers Blog*

'Chilling… compelling… indicates how truly terrifying the human mind can be when it develops a warped perspective… extremely thought provoking and shocking.' *Jera's Jamboree blog*

'A sinister novel with a build that [is] totally unexpected… a quite unique thriller.' *A Knight's Reads blog*

'The kind of creepy disturbing read that stays with you… it's dark psychological crime fiction with no ground rules or boundaries. Whatever the reader expects to happen, well don't get too comfortable because it probably won't happen the way you expect it to.' *Cheryl MM's Book Blog*

'This novel grabbed me from the very first page and refused to let go… wonderfully quirky yet frightening… the atmosphere that Iain Maitland creates with his writing is incredible… he is a master of suspense.' *Bookaholic Confessions*

'Pure creepy gold… a superb storyline, brilliant characters and subplots that tweaked my adrenaline… this is a stunner!' *Books From Dusk till Dawn*

THE SCRIBBLER

'Very few authors could sustain the tension of a final scene over one hundred and eighteen pages. Maitland, however, has the reader bound up as tightly as a hostage, and he never loses that grip… this is an outstandingly good book.' Rosemary Kaye

'A brilliant read [on] LGBTQ+ crimes that traditionally were underreported. Thankfully, times have changed.' Neil Boast MBE, former LGBT Liaison Officer, Suffolk Constabulary, and former head of task force on sexual exploitation and trafficking

'One seriously weird killer and an engaging cop-partnership dynamic. Exciting.' *Sunday Times*

'Brilliantly creepy.' *Scots Magazine*

'The cavalier approach to the investigation brings tragedy and further killings in its wake – an interesting twist.' Jon Morgan, *Shots Magazine*

'*The Scribbler* is a slow burning, tense and downright creepy thriller. Likeable, engaging protagonists and an unusual villain… shocking, providing more than one OMG moment.' *Suze Reviews*

'I feel like I have just made one of the greatest discoveries on earth… What a mind this author has… a fantastic… dark, gripping, creepy and tense read… another book to add to my favourites of the year.' *A Lover of Books Blog*

'*The Scribbler* is well-paced, engaging and punctuated by… unexpected humour, leading to a compelling and incredibly satisfying crime read. Watch out for that ending… highly recommended.' Raven Crime Reads

'Intriguing… it's a great read.' *Cheryl MM*

'A creepy read with an explosive ending, I was engrossed from start to finish.' *Jera's Jamboree*

'Iain Maitland has a delicious and dark style of writing, he tricks you into thinking you are just meandering along nicely… then he jumps out behind you and knocks you sideways as he delivers some dark and deadly punches, then lets you breathe before he does it all over again.' *Chapter In My Life Blog*

THE GIRL DOWNSTAIRS

'*The Girl Downstairs* is a very well written book, so well that I've finished it and am wanting more. I need more! This is one of those books that sits with you for a while after you read it. It definitely plays with your head! Excellent read! *The Book Booth*

'I did enjoy this book. I really wasn't expecting that. Read in one sitting. Brilliant.' *Sue Loves to Read*

THE WICKHAM MARKET MURDER

'A well-crafted murder mystery, weaving a family saga with engaging protagonists and a clever twist.' Thomas Waugh

'*The Wickham Market Murder* was an entertaining novella.' *Loopyloulaura*

'If you like TV shows such as *Murdoch Mysteries, Midsomer Murders* or *Father Brown* this book is a perfect one to read. The characters and writing are described well, and it feels very easy to read, to get into and follow.' Steph Louise On Instagram

'I really enjoyed the plot and the pace; it was easy to follow, and

I was fascinated to see how they might solve this case without clear cut evidence. What was even better is that the story really highlighted justice, or rather injustice at times, and how difficult it would be to solve some cases.' *David's Book Blurb*

'... the dramatic climax. It's a shocker. I really enjoyed this book and hope to see our intrepid duo again soon.' *Lynda's Book Reviews and News*

'I won't say too much, but it's engaging and gripping right to the end. The pacing is perfectly matched to the story, it speeds headlong like a high-speed train from the first page until you are closing the last.' *Chicks, Rogues and Scandals*

AS A SPEAKER AT LITERARY & MENTAL HEALTH EVENTS

'Breathtakingly magnificent... his deadpan delivery of a dry wit that will leave you with tears streaming down your face but at the same time his own life experiences shine through his narrative making it totally unique, relevant and thought provoking!' *Chapter In My Life*

'Marx Brothers on speed.' Douglas Skelton, Author.

'So much fun, and a bit bonkers.' Bloody Scotland Attendee

'Iain Maitland... a hilarious and, frankly, show stealing turn in a panel at last year's Bloody Scotland book festival.' *Suze Reviews*

'Brilliant and heartfelt talk.' Ipswich Samaritans AGM Attendee

'A brilliant speaker... Iain is open and frank and his moving account endears him to his audience straightaway.' Stem4

For Jonah and Halley - I love you this much… and more.

PART ONE:
HOME SWEET HOME

1
THE CUPCAKES

The thing Ian loved most about the house, the garden really, was the magnolia tree. Kate had planted it when they bought the house – their home – 30 or so years ago. By now, it had grown and bloomed and spread until it created a shady corner that was just perfect for a picnic on a Sunday afternoon in these last few weeks of spring.

It was more than just an al fresco late lunch for the two of them and Bernard the Jack Russell though. It was a family get -together over afternoon tea. Their three children, Alex, Beth and Joe, and their respective partners, Hannah, Glenn and Yasmin, came along at the same time, almost as though they had rehearsed their arrival. They each carried something to put on the table or the blankets – including a six-pack of beer, a bottle of fizzy pink drink and some gaily coloured serviettes featuring dancing dogs in ballet costumes.

As they fussed about with trays of sandwiches and cakes and drinks, neither Ian nor Kate thought there was anything out of the ordinary, anything particularly special, about this afternoon. The three children and their partners all lived locally, and they got together at The Cape, as it was known, on a Sunday afternoon or evening every month or so. It was just a chance to catch up, to joke and laugh and to listen to some of Ian's tall tales; same as it ever was. A happy day.

They did not notice Hannah, Alex's partner, sitting quietly with a Tupperware container of cupcakes on her lap, casting anxious looks at Alex who sat there beaming at everyone. They did not see Beth, their only daughter, checking her phone and repeatedly filming everyone. "She's always fiddling with her phone," they'd have joked. They only really noticed Joe pulling faces at his partner, Yasmin, when he thought no one was looking.

"Your face will get stuck like that if the wind changes," Kate said.

"It changed years ago, that's why he looks like that," Ian added.

Joe and Yasmin laughed.

Their family home, where they'd raised their three children, overlooked the sea at Felixstowe in Suffolk, some 70 miles north-east of London. Felixstowe Ferry, to be precise, was the hamlet that time forgot. It was at the far end of the bay, beyond the woods and the golf course, and away from the pier and the amusement arcades. Further round, there were the relentlessly busy docks.

The Ferry was an olde-time world. A pub, a couple of cafes, a ferry where children and adults alike fished for crabs, and a boat service to take you across to Bawdsey Manor and back at weekends and weekdays in summer, too. That was about it, other than a small car park, always overflowing at weekends and through the summer holidays, a block of toilets, a row of bins and, a little further along, a long line of boats down by the sailing club where Ian walked Bernard out to the old 1800s Martello Tower and back, mornings and evenings.

There were 13 houses in all, from a higgledy-piggledy row of wonky terraced ones around the car park to half a dozen detached places with lawns running down towards the sea. The Cape was one of these and it was a comfortable old home, despite the endless lashings of wind and rain from the North Sea throughout the never-ending winters.

The Cape – its look, its location – had always given people the impression that Ian and Kate were rich and successful. As a recently-made-redundant marketing manager and a specialist diabetes nurse respectively, they were anything but. There were times when it had all been such a struggle. They had bought

4

the house when it was worn-down and sold at just above the reserve price at auction in nearby Ipswich. They had paid the deposit with their savings and an inheritance from Ian's nan and grandpa, and the rest with a mortgage they could barely afford.

"Ready?" Beth asked Hannah.

"As I'll ever be," Hannah replied.

Alex and Glenn exchanged glances. Joe and Yasmin did too.

"Sit down, Mum... Dad," Alex said, waving towards two deckchairs that had been left empty for them.

Sitting in the semi-circle − deckchairs, rocking chairs, even two chairs carried out from the kitchen − the eight of them faced outwards, looking down the long slope of the garden towards the sea. Fishing boats drifted in and out. Bernard sat up, resting his head on Ian's lap.

"Now," Alex said quietly to Hannah.

Beth lifted her mobile phone and started filming.

Hannah stepped forward and handed Ian a clear Tupperware container with a blue lid. Ian could see there were cupcakes inside. He did not notice Beth filming him on her phone. Nor did he see everyone was now watching him, including Kate, who had a puzzled look on her face.

Ian pulled back the lid and saw six cupcakes sitting there, two-by-two-by-two. On each cake was a blob of light blue icing with cut-up pieces of strawberry-red liquorice laces on top of that.

From left to right, top to bottom, he could read what it said. *B A B Y ! !* It took him a moment or two to realise what this meant, before he angled the container towards Kate so she could see. He looked up at Hannah and asked the question.

"Are you pregnant?"

"Yes," she replied.

And that was how it all began.

***

Later that evening, Ian sat up in bed, put his Agatha Christie novel on the side cabinet and his reading glasses on top of that. He folded his arms across his chest.

He then looked over at Kate sitting at the dressing table, doing all the things she did before coming to bed. Her beauty regime, as she called it.

He ran through them in his head, the things she did, and could remember each and every one of them in the correct order. Eleven in all. They always seemed to take longer each night.

"I thought that went well," Ian said, clearing his throat. "The announcement."

Kate turned and looked solemnly at him over the top of her glasses. Like a judge might gaze at a prisoner in the dock. She made a huffing noise at the back of her throat. She then turned back to the dressing table as though searching for a black cap before passing sentence.

"I think it was okay," Ian added, "I mean, nobody said anything... you know."

Kate looked at him through the reflection in the dressing table mirror. Just sat there brushing her hair, first one side, then the other, and then flicking at imaginary strands of hair across her fringe.

"I mean, obviously, I was excited... you know, first grandchild... and... and," he searched for the phrase he wanted, "the surprise of it, really... they've not been together long... and she's quite young. And a bit... um, feisty. I thought Beth would be first. I wanted her to be."

Kate took off her glasses and started rubbing cream into her face, first her forehead, then her cheeks and, pursing her lips, just below her nose and above her chin. Ian did not add anything about Beth having a baby, knowing she and Glenn had been trying for some time without success. The word IVF had been mentioned lately. It was all rather... What was the right word? Fraught. And uncertain. Beth was a nuclear bomb

6

ready to explode at any moment at the best of times.

"The hugging thing with Hannah was just…" Ian hesitated, "… in the moment really… and I thought she'd turn her head so I would kiss her on the cheek… maybe I was just too fast."

Kate continued putting cream on her face and her neck. This was a new part of the routine after Ian had told her she had lines around her neck. He wished he hadn't said anything. "Goosy-Goosy neck," he'd said, as a joke. He thought it was, anyway. She had not laughed.

"And telling her about your pregnancies and births… and… everything was just to, I don't know, help to prepare her for it… so she knows what to expect… all of it."

Ian thought for a moment or two as he watched Kate do the tying-up thing with her hair that pinned it down for when she got into bed and went to sleep.

"And, obviously, I mean, the rest of it… I just got a bit carried away… because of the thrill of it." He paused, trying to remember all that he had said and done and how everybody had reacted and what they had said in response. He thought – no, he was sure – that everyone was happy. Happy enough. "I'm not really going to deliver the baby am I… and use a Swiss Army Knife to… whatever."

Kate finished what she was doing and rubbed cream from a different, small and expensive-looking, pot into her hands and onto her elbows. Then she reached across and pressed a button on her phone and another.

"Beth put the video on the WhatsApp page," Kate said. "Just for the family. Thank goodness."

Ian listened to the shouts and yelps, mostly from himself, getting ever higher and louder.

When he heard himself singing "Congratulations" tunelessly, he asked Kate to turn it off.

She did.

He turned over.

And was asleep by the time she got into bed.

The next morning, after Kate had headed off to work at Ipswich Hospital, and before he went for his morning walk with Bernard, Ian stood naked in front of the full-length mirror in the corner of the bedroom. He looked himself up and down. He had seen better days, he thought.

"Vintage…" Kate would say if he asked her. Then add "Skoda". Not that she ever looked any more.

He sighed. He wasn't much to look at. Never had been really. And he was all out of proportion with himself.

"Salt and pepper," he said aloud, looking at his hair.

"Grey-haired. Well-seasoned," he added. "Blue eyes, watery. One slightly off-centre. Firm-enough chin. Sagging jawline. White…"

He thought for a moment. About the word he wanted to use. Searched for it. But it was not there.

"Big head. No neck. Frog-faced."

He had seen film of himself a while back. Up close. On Alex's mobile phone. Alex had come round unexpectedly to borrow the lawnmower and had crept up on Ian whilst he was snoozing in an armchair. He had filmed Ian jumping and shouting in surprise.

"Nuts!" Ian had shouted. He did not know why. He could not believe how he looked when he was asleep.

Like a toad. All big head sat heavily straight onto shoulders. He held his mouth in a funny way too, as though he was pursing his lips permanently. It took some getting used to.

"Broad-shouldered."

He remembered that as a child he could not pronounce "soldiers", and instead it came out as "shoulders". He could not pronounce "assume" properly either. Still couldn't. It would always come out as "ashume". As he got older, he learned to avoid the word or, if he needed to use it, he would focus on the "ass" syllable and follow it with "ume". It never sounded quite right.

"Sagging chest."

He did not know the correct words to describe his fatty chest. "Moobs" came to mind, but he was not sure if that was a real word or just slang. He had first noticed them when he was a teenager. They were just like his father's. He always thought he would exercise them away as he got older, but he never had. They just hung there, two big hairy saggy things.

"Barrel stomach."

There was no getting away from it. He was overweight and most of it seemed to be round his middle. He did not know how he had let himself get like this. "In the shallow waters of diabetes," his GP had said after last year's annual blood tests. A little man with a bow tie. Nondescript without his affectation of clothing. Kind though. He had gentle eyes. Ian did not tell Kate what the GP had said, only that all was well. "Okay?" she'd queried briskly. "Okay," he replied emphatically and gave a thumbs-up. And that should have been that for another year.

"Small. Shrivelled."

He searched for his third word. All he could think of was "hamster" or maybe the other one. Not guinea pig, that was too big. The mouse thing. Not a field mouse, a thing mouse. He paused, no, he could not think of that either. Tit mouse was all that came to him, but he knew it wasn't that but something like it.

"Strong arms. Long legs. Feet."

His arms and legs were taut enough because of his morning swims. And they were in proportion. It was his body, his great big, back-to-front, S-shaped body, that was out of proportion. Always had been. It bothered him when he was younger, not so much now though. If at all. He just looked at himself with lugubrious eyes.

He did not know how to describe his feet. They were just feet. He used to be a size nine but, more recently, he had been wearing 10s. He thought the weight of his body must have flattened them out over the years.

He turned slightly to the side and glanced at himself from behind. He sighed again. "Not a pretty sight," Kate would have said in years gone by, and only half in jest. He had never been good at knowing when she was joking or not, even after 30 or more years together.

"Baldy head."

He had always been rather proud of his full head of hair. He had been known for it around town when he was younger. People who met Kate and got into conversation would sometimes say, "Oh, you're married to the man with the hair." It was big and bouffant and long at the back. It was so long that he could put his hand up and grab a thick handful of it. A mullet. That was what it was called, and he stuck with it long after it had gone out of fashion.

On reflection, he thought, most probably, that he looked rather silly, but no one had ever said. Into his 30s and 40s, he had it cut shorter, more in keeping with an older man. In the past few years, it had thinned at the crown, and this seemed to get wider and further, back and front, every time he looked. There was no disguising it now. It had spread right through and in sunlight you could see his whole scalp quite clearly.

"Round-shouldered."

From this angle, he was distinctly round-shouldered. A woman at a party once told him that, and he had laughed and done a fleeting impression of the hunchback of Notre Dame. She had laughed politely enough. Now, he thought, she may have been serious.

"Bottom. Mega Bottom."

His backside was huge. He had always been conscious of it. At college, he was teased about it by a group of girls. And there was a boy he did not like, Wellman, who had come up through the school with him into sixth form and called him "Jumbo" all the time. He could not help but think that this was a reference

10

to his over-sized bottom. Throughout all these years, he had never left the house without a loose hanging shirt or a jacket to cover it. It was always there, a constant source of possible embarrassment to him. He then looked at his shoulder. It was still there.

"Big. White. Lump."

"Hard to the touch. Moves slightly."

"Frightening. It scares me."

And he remembered what he read on Google and said it out loud, word-for-word. "A shoulder lump might indicate soft tissue sarcoma. This is a rare cancer."

He paused, dipping his head, pleased that the words had all come out right. Just his bloody luck though. Having a rare cancer like this.

"I am Ian... my mother chose this name. Charles... my maternal grandfather's family name. Wilkerson... my father's name. I am 54 years old. And I am going to be a grandpa," he said, looking into his eyes in the mirror. And, quietly, "I am losing my mind."

2
THE FATHER'S DAY
PRESENTS

A few weeks later, Alex and Hannah dropped by on Father's Day morning. Just the two of them, each holding a carefully wrapped present for Ian. Alex had a card too. They stood there, both smiling widely on the doorstep.

As he led them through to the orangery where he and Kate were reading the Sunday papers, Ian couldn't help but notice that neither of the presents were book- or DVD-shaped. And they weren't chocolates, jelly beans or coconut ice, otherwise Bernard, trotting along behind, would have been sniffing at the packages.

They'd obviously gone off the list that Ian gave to Kate to circulate to the children every year. Had gone rogue as it were. He hoped these would be presents he liked. He always struggled to feign pleasure, let alone delight, when receiving presents that he did not really want. A tie with a funny motif, socks, any types of socks, and a fountain pen, so many fountain pens over the years.

"Happy Father's Day," Alex said, kissing Kate and sliding into one of the battered old armchairs opposite Ian.

Hannah wasn't the kissing and hugging sort, as Ian now realised, but she smiled and said something cheery enough before sitting in the other armchair next to Alex.

"Are you showing yet?" Kate asked as Hannah shook her head and smoothed her top across her stomach as if to say, "Look, there, nothing."

"Work okay?" Ian asked Alex as he sat down next but one

to Kate on the sofa, with Bernard jumping up and sitting in between, his head resting on Ian's thigh.

"Yeah, got a full week coming up." Alex was a tattooist in the town, had been since he'd put his issues behind him. Tattooed from neck to feet, his aggressive appearance was at odds with his gentle nature.

Neither Ian nor Kate were keen on Alex's tattoos, a mix of ghoulish faces and Chinese letterings for the most part, and they avoided saying anything when a new one appeared creeping up his neck towards his face. But, as they snapped back whenever someone they knew made a discouraging remark, "We'd rather have a happy tattooed son than an unhappy dead one." And that, at least for those who knew Alex's history, and that of the family's, was enough to stop them in their tracks.

There was a moment's silence. Not an uncomfortable one.

More a recalibration of why they were there.

Kate offered drinks, hot or cold, some toast maybe, if they had not eaten breakfast.

Alex and Hannah declined. They were going somewhere or other for the day. Over to Cambridge to tell uncles, aunts and cousins of Hannah's about the pregnancy, then back for an evening meal with Hannah's parents. They just wanted to say hello and drop off the Father's Day presents.

And so they all came to be sitting round the little coffee table piled high with cartons of orange and apple juice and glasses and cups and plates and half-eaten pieces of toast. And the two presents. And the card.

Ian always liked giving presents. He liked receiving them too, but always struggled to put on the right face, that flash of delight, whenever he opened them. Kate had told him many times over the years that when he smiled he looked like Norman Bates in *Psycho*. He always replied that she looked like Norman Bates' mother (and, although that wasn't 100 per cent accurate, there was a look about her).

Anyhow, as a rule, Ian tried not to smile when opening

presents but just attempted to look jovial. It was harder when he knew he was being watched. Kate and Alex realised this and smiled vaguely in his direction as he opened presents.

Hannah did not and, as Ian glanced at her, he could see she was looking at him. Not in an unkind way, just more closely than he would like. Perhaps she was expecting something close to a whoop of delight.

Ian opened the envelope. Usually, Alex would give Ian a funny card, most often with a picture of a gorilla on it. And he'd put *Hey Old Man!* and then write something bright and breezy inside, words that would look insulting to anyone else.

This card was different. *To My Grandpa to Be* was printed on the front in delicate gold lettering, against a white background. A little red heart sat below this and, in smaller letters still, *Happy Father's Day, Lots of Love, Pudding xxx.*

Hannah's influence, thought Ian. The sentiment. The emotion of it. An art degree and now a trainee primary school teacher, following in Beth's footsteps funnily enough. An arts and crafts girl – or woman, he should say these days, correcting himself.

"We're calling the baby Pudding for now," said Hannah.

Ian stopped and smiled and laid it carefully on the table, unopened.

"Very nice," he replied. "Thank you."

Hannah looked flustered and was about to say something before Alex put his hand on her arm. The vaguest shake of his head.

Ian opened a present. A small, rectangular piece of wood with *Happy Father's Day Grandpa* across the top in fancy lettering. Homemade. A clumsily written but sweet poem by Hannah, Ian assumed, below.

I wanted to tell you Grandpa, that I am doing swell
Here in Mummy's tummy,
Feeling safe and warm and well.

15

I'm looking forward to meeting you, so gentle, kind and mild,
You're my lovely grandpa
And I'm your first grandchild.

Love,
Pudding
x

Ian only glanced over the words. He knew he could not read the poem properly. Absorb it. Not now anyway. The emotion of it would get to him.

"That's lovely," he said, putting the present next to the card, "thank you."

He could see and feel the tension from Hannah, sitting upright, her hand moving across her tummy. He knew that he needed to say a few words, to show something, some sense of how he felt. To claw back the moment.

Ian picked up the other present and ran his hands over it. A similar size to the first present but thicker. "Mmm," he said out loud, two or three times, as jovially as he could. He did not look across at Hannah, keeping his head down, focusing on the present. He hoped it would be something less sentimental. Not as emotional. Nor heartfelt.

It wasn't. It was a blue-and-pink booklet headed *Letters to My Grandchild* with *Write Now. Read Later. Treasure Forever* beneath. Letters he should write to Pudding. With words of warmth and advice and love. He knew he needed to look through it, show interest and delight. And so he did as best he could, looking at headings such as *The Best Advice I Was Ever Given Was…* and *My Wishes For You Are….* He knew as he looked at them that he could not read them out loud. His voice would betray him.

He realised, as he put the booklet down on the table next to the card and the wooden sign, that he had done something terribly wrong. That he had upset Hannah and possibly even Alex.

And so it proved. Within a few minutes, after some small talk between Hannah and Kate, they were up and going. Far too soon. Out the front door with barely a word to him. Alex simply pulled a "Dad, eh?" face and patted him on the shoulder.

As Kate shut the door behind them, she turned and shook her head at Ian, then headed off to her study without a backwards glance.

It was going to be one of those Sundays, Ian thought. The other children coming and going, dropping off presents and then heading on to see the other fathers, Glenn's and Yasmin's. Kate doing her own thing. Him watching sports on the television. A quiet evening meal with little more than the bare bones of a conversation.

He'd have liked a proper family get-together what with it being Father's Day and all, but they had had that last year and it was the turn of other fathers this year. So that was that. A long and lonely week stretched out ahead with him filling his days with mundane odd jobs.

***

"My name is…"

Ian spoke to himself in a clear, strong voice as he sat on the edge of the bed the next morning. He was fully dressed and ready to tackle the *To Do* list on the fridge in the kitchen. First, he had something else he needed to do. He did it every week or so. Had done for the past couple of months.

"Ian. Charles. Wilkerson. Not Wilkinson. Or Wilkins. Tweedy. Tights. Or Wilkes. Wilkerson. W. I. L. K. E. R. S. O. N."

He took a black fine-line pen and an A5-sized notepad from the drawer of his bedside cabinet. He then stopped for a moment before writing in small and neat block capitals on a page in the notepad.

IAN CHARLES WILKERSON

"I am 54 years old. I have lived in Felixstowe all my life. I worked for the council as a… in marketing… for… doesn't matter how long… far too long… and have just been made redundant. Let go. Dumped." He paused and thought for a moment, then spoke again. His voice steady.

"This is a fresh start for me. I am going to be a happy man again. I am going to put everything right at last." He stopped and wrote another name just below his on the card.

KATHERINE JAYNE WILKERSON

"My wife… Katherine Jayne Wilkerson. Kate. Born Towner." He paused, then added, as if for himself, "born 18th November…"

He could not remember the year. No, that had gone. He'd come back to it.

"Works for the NHS. A… specialist diabetes nurse." He gabbled the last few words and nodded to himself before carrying on.

ALEXANDER JAMES WILKERSON

"Alex James Wilkerson. 28. A tattooist. Lives with his partner Hannah. Brightwell Close. They are expecting their first child." He paused for another moment. "Pudding… they are going to call it Pudding until the baby is born."

He then went on, after a moment's hesitation, "Anxiety. Depression. Drugs. Hospital. The Priory. Alex has turned his life around. Today he is happy, and I am proud of him. I could not be prouder." Perhaps I should tell him, Ian thought. I never have. Nor told him I loved him, come to think of it.

Ian got up and wandered to the bedroom window, looking out towards the sea. Another sunny day ahead. A day with nothing much to do.

He sat down on a stool and thought how miserable all this was. The writing. The speaking out loud. But he needed to do it. To remember. To have it clear in his head. To check and test himself regularly. That he was still where he was. At the top of a long and downward slope. Yet he knew, in a way, that this was holding him back. The repetition. The endless going over of it. The never letting go.

But he could not seem to help himself. In a way, it reassured him. Soothed him to know that he could still remember everything just fine, more or less. Odd bits and bobs he missed. He tried to add new things to remember and say out loud each time.

He looked at the card that Kate kept on her dressing table – a single rose on the outside and small, spidery handwriting on the inside. He did not know who had written it. One of Kate's friends, he supposed. He did not recognise the handwriting.

On the inside left page, in that spidery hand, was the sentence. *Turn your face to the wall and you will die.* On the right, *Turn your face toward the sun and the shadows will fall behind you.*

He had always thought of himself as a happy man. It was true that the past years had not been so good. It – the tragedy – had knocked him sideways, and he had turned his face to the wall. They all had in their different ways. But it was not all doom and gloom. There would be happy times ahead. With Pudding. He paused and went on writing.

BETHANY LOUISE WILKERSON

"Our Bloody Big Beth," Ian said. "Scholarship to Ipswich School. 2:1 at Durham. Psychology." He laughed to himself and thought, "What we could have done with a psychologist these past years."

"Trainee teacher of the year…" He forgot the year. He was never very good with dates and things, even before all of this…

brain stuff. Nor could he remember who awarded it. East Anglian something or other. Hannah was now on the same course a few years behind.

"Lives with Glenn, her fiancée, six doors down to Alex and Hannah." He stopped, his mind a swirl of emotions. "Lost... pregnancies. Can't have babies. Must be hell," he thought, and gathered his breath. Wrote again in the notepad.

JOEL CHARLES WILKERSON

"Joe," Ian laughed. "Three weeks on a degree course until he discovered he'd been attending lectures on another course on the wrong campus. Two weeks on an electricians' course. Departed after the fire. One week as a pizza delivery driver... left after he crashed the car.

"Warehouseman at docks. Lives with Yasmin. She works in a care home. They rent a bedsit in Ranelagh Road... a bit..." He struggled for the word. "Grungy."

A happy couple, he thought. Joe and Yasmin. They looked a bit odd together. He was big and gawky and gormless. She was short and elegant and busy-busy-busy. Yet, somehow, they seemed a good fit. And she made cakes, lots and lots of cakes, which she brought round most times they visited. They always tasted a bit odd. Too spicy for Ian, anyway.

BERNARD ALOYSIUS WILKERSON

"Bernard. Our Jack Russell.

"Got him from the Blue Cross 11 years ago... the 15th of April. His birthday.

"Twelve years old. My best friend."

"There," he said to himself. "I remember everything."

He then paused for the longest time and wrote one more name and three more sentences without speaking.

ADAM JOHN WILKERSON

Our darling boy.
Died.
Four years old.

***

Ian looked at the week's *To Do* list, stuck behind the New York magnet on the fridge. Wherever he and Kate holidayed, they always brought back a fridge magnet and put it on the side of the big old Smeg. There wasn't a lot of space left these days. Not that it mattered, they'd not been on holiday for such a while now.

He ran his fingers over each magnet, left to right, top to bottom – Calpe, Paris, Maine, Milan, Tarragona and so on – and tried to remember something memorable that had happened on each holiday. Many of the holidays blurred into one another. They were happy, relaxed times. Up until the last one.

Ian went down on his knees. The magnets at the bottom of the fridge were from Britain. Caravan sites and lodges, usually. Ian stopped at the last one, Hunstanton, up on the Norfolk coast. Put his finger on it. The final family holiday. The one they never talked about.

He got up. Looked down at the *To Do* list. *Mow the lawn* was at the top.

Made his way outdoors to the garage. Got the lawnmower out. The grass was still damp, but he had nothing better to do.

Started mowing the lawn. To and fro. Back and forth. He liked the rhythm of it, which he found relaxing, soothing even.

From the moment they'd arrived, the six of them had loved Hunstanton. Ian, Kate, and the four children. An old 1950s seaside resort with a pier and a prom and a few shops and amusements. But not too many. The kind of place you could just wander about without being disturbed by gangs of teenagers, and motorbikes, and endless cars racing round and round.

They had rented a holiday home out at Old Hunstanton. Spent mornings on the beach there below the cliffs, exploring, swimming and walking along the sandy shore to the main part of town. They'd then buy sandwiches and sausage rolls and cakes and cans of drinks before sitting down on the green looking out to sea.

They were only there for the week. Saturday to Saturday. It was warm and sunny every day and they did not really do anything much, just mooching and meandering about in their own sweet ways. They were in the moment. Such a happy family. Up until the Friday afternoon.

This was his life from now on, thought Ian, as he emptied the cut grass into the big green bin. He hated how the still-dewy cuttings stuck to his hands and clothes and just about everything.

Household chores. Doing the garden over and over. Getting milk and bread and other bits and pieces from the local supermarket. Watching TV and Dad's Army and other old-time DVDs to pass the time. An endless loop. A dreary, next-to-nothing of a life.

Finished at 54. Kate was still working away, probably would be for another decade. The children were all busy with their own lives. It was just him and Bernard at home all day.

The Friday afternoon of that holiday, after they'd sat on the green for simply ages, the children disappearing and returning time and again, they made their way back along the clifftop towards Old Hunstanton. Beth and Joe in front. Alex next, holding Adam's hand. Ian and Kate following behind. Holding hands too. They did that in those days.

They stopped at the café on the clifftop at Old Hunstanton for ice creams, the six of them taking an age to choose what they wanted. Alex and Joe swapped with each other as they all made their way back to the beach for one last paddle.

It was in the dunes that they lost Adam. Playing hide and seek on their way for a paddle, each assuming one of the others had him. They had come out the other side, looking at one another, all suddenly saying "Adam!" at the same moment. It was in the sea that they found him, face down, too late.

Ian sighed as he finished mowing the lawn. The big green bin was now more than half filled with grass cuttings.

He put the bin back in its place by the side of the garage, and packed the lawnmower away.

Then he looked around the garage to see if anything was out of place, or needed tidying. But there was nothing. Everything was just so. Same as last week. And again next. The same every bloody week.

Alex blamed himself for what happened with Adam. Looking back, that was the start of his troubles. He went off to university that autumn seeming, if not exactly happy, at least all right. With hindsight, he was anything but. They were all distracted and looking the other way. Until, some time later, they got the late-night text from his girlfriend at the time. He was on his way to hospital in an ambulance.

Ian could not remember when he had last held hands with Kate. They held hands at Adam's funeral, he remembered that. Was sure of it. But after? What they were like together then compared to now seemed a million miles apart. But they had gone from one to the other so slowly, almost imperceptibly, that it did not seem possible. He wondered if it could ever be turned around.

Adam was always there. An unspoken presence. Everyone seemed to tense whenever his name came up in conversation. They stopped talking about him not long after the funeral. Until it became hard to mention Adam naturally in conversation. And then almost impossible unless his name had to be said. Ian did not know how things could have got this bad.

Ian whistled to Bernard. He'd walk him along to the Martello

Tower and back now. Something to do.

He thought about the baby, and wondered whether Alex and Hannah might name him Adam. And whether that was a good idea or not.

Ian hoped that the baby might somehow save him. And his marriage. And the whole family for that matter.

3
THE GENDER REVEAL

Hannah's family home was a self-built house on a large, set-back plot of land near the Docks. Kevin, the father, worked there hitting things with a hammer. Deborah, "Debs", the mother, was a dinner lady at a primary school near Ipswich. Hannah's sister, Sophia, two years younger, did something with Botox and face-fillers at a beauty therapist in Felixstowe town centre.

Alex had described them to Ian and Kate as "salt of the earth" people. That, thought Ian, was probably a polite way of saying something else. He had looked through social media and could not find out anything about them.

It was here, at The Cartwrights, that Hannah and Alex had chosen to have the gender reveal for the baby. Just the two families and a few close friends. The first Sunday afternoon in July. Sandwiches, cakes, and drinks. Outdoors, under a home-made gazebo. The father was useful with his hands, said Kate on arrival. Ian wasn't. The list of his DIY disasters was long and varied.

Alex and Hannah did not want to hold the reveal at their own home. Their end-of-terrace on the Orwell Green estate was too small, they had said.

No one had asked about having it at The Cape. Ian would have liked to have held it there. Been the ringmaster. Made a funny speech. But he did not want to suggest it and be rejected.

Hannah's mother seemed to be very much involved in everything. Ian sensed that it was held at Hannah's home to please her. Placate her, possibly.

At the baby scan earlier that week, Hannah, armed with a

pen and paper, had asked the nurse to write the gender down – "M" or "F" – and put it inside an envelope, which she then gave to her mother.

She, the mother, and most probably the father too, then set about making the gender reveal party just so. The centrepiece of the afternoon was a huge white pinata hanging from the top of the gazebo. When struck, blue or pink pieces of tissue would tumble and flutter down revealing the baby's gender.

"They're not in," Ian said, as he rang the front doorbell for the third time. "We'll go home."

Joe and Yasmin, standing behind, both laughed. Kate pulled a "no we won't" face.

"We'll go round the back," Kate answered. "Beth and Glenn said to meet them there."

And there they all were. The Wilkersons – Ian, Kate, Alex, Beth and Glenn, Joe and Yasmin. Hannah, centre-stage in her finery. And the Cartwrights. The mother, a fake blonde with an improbably pneumatic chest, looking fit to burst. The younger sister, with a permanently startled face, playing with her mobile phone. The short and stumpy father, with his impossibly jet-black hair, bustling about all shiny-faced to and from the barbeque.

"You know what it is then, the baby?" Ian asked Hannah's father cheerfully enough early on. Something to break the ice as it were. To start a conversation. Hannah's father just pulled a "what, me?" face, laughed, and then sauntered away.

He obviously did know, thought Ian, as he would have made and filled the pinata with blue or pink pieces of paper. And he seemed so pleased with himself. This little man with a big secret.

That annoyed Ian somehow, not so much because the gender reveal was being held here (although that was bad enough), or because the Cartwright family knew about the baby's gender and the Wilkersons didn't (which was worse). It was just their – what was the phrase? – sheer bloody smugness.

26

It became apparent, as the afternoon progressed, that Ian wasn't taking part in the chatter or the laughter and sheer enjoyment of the celebrations. Not only that, he was barely speaking.

If someone spoke to him directly, as Hannah's mother and father did once or twice, he answered as briefly as he could, ending his replies with a "thank you" that sounded more fake than genuine. Other than that, he just sat there. He did not start any conversations or seek to join in any that were going on around him.

And he ate and drank sparingly. He took a burger in a bun and had that. And he sipped at a glass of water. But he ignored the fries and salad on the plate and the offer of slices of various cakes that Hannah's mother had made. "I'm on medication," he murmured on occasion, even though he wasn't.

Beth looked across at Kate and nodded towards Ian as if to say, "What the hell?"

Kate just shook her head slightly as if to say, "Who knows?" and carried on chatting to Hannah's mother.

Ian sat there, staring into space, on and on. This big forbidding presence in the middle of all the jollity.

Eventually, Hannah and Alex got up and moved towards the pinata. The mother hustled and bustled forward so she was standing next to Hannah. Literally pressed against her like a Siamese twin. The father, with his great big gurning red face, stood next to Alex and put his arms round his shoulders. Like he was Alex's father.

The surprised-looking sister, at the mother's signal, took her mobile phone and stood in front of the four of them. Ian could not see as Alex and Hannah raised a hammer together and hit the pinata.

Little pieces of blue confetti flew out and fluttered away on the breeze.

Everyone moved forward to congratulate Alex and Hannah and, so it seemed, the mother and the father as if they had something to do with any of it.

Except Ian, who just sat there wanting to go. He clapped, feeling he should do something. As they drove home afterwards, he thought that maybe he should have clapped a little faster, as it had sounded as though he were slow-hand clapping the whole damn thing.

***

The next morning was not a good one for Ian. In fact, it just went from bad to worse. It began, after breakfast, with Ian going into the back garden in his flip-flops to do some weeding; a particularly overgrown long bed of, well, dirt and weeds really.

He had trodden almost straight away in a pile of Bernard's mess from earlier that morning. He took off the flip-flop and threw it as far away as he could.

He went to take off the other flip-flop to avoid the up-down walk that would have resulted from having one flip-flop on, one-flip-flop off. But then he saw that, somehow, he had already trodden it in another pile of dog mess. He threw that flip-flop to the other side of the garden and went indoors in a temper.

Ian then took Bernard to the vet. Bernard's teeth needed cleaning and the usual, older, assistant said that they wanted to do blood tests before giving him a sedative. Bernard being an old dog and all. Just in case. Nothing to worry about. Only routine.

He was told to telephone at lunchtime before coming to collect Bernard. Ian never knew what time that was. He always had his lunch at 12.30. Most other people, he thought, had it between 13.00 and 14.00.

The other assistant, the jollier one he liked, had telephoned just after 11.00 to say Bernard's blood levels were high but not to worry, and could the vet do an X-ray? He'd have liked to have had a moment to gather his thoughts, ask to talk to the vet and phrase some questions. But she seemed breezy and dismissive as if it were something and nothing and so he had agreed. And that he'd come and fetch Bernard at 16.00.

It had nagged at him all through the morning as he pottered and fiddled about, then right through his lunch (which he did not really eat) and all afternoon.

He knew that Bernard, aged 12, was old, but had read somewhere that some Jack Russells lived to 18 years. And he'd got that into his head.

That they had six more years together at least. Him and his pal. Not that it was all about to end now. When he wasn't ready. He had not even started to prepare for it.

Ian went back at 16.00 and, after some to-ing and fro-ing behind the scenes, the vet opened the door to the examination room. The vet seemed young to Ian, but then more and more people in positions of authority seemed to these days. He didn't mind that so much but just wondered, with this vet fresh out of vet college or whatever it was called, how good he actually was. How experienced. Or whether it was all just textbook know-how.

"Ian?" the vet said as though they had met before (they never had). "Please come through."

Ian had expected to see Bernard in the room with the vet and had a sudden sense of panic when he saw he was not there.

"Where's Bernard?" he said, slightly louder than he would have done if he'd had a chance to think about what he was going to say.

"Ah, he's in the kennels. We'll fetch him for you in a moment."

The vet, who had not given his name, now had his back to Ian and was reading notes on a computer screen as if he had not examined Bernard and had no knowledge of him.

He turned around and glanced briefly at Ian and then looked back again towards the computer, pressing buttons as if to avoid the conversation.

Ian knew what was coming. Bad news. And that he did not want to get upset in front of this young and nervous man. He went to say, in a light and almost carefree way, "So what's the problem?" but then stopped as he knew his voice would crack and betray him. So he waited.

"Ah, the thing is," the vet said, glancing again at Ian, "I'm really sorry, but the X-ray shows a, ah, growth on... on... the dog's liver."

"Bernard," Ian said. "My dog's name is Bernard."

He looked at the vet who turned and pointed at the X-ray on the screen and talked quietly and seriously for the best part of two or three minutes about the growth. It was all babble to Ian, who could not take much in, this jumble of Latin words and such. He only really wanted to ask one question.

"Is it benign... or... the other?" He could not think of the word. He thought "terminal" and "rampant" but knew neither of those were quite right. And "transplant" wasn't either.

"Malignant," the vet replied. "It looks to me... yes... you'd be welcome to get a second opinion if you wanted."

"No, no." Ian shook his head. He wanted a second opinion, but did not wish to be rude to the young vet who, he could now see, had a kind and gentle face. A pudgy boy face. "If you say..." His words tailed away. He did not know what to add.

Ian turned to go, to say, "Let me pay... at the desk whilst you get Bernard." But the vet did not move. Instead, he just said "Um," as though that wasn't the end of it. He wanted to say something else. Something even worse.

"Um, if you wanted me to, it could be very aggressive, you see, the tumour, and he may start suffering soon... already. If it bursts, he will be in a lot of pain. Ah, agony. I could put him to sleep for you... best thing really."

"Now?" Ian asked.

"Yes."

Ian cried. He could not seem to stop himself.

And the vet did not know what to do.

***

After the visit to the vet, Ian drove to the marshes at Trimley St Mary. Bernard's favourite walk. The circular route took about an hour, what with Bernard's sniffling and snuffling all the way round. Plenty of time to think, to decide what to do. "I'll need to think about it," he had said to the vet.

"Not too long," had been the reply. Ian felt like punching him.

Ian mulled things over as Bernard trotted ahead, darting in and out of the long reeds time and again and reappearing further on a few minutes later. Then Ian went back home with Bernard to lie down and make a decision.

He knew if he told Kate, she would say go back to the vet tomorrow and put Bernard out of his misery. But, thought Ian, as he stroked one of Bernard's silky ears, there was life in the old dog yet. In him too. Fact is, neither of them were ready to call it a day. Bernard with his lump. Ian with his rare cancer. Even though that day was coming soon, one way or the other, he thought, for both of them.

So he laid down on the sofa, his head on three or four comfy old cushions.

And Bernard, with a little help, climbed up and sat next to him.

They sat there looking at each other and thinking things through.

An hour or so later, Ian woke up on the sofa, Bernard stretched out his full length behind him, against the warmth of his body. It took him a moment or two to realise where he was and why, and what day it was. And what he had to do for the rest of the day. Nothing. Absolutely nothing. Whilst everyone and everything around him went on as ever. Moving forward. With a sense of purpose.

Bernard growled in his sleep as Ian sat up and ran his fingers through his hair, turned his neck from side to side, and then stood up and stretched his arms and legs. He felt instinctively for the white lump and it was still there.

Same size as it was. Hard and solid. He could not get his fingers around it at the back. Larger than it was when he first found it. Growing silently when he did not notice, the cancer within it sneaking its way into his bloodstream and on to other organs all around his body.

He thought this growth was much the same as Bernard had inside him. And that it would get bigger and bigger. The cancer ever more poisonous. Whilst they both just sat there and waited for it to happen.

He glanced at the clock on the wall and saw it was 15.50. He had wanted to talk to Kate about the gender reveal party before she left for work, to explain, to reason with her, but she had gone by the time he woke up. She'd be back soon, but then out again for a yoga class, or Pilates, or one of the other activities that filled so many of her evenings.

She was always busy, busy, busy.

Had less time for him these days when he said or did anything wrong.

What was once humorous to her was now annoying, and embarrassing to family and friends.

Ian went into the kitchen to make a cup of tea. As he went to fetch milk from the fridge, he noticed a post-it note stuck on the door. A sentence from Kate, in block capitals, on it. *SAY SORRY TO HANNAH AND ALEX*. Hannah was underlined.

Ian sat down with his cup of tea at the kitchen table, Bernard by his feet, sitting upright. He stroked the dog's head and rummaged in his trousers for a treat. There was nothing in his trouser pockets except a folded-over postcard.

Ian sighed as he took it out. The postcard was torn and crumpled and had scribbled notes on it. Top to bottom on one side and halfway down the other. He'd had the card for about three months and carried it with him and made notes on it whenever he forgot something.

He counted the number of comments, 14 on one side, six on the other.

He thought that was a lot of things he had forgotten in three months.

What bothered him was that they were all little things, not big and important matters like birthdays or anniversaries but silly, everyday bits and pieces. It was as though his mind was fraying around the edges.

The first comment, *Barry – swimming*, reminded him of when he started to notice he was struggling with his memory. He had swum every weekday, on and off, for the past few years, although it had tailed off these last weeks. It was an opportunity to get some exercise. And mix with people. His friend David. He said hello and passed the odd comment about the weather and had conversations about football with another half a dozen regulars there. Barry was one of them.

One day, Barry was swimming towards him as he got into the pool.

Ian went to say, "Good morning..."

And he could not remember the man's name. It was as if his mind had stuck in a groove and however hard he thought and worried about it, the name would not come.

It came to him later, an hour or so on, when he had stopped trying to remember, to force it into his mind, and had forgotten about it. Then it popped up just like that and he noted it on the card along with the date. Three months ago, give or take a day.

He looked down the list and some of the notes made sense to him. *Penny – surname* was one. He remembered writing the family birthday card to Kate's oldest friend and had put *Ms. Penny* and went to write "Black" but stopped as he realised that was wrong although he could not remember the correct surname.

Penny had changed her name to take that of her partner, an Asian woman who worked in HR somewhere near the Shard in London. He could remember all that now and the woman's first name, Nihara, and spoke it out loud to check his memory, but could not recall the... No, it was not there.

33

Other notes about fleeting moments of forgetfulness he could remember nothing about. *Chocolate, Sainsbury's* was one. *Boiler woman???* was another. Moments that troubled him at the time but meant nothing now other than this worrying, lengthening list.

He had put the dates next to each note.

Twenty in all. Or was it 21?

Either way. Fewer at the beginning, more at the end.

He sat there, mulling this over, as Bernard put a paw up on his knee, wanting to go out again. Then he heard the clatter of letters falling through the letterbox onto the doormat. He got up and walked through into the hallway.

There were two envelopes on the floor. One from the council, no doubt detailing his redundancy package, such as it was. A standard, automated letter setting out this and that with a final figure at the bottom telling him what he knew already. He was going to have to find a job in a supermarket or wherever to help pay the bills.

The other was from the local medical centre where he'd just had his most recent annual blood tests. Sent by first rather than second class post. He had received text messages and calls on his mobile phone from the centre this past week and had not responded, knowing that the repeated calls meant the news was not going to be good. That this lump was the visible sign of the cancer spreading silently inside him.

Ian hesitated for ever such a while, thinking, before putting the two unopened letters on the shelf in the hallway, and laying his mobile phone on top. Then he went into the kitchen, scribbled a note to Kate, and left it by his mobile phone.

After that, he went upstairs to his bedside cabinet and took a bundle of £10 and £20 notes he'd started putting aside for Christmas. He thought there must be a good £300 or £500 in all.

He put on his jacket and canvas boat shoes and whistled for Bernard who trotted out the front door just behind him. They did not look back.

The wind from the door that Ian slammed shut behind him blew the note from the shelf onto the wooden floor. It landed message-side up. *Taken Bernard for a walk. Be back sometime. Ian PS. Sorry about the flip-flops*

PART TWO:
THE JOURNEY NORTH

4
FELIXSTOWE FERRY TO SUTTON HOO

MONDAY 4th JULY

(9.9 MILES, 3 HOURS, 14 MINUTES)

Ian started striding out, Bernard close behind, by the side of the road that made its way from Felixstowe Ferry up through the golf course and towards Felixstowe town centre.

Usually, the road, twisting and turning with the greens to either side, was relatively quiet. But now, just when he wanted peace and time to think, it was one car after the other.

He had to lift and carry Bernard, stepping onto the grass verge and out of harm's way. They stumbled along. It bothered Ian, this traffic, and the thought that, on main roads, he'd have cars coming at him or behind him all the way to Hunstanton.

That's what he was going to do, though. Walk to bloody Hunstanton and celebrate Adam's life. He wasn't quite sure how he would do that. Get there. And celebrate wasn't the right word anyway. Pay tribute wasn't either. Something like it though. He did not know what he would do when he arrived in Hunstanton. He was not religious so he would not say a prayer or anything like that. He'd have to think about it on the way. Plan something out.

What he wasn't going to do was to worry himself to death. He was not going to think about his fading mind. His brain. Or memory. Whatever it was, is, that made him forget things. Well, not things. Words. That was it. He could not remember words that should be obvious to him. And people. Their names. The names of people he should remember. He was not going to think about that. At all.

And all the other stuff. The lump thing. He thought, when he was feeling okay, that it was just a fatty lump. A congealed mass of blubber. When his mood dipped, as it did so often these days, he thought it must be cancer, and with each cough and splutter and ache and pain in his back and arms and legs and each twinge and growling noise in his stomach, he was sure it must have spread. He knew, once it had spread from wherever it had started, you were done for. That's what his mother used to say about cancer. And she was right. So he was not going to think of anything like that either.

Ian knew that, if he was going to do this, the walk to Hunstanton, he had to keep going tonight on and on, as far as he could. If he hesitated, stopped, or had second thoughts, he would give up and go back home and this endless, what was it, this endless... self-torment... would continue and he would keep spiralling downwards. And also, he realised, he had to get himself far from roads and taxis and buses and trains and anything that would make it easier to go backwards rather than forwards. He had to move away from civilisation. Yes, that was it. Out into lanes and fields where he'd have no choice but to keep going.

What he had to do, on this journey, this adventure, was to, what was it, "rejuvenate" wasn't the word. Nor was "cleanse", although it felt closer. He had to put things right within himself, make his life better, happier, as it should be. This had to be joyous. A caper. A glorious escapade. He had to be in the moment and live it. Yes, that was it. Not think about his redundancy and his God-awful boring and mundane life with its stupid *To Do* lists full of nonsense and his endless mowing of the lawn and treading in dog mess. Nor the letters on the side from his old employer and his GP telling him what he didn't want to know and confront.

And he had to try very hard indeed not to think about Kate and what had happened to them, what their marriage had become, because of him. What he had done. Or not done. And what he had turned into. This floundering marriage that had once been everything they had hoped for. And he could not think about the children and how he had let all that… love… falter and fall away over the years. Their partners who he hardly knew, and had shut out really. And this baby. Pudding. His first grandchild. He could not think about him. This little baby boy. It would make him cry. Everything was such a mess. And it was all his fault.

He rallied, trying to wrench his mind back to this adventure of a lifetime. Him and Bernard, his best pal. Two old men, in the autumn of their years, with winter approaching, on one last long trek together. What a time they would have. Through Suffolk villages bathed in sunlight, by apple trees in orchards, up gentle hills and down into dales where they'd eat whatever they had foraged that day sitting by a hedgerow. And up the coast into Norfolk, on sandy beaches and through dunes and paddling by the shore to ease their aching feet (and paws). The glory of it all!

As if out of nowhere, a lorry roared up behind Ian as he was treading carefully through the bumps and dips on the verge.

And, holding Bernard and being half off one foot and half on the other, the whoosh of the lorry knocked Ian clean off his feet.

Ian and Bernard sat on the verge for a minute or two as Ian gathered his thoughts. Then he stood up, dusted himself down, said something sweary to himself under his breath as he picked up Bernard and turned around, marching back towards Felixstowe Ferry.

***

Anyone who saw Ian striding back, with Bernard tucked under his arm, would have assumed, not unreasonably, that he had given up on his walk and was going straight home as fast as he could. That he had changed his mind already.

But they would be wrong. He marched straight by his home, the pub, the block of toilets and the cafe and went to the end of the jetty looking across the river to Bawdsey Manor, the old wartime radar station, on the other side.

It was anger, having been swept off his feet by the lorry, that drove Ian on now. And it gave him the determination to get as far away by nightfall so there would be no turning back.

As he stood there, fuming inside, he checked the pockets of his trousers to see what he had on him. A piece of folded-over kitchen roll in his left pocket; a modern-day handkerchief (or possibly toilet paper). That wodge of bank notes in his right pocket. He'd split that up and spread them about different pockets later.

The lightweight jacket he'd put on over his shirt as he'd left the house had a piece of string of about one metre in length in one pocket. The other pocket was empty. He thought the string might come in handy but was not sure when or how.

In the inside pocket of the jacket, he had his library card tucked inside that *Letters to My Grandchild* booklet and a pen from when he'd last sat in the garden and had been flicking through it. He put those back for now as he did not want to think about them.

Ian had intended to begin his walk by going through Felixstowe town centre and out north beyond the two villages of Trimley St Mary and Trimley St Martin before heading eastwards over towards Kirton and up north again to Brightwell and Martlesham and up the A12.

But that, even via the back ways, would be full of traffic. And it just made him edgy and twitchy. It made him feel unsafe. He wanted Bernard to be able to trot along by his side, not have to be carried (not least because he was a sturdy little fellow and too heavy to carry for long).

Ian felt that, at the jetty, where the River Deben joined the sea, he could turn left and walk all the way up the river, north to north-east, to the pretty little village of Waldringfield and maybe somehow cross the river up near Sutton Hoo.

Ian thought for a moment about what he should really have liked to have in his pockets. For the journey. Had he thought about things. Planned it. Not just got up and left just like that on the spur of the moment.

A mobile phone and a debit or credit card would probably have been most useful. The "most sensible", as Kate would put it.

But a mobile phone would mean he would never have got away; he would always be tied to home. Besides, he could send postcards to Kate and the children as and when he reached different places.

And he did not need a debit card or credit card; not really. The cash he had – a nice, thick bundle of notes – would last him long enough. Until he went home. Whenever that might be. When he ran out of money, probably.

Ian wasn't too sure, if he walked north to north-east on this side of the river, where or when he might cross. The river was so wide in places and there were no bridges that he knew of. He might have to keep going until another tributary flowed into the sea somewhere up the coast. He had no idea where that might be, but he was pleased that he could remember the word "tributary", although he was not absolutely sure it was the correct one to use in this instance.

He knew the river flowed close to Sutton Hoo. He had been there once with Kate and the children when they were small and the elderly lady with a bright-blonde wig and comedy glasses who showed them round the lumps in the fields and other dreary sights made a big thing of how the Vikings would have brought their longboats up the river. "Over there," she had said, her hand sweeping vaguely towards the plains.

But he wasn't sure if he would be able to get to Sutton Hoo as it might be the other side of the river. He could try to cross and end the evening up to his knees and neck and head in marshes and simply be sucked into the ooze and slime and never be seen again.

A change of pants and socks was what Kate would have added to his list of things he should have taken with him. "You don't want to smell do you?" she'd say, as if that were his intention. He would make do, rinsing his whatnots at night and hanging them over the branch of a tree to dry by morning.

A Swiss army knife. Plasters and Vaseline for his feet. Poo bags for Bernard and, most likely, himself. A bottle of water. Some high-energy bars. The more Ian thought about it, the more he realised how much he needed. And did not have.

He thought that somewhere, out there, he would have to try to buy something like a rucksack and keep re-stocking it each day. If he could get to Sutton Hoo tonight, they could head towards Aldeburgh tomorrow where there were plenty of shops.

As Ian and Bernard stood by the jetty, they watched the ferry coming towards them across the water from Bawdsey Manor on the other side of the river. The word "ferry" might suggest something like the big ships that go from Felixstowe to the Hook of Holland, or perhaps the pretty steamboats that travel up and down the Mississippi River.

Not so. The ferry was little more than a big rowing boat with an engine and a waggly thing, as Ian thought of it, steered by the skipper, a gnarled old man with a pipe and a bucket hat. He had four passengers, a family. Mum, Dad, and two children (maybe eight and 10 years old), with lines and buckets for crabbing. The ferry went back and forth every half hour or so, or whenever the boat was full, at this time of year.

And so, some 10 or 15 minutes later, Ian sat at the back of the boat going over to Bawdsey Manor, Bernard on his knees and the wind in their faces. The only other passenger was an old-fashioned looking man in a sailor's cap with beige shorts and leather sandals who kept sniffing and snorting and spitting over the side. Ian gave him a look, but the man did not seem to notice.

They got off on the other side of the river, with Bawdsey Manor to their right and a road stretching out in front of them. They set off towards Bawdsey and Alderton and Shottisham and on to Sutton Hoo, hopefully by nightfall. They'd make camp there somewhere and somehow.

Then on towards Aldeburgh the next day, where they'd get their supplies and have fish and chips and an ice cream and sit on the beach and just recharge their batteries. The journey, their brilliant caper, had begun!

***

Ian lay down in a ditch that night to sleep with Bernard at his feet. His bloodied and aching feet.

The ditch was dry enough and full of bracken stuff, which he pulled and tore to form a pillow-type shape beneath his head and neck. Trying to get comfortable enough to sleep.

And he lay there on his back now, wide awake, Bernard resting his head on his thigh, looking up at the moon. Feeling utterly spooked.

This wasn't how it was supposed to be when he first set out from Bawdsey Manor however many bloody hours ago. It was meant to be glorious and exhilarating. An adventure. Something to write home about. Perhaps he could even write a book. Make notes in that *Letters to My Grandchild* thing. He had always loved reading stories of people on crutches and in wheelchairs, who had travelled against the odds from Lands' End to John O'Groats.

This should have been like that. Not as far, but just as epic. Romantic too, in its way. As he had set off towards Bawdsey and Alderton, with Bernard a step or two behind, he decided that it would be a back-to-nature walk. He and Bernard would drop out of sight, sometimes sleeping by day and travelling at night. Without the trappings and paraphernalia of modern life.

They would sleep in home-made shelters in the woods. Eating whatever he could find. Mushrooms maybe, although he wasn't sure if they were all safe to eat. He had heard of magic mushrooms and didn't want to eat any of those and risk wandering about singing sea shanties at the top of his voice. And rabbits. He doubted Bernard could catch one. Nor would he know what to do with one if he did and it were still alive. He could not imagine strangling it nor even giving it a good shaking for that matter.

If it were dark now and the moon were behind the clouds, he thought he would be able to sleep. But it was like sleeping with the light on.

And Bernard was a dead weight on his legs, snoring away in that peculiar stop-start way. Ian moved his legs to rouse him.

But then, after less than a minute, Bernard was asleep again, leaving Ian to twitch and shiver at every noise. Each rustle, creak and crackle near and far.

He had thought, as they had walked along towards Alderton, about Hunstanton. Where they had all last been happy so many years ago. He had the almost overwhelming feeling that, if he could get there and just wander around for a while reminiscing, he could somehow come to terms with what had happened, terrible though it was. That way, he could reset himself and come back to start over. That was the idea anyway. The plan. As good a plan as any.

He did not know how long it would take, but the weather had been fine and sunny for a while now and that stretched out in front of him for days, maybe even weeks. He guessed it was maybe 90 or 100 miles to Hunstanton and that he could walk 10 miles or so a day there. Have a day there. Then walk back. A few weeks then, he thought, that's what he'd allow himself. A few extra days for mini adventures, although he was not yet sure what these might be. Unhooking a rabbit from a snare, helping an old lady across the road. Stuff like that.

He felt somehow that this whole thing – this epic journey with adventures along the way – might allow him to be renewed, to shake off the lethargy and low moods of late, and to slow or even reverse the failings of his mind. And it would do the same for Bernard, he thought. Fresh air, sunshine, the fruits of the woods and the seashore all rejuvenating both of them.

"Ssshhh," Ian whispered urgently to the snoring dog, nudging him awake again. Bernard lifted his head slowly, looked around vaguely and lowered it.

Ian could hear footsteps. Far away to start with. But coming closer.

He held his breath, listening carefully. Ready to grab Bernard and to jump up out of the ditch and run.

He had intended to walk all the way along the coast, coming inland at night to sleep in a copse, the woods or a forest, depending on where they were. He hoped to get to Aldeburgh tomorrow. Have those fish and chips on the beach. Then walk towards Thorpeness and sleep somewhere down one of the lanes amongst the trees near the old windmill.

It had seemed to take an age to walk from Bawdsey Manor through Bawdsey and up to Alderton. Far longer than he thought. And he felt alone as he saw nobody else about and the cars that went by were few and far between. He reached a fork in the road halfway along and was not sure whether to go on or veer right. He thought Sutton Hoo was straight on, and Hollesley and the coast, where he wanted to go, were to the right. But he had it in his head to stop off at Sutton Hoo (he did not know why) and, besides, Hollesley had the prison and there always seemed to be a lunatic escaping most weeks according to the local paper. It always included a photo of a wild-eyed man with bolts in his neck. And he did not want to come across a madman with a carving knife who would strip the flesh from his bones as he lay there terrified and unable to move.

On he went. Straight on. He stopped and started. Carried Bernard. Stopped and started again. Stumbled over. Rubbed his feet. Stroked Bernard's paws. And just kept going. For what must have been the best part of five hours or more. Until it was dark. He knew he had to press on and get away before his confidence wavered and he changed his mind. But he was confused about where he was. He had no real sense of direction. Then, quite by chance, he saw a sign for Sutton Hoo and turned and followed it.

And that's where he was now, at Sutton Hoo. In the ditch. Listening to footsteps coming towards him.

With a madman approaching. With a big carving knife. Ready for disembowelling. Bernard with his little guts. And Ian with his big guts.

Ian had read somewhere that the average human has about six metres of innards to unravel. He did not know what that was in feet and inches. Twenty feet or more, he guessed. And that would be a heck of a lot of entrails spread out across the grass. And he'd probably slip on one end of them as he ran away trying to push the other end back inside himself.

5
SUTTON HOO TO ALDEBURGH

(14.7 MILES, 4 HOURS 48 MINUTES)

Ian could not begin to describe the agony of waking up in a ditch just after sunrise.

His elbows and knees pressed against the sides. His head at something close to a right angle to his neck. Bernard somehow sleeping on his chest and snoring in his face.

He could only wonder, as he moved with creaking and aching bones, how he ever got to sleep in the first place.

The previous night, into the early hours of this morning, was a blur of terror and utter exhaustion. He recalled hearing footsteps and sitting up and peering out of a ditch, much like the one he was in now, but a mile or two away, and seeing what looked like a figure, a horned Viking, in the distance amongst a thicket of trees. It did not do anything, this figure, it just stood there in its ghostly way, watching him.

Ian knew, in the rational part of his brain, that he was imagining things. There was not really a Viking standing amongst the trees. He knew it was simply a trick of the night – the moonlight between the trees creating a mix of shade and light and shadows that his befuddled brain, trying to make sense of it all, turned into a big horned Viking. Because his brain, fraying and unravelling, had been thinking about Sutton Hoo and Vikings and longships and helmets. And a madman with a carving knife.

But then the Viking moved, as if he were drawing a sword and turning slightly behind him to call other Vikings forwards to attack. At that point, moonlight and trees and optical illusions and brain neurons and pulses be damned, Ian grabbed the snoring Bernard and was up and away out of that ditch, stumbling and staggering for what seemed like miles in the opposite direction. Until, sweating and exhausted, he lay down by a row of trees and, later, when the sweat had dried stiffly into his clothes, climbed into this ditch where he stayed awake, listening to every click and clack for hours. Until he dropped off, utterly exhausted.

And now Ian was up and out of that ditch and Bernard was doing that stretching thing that all dogs seem to do after they wake up.

Ian felt dirty, dishevelled, thirsty and hungry, and he did not know where he was.

So he had a long wee over by a tree and gave it some thought. Wherever he was, he needed to go east towards the coast and north up it. Or north a while. Then east. Whatever.

Ian knew that he really had no sense of direction at all. He remembered, years ago, going on holiday to Spain. They landed at Alicante Airport and hired a car there for the 45-minute drive north, up the coast to a villa in Calpe. Some 50 minutes on, having yet to see a sign for Calpe, he realised the sea had been on his left the whole time and not the right, and so he had driven south for miles and miles and miles.

He knew, one way or the other, he now had to go east until he reached the sea and then keep walking north with the sea still on his right. When he ran out of land somewhere near Cromer, he had to turn left, westwards, with the sea on his right, and that way he'd get to Hunstanton. And he thought he could do that well enough when he could see the sea or feel the sunny, windy emptiness of it on that right side.

But now, half awake and full of aches and pains and rather confused, he was not sure which way to go.

Ian remembered that the sun rose to the east and set in the west. At least he thought so. He recalled, from somewhere or other, that Japan was the Land of The Rising Sun, and that Japan was in the East and so that was where the sun rose. But he was unsure and thought perhaps that was just east of Japan. He tried to recall where Japan was exactly and was pretty certain that, on a flat map, it was over to the far right of England, beyond Russia. And that put the rising sun to the east of England. Then again, on a globe, he thought it was near Australia on the other side, the bottom of the Earth. As if it were moving about a bit. And he was not sure that any of this flummoxy flim-flam helped at all.

And so he set off that way, Bernard by his feet, away from where he had been, at Sutton Hoo.

They would keep walking until they reached a road with a signpost or saw someone who could point them in the right direction.

Towards Rendlesham and on through Tunstall and Snape until they could turn and make their way to Aldeburgh on the coast. And up the coast and all the way to Hunstanton. Possibly.

***

The walk – and this was the proper start of it, what Ian thought of as their epic thing, their legendary adventure – began well enough. An... what was it? An idyllic walk. Yes, that was it, through the Suffolk countryside on a perfect summer morning.

He'd been down this road before many times in a car with the family, on days out when the children were small. To forests and beaches. To fun and happiness. A road that weaved its way from Sutton Hoo through woodland, by a golf course and caravan parks, and on to farmland and fields and the village of

Eyke.

An hour's walk, no more than that, with the sun on his back and his pal by his side and cars going by now and again, but not too fast. He stopped at the village stores where he picked up bottles of water and chocolate bars and sachets of dog food and a small bag of dog biscuits which he put in his pockets for later. (A bowl of water outside the stores was lapped up by Bernard.)

And what he decided, as he walked along, was that he was most definitely just going to live in the moment. Look up and feel the sun on his face. Look down and feel the ground beneath his feet. Smile and encourage Bernard along. Just be happy.

He would not dwell on what had happened. Nor look forward to what might come. Not think about Kate and the children or their partners or Pudding. Nor Adam. Not think about his redundancy or his dreary life or his failing mental and physical health.

And so he walked, slowly and steadily, with Bernard trotting along contentedly, beyond Eyke and up towards Rendlesham and the Bentwaters US Airforce base and, some way on, the halfway point of today's walk, Tunstall Forest.

As he walked, his mind skipped from one thing to another as it always did. It struck him, out of the blue, that this was the first proper exercise he had taken since he stopped swimming in the mornings, weekdays, 7.00 to 8.00, a while ago. But he knew he did not want to think about that, the swimming, and he knew why, so he pulled his mind back to the here and now and looked all around as they went on their way.

He counted trees, not that he really knew any of them. He could spot horse chestnut trees, if that were the correct name, in the autumn when conkers lay all about. But that was about it. Oak trees maybe. And conifers. But not much more. He looked at the clouds, but he did not really know what the different types were called. Nature-wise, he was a bit clueless.

The swimming, the thing he wanted to avoid thinking about,

kept coming back to him as if to grab him by the shoulders and yell, "You've thought about me. You know why! You can't blot me out now." But he tried, straining his mind to think about trees and clouds and birds and flowers and plants and all those things that he should know something about but didn't.

An hour and a half or so on, when Bernard had slowed and stopped, sat down several times and eventually had to be picked up and carried, they arrived at Tunstall and Ian decided to have a breather.

Ian sat on a bench and emptied a sachet of dog food on a clean, dry spot by his feet. Bernard ate hungrily and Ian poured water into his cupped hand so Bernard could drink.

And Ian made a mental note that, when they reached Aldeburgh later that day, he'd buy a rucksack and stock up with paper plates and bowls and all that doo-dah.

It was the next part of the walk, from Tunstall to Snape Maltings, maybe 40 to 50 minutes at the pace they were walking, that the whole swimming thing crowded into his mind. Pushing and shoving its way to the front. And, because Ian was starting to tire already, it seemed to fill every corner of it. How he'd swum for an hour or so from 7.00 every weekday for five or more years, alongside a man – a friend – called David. Dear David.

Over that time, they'd become friends, best friends really, starting off by swimming beside each other in different lanes, slow and medium, separated by a bristly orange rope thing, and passing the time of day. And that had rolled into general chit-chat about holidays and football and, as you might expect, on to family stuff and shared thoughts and feelings. Ian had talked to David about Adam, the only person he'd felt comfortable sharing the story with.

David suddenly disappeared for a whole week and Ian was about to go and knock on his door the next morning when he received a text from his son Liam saying David wasn't well and wouldn't be coming swimming any more. Ian and Liam texted for a while. David had been diagnosed with pancreatic cancer and taken to hospital where they'd tried to fit a stent or something (Liam wasn't terribly sure), and that didn't work so they tried something else and so on. But nothing seemed to fix things, and the hospital sent David home to die. And he was at home for what must have been two or three weeks. And he died. And that, the bare bones of it, was about all Ian could manage to think about now. It was so awful.

Ian forced thoughts of David out of his mind, and tried to distract himself. Get himself back into living in the moment. He looked at the houses as he went along, each in turn, naming the various parts of each house from top to bottom. Chimney. Roof. Windows. And so on. He did that well enough.

Then he watched Bernard, taking pleasure in the dog's slightly rolling gait. The way he strode along confidently on the pathway. How he tiptoed on grass, feeling his way through lumps and dips.

And Ian focused on himself. The slight sheen of sweat on his forehead. The sweat beneath his arms and between his legs. He took off his jacket and tied it round his neck and shoulders. He touched the lump and that felt much the same. He wanted to roll up his trouser legs and roll down his socks. So he did. His feet ached but not too much.

They arrived at Snape Maltings and Ian strode into the complex, Bernard close behind, with an almost overwhelming sense of triumph. He wanted to punch the air as if he had just won Wimbledon or the 1,500-metre race at the Olympics. It – Sutton Hoo to Snape Maltings – could only have been about 10 miles or so, he thought, and it had probably taken him four hours or so to do it. But he felt now, having done this, he could do anything.

He had been to Snape Maltings only once before. A Christmas time about five years ago when the family had gone to see a live orchestral performance of *The Snowman* followed by *Paddington Bear*, where the orchestra had played along to the cartoons on

54

screen. It seemed a bit pointless to Ian but the woman next to him said she was the "very proud grandmother" of the little boy on stage who sang "Walking in the Air", and she had cried all the way through the song. And Ian, seeing the boy looked a little like Adam, did too – although he blew his nose several times to disguise it as a cold .

Ian decided they would stop at Snape Maltings for a while. It was the type of place, with little fancy shops dotted around the complex, where Ian could buy a change of clothes for later and a rucksack and maybe one or two other things he might need for the journey. If nothing else, he could purchase some food and drink here and they could sit outside somewhere and have a makeshift lunch.

**

Ian and Bernard sat, both upright, by the side of a field at Snape Maltings looking out towards a river. Ian was not sure which one it was. The River Orwell. The River Deben. The River Alde. He guessed, correctly as it happens, that it was the River Alde that went on its way to Aldeburgh. It had to be really.

He had, from the various shops and places to eat, and with Bernard sitting patiently outside, bought what he needed. At least for now. A rucksack, rather small and twee, a map of East Anglia, more bottles of water, a BLT sandwich, a sausage roll (to share with Bernard), plus some more chocolate bars. (You can never have too many, thought Ian, either for sustenance or a treat.) The woman behind the counter gave him a look when he held out his hands with three chocolate bars in each. He could not think of anything witty to say so he just smiled at her as if it were all perfectly normal to have six chocolate bars as a snack.

So here they were, looking out, with Ian wondering if something magical might happen somewhere in the bleakness of the landscape. All he could see, to where the sky met the land, were reeds and mud and the river. It could be 1066. No, not that. 1966. No, not that either. Whenever it was that the Vikings arrived. Various birds floated and soared in the sky and some gulls were by the riverbank strutting about searching for the wiggly things. The worms. At the bottom of the garden. Wiggly Woo.

Ian tried to blank his mind. To not think about anything, and instead just be in the moment. Free from the stress and tension he always seemed to experience one way or another whenever he was thinking, really thinking, about important things.

He knew that if he thought at all about his life and everything in it right now, he would just feel negative and miserable. He did not want to feel sorry for himself. He wanted to be happy.

He decided, quite randomly, to think of three things that kept him in the here and now. And that made him feel good about himself. The sun in his eyes. The wind on his face. The sound of the birds above.

As Ian sat there, with Bernard beside him and rolling onto his side, he heard a rustling in a nearby tree. An oak tree possibly. He was not sure. A big solid one just up the riverbank. Mighty oak-ish for certain. He watched the tree, not knowing where the rustling was coming from, somewhere in amongst the branches and the leaves.

And he saw a squirrel, a big, grey solid-looking one with a long and arched, fluffy tail. It came scurrying down the tree trunk almost vertically. Ian reached out and put his hand on Bernard so he could not chase the squirrel – having once chased a rabbit across two fields and out of sight and disappeared for ages when he was younger, it was not something Ian wanted him to do again now. Bernard rolled back further expecting a tummy rub. Ian obliged.

The squirrel sat up by the trunk of the tree, looking around, his head going this way and that. It stopped for a moment and seemed to be watching Ian who sat as quiet as a... thing... a whatsit thing. Then the squirrel was off, across the field away from Ian who lost sight of it. He sat there for a while, waiting to see if the squirrel came back. But it did not.

The thing Ian wanted most from this walk, this epic journey, was to somehow find peace. To cleanse himself, and start over.

He did not know whether blanking everything out was the way to achieve that serenity.

Or whether he should think about things in turn. Kate. The children. His mental health. The physical stuff. Rearrange it all in his mind into some sort of order.

But then the squirrel was back, his tail appearing first, poking out from the long grass, as it returned from wherever it had been. It stopped at the trunk of the tree and took another close look at Ian. To see if he were a threat, most likely. Ian looked back and wished at that moment he had brought his mobile phone. He would have liked to have filmed the squirrel which made him smile.

It looked to Ian, and he would be the first to admit that his eyesight was going a bit but was too vain to admit it, as though the squirrel had food in its cheeks and also in its hand things, its paws. Claws. Jaws. He did not think that was likely if the squirrel was going to go back up the tree and needed to grip the bark as it went.

Ian thought, decided, that this big old squirrel was a daddy squirrel and that the mummy squirrel and the baby squirrels were somewhere up in the tree. And he felt that was rather magical. He watched as the squirrel scampered back up the side of the tree and listened to the swishes and rustlings as it ran along branches although he could not see where it went.

He felt at peace for a moment, unexpectedly, and decided he could sit here a while, watching the squirrel's comings and goings. It was a chance to relax.

But Bernard had heard the noises this time and sat up and looked around. He did not bark – not Bernard's thing, that, barking – but Ian knew that if the squirrel reappeared, Bernard would give chase.

And Ian would end up running after Bernard along the riverbank and into the reeds and probably the river. One way or another, he'd end up flat on his face in mud. And so, with a sigh, he got up and, after a quick wee in the toilet inside the, you know, the centre thing, Ian and Bernard were on their way.

***

Snape Maltings to Aldeburgh looked to be about six or seven miles, according to the map. Maybe a two-hour walk. Ian decided they would walk for half an hour. Then stop for 15 minutes. Another 30 minutes walking. And so on. So, maybe, three hours in all.

He'd get there before the shops shut. Fill the thingammy with whatever they'd need to keep going – the basics, as it were, and enough food and drink until their next big stop at Southwold the next day. They'd have fish and chips on the beach at Aldeburgh, then head up towards Thorpeness and its windmill and fields and woods to find somewhere to sleep tonight.

It looked a simple enough walk on the map, northwards along a country road, with the sun high and bright in the sky, and a gentle breeze on his face. He had to turn right somewhere up the road, to cut off a corner so to speak, before heading eastwards towards Aldeburgh. From there, it was all the way up and round the coast to Hunstanton – easy enough to do; just stay close to the sea, on the right, to the east, without falling in.

And off they went. Ian and Bernard. Just ambling along. These two old boys. Out of Snape Maltings down Bridge Road and, a way along and umming and aahing, a right turn to Snape Street rather than going straight on up Bridge Road (this turning right being the cutting off the corner bit).

Still going northwards and knowing that at some stage, they would reach a junction and go right again. And that road, the something-or-other road that was too small to read on the map, took them along into Aldeburgh. Yes, that was it. He had that clear in his head. Sort of.

As they went along, Ian thought of what they had done at Snape Maltings and repeated the doings one by one. "I went to the toilet first. Bernard waited outside. I then bought a latte from the café." And so on. And he did these rememberings all well and just so. But then, suddenly, he could not remember the name of the thing, the whatsit, on his back. He took it off and looked at it and checked the receipt. Rucksack. That was it. Christ, he thought. What the hell, his children would have said.

What Ian feared most, more than anything, was losing his mind. Forgetting things. Like this thing now. They never came to mind if he really focused and tried to think of the word or phrase immediately. That, the forgetting thing, did not really matter. It was just his mind fraying at odd moments. As long as he could remember most things, the main things, that would be okay.

He thought again of his friend David, and what happened to him. How fast it had all unfolded. Swimming just as he'd always done. Off for a week when Ian had assumed he had a cold or something like that. A week of fiddling about desperately in hospital and then back home to die. Gone within a few weeks. Ian could not bear thinking about it.

There came a point on this road, this whatever it was called, too small to read on the map road, that Ian stopped, Bernard by his feet, and was suddenly not sure where to go. It was a dithery moment when Ian seemed to quite forget where he was going. Perhaps even what he was doing.

He'd gone by a sign for Friston along a road that kind of went north-east back on himself. Then, further along, where he was standing now, there was a sign for a road to Aldringham and Thorpeness which went north-west. And this road, the one he was on, was still going to Aldeburgh although it seemed to curve southwards. And he wanted to go north, not south.

It was the curving southwards that threw him, confused him. And he thought that the heat, the sun on his back, the sweat on his body and the lightness in his head had all combined to bewilder him. He drank some water and cupped some in his hand for Bernard. Then he took out a Mars bar for himself and a dog biscuit for Bernard and they ate, before walking on – still on the road to Aldeburgh. His mind went back to David again.

It was not the fact that David died that bothered Ian most. He knew it was sad. One moment he was here, fit and strong, and then the next, he was gone. And he left behind a wife and a daughter and a son. But Ian could not say he was particularly upset by it. Not really. He thought about it a fair old bit but not because he was distressed at all. He did not cry.

Ian wondered whether that made him a heartless man. He had swum alongside David for an hour every morning, 7.00 to 8.00, for more than five years. And they had chatted away about all sorts of things. And they gave each other lifts whenever their respective cars were in for an MOT or whatever. And ate fish and chips and drank a beer or two before Christmas with some of the other swimmers. And, after all of that, Ian did not care that much about his death.

What did bother Ian, and he knew why, was the fact that sometime between coming home and dying, Ian had seen David up the town being pushed about in a wheelchair by his short and stocky, orange-haired wife, Glynis. She had stopped as she approached Ian and said to David in a too-cheerful voice, "Look, David, do you know who it is?" And David, waking with a start, had looked up at Ian with dull eyes and slowly put out his hand as if told to do so, to be polite. Ian babbled away for a minute or two and it seemed that David had no idea at all who he was. Whether it was the medication or his mind had gone, Ian did not know, but he walked away with tears in his eyes.

It was this part of the walk, going slowly southwards towards the town of Aldeburgh, that Ian found the hardest going so far. He just felt they had been walking for ages and were not really getting anywhere.

The road twisted and turned, and it was pleasant enough. The sun and the wind were just right and there were fields and woods and places to stop for a breather every half hour or so.

But it felt as though he was marching on the spot and everything – the cars, cyclists, even a little putt-putt-putt scooter – was racing by him.

And he could not shake the sadness from his mind about David. The reason Ian was so bothered by the encounter with David up the town was because this was how Ian feared his own life would finish. He worried that he would spend his final days in a wheelchair unable to feed himself or go to the toilet without assistance. The thought of Kate, Beth or anyone else for that matter changing his pants filled him with horror.

It was losing his mind that made him feel sick with worry. He remembered, years ago, visiting a great-uncle of Kate's in a home and he would alternate between shouting racial obscenities at a black nurse and sexual suggestions to a white nurse. It seemed funny to Ian at the time, as a gauche man in his early 20s, but now he worried this would be how he would end his days. That somehow the shutters of his mind would open, and he'd just spill out his innermost thoughts. Telling Alex he had raisin eyes. And that Beth had a huge, massive, great wobbly backside. And yes, really, Joe did have the fattest neck he'd ever seen.

It came to him suddenly in his mind's eye. He would be in a wheelchair with his family round him trying not to look revolted by the stains on his trousers and that stale smell of old, sat-on poo. He recalled being violently sick on a coach on the way to Heathrow Airport for a holiday once and how they all looked when he got off with his vomit dripping through a carrier bag. They'd look like that again. And he'd be sitting there shouting about raisins and arses and fat necks with poo stuck to him right the way down to the back of his knees. Really, he could not bear to think about it.

Ian and Bernard went by a library on their right and, a little way on, a church on their left. Then, the road sloped downwards to a T-junction and, at last – at long last – they were in Aldeburgh.

Ian picked up Bernard and they crossed the road. To the left, the road ran along the coast a mile or two to Thorpeness. To the right, it went up by the old bookshop and the ancient cinema to the town itself and its mix of ordinary shops and tat stores for tourists.

And ahead, just by that creaky old cranky building, there was a coffee kiosk and a little boating lake. And Ian hoped, more than anything else, that there was nobody about and he could strip off his bloody socks and battered shoes and just put his feet in the water. But he thought, correctly as it happened, that it would be far too busy to do that. He'd have to hobble that bit further to the stony beach and down to the shore, where he could soak his feet for an hour. Bliss. He might even fall asleep if there weren't too many people about.

***

Ian filled his rucksack, had a wander about Aldeburgh for a good while, had those fish and chips on the beach, two plain sausages for Bernard, and headed towards Thorpeness, a mile or two up the coast.

He had walked by the Scallopy thing – a big ornament, an exhibit thingy – on the pebbly beach on the way and went by the Meare at Thorpeness to see The House in the Clouds and the whirly window opposite... the... the... the windmill.

He could not see anywhere obvious where he and Bernard could tuck themselves away to sleep at Thorpeness and, besides, it was still light. Instead, he decided they would keep on walking as far as he could, up by Sizewell and towards Minsmere, the bird place, until it was dark, and he was ready to sleep.

And now he sat leaning against a tree in a copse on the banks of a river somewhere between Aldeburgh and Southwold. Bernard sat up straight next to him as if scanning the horizon for seagulls or ships or maybe even pirates.

Ian realised that it was at this time, at the setting of the sun, that his mood dipped each day. Like clockwork, as it were. He was already brooding, thoughts flying in and out of his butterfly mind. All negative ones.

He knew he should keep walking a bit further to try and shake off his gloom, but his feet hurt too much. So he pulled his shoes and socks off, staring into space whilst massaging his aching feet.

His mind, his memory, seemed to have been a little better today, since he started his walk even. He wondered why this might be. He thought it could be because he had a clear and singular purpose – to get to Hunstanton – and that he could free his mind from all the petty, day-to-day nonsense, the detritus of life, that dragged him down. The *To Do* lists. Changing the hard-to-reach light bulb on the stairs to the attic. Chasing a crisps packet that had blown into the garden. All that nonsense.

What he had to do now was to walk, one step in front of the other, as slow or as fast as he wished, along the coast, with the sea on his right at all times, until he arrived in Hunstanton. He could stop and start when he wanted, detour for supplies as needed and find a tucked-away bush or a tree or even a ditch to sleep at night. His biggest concern was where to do his business. He wished he had one of those trowels Kate used to plant daffodil bulbs. He did not like to just leave it, where he had just been over there, crouched down and pushing his bottom as far as he could under a bush. With the ever-present risk of losing his balance and falling backwards.

The physical exercise, the feeling of the sun and the wind on his face on a bright and breezy day, the pleasure of walking (when he did not push himself too hard) was all just... What was the word? Joyous. He was already getting into a routine, to pace himself, to take care of his body, his feet and his legs and his back. And his shoulders. He did not know why his shoulders sometimes ached, but the big white lump did not. From now on, he'd get up as the sun rose each day. Walk a while. Take a break. Another long-ish walk. Have something to eat. Then search for a place to sleep. A simple life.

He was looking forward to arriving at Southwold some time tomorrow. He was going to buy himself a change of clothes there. Trainers too, if they weren't too expensive. He'd try a charity shop. He had not thought to look in Aldeburgh. He did not know why. It never came into his mind. He also liked the idea of getting a hat, a bucket hat maybe, if he could get something big enough to fit his huge old head.

And he'd walk on the tiddly-om-pom-prom and sit on the beach for a while. He'd go on the pier and get an ice cream to eat. Bernard could have some of the cone. They'd just have a jolly good time. An afternoon off.

If he didn't have Bernard, of course, he could have gone up… the whatchamacallit. The red- and white-striped thingy that went up into the sky. Uh. It was no good. He could see it so clearly in his mind but could not name it. The thing. With a beam at the top. That shone out to sea. At night-time. To warn the ships.

Ian reached into his jacket pocket and took out the baby booklet. He peered closely at it, wishing he had brought his reading glasses with him. Then dug deep again to find the pen that was somewhere in there too.

He opened the booklet, flicked to the spare pages at the back, and drew the stripey thing. It was so strange that he could see it in his mind's eye but could not name it. Yet he could draw it, near enough.

He looked at it. The word "penis" came to mind, but he knew it was not that. He added some shading on the stripes. There, a stick of rock. Not that either. The name. What was it really called? And was it red and white? Or just his imagination?

Ian thought for a minute. The name would come to him

later. Maybe overnight, if he did not strain for it. He turned over the page in the baby booklet and started writing. *Ian. Kate. Alex. Beth. Hannah. Glenn. Joe. Yasmin.* He looked out to the river and the sea beyond and remembered and wrote down one inconsequential fact about each of them. *Yasmin makes cakes with custard creams on top.* Checking himself and his memory.

He stopped for a while, feeling sleep coming on, and then wrote the word *PUDDING* in block capitals. He underlined the word, and it struck him he had not really thought about the baby since he set off. Ian wondered why that was. He sighed as he tucked the booklet and pen back into a pocket. Pulled on his socks and shoes. Then, he took off his jacket, rolled it up, and put it behind his head.

He leaned back on the jacket between his head and the tree. He knew he could not sleep here, in this copse, with the riverbank in front of him and stretching out to the other side and beyond. It was too exposed. He still had memories of the Viking warrior from last night. And there might be passers-by. And cut-throats and villains and highwaymen. Dick... whatsit. Dickie Doughnut. Dick Turnip; no, not that either. He knew he was nodding off, so decided he would stay put for a while before going to find some bushes for their night's sleep. A thicket. That was it. A thicket of bushes.

***

It was Ian who first saw the children in the river, two small heads bobbing away in the strong, fast-moving current. Heard their plaintive cries for help.

Two young women picnicking on the riverbank, the mothers of the two children, were chatting away and looked up as Ian raced by, already on his way to save the children. He was somehow younger, fitter, leaner. More heroic. And strong enough to reach the children before they were swept out to sea.

"Call for... Air Sea Rescue," he shouted back at the women,

the word "Thunderbirds" on his lips but not out of his mouth.

"999!" He kept running. He could see the children, just their heads anyway, as they were pulled further and further away down the river. Ian looked desperately across to the other riverbank, hoping that, somehow, there may be someone there, further along, who could dive in and rescue the children. But there was nobody in sight.

He could hear, behind him, the desperate cries of the two young women, one of them screaming into her mobile phone that her children had fallen into the river, were being swept away, would drown. A moment's ragged and breathless silence, a calming and measured reply, as Ian just kept going.

No, she did not know the name of the river. A day out, she was saying. Somewhere near Aldeburgh. Where the river ran into the sea. Hurry! Please! Send a helicopter. My children are drowning. And Ian ran and ran, knowing that if he did not save the children, no one could.

He tore off his jacket. Then his shirt, dropping them on the ground behind him.

Knew he needed to be wearing as little as possible. No extra weight. Nothing to drag him down.

He would slip off his trousers and his canvas boat shoes just before he dived into the river.

The young women were behind him now. Chasing. Ready to dive in too; to help as best they could. But Ian was stronger and faster and as he raced along the riverbank, he could feel himself getting further away from them. They called and shouted to him, their frantic words blown away in the wind, but he just kept on going, focusing on the children.

He was just about keeping pace with the children, maybe edging a little closer. The river was strong and relentless but so was Ian. The river would never voluntarily let them go. Ian would have to tear them from its clutches. And he would, he thought. He would never give up, not as long as there was breath in his body.

He had to decide – quickly, instantly – whether to carry on running along the riverbank or to dive into the river. He was moving so fast, and closing the gap, but the ground was so rough and uneven that he feared he might stumble and fall, losing precious seconds. He made his split-second decision.

Slowed, pulling off first one shoe and then the other.

And his trousers.

Dived into the river in his pants and socks.

Ian could see ahead, not so very far away now, the children, just their heads, struggling to breathe, still fighting against the strong current. Neither of them crying out any more, just trying to stay alive. And beyond that, what Ian feared most, the wide-open sea. He knew, somehow, that he had to reach them before the river broke out into the sea. That once the waves and the current had them, they would be lost. Recovered somewhere, too late, in a sheltered cove, in two or three days.

Ian concentrated on swimming as hard and as fast as he could. He was a strong swimmer because he had swum so regularly for so long for so many years at the local leisure centre. He knew it was not the same as swimming in the open, but he felt it gave him the strength to keep going. And it did. He could hear the women running along the riverbank, so far behind now, but still screaming. He did not know how he would face them if the children were lost at sea.

Somehow, as the river swept the children along and away, it did the same for Ian. But, as he was heavier than the children, it seemed to sweep him along faster. He could see the sea now, just beyond them. Heard their sobs and cries as they saw it too. But the gap between him and the children was closing. Not fast enough. Not close enough. It was touch and go. The sea was there pulling them in.

"Got you," Ian cried, as he somehow managed to grab the boy with his left arm.

"And you," as he got his right arm around the girl's neck.

He pulled them close, managing to turn over onto his back,

one arm around each child.

It was not over though. Not yet. Far from it. The river was pushing him out to sea. He knew if the three of them were swept into the sea, they would not survive for long. However strong he was. It was cold in the water even at this time of the year, and the undercurrents were strong. He might survive. At least for a while. The children would not.

He somehow turned his body and the children away from the fast-moving current of the river and the pull of the sea and towards the riverbank where the women were still running to him. With his legs, he kicked with all his might. Hoping and praying that it would be enough to break the push and pull of the water. It was the make-or-break moment. He and the children could soon be lost forever.

Slowly but surely, his body stayed strong and unmoving against the currents. As though he defied them both with his strength. For a minute or so, maybe even two, it was an evenly matched struggle. He thought it could go either way. His body was at breaking point. Suddenly, he let out an almighty yell, and heard the children splutter and squeal in the cold and stormy water. And then he was away and kicking towards the riverbank.

The women were at the edge of the river, sobbing with relief and joy.

They dashed forward, wrapping arms around the children, smothering them with love and kisses.

Then they looked up, two or three minutes later, to thank this man, their hero. Ian. The legend. But he was gone. All that was left behind was a single sock with a hole in the heel.

6
ALDEBURGH TO SOUTHWOLD

WEDNESDAY 6th JULY

(16.3 MILES, 5 HOURS 20 MINUTES)

It was this part of the Suffolk-Norfolk coastline, Aldeburgh to Southwold, that Ian knew best. They had, as a family, been here so many times over the years. When the children were small, anyway. It had been a fair old while, to be honest. Longer than Ian had first thought.

Aldeburgh. Sizewell. Dunwich. Southwold. The two rather quaint, old-fashioned 1950s resorts at either end. One long bleak and windy beach stretching in between. It seemed to go on and on forever.

Early the next morning, Ian made his way to the beach with Bernard not so far behind. He decided that, if he could, he would walk all the way along the beach to Southwold. It must be the best part of 15 miles.

As he walked, he checked his jacket pockets, taking a handful of whatever was in each, holding the items in his palm and naming them. Just so. And then he did the same with his trousers, left and right. Correct again. Finally, almost absent-mindedly, he slipped his hand into the back pocket of his trousers. Habit, really. Not expecting to find anything there.

He pulled out a folded-in-four piece of white paper. A cheap sheet from a ream of typing paper that he had obviously torn in half, so that it was now A5 in size. He had written several notes on it, including *Tuesday* at the top. Then below, *Petrol cap off* and *Man in Shop* and *Blueberries!!* and beneath that, a squiggled star shape next to, ah what was it, what a princess wears on her head. Not a crown. The other thing. Spikey. Not a tiramisu. And *007 2!!*

He stopped thinking for a moment, striding along, knowing that the harder he thought, the more he searched and probed his mind, the more difficult it was to remember. All he could recall was the petrol cap note. He had filled the car with petrol. Whenever. Then driven along the A14 to wherever and a passenger in a car going by leaned out of the window shouting and pointing behind Ian. He assumed he had a flat tyre and pulled over at the next lay-by to discover his petrol thingy bouncing about. The cap? He could not remember anything else about the other notes. That frustrated him.

Walking on the beach was not easy. It was sandy, this part of it, and he had to lift his feet up and down like a soldier marching outside of Buckingham Palace, rather than just strolling along normally; it made him think that he must drag his feet usually. Like a caveman.

And Bernard, rather than moving along effortlessly, his paws gliding through the sand, had fallen behind. Plod. Plod. Plod.

Ian stopped and took off his shoes and sock. Somewhere or other he had lost a sock but did not know where or when. He tucked these into his jacket pockets; one shoe and one sock on one side and one shoe on the other. Then picked up Bernard and continued walking. They'd do this together.

As he walked along, he heard Kate's voice, as clear as can be, in his head. Well, not exactly Kate's. He did not actually have Kate's voice in his head telling him what to do or think. Nothing like that. Nor anyone else's for that matter. Norman Bates, for example. Or, heck, the other one. Not Anthony Hopkins. The character he played. Rumpelstiltskin. No, not that either. Whatever. But he could imagine – imagine, yes that was it – Kate as if she were here now and what she would be thinking and saying to him.

"Now you know what's going to happen next, don't you?" she'd say in that slow and polite "I'm talking to the village idiot" voice. "You know what will happen if you walk along this beach for miles with your size 10 shoes in your jacket pockets?" Then she'd say that "actions have consequences" line (the one that really got on his nerves). And she'd be right, of course. As ever.

What would happen would be that one of his shoes would fall out and land on the sand and he would not notice it and just keep walking on and on until he got to Southwold where he'd stop to put his sock and shoes back on. He'd then have to go round the shops with one shoe on and one shoe off, bobbing up and down, until he could find a replacement pair. Which would probably be flip-flops, and they would look quite stupid with just one sock.

So, he stopped and sat down and, as Bernard limped slowly up to him, he realised that this had already happened; that his left shoe had fallen out.

He left his rucksack and right shoe and sock with Bernard and started walking back, following his footsteps. He turned now and again and could see Bernard sitting upright and staring out to sea on this vast and empty beach. As though he were too embarrassed to watch Ian retrace his steps. To even be seen to be with Ian.

It took five minutes to find it and another five minutes to walk back and, as he put his shoes and sock back on, patted Bernard on the head and gave him a dog biscuit from the rucksack, he felt tired and utterly fed-up.

But, as he looked out to sea, the great big greyness of it with white ripples by the shore, it suddenly struck him what *007 2!!* meant. He'd had in his head, whenever he wrote the notes, an image of James Bond coming out of the waves. Goodness knows why. But he did. And it was not Sean Connery when he came out of the sea in Doctor Who. Not Who. No. Doctor

No. And it wasn't the one with the potato head either when he did much the same thing in some other film. It was the one he could not now remember. Nor the film. Or when he came out of the sea. But he definitely did. James Bond. The second James Bond.

It was the Australian actor who played Bond after Connery. And Ian, right here and now, could remember back to when he wrote the note, and could see the actor in his head. And saw him coming out of the sea. Although, in his mind, the actor was wearing an old-fashioned three-piece suit and a bowler hat, holding an umbrella, and speaking with an English accent. And was married, or got married, to Diana Rigg. And she was called Tracey, which was a classy name years ago (what with it being the name of a character in a Hitchcock film), but was not any more for some reason or other. Something to do with Sharon; whoever she was.

He remembered all of this, this jumble of nonsense, back then when he had been thinking about it (for whatever reason). But he could not name the actor then even though he saw him clearly. But now he could name him. And see him. George Lazenby. And that made him feel good. Or at least better. That he could recall it now, even though it was two or three weeks on. But, of course, he could not now remember the name of the other James Bond. The potato-headed man in the budgie smugglers. So that bothered him instead. Endless, this was. Blurry memory stuff.

Up he got, swinging his rucksack onto his back, calling to Bernard, and going on their way. More trudge-trudge-trudging along the beach. With the wind in his face. And the sun rising to the top of the sky. And the sand getting into his shoes and sock. And, not long after, carrying Bernard again, which he thought would soon become a regular feature of this adventure. Sludge, more like. No, trudge.

He decided that, as soon as he could, when it looked like they were close to civilisation and signs for pubs and shops and public toilets appeared, they would walk up from the beach and make their way to Southwold along the road.

***

Many more days like this, Ian thought, and he would just give up or at least hitch a ride or take a bus or whatever – anything other than this endless, um, endlessness… trek. That was it.

The sun was high and hot in the sky and the day was dry and dusty. His feet hurt. And the rucksack straps cut into his shoulders.

And he was walking along a wide-open road with fields rolling away for miles either side, and there was no sign of a village or anything ahead. He'd come inland and followed the road right and northwards. But still. It was never-ending. He should have stayed on the beach.

Bernard had slowed and stopped a mile or so back. So, he was now carrying the wretched animal in his arms, and Bernard held his head up to look ahead, which made Ian think of one of the late Queen's corgis being carried on a red and gold cushion by a supercilious-faced flunkey.

Except Ian was sweating profusely. His shoulders and arms hurt, and the back of his legs and feet ached so much. He just wanted to lie down by the side of the road for a while and not do anything. The verges were wide and inviting.

But he carried on. He thought that if he did lie down and fall asleep, it might seem to drivers passing by that he was dead. And someone would call the police on their mobile phone and the next thing he'd know he'd be prodded and pushed by a traffic cop's boot to see if he were dead or alive. And it all just seemed to be more trouble than it was worth when all he wanted was a 10-minute kip.

On he went. And on. Up that long and dusty road with a shimmering mirage of a village ever in the distance.

And he thought for a minute that he felt dizzy and that he might be sick. So, he stopped and put Bernard on the verge so he could put his hands on his knees and lean forward to get his breath.

He expected Bernard to take the opportunity to cock his leg against something but there were no trees or fences, just an open ditch, and the dog looked at him with a long-suffering expression as if to say, "What am I supposed to do?" until Ian picked him up and carried on walking.

Bernard was not, it had to be said, an overly affectionate dog. He did not, whenever Ian returned home from anywhere, come walking, let alone running, towards him, for example. He would allow himself to be lifted and put on Ian's lap and would then sit there staring into space. He would, on occasions, stretch out alongside Ian when he lay down on the sofa. But Bernard was passive in all of this, not outwardly active.

"Stoic" was the best word to describe Bernard. He would look at Ian as he talked to him, as if he were polite but essentially bored. He would, as if with a sigh, roll out of his basket and walk wearily towards Ian if he gestured and whistled to him. The only time Bernard ever seemed animated was when he broke wind and would walk briskly out of the room, looking over his shoulder at Ian as if to say, "You did that, not me."

Now, as Ian stumbled along avoiding potholes in the verge, Bernard just seemed indifferent, looking at some vague point on the horizon. Lorries raced by, almost blowing Ian off his feet. But Bernard remained exactly the same, aloof and ever-so-slightly put out, as if Ian had offended him in some way.

At last, the wide-open road began to narrow, and pavements appeared on either side, followed by bungalows and cottages.

In the distance, the mirage of a village started to take shape and Ian could see a village stores. That was about it.

But it was enough. He could stop there and get some water and fruit and something for Bernard too. He put Bernard down and they walked on slowly side by side.

It was as Ian passed one of the cottages that he heard a noise. A tap-tap-tap on glass. Like a woodpecker peck-peck-pecking at the bark of a tree. It took him a moment or two to stop as another lorry roared on by and he stumbled over and then picked up Bernard. Just in case the next lorry came closer.

He looked to his left and saw a neat and tidy, small bungalow. A black garden gate. A crazy-paving pathway. A door with a slope up to it and a handrail to one side. Two bay windows. Net curtains. Quiet and peaceful. He wondered if there were squirrels in the loft, running about, tap-tap-tapping. Or rats. He swallowed. He hated rats. Just the thought of them let alone the sight.

He stood for a moment, listening. Then saw movement. A hand. A claw more like. At the window to the left, behind the net curtain. It was an old woman. White hair and a faded face, an almost ghostly apparition, with her black funereal clothes. She raised her hand and beckoned him towards her.

He hesitated for a moment, not sure what to do. Thought maybe he'd feign deafness and keep on walking.

She beckoned again with greater urgency.

Great, he thought, it's the woman in black and now I'm going to die.

***

Two to three hours later, Ian and Bernard were on their weary way again to Southwold.

Ian had a piece of paper in his hand, a sheet of old-fashioned Basildon Bond writing paper.

B1125 North B1387 East Ferry Across 8 Miles was written on it in wavery writing below a squiggle of lines.

The old lady in the bungalow had opened the bedroom window as he and Bernard had walked up the path. It was an old, original window, no double glazing, and it creaked and then screeched as she pushed it open. This woman looked so fragile that it seemed as though her wrist would snap at the repeated pushing. She had, in her gasping, raspy voice, told him something about her son being away on holiday and a neighbour who usually did her shopping but was in hospital, and could Ian get her some things from the village stores. She handed him a list and a £20 note, then looked at him with watery eyes that reminded him of his late nan.

And he did just that as Bernard sat outside the village stores. He went up and down the aisles with the list and peered at it and guessed at the type of milk she wanted and bread and whether she wanted the free range eggs or the other ones. He worked his way down the list and just got the cheapest of everything, but even then it came to more than £20, or £22.67 to be precise. He put it all in the carrier bag she had given to him and took it back with her £20 note tucked at the bottom and the receipt laying near the top.

When he returned, the front door had been opened and he went up the slope with Bernard behind him and he called out and she replied to come in. She was in the kitchen at the back of the bungalow making a pot of tea and putting rich tea biscuits onto a plate. She was using a walking frame and her hands seemed very shaky, and he thought she might fall over at any moment. So he carried this and moved that and put this down here and that over there, and they sat at the little table in this 1950s kitchen. She smiled at him, thanked him, and they talked for a while. Polite, weather-related conversation. And she asked where he was going with his rucksack on his back and his dog by his side.

The walk from the village of Westleton up the B1125 was pleasant enough. It was a rural B-road and Bernard walked most of the way although Ian lifted him up whenever a car came accelerating up behind them.

And the sun was now dropping in the sky, it was comfortably warm rather than being what Ian thought of as a sweaty heat. The one where he had to walk with his legs slightly apart.

But he was meant to turn right on to the B1387 at some point and along to somewhere, the name escaping him. And he worried that he might miss the turning. His mind was still on his meeting with the old lady.

As they sat there having tea and old biscuits, he told her what he was doing. Walking from Felixstowe to Hunstanton and back with Bernard. He said it as though it were perfectly normal for a man in late middle-age and his elderly dog to just walk 90, 100 hundred miles there and back. As he said the words, he knew they sounded mad; made him seem insane really. As though he were having a mental breakdown. He did not think he was. But perhaps he was wrong.

And he had dipped his rich tea biscuit into his tea to soften it, but not too much, then broke off a bit of the mulch and passed it to Bernard who ate it in a "well-if-I-have-to" kind of way. Ian blinked and looked around and swallowed and smiled at the woman who seemed to be watching him and was about to say something. It struck him that he knew her from somewhere, was familiar in a way, although he could not think where or when. He had introduced himself as "Ian... and this is Bernard," and she had said she was "Mrs Parker", but the name meant nothing to him. But still.

"Rough camping," she had said, and he must have seemed confused because she added, "that's what you're doing. Rough camping. Sleeping in fields," and she had gone on to explain that her husband used to do it, ooh, years ago, with a friend. "Before he died" – as if Ian might otherwise think that the friend had, for some reason, dragged along the festering corpse of her husband whenever he went camping. And she said he – her late husband – was a big man and that was his undoing. The diabetes. A stroke. Heart attack. She looked at Ian, up and down, and he felt spooked, but he talked on for a little while, being polite, whilst she drew a little map for him, and he then said they must be going.

Ian was thinking about this – the spookiness of the

encounter, the otherworldliness of it – whilst he was walking northwards on the B1125.

He kept replaying parts of it in his head. The meeting. What was said. And so, turning right on to the whatever the road was went completely out of his head and he just ploughed on. And on. And on.

When he got to the country crossroads – and could go straight on to Blythburgh or right to Walberswick or left to somewhere else – he went straight ahead without a moment's thought. He did not realise his mistake until he was on the busy A12, and the cars were hurtling by.

The old lady had seemed sad when he said they must be going, and she asked him to sit there for a minute. She got up, bones aching and creaking, as though she was going to put the kettle on to top up the teapot. So, he did it for her. Whilst the kettle was boiling, she shuffled her way out of the kitchen. He asked if she was alright, and she said yes, she'd be back in a minute, and he wondered if she were going to the toilet. Ian did not want to get involved with that sort of thing at all. Instead, he poured boiling water from the kettle into the teapot and fiddle-faddled around making two fresh cups of tea.

A few minutes later, she came back with a carrier bag hanging from her walking frame and he could see that there were clothes and things in it. "My husband's," she had said. "About the same size as you." He wondered when her husband had died. And how old-fashioned they might be. And if these items had been washed. Because he had a recollection from somewhere that when someone dies their bladder and bowels emptied themselves. He did not want to wear unwashed, dead men's trousers.

She handed them to him one by one. Waterproof top and bottoms for putting over clothes when it was raining. A compass. A Swiss Army knife. A pair of socks (which he would change into). And a bucket hat which he could see would be too small (and he thought it probably smelt anyway). He tied the carrier bag to his rucksack and thanked her and suddenly felt ever so emotional but covered it with a cough and a sniffle and a wipe of his eyes as if he had some grit in one of them. They talked a little more, about nothing in particular. Tomorrow's weather forecast mainly, and then he got up and left with Bernard.

It took him ages, an extra hour or so, going up that busy A12 and off to the right on another long and endless road towards Southwold. And, as he went, all he could do was replay bits of conversations he'd had with the old lady.

By the time he arrived his mood had slumped, and he simply bought some fish and chips for himself and sausages for Bernard. They headed northwards again to find somewhere to rest up and sleep the night.

Then he remembered the last thing she said to him. "I hope you find what you're looking for." She had handed him a small credit-card sized mirror from the bottom of the carrier bag. And he thought, he could have sworn, that she had added, "God bless," followed by "Adam." Although he was not sure if he had simply misheard her. He went to ask but she had already closed the door and he was on his way. He was trying to remember if he had mentioned Adam or not. He thought not. That spooked him.

***

Ian had always had the ability, so Kate had often said, to fall asleep on the spot. Literally. Well, almost. He had, in the past, once slept with Bernard laid out on his chest (more than once, actually). It was certainly true that he could usually go to sleep easily.

Not tonight, though. The third night of... what was it called... the word phrase thing. Sleeping out in woods and fields stuff. He just felt rattled by it all. Owls and rabbits were okay. Rats and things were not. He also had a fear of a spider crawling into his ear in the night and laying eggs and baby spiders crawling out of his nostrils and mouth in the morning. Rough camping. Yes, that was it. It could be spooky.

Ian had tried to sleep in a wooded patch of trees outside of Southwold. The other side of it. Northwards. But the crickle-crackle all around had made him feel uneasy. They were now in the middle of a maize field and, having checked the lump, the same size as ever, he was peering without his glasses at the baby booklet until he felt tired.

All About Our Family was the first page where he could write something.

When I Was a Child was the next one.

When Your Parent Was Young was the third page. Ian was surprised it did not say *Parent/Carer* these days.

He took out his pen from inside his jacket, then angled the page in the moonlight so he could see it. *All About Our Family* in fancy handwriting across the top. He hesitated, not sure what to write. He could not help thinking that, if he gave the booklet back to Alex and Hannah, it might become a family heirloom handed down through the generations. It could not be full of scribbled writing, spelling mistakes and crossings out. Then again, it may lay at the back of a kitchen drawer for 20 years before being thrown away.

He flicked to the back of the booklet, remembering he had already used one of the blank extra pages to make notes, drawing what looked like a large penis and also to write a *To Do* shopping list. He could not recall doing that which worried him. And he was not sure *Big Plasters. Vaseline. Poo Bags. Big Bottle* etc. was something he wanted to be remembered for. He thought he would use these extra pages as and when needed, for reminders and stuff, and would then pull them out later if he could do so without removing the front pages as well. If not, he would buy some big white stickers somewhere and put them over the list and anything else he might write there.

He could maybe write a poem or something like that on top of the stickers. Not that he ever had. Written a poem. But an amusing poem, maybe a limerick, might make the child – Pudding – laugh at a certain age. He'd have to give it some thought. The only limericks he could recall were rugby-type ones and he did not think any of those would be suitable. Besides, he should make one up. *There was a young child called Pudding.* Of course, that would not be the child's actual name. Hopefully not anyway. They picked such funny names these days. Mississippi. AJ! Attila. BK! Einstein-Agogo.

Ian put the booklet and his pen on the ground beside him and Bernard, then lay back and looked skywards. The moon and the stars and the, what was it, the clarity of it all, surprised him. The clearness, if that were a word.

He wished he could name the stars, even just one or two, but he could not.

He thought there was a great star one and another that looked like a bear, and one more that looked like a soup ladle. He gazed across the sky but could not see any of those.

Sitting up and taking his pen, he drew, as carefully as he could, the family tree – *Ian* and *Kate* at the top, then little lines to *Alex* and *Beth* and *Joe*. He hesitated for a long time and added *Adam*. He put a dash to the side of Alex's name and added the name *Hannah* and a dash down where he hesitated again and wrote in *Pudding*. He thought for a while deciding if he should add in Glenn and Yasmin's names but didn't – just in case they broke up and Beth and Joe had different partners by the time Pudding read this.

He thought for a second or two that he should add Hannah's family names – that he should start again with Pudding at the bottom in the middle and work upwards and outwards. But he could not bring himself to do that; the memory of their smug, self-satisfied faces troubling him. He also remembered overhearing what Alex had said about them a while back when he was talking to Kate about Hannah having the baby. "They'll be in the car park outside the hospital waiting to run in just as soon as the baby's born." Elbowing Alex out the way. Tearing

81

the baby from Hannah's arms. They made Ian feel sick.

And he did not really want to add in the names of parents above himself and Kate. Ian turned his wrist in the moonlight and could still see, faint but definitely still there, the scar that had been made by his father's cigarette. The only just-about-visible scar. On the outside anyway. His mother had long since gone. Walked out, his father had said, although he discovered the truth – and the awfulness of it – later.

Her place was filled by a much younger woman soon enough, his stepmother, until Ian left home for university and never went back. Kate was an only child too. Her father had died in a road accident when she was eight or nine. Her mother sought solace in drink. She was still around but they saw her rarely, once or twice a year. A cold and distant woman who made Kate feel tense and edgy. So, Ian just left their own names at the top like Adam and Eve. As if they were the start of it all.

Ian sat there for a moment thinking. Bernard was by his side, stretched out now and asleep, snoring oh-so-gently deep into his dreams of chasing rabbits.

He doodled a little stick man to the bottom right of the first page of the booklet. Then again and again on each subsequent page until, flicking the pages, the little figure made its jerky run from beginning to end. He put the booklet and pen back in his jacket pocket and sighed.

Ian rolled over, lay down, waiting for sleep to come. The horror of *When I Was a Child* and the guilt of *When Your Parent Was Young* and all the rest of it could wait for another night.

7
THE FAMILY GET-
TOGETHER

WEDNESDAY 6th JULY

(19.30 ONWARDS)

The six of them sat around the table in the orangery at The Cape, eating Chinese food, dipping chopsticks or knives and forks in and out of foil containers, taking what they wanted onto their plates.

Kate, Alex and Hannah, Beth and Glenn, and Joe. Yasmin was working at the care home this evening and was no doubt pulling emoji-type faces and giving thumbs-up galore to amuse the elderly residents.

They all met like this once a month or so to catch up on each other's news. But this get-together, suggested – demanded – by Beth, was an extraordinary one. It began as if it were a "same as usual" type of evening. But they were all really waiting for Kate to raise what they wanted to discuss – Ian and Bernard's disappearance.

Alex was the calmest of the three children and had started the evening by talking about the tattoo he had done that day – a girl's smiling face inside the wide-open jaws of a wolf. "Sounds delightful," Ian would have said instinctively if he had been there, and they would all have laughed and teased each other about this and that and the other. There was a moment's silence as Alex finished talking and Joe, in an all-purpose Eastern

European accent – he always did a foreign accent when he felt embarrassed about anything – said "Charming, Comrade, charming," and everyone smiled but did not laugh.

Beth was by far the most volatile child, quick to drama and straight on to melodrama without a moment's hesitation. She would probably have claimed she loved her dad the most. "Much more than any of you!" she would have screamed or at least shouted inside her head. "I make all the cakes for Father's Day and his birthday," she might have added, as if that were conclusive proof. She twitched and huffed her way through the meal, throwing glances and sighs all around as if to yell, to demand to know, "When are we going to talk about Dad?"

Glenn, of course, sat there ramrod straight and ready to make polite small talk. He was a practical fellow who knew that fitting stairlifts for old folk for a living wasn't much of a conversation piece and that there was limited interest in what some old lady had said to him that morning or the fact that an old boy had to shut his Alsatian in the kitchen in the afternoon. But he smiled and nodded at the right times. He was, more than anything, a black-or-white type of man who did not believe in ghosts or UFOs and, in olden days, would have claimed the earth was flat because he'd not seen anything to show him otherwise. He did not do feelings or emotions or anything like that. But he was a nice enough sort in his own way.

Hannah, almost shyly, and encouraged by Alex who touched her gently on the stomach, took out a scan photograph of the baby. Of Pudding. A new one. Done privately. In 4D!

She looked around the table and showed it first to Kate who made some sort of whooping noise as she rummaged in her apron and put on her glasses and peered at the photograph. "Today?" she asked and Hannah nodded.

"Bigger," Kate said, smiling almost triumphantly at Hannah. "And clearer. Such a nice scan," she added, passing the photograph on to Joe.

There was a moment's pause as they waited for Joe to

say something as inappropriate as Ian usually did. Working at the docks, moving stuff about in an effing and blinding environment, he was used to rough-edged conversations and sometimes struggled to let his real personality shine through at family times. They expected him to do a funny voice if what he had to say were kind and gentle, as though he needed to keep up the pretence of being tough and strong. He thought for a while as they waited, and simply said, in his normal voice, "The baby has the Wilkerson head. Dad's big head."

There was a silence (slightly surprised) and they all then seemed to talk at once. Kate said something about all babies having large heads in scans and patted Hannah's arm encouragingly. Hannah just gave Joe a look – not an angry or upset look but, well, more of a puzzled look as if to say, "What on earth are you talking about?" Glenn suggested in his way that it might be a trick of the light. Beth kicked Glenn under the table and called Joe an "idiot". And Alex just said, "Shut up, fatneck." Joe then passed the scan photograph to Glenn and pushed a whole sweet and sour chicken ball into his mouth.

And there it was, out there. The mention of Ian (and his big head), and they all knew it now had to be addressed. They waited for Kate to gather her thoughts as they passed the scan photograph from one to another with Glenn and Beth both saying the right thing, more or less. Beth did pronounce, after careful consideration, that it was definitely a boy. Joe, not sensing the trap, blundered in, and said that was stupid and how could you possibly see "it". Beth then paused for effect and added that "it was incredibly small and hard to see… much like yours". To which Joe replied, "ha ha" and everyone was then pretty much even-stevens.

"Where the hell is Dad?" Beth blurted out suddenly, turning around as if to say, "you all know but me!" Alex shook his head and shut his eyes as if to say, "for God's sake, don't". Joe did the same a second or two later. Glenn knew better than to challenge Beth and just sat there smiling vaguely at nobody in particular.

Hannah, tucking the scan photograph away, turned and smiled at Kate. She patted Kate's arm. The two of them had just started doing this touching thing with each other as if they both really, really wanted to hug but were too polite to do so first.

Thing is, that's what Kate needed right now. A hug. More than anything. A great big *there, there* hug. But she knew if anyone did hug her, she'd start crying. And she'd probably never stop.

***

"What did that note say again?" Beth demanded. "The one Dad left behind?"

Kate knew it from memory by now. "Taken Bernard for a walk. Be back sometime. Ian. PS. Sorry about the flip-flops."

"So, it's a suicide note," Beth stated, fighting back tears. "He didn't put love and he didn't put kisses."

Kate rolled her eyes. You could almost hear her groan. No one said or did anything. There was a frozen tableau for what seemed an age. Then Alex picked up his phone, pressed buttons and scrolled down. "Tony Hancock... Dad's favourite comedian... left a suicide note that ended, *Things just seemed to go too wrong too many times.*" He scrolled further. "And the actor Kenneth Williams' note ended, *Oh, what's the bloody point?* That's how you end a suicide note. Not *PS. Sorry about the flip-flops.*"

"The flip-flops," Kate explained, "had been thrown across the garden; one to the left, one to the right. As if in anger. There was dog mess on both." She laughed suddenly at the ridiculousness of it. Then raised her hands and shrugged her shoulders as if to say, "I don't know what to think." And the children, and Glenn and Hannah, all looked at her and could see that she was on the brink of tears. Hannah patted her on the arm again and Kate leaned her head towards Hannah, who responded in the same way, their heads now almost touching.

"I imagine," Kate began, sitting back up and laughing

86

through tears, "your father trod in Bernard's mess with one foot. Took the flip-flop off and threw it across the garden. Then stepped back and trod in it again with his other foot. Threw the other flip-flop away. He probably then fell over and rolled in it. Just for good measure, knowing him. You know what he's like. Laurel and Hardy in one body."

Alex said something about Ian's home-made ladder for painting the outside of the house, comprising a kitchen table chair on top of a garden bench. And how Ian had fallen off and hurt his ankle and had to be taken to hospital.

Beth cried her way through the story of Ian storing Christmas decorations away in the loft and putting his foot through the ceiling so all you could see was his sock and his hairy leg up to the knee.

Joe mentioned, somewhat off-topic, the time his friends at school had seen Ian singing loudly alone in his car. This was apparently the most embarrassing thing Joe had ever experienced in his whole life.

Kate sighed and pushed her plate away. She took a swig of her glass of gin fizz and ummed and aahed for a moment or two before deciding what to say. "I've not heard anything since I texted you... sent you all that photo of his note. I haven't heard a thing. I don't know where he's gone. I don't know what he's doing... I don't know when he'll be back... I'm sure he will come back," her voice wobbled slightly as she put her glass back on the table.

A barrage of questions followed from Alex and Joe, relatively calmly, and from Beth, relatively loudly (if not deafeningly). Hannah and Glenn remained silent. Kate answered each of them in her sensible, to-the-point way. "Has he taken any money out... used his credit cards?"

"No – they're all here so far as I can see."

"What cash does he have?"

"Maybe a few hundred from his Christmas pot."

"What else does he have on him?"

"Not sure. The clothes he's wearing and the cash… he's not taken his cards or his phone… that's on the side over there." Alex went to have a look but could not get by the thumb-print security.

"Where's he gone?" was the next main question, asked in various ways – "Where do you think he's gone? Where might he have gone?" – all of them coming at it from different directions.

"Don't know."

"Not sure."

"He could have gone anywhere."

"Is there some place he has always wanted to visit?" asked Glenn innocently.

Beth swore at him and said something about "My Dad's having a breakdown, he's not gone on his effing holidays, has he? D'uh." Both Kate and Alex, echoing each other, told her to calm down.

"Do you think he might have killed himself?" shouted Beth, her voice rising ever upwards now in a mix of anger and fear. "Have you two had an argument?"

Kate shook her head. "No. And no, he won't have taken his own life." She paused and added, more lightly: "Not intentionally anyway. He's capable of tripping over his feet on a railway platform when he's checking the train that's coming in… or leaning too far out and falling off a bridge watching a duck swimming by. Anything ridiculous like that is completely plausible."

She stopped and drank from her glass again. A little stronger now. Less likely to cry. The thought – the certainty – that he would not take his own life somehow encouraging her. But then she thought of the time Ian had fallen off that home-made ladder and twisted his ankle. And he was always tumbling over the edges of pavements. And bumping into bins and lampposts. She hoped he'd not be walking near a cliff edge. It would be touch and go.

The six of them talked it all to, well, death, really − if that wasn't too inappropriate a word. Kate being comforted by Hannah. Alex and Glenn calm and sensible. Joe trying to lighten the mood with jokes as best he could. Beth was Beth.

And they finished the Chinese takeaway and scraped leftovers from their plates back into the tinfoil containers. One or two containers of rice − but not the chicken, "we don't re-heat chicken," said Kate − were placed in the fridge for another day. All the rest were put back in the cardboard box and that went straight out to the grey bin by the garage.

They sat down again with bowls and spoons and serviettes to choose from profiteroles (Joe and Glenn) or raspberry trifle (Beth) or fresh fruit (Kate and Hannah). And it looked as though Ian and Bernard were going to be left to sort themselves out, but then Beth demanded, in that "I must know everything" way of hers, "Has he ever done anything like this before?"

Kate thought for a bit, swallowed a mouthful of banana and said, "We had an argument over at Waitrose in Ipswich once about the sell-by dates on half-price raspberry trifles and he, er, decided to walk home rather than come back in the car with me." She laughed out loud at the thought of it, a joyful, tinkling laugh.

"It took him about three or four hours, and it was getting dark by the time he got back. He stood in the kitchen whilst I was emptying the tumble dryer and he had thick mud all down his right side, his clothes… all over his face… in his hair. And he'd thrown his shoes away. So, he stood there expecting me to say something sympathetic and consoling, but I turned round and took the washing up to the ironing room. And just about kept a straight face."

She laughed again at the thought of it. Threw her head back and roared this time. The others watched her, not sure how to react − whether she was then going to burst into tears. But she did not. "He went upstairs and had a bath, put his clothes in the usual place in the corner of the bathroom and came downstairs, and we watched TV and just carried on and never spoke of it again." She shook her head with even more laughter.

"Well, he's not going to get far then, is he?" Alex said. "He's probably sitting in Rendlesham Forest in his underpants. Bernard's his hot water bottle. He won't have got any distance with Bernard anyway."

"He won't have taken Bernard on a bus or a train or anything like that," Joe added. "He'd have just gone walking... camping..." Joe was going to say "up the coast to Great Yarmouth. Maybe even to..." and the word "Hunstanton" popped into his head. He held it there and just said "... somewhere."

"He'll come back," Kate concluded. "What worries me is if he has an accident. If he falls over and breaks his ankle this time and can't walk. Remember the time he tried to put his pyjama bottoms on at the top of the stairs?" Alex, Beth and Joe all laughed and mock shuddered.

"Don't ask," Alex added to Hannah and Glenn. "No pants."

They were all quiet for a moment or two, thinking about Ian and Bernard out there somewhere (or possibly just about Ian falling down stairs without his pants on). "We should call the police," Beth said suddenly, anger still in her voice. "We can't just sit here and do nothing."

A babble of voices, each of them seeming to offer a different view. Kate cut through it as they all finished speaking. "He's a grown man. There's nothing to suggest he's going to harm himself. They won't want to know," she concluded. "Not yet, anyway."

"The papers then?" Beth insisted. "He always reads the papers every day. The local one, at least. We can make an appeal for him to come home." Again, another babble of noise. This time, more of a consensus of agreement that this might be a good idea. Joe ventured that Ian wouldn't want his business spread all over the newspaper, to which Alex replied that Ian had probably already done that if he were now living as The Wild Man of Rendlesham Forest.

Kate settled the matter. "Let's leave it for now. Give him a few more days to sort himself out and come back. If we've not heard anything by the weekend, then let's see if we can get something in the newspaper. In case he's round and about and might spot it. Agreed?" She watched as each of them nodded in turn. Some more enthusiastic than others. Beth, of course, was the last to nod her assent, reluctantly.

So they were up and hugging and kissing each other goodbye. By the front door, Kate and Hannah both hesitated for a moment before lunging at each other, patting their backs and all that stuff.

Beth and Glenn were out of the front door and away down the path. Glenn did not do the huggy-kissy type of thing. And Beth was still glowering and on edge. The sooner Glenn could get to bed and to sleep the better, although there was not really much chance of that for ages. Beth would be awake for hours yet, prodding Glenn with her elbow if he fell asleep first.

Joe touched Alex on the arm as he left and mouthed the word "Hunstanton" at him. Alex seemed to know what he meant, as if had already thought of it, and just said "Text me" under his breath. The two sons were going to find their dad.

8
SOUTHWOLD TO GREAT YARMOUTH

THURSDAY 7th JULY

(22.4 MILES, 7 HOURS 23 MINUTES)

There were mornings like this, thought Ian, when it was a joy waking up.

The sun on his face. Warmth on his body. The comfort of bracken for his bed.

He pulled his shoulders forward. Stretched out his arms and legs. Heard his body clicking and reached out to stroke Bernard.

Then he sat up, rubbed his eyes, and turned around to see where Bernard was. Not to his left. Nor to his right. Not by his head. Nor by his feet.

Ian stood up. He was in a little dip of land in the middle of a field of maize somewhere north of Southwold, with trees circling all around high and wide and stretching to the sky.

He had made himself a bed from bracken and leaves and, what was the word, the debris of nature. No, that wasn't right at all. Detritus. No, not that either. No matter. What mattered was that Bernard wasn't there. Just the rucksack and the old lady's carrier bag of bits and pieces.

Ian assumed Bernard had simply gone off to have a sniff, a wee, and to do his business. He felt a sense of alarm deep down inside though. But he knew it was foolish.

He whistled. The special whistle that called Bernard back. Two short whistles. One longer one. Come on!

He expected Bernard to come bursting through the trees, hot and panting, on the third whistle.

But nothing happened. Ian stood there for a minute or two and swallowed, realising how dry his throat was. Then he reached for the bottle of water by his bracken bed and took a swig. One. Two. Three. Thinking. Worrying. Considering the options. Weighing things up. His mind coming to sudden, and the most awful, conclusions.

Perhaps Bernard had been snatched in the night. Taken away as bait for a dog fight. He had no idea what made him think that. But he knew, the commonsense part of him anyway, that this was ridiculous. He had been taken by a fox, then. A pack of foxes. He also reckoned, in that calm part of his mind again, that this was just as unbelievable. Bernard, even in his diminished state, would fight back. Ian would have been woken by the snarling, the scratching, the fighting for life.

He looked at the ground where Bernard had been when he went to sleep. There were no signs of any disturbance nor any spots or smears of blood. Nothing untoward at all. He put the palm of his hand on the little bracken bed he had made for Bernard, but there was no feeling of warmth at all. So, Bernard had been gone a while. Just got up in the night and wandered off. Maybe chasing a rabbit, then got lost out there somewhere.

Ian stood, his head down, his eyes shut, on the edge of despair.

He listened to the sounds of the fields and trees and woodland waking, hoping to hear Bernard rustling through the undergrowth, maybe even barking to him.

But there was just a twitching restlessness out there. No more than that. And Bernard never really barked anyway.

Ian slipped the rucksack onto his back and set off to search. He slipped through the space between the trees where they had squeezed in last night. To a pathway where he could go left or right, the way they had come or the way they should be going that morning. He looked both ways as if he might see Bernard in the distance at one end or the other. But he was nowhere to be seen. Ian turned right, where they should be heading next towards Great Yarmouth.

He walked along the path, looking left and right into the trees and whistling and calling Bernard's name over and over. He stopped every so often to listen, hoping to hear some sounds of Bernard. But there was nothing, and on he went. A sick feeling in his stomach coming up into his throat. He could not bear to think of what might happen to Bernard out there on his own. Nor what he would tell the family when he got back. And he would have to go home if he could not find Bernard. He could not bear to go on without him, nor leave him behind like this. He shouted time and again, hoping to hear a single bark back.

Unlike most Jack Russells, Bernard never really barked. Not when the postman clattered letters through the letter box. Nor when the Amazon delivery driver threw three parcels one after the other over the garden gate. Not even when the blasted window cleaner kept bloody whistling "Whistle While You Work" over and over again. Ian could only remember Bernard barking three times ever. Once, when Ian had a new lawnmower and the noise enraged Bernard so much that he ran alongside trying to bite the black rubber wheels. Another time when they saw a frog in the garden and Bernard circled it, barking endlessly. And the third when they saw a hedgehog and Bernard raised a tentative paw to its prickles, then retreated, growling and barking.

Ian got to the end of the path and stepped onto the main road. Where they should turn right to go on up towards Great Yarmouth.

Looked up and down the open road, the woods to either side, hoping to see Bernard out there somewhere.

Nothing. All Ian could see, far away to the left, was a bus stop where he expected he'd have to wait for hours later, broken-hearted, to set off home. Alone.

Ian turned back to retrace his footsteps along the path, to pick up his belongings from the little clearing and to have another desperate look for Bernard the other way along the path. He kept on calling, turning round repeatedly and stopping and listening frequently for a noise, any type of noise, that might mean Bernard was out there somewhere. But he heard nothing.

Halfway along the path, on the way back to the clearing, he saw a woman of indeterminate age appear from between the trees, walking towards him. Wild grey hair, a heavily lined face, olive-green trench coat, black leggings and boots. A whippety-greyhound mix of a dog trotting beside her. "I've lost my dog," Ian blurted out. She carried on walking as if she had not heard him. He turned back towards her and raised his hands in despair.

"Lots of dogs in these woods," she said, calling back over her shoulder as if the matter were something and nothing. "Plenty to eat." He did not know what to say to that. The idea that there were dogs roaming about unseen seemed unlikely to him. There were trees. A woodland. Hardly a wood or a forest. That Bernard might somehow meet up with them and have some adventures just made him feel sick. The reality would be that Bernard would walk round and round in circles eventually dying out here under a tree. Starved to death.

Ian's head dropped as he continued walking. He had hoped the woman might be sympathetic. Maybe even help him search. But she was gone. And he was alone. He wished more than anything that his family were here now to help. Even Beth with her endless, blood-curdling yells.

He focused on putting one foot in front of the other. Trudging back to where they'd slept. Close to despair.

Ian thought about what he could do. He'd given up calling and whistling as he walked along. Bernard would be too far away to hear him. Ian knew he could not just head for home.

However he felt, he could not bear to give up and go straight away, knowing he'd never see Bernard again.

But what was the alternative? He could spend the day criss-crossing the woodland and the fields, guessing it was probably four or five miles one way, four or five miles the other, before he reached a town. Or he could try and find the edge of the woodland and fields and walk all around. Shouting and whistling as he went. But he realised the chance of stumbling across Bernard was, in all honesty, nil. At some point, Ian would lie face down in the bracken and have to give up.

As he reached the trees where he'd turn to the clearing, he wondered, hard though it was, whether he should go home now, as fast as he could, asking everyone to come back here with him to search tonight. Until they found Bernard's body, wherever it was. But he did not want to go home. He saw, in his head, how everyone would be there as he limped up the driveway on aching feet, waiting for Bernard to appear behind him. "Where's Bernard?" They would ask. And he would choke out the words "I've... lost him. I think he's... dead."

He turned, pushed his way through the trees, and reached the clearing. Ready to walk across to the old lady's carrier bag beside his bracken bed.

He would just lie down there and die.

Then, he looked up in utter despair. And saw Bernard sitting there panting, a rabbit in his jaws. He dropped it by Ian's feet. Ian hoped it did not twitch.

***

The day, truth be told, did not get any better than that. The rabbit that did not twitch. It meant that Ian did not have to touch it, nor do anything unpleasant with it. He could just leave it there as if it had simply fallen over and was having a rest. And they could be on their way. An early start. They'd need it. So that's what they did. They got going. And it was a long time

– too late to go back – before he realised that he'd left the old lady's carrier bag behind.

Ian had set himself the target of reaching the Pleasure Beach at Great Yarmouth, with its lights and rides and noises, by the time it got dark. He reckoned, from road signs, that it was a good 20 miles. He did not think they had walked so far in a day. Moreover, he was not sure that they could. He would have to carry Bernard much of the time; no doubt about that.

He ticked off the route in his head. Up the busy A12. Kessingland. Pakefield. Lowestoft with Pleasurewood Hills just the other side of it. Then Hopton and Gorleston. Or maybe Gorleston before Hopton. He was not sure. The map he had got from Snape Maltings did not go that far. And finally, Great Yarmouth itself.

He knew they had to pace themselves properly. Three miles an hour with short rests every two hours or so should see them there by 17.00.

Ian would pass the time in daydreaming reveries, stopping whenever he felt light-headed.

He realised he had to be careful, constantly monitoring the ground and the weather and the sun above. And the lump on his neck. And his feet. Bernard too, of course.

The first part of the walk, towards Kessingland, was a pretty one. Ian and Bernard walked steadily along a B-road, a world of lanes and fields, Ian picking Bernard up whenever he saw or heard a car approaching.

They then turned north to head up the A12 at Wrentham, where Ian bought supplies and some treats, including a rubber bone for Bernard, from a village store. Pasties, sausage rolls, pork pies. Emergency meals for both of them. They stopped for a rest just along from there before carrying on.

And on and on. Stop start. Stop start. Bernard up. Bernard down. The A12 was not a pretty road and seemed to just go on for ever and ever. Eventually, just as he was feeling dizzy and thought he might keel over, Ian saw signs for Africa Alive, a wildlife park just off the A12 at Kessingland. He decided they'd stop there for a while for a proper get-your-breath-back sit-down. Maybe even a short but restorative snooze.

He thought it was a funny place for an African wildlife park, out here in the sticks of East Anglia, in the middle of nowhere. He was tempted to go and have a look, or maybe even a walk round (if dogs were permitted), so Bernard could see the wild animals.

But he remembered Bernard's reaction when he first saw cows in a field in Felixstowe. The stepping back. The hurrying away. He was most put out. Indignant. Almost outraged at the sight. These big brown and white mooing beasts that came ambling across as though they knew him. So, Ian decided they'd be better off sitting here on this bench.

He'd shut his eyes for five minutes whilst Bernard chewed and licked and fiddled about with the bone-type thing, it was the only way to describe it, that he'd bought at that village store. Forty winks would see him right. He could feel himself nodding off.

It was Bernard, sitting up and staring, dropping the bone thing, that alerted Ian to what was happening. Ian glanced at the dog and then saw, over the way, a lollipop lady watching a line of young mothers and small children across the road.

One of the children turned and looked beyond Ian and screamed. One by one, all of the children, the young mothers, and finally, the lollipop lady, all turned and screamed too.

Ian looked and saw a huge whatnot... you know, stripes and teeth and rippling muscly bits. A tiger, yes, that was it.

The screaming children, young mothers and the lollipop lady had caught the tiger's eye and it was moving forward, low to the ground, ready to attack.

Ian stood up, stepped in front of Bernard, and put himself squarely between the tiger and the screaming... ab-dabs. You know, them.

Ian had once hypnotised next door's cat, crouched and ready

to do its business in his garden, by staring at it and making a high-pitched humming noise. Not humming really, more piercing than that. But he had done it to see what happened and the cat just stared at him. Then turned and ran away.

He would do the same now with the tiger. Leaning forward. Making a screaming noise in his mouth.

The tiger stopped and looked at him. Their eyes locked ready for combat. Ian held fast. On and on. He would not break his gaze first.

He held it, for ever and ever it seemed, until he felt that he could do it no more.

He sensed his eyes shutting and knew, in that terrible moment, the horror that would follow – the slaughter – if he could not continue.

A second more. And another. One last second and it would all be over. He would have failed the children.

Then, such a moment of joy, a marksman from the zoo, marksperson these days most probably, appeared as if from nowhere, running at the tiger, stopping, kneeling, and taking aim with a stun gun thing.

And it was all over so fast, just like that.

Everyone cheered for Ian. Their hero.

He smiled modestly and waved at the small children.

Ian woke with a start and, remembering where he was, made a click-click noise to Bernard who looked at him wearily. Then they were up off the bench and on their way. Slowly and steadily. More of the same. Mile after mile after mile. This never-ending trek. Ian carried Bernard more than he didn't.

Up that A12 road for an hour to Pakefield, past the old holiday camp, and another hour or so on to Lowestoft where they got a McDonalds and sat on the beach by the pier sharing burgers and chips. Thinking about nothing much in particular other than aches and pains and how far they still had to go.

Then, click-clicking Bernard again, Ian wandered down to the sea for a paddle to ease his sore feet. He watched as their foot and paw prints in the wet sand were washed away by the tide. Ian walked up and down kicking the spray. Bernard followed him neither excited nor frightened by the sea. He was, after all, a stoic little chap.

Ian wondered why Lowestoft beach was sandy whereas Southwold was mostly stones and gravel, even though it could only be 10 or 12 miles away. He thought maybe there was a point at which it switched. Where the shingle stopped and the sand started.

And so, a little while later, as the sun was on its downwards descent, Ian and Bernard were on their way once more. The A12 seemed to have morphed into the A47 (although it looked the same), as they headed towards Pleasurewood Hills on this exhausted blur of their endless journey.

***

The beginning of the second half of the day's walk, up by the turning to the amusement park and beyond, was surprisingly joyful for Ian. So unexpected! It was if he had got his second wind and was hitting his stride. He thought perhaps it was the chips that had done it. Even Bernard seemed to be full of energy. He estimated they were doing closer to four miles an hour than three. Not that that would last for long.

The road, to be honest, was not one that he had imagined walking along on their journey. It was not the stuff of dreams. He had thought they would make their way on beaches and cliffs and through woods and fields and really get back to nature.

He believed somewhere above Great Yarmouth there was a coastal path, the Norfolk Coastal Path, that he had heard of, and thought this was more, what was it, more natural. He could walk along that – if he could find it, of course. Until then, it was all pavements and petrol stations and parades of shops and cars and lorries and hullabaloo.

Suddenly, the A47, or whatever the stupid thing was

101

called, seemed to turn from a busy but urban road into a dual carriageway that was more like a motorway in places. And, carrying Bernard now, Ian felt more and more edgy.

So, he came off the carriageway and went east towards the coast, spotting signs for Hopton one way and Gorleston the other. He decided to head northwards towards Great Yarmouth, and got lost and retraced his steps more than once. (Four times actually.)

Through back streets and over roundabouts. Down side streets, backwards and forwards. Over and over again. Getting angrier and angrier.

And on he went. His mind, he felt, was a mush now. No thoughts or daydreams or worries, nothing. All he could focus on was his feet. It was a matter of putting one foot in front of the other just as long as he could, until he either arrived at his destination or stopped and slumped by the wayside, somewhere out of sight.

Finally, after hours of aches and pains, sobs and tears, and exhaustion (although Bernard seemed quite happy in his arms), Ian reached the outskirts of Great Bloody Yarmouth, all wide-open roads and roundabouts (so many wretched roundabouts) and cars whizzing by at 70 miles an hour. It was not as he remembered the town.

Some 10 to 20 minutes later, he staggered across the river and recognised the old buildings and the space where they used to have the market. Ian went by a multi-storey car park and underneath some archway thing (he could not think of the correct word as he was growing far too tired), then down a road to the seafront, the cinema, and finally the Britannia Pier.

And he was crying by this time. They had done it. So far and so long. And his head hurt. And his neck and his shoulders. And his feet. God, his feet hurt so much.

But if he could just go a little way along the prom and maybe come off onto the sand by that beer garden place, he could sit there in triumph. He would see the Pleasure Beach and the rides and everything and just think, there, I've gone and done it. Well done, Wilkie.

And he lay on the sand with Bernard next to him for ever such a long time, until it was properly dark. He wondered later if he had fallen asleep or had maybe even passed out (which was by far the more likely).

And then they wandered a little way along the front. Ian went in the toilet block whilst Bernard sat outside. Then Ian picked up hot dogs and bottles of water from a souvenir shop on the front. And that was about it.

And they walked, limped and stumbled really, out of town and into the sand dunes to the north of Great Yarmouth. And he thought later that he had fallen over there or possibly even collapsed (which was closer to the truth).

***

As Ian lay in the dunes beyond Great Yarmouth, Bernard stretched out alongside him asleep, he remembered a vivid dream from his childhood. He would have been eight or nine, and sleeping alone in his small bedroom, a box room really, where he lived with his father and his much younger stepmother who he did not really like; nor her him – not at all. She called him "the nuisance".

As Ian came out of the deepest sleep, he saw a woman, covered with a colourful head-dress, and swathed in silk scarves, standing in front of him. She raised a gun and aimed it at his face. Then said, "Lyndon Berry, London." And pulled the trigger. Ian turned his head instinctively to the side. The shot missed him. He lay there breathing heavily. Sweating. Waiting for the second gunshot. But it did not come. And, eventually, he sat up. The woman was not there.

He recalled this dream so vividly as if it were real. He clearly remembered waking and feeling a presence in the room. He opened his eyes. She was at the end of his bed. As if she had been waiting for him to awake. To see her and hear what she had to say before she shot him. "Lyndon Berry, London," – although the first two words sounded as though they were one, "Lyndonberry". He had no idea then what it meant. Did not know anyone or anything with that name. It was the words as much as the vision that he remembered all these years.

Ian sat up in the dunes and looked around. It must now be 1.00 or 2.00. He was still exhausted by the previous day's walking. More than 20 miles. It was too much for him. That distance. And Bernard. He needed to pace everything better.

And here he was – here they were – exposed somewhere in what seemed to be mile after mile of dunes. They would be seen if anyone were to wander in and along. A young couple coming home from a nightclub. Whoever. He preferred to be hidden away somewhere out of sight. And they were not; not really.

But he was too tired to care as he lay there. It was at least out in the open and that was better than hiding in a car park or behind the bins of a supermarket or in a shop doorway. This was, what was it, he could not think of the word at all. Better, maybe.

The second dream Ian could remember from childhood – teenage years really – was when he had come back alone from a pub after celebrating someone's 18th birthday party. Down a wooded country lane. In the sky above him, he saw a row of lights gently throbbing, and heard a deep humming noise alongside it. Screwing his eyes up and looking beyond the lights, he could make out a silver shaped object. He threw stones at it as it rose and accelerated away out of sight.

That night, he dreamed he was on board an alien spaceship and was being subjected to medical examinations, as his mother would have put it, "down there" (front and back). They stretched things out as far as they could and pushed other things in as far as they would go. And they leaned over, these spindly grey stick creatures with the big dark eyes, and studied him.

They were talking to him, in his mind, but he could not make out what they were saying.

He woke, with sick on his pillow and in his hair and two thirds of his genitalia hanging out of his pyjama bottoms. He thought this was most likely a consequence of a missing button rather than an alien's clumsiness at tidying him up. But he could never find a missing button and could not work out how so much (one meat, one veg) could have squeezed itself through such a small space between the buttons. It was – they were – painful and ached the whole day.

Ian wanted to move out of the dunes because they made him feel bad in some way. Really bad. Uneasy. He was not sure why. It was more than just the thought of being found. Maybe being robbed. Bernard being stolen.

That, either of those, was bad enough but... no, it was not there. He was fighting sleep now, well-deserved sleep, but he wanted to stay awake and get his thoughts in order.

He hated dunes. That was it. He really did not like them. The ever-shifting spread of sand pushing into bushes and forever changing shape. Shape-shifting. Monsters. Ah no, it was too much. He could not think, the tiredness was spreading through his brain.

And Ian was in another dream, every bit as vivid as those from his childhood and teenage years. A nightmare really. He stood in dunes, much like these, and had a 99 cone which he licked and turned and licked and turned. He was enjoying the sheer pleasure and joy of it so much. But he did not touch the chocolate flake. He was saving that. He was not sure why, just that it was important that he left it.

Ian was moving through the dunes. Hurrying. He did not know why he felt such a sense of utter dread. And he was running now. Just Ian on his own with no one else about. And he knew that something very bad, something terrible, was going to happen if he did not keep this chocolate flake upright as he ran. Wherever it was he was going to.

And he was suddenly through the dunes. And he realised then why he hated them so much. And why he had been saving that chocolate flake. And why it was just too late. Adam. Out there. Beyond the dunes. In the water.

And Ian sat up again, his face twisting and sobbing in pain, and he grabbed his rucksack and Bernard and made his way out of the dunes along the beach. He walked and walked and walked until he was so exhausted that he lay down on the sand with Bernard next to him and finally fell asleep.

People, young people, did walk by him and Bernard and smiled to each other. One little group had a whip-round and put some notes and coins inside the edge of his right shoe.

9
GREAT YARMOUTH TO SEA PALLING

FRIDAY 8th JULY

(15.9 MILES, 5 HOURS 11 MINUTES)

Once Ian was up and ready to leave the dunes the next morning, he decided that today, at least until the afternoon, was going to be a good day. He had found £11.55 in his shoe – no idea how that came to be there – and he was going to spend time having fun in Great Yarmouth. The whole Great Yarmouth – Caister-on-Sea, Hemsby, West Somerton, Horsey, Waxham, Sea Palling list; the great big flipping endless… thing of it – could wait until later in the day.

He'd been walking all day every day since the beginning of the week. He'd kept his focus, covered the miles, stuck to his schedule, and shredded his shoes and socks and feet in the process. His clothes, which he had forgotten to wash each night and hang over a tree to dry, were stiff in places, especially under the arms. He did not want to think about his pants. They felt as though they had been starched.

Besides, apart from a change of clothes – he'd throw away his old shirt and his pants and sock afterwards – he wanted to buy a sun hat and a cane. He'd go for the biggest bucket hat he could find, tearing the fabric at the back to fit his head, if need be, and a stout cane. Not a fancy one like a magician might have but something that was practical. Well, maybe a bit twisty and Harry Potter-ish. He'd have to see. He'd not buy sunglasses; they were always too small for his head, even women's larger glasses.

Off they went back along the beach towards the pier and the main stretch of the front along to the Pleasure Beach. They'd come here, as a family, once or twice a year for the day in summer, up until the Hunstanton holiday. A full English and a big white mug of tea and platefuls of white bread and butter to start with. Then up and round the shops in the town, checking out book shops and sweet shops, and back down to the pier where they'd play on the tuppenny slot machines for ages. No lunch, well maybe fizzy drinks and candy floss on the pier, nougat sometimes, popcorn too, before they did something else in the afternoon.

If the weather was good, Ian and Alex would walk to the car, parked up in a road opposite the Pleasure Beach, and come back with a picnic basket of goodies and those coconut thingamajig things – mats – and they'd sit on the sandy beach and look out to sea and, later on, Beth would throw something at Alex or Joe or Adam, a satsuma usually, and look away quickly (although everyone knew it was her). And they'd chase each other and run in and out of the sea and push each other over and have a good, squabbily time.

If the weather wasn't so good, they'd go to the cinema down by the pier – there were so many Disney films that Ian nodded off and slept through and woke up blinking at the end – or, if there was nothing much on, they'd do something else. The Hippodrome circus just off the prom one year, or a theatre show – they'd seen The Chuckle Brothers so many times there. And then, at the end of the day, fish and chips and home with everyone asleep in the car (except Ian, of course, who was driving).

Ian thought he'd do the same today, at least up until lunchtime, or just after, when he'd head on off to Sea Palling instead of the cinema and fish and chips. He'd find a chip shop somewhere by nightfall for sure. So, he went and had his breakfast at a café on the prom eating his full English (sausages for Bernard) and swilling down two mugs of tea.

Then a big wee, as Bernard waited outside, at the block of toilets just along the way. And up the street towards the town, where he bought a white T-shirt with "69" in red letters on the front, and a pack of white, fluffy-looking socks and some black trainers from an open-fronted shop that looked like a market stall.

He had wanted to go to Marks & Spencer in the town and get a proper set of replacement clothes but knew it would be busy there and he could not risk leaving Bernard outside. Instead, he carried Bernard and went back to the toilet block where he changed and shoved his old shirt and sock and shoes into a bin outside and then stood there on the prom deciding what to do next.

It was at this point, this instant, that Ian suddenly saw Adam. He was walking along the prom, away from Ian, up by the green and going towards the Sea Life Centre. This stunned Ian because he'd not seen Adam since Hunstanton, and he was totally unprepared for the moment.

His little head with the blonde hair that never really settled because he had a double crown. The blue and white stripey top. His favourite − the one he always wanted to sleep in at night. Navy shorts and white socks and sandals.

He was walking along with his hand up, holding on to the jacket of the woman he was with. In his right hand, he had a little red bucket and spade, and Ian could hear the spade clack-clacking against the bucket.

Ian picked up Bernard and started following the woman and Adam. The woman did not look anything like Kate from behind; she was shorter and stouter and had gingery hair under a light blue hat with a matching linen jacket and navy shorts and solid, tree-trunk legs. And boating shoes. No, nothing like Kate at all.

She was singing something to Adam, a song that sounded familiar to Ian. He could not quite hear it and moved ever closer so that, eventually, as they approached the Pleasure Beach, he was walking just a few steps behind and keeping pace, left foot, right foot, in time with the woman's steps. "Wheels on the bus," that was what she was singing. "Go round and round," Adam's favourite.

And Ian was crying now, rubbing his face into Bernard's neck, and people coming the other way were looking at him strangely and he did not know what to do. So, he just kept going, behind and in time with the woman and the child. He wanted to stop the woman putting his hand on her shoulder, so that she would turn. And the boy would too, so that Ian could see his face. He could smile at Adam and say something. About loving him so much. He'd never really said it, and he always wished he had.

Suddenly, unexpectedly, she did stop and turn, and he was not sure if he had touched her on the shoulder or if he had just imagined it. Or if she had noticed the passers-by reacting to him. She looked at Ian and seemed shocked. Alarmed, really. He thought, through his tears, that she had a kind and friendly face, and he must have frightened her in some way. And so he said he was sorry in a voice that was maybe a little too loud.

She replied that it was okay, don't worry, and turned back to the little boy. He was looking up at her and Ian could see now that he was nothing like Adam. His face, anyway. A nice, sweet face. But completely different to Adam's. His hair was not as blonde, and it was long and held up with a clip on the top of his head. And his stripey top was not stripey. More checkered really. And Ian suddenly felt very stupid. And horribly embarrassed.

The woman glanced at Ian again, a worried look really, as she bent and lifted the small boy into her arms and said something to him under her breath. Then she was hurrying away, and the boy turned and watched Ian standing there, holding Bernard, and crying.

Ian decided, on the spot, that he had had enough of Great stupid Yarmouth and that this – wandering along looking at family-orientated places and things to do – was not for him. Not today. People would think he was odd or weird and maybe even dangerous.

He knew he was none of these things. He was simply sad and fed-up and miserable and this, seeing and thinking the little boy was Adam, meant his mind was almost certainly now playing tricks on him. He was probably going mad.

So, he walked back a little way along the promenade and sat down again at the table outside the café where he had eaten breakfast. He would gather his thoughts here, and compose himself. Get ready to restart the walk. By the time the waitress had brought him a cup of tea he was feeling a little better, so he asked her for a muffin, which he would share with Bernard. He'd have the chocolate bits and Bernard could have the thingy. You know, the bready stuff.

***

Next to the table where Ian and Bernard were sitting was a big white whatsit. A wire mesh swing round thing. A stand, yes, that was it. With all sorts of postcards of Great Yarmouth on it. Ian thought for a moment, remembering suddenly that he had planned to write postcards to everyone. He had forgotten. His mind was like an old man's holey vest.

He shuffled through the cards on the stand, ignoring the McGill postcards of heavy-breasted harridans and small, bespectacled men. And the children's ones with teddy bears and googly eyes. He just focused on those with views of Great Yarmouth, the pier mostly.

Kate. Alex and Hannah. Beth and Glenn. Joe and Yasmin. He'd need four. He chose two with a single, but slightly different, view of the pier and two with four little photographs of other views of the resort. He gave some money to the waitress when she came back with the muffin and asked her if there were any stamps. She had some in her handbag out the back, and so he bought four from her for a handful of pound coins and sat there, ready to write.

He flicked through the four postcards again, looking at each in turn, and thought they were rather dull and uninspiring. They all looked, what was it, not dated – outdated. Something from the 1980s, maybe even earlier.

He sighed and took a pen from his jacket. *Kate*, he wrote on one of them. Went to add *Dear* in front but he hadn't left enough space. So, he squeezed in *Hi* instead, and thought for a while about what you should write on a postcard to your wife of 30-odd years. *Hi Kate… I've gone mad. Love Ian x.* Then he shook his head and put the postcard to one side.

He put two more side by side in front of him. One for Beth and Glenn. The other for Joe and Yasmin. Try as he might, he could not remember their addresses. He could see Beth's terraced home and Joe's block of flats in his head but could not recall the numbers or even the roads. He put those postcards aside too.

But he could remember Alex and Hannah's address. The road and the number. He did not know the postcode beyond IP11, but it would get there just fine in a few days. He wrote *Hannah* and *Alex* and the address on the right of the back of the postcard. Stuck a stamp on it, then sat and thought.

He knew he had to say he was sorry for what happened at the gender reveal. They – Kate, the children and their partners – had obviously all decided he had been rude. He did not think he had. Not really. They – the family – had not seen what Hannah's parents were like. The smugness. The smirks. The asides. The whole control-freakery-ness of it.

Kate had said he needed to apologise though. If not to her family – no chance of that! – at least to Hannah. Kate had said, word for word, after the gender reveal, "You have to be nice to her… *whatever*" (as he tried to state his case) "… otherwise

112

you… we… won't get to see the baby. She's tough as old boots, that one. She won't let us near him."

He turned the postcard over again and again, thinking about what to write. There was not much space really. He decided he would not put *Dear Alex and Hannah* at the top as that would waste a line. Nor *Love Dad/Ian x* at the end, as that would be another wasted line. He would just write a three- or four-line apology in a large, easy-to-read hand rather than his usual spider-ish scrawl.

He hesitated, looking at the ridiculous photograph of the pier on the front of the card; it must be at least 40 years old. A lifetime ago. When the world was a simpler place. Maybe happier too. He scribbled a little shaded-in figure, a stick man, on top of the theatre at the end of the pier and was tempted to add a speech bubble, "aarrgghh", but thought that would be childish. He then flipped the card over, having decided what to put.

It had to be an apology, straight and to the point, with some other kindly words. Nothing too personal, he did not want the postman reading it and wondering what that was all about. So he wrote, in a large and careful hand, as if it were not his own, *I am sorry.* He thought for a moment and added, *I hope your pregnancy and Pudding and everything go well for you.* And he drew a little heart in the space that was left and shaded it in.

And that, he thought, was that. He finished his mug of tea, gave Bernard the last piece of the muffin, and he was up, holding the postcard to Alex and Hannah, click-clicking to Bernard and was on his way back along the prom towards a post box by the toilet block.

The waitress, coming out a moment or two later and noticing he had left the other postcards on the table, called after him once and then twice, a little louder the second time. But he was out of earshot and, quite frankly, she could not be bothered to go after him, as she had been on her feet all day and her legs hurt. She had varicose veins all down the back of her legs and, from a distance, they looked like a route map of the Elizabeth Line.

When Ian had put the postcard in the post box, he went for another wee in the toilet block whilst Bernard sat patiently outside. Then he came out and decided that these trainers were far too stiff and tight. So, he rummaged through the bin and, some way down beneath lolly wrappers and fish and chip papers and what felt like a warm nappy, he found his trusty old canvas boat shoes. He put them on, whistled to Bernard, and they were on their way. And he suddenly remembered he had not bought a hat or cane and that his pants still felt stiff. And the new T-shirt was too tight and made him look rather bosomy. He sighed.

It was a shame really, more than that, a great pity, that Ian and Bernard then left Great Yarmouth. That they did not walk as far as the Pleasure Beach as Ian had first planned. That they had turned back by the Sea Life centre. Ian had completely forgotten about the rides what with the whole Adam sighting and everything.

Had they gone further along the prom, Ian would surely have seen, stuck on telegraph poles and lampposts and walls up by the Pleasure Beach, the A4 sheets of paper with his photo on them – a blow-up of an old photograph where he looked like a sour-faced prisoner – and DAD in big black letters above and PHONE HOME below. And he would without doubt have telephoned home and things – all that happened next – would have been very different.

But he did not. And the time – yesterday, the Thursday – that Alex and Joe had spent driving around and putting up posters in places that they thought Ian might visit in Aldeburgh and Southwold and Lowestoft and Great Yarmouth was all in vain. And they had turned back from Great Yarmouth, tired and somehow angry with Ian, the posters all put up, and headed for home. Agreeing they'd give it a day or two before going – if need be – to Hunstanton at the weekend, after the next family get-together. To do it all again. Until the silly old man saw a poster and realised how much they loved him.

***

Ian and Bernard walked side by side along a wooded path, through fields and woods and farmland, and Ian was completely and utterly spooked by the darkness and the silence and the dead of night.

They had not, other than that first evening when he had been driven on by a mix of rage and pride, walked at night-time. And that had spooked him too. The horned Viking at Sutton Hoo especially.

Ian liked to check all around and be settled in a tucked-away hidey-hole by the time it got dark. A copse. Behind a tree. In a ditch. Somewhere he felt safe and hidden.

The first part of the afternoon's walk, Great Yarmouth to Caister-on-Sea, maybe four miles in all, had been on the beach, striding along through golden sands. Ian was troubled, his thoughts all over the place.

He decided, after a while, with that rational part of the brain, that to be happy – to stay sane, really – he had to keep his focus on waking, walking, stopping, eating, walking, stopping, eating, sleeping; and starting over again. Anything but thinking himself into a miserable mood.

As he moved inland, to the town centre and the Co-op food store to top up with supplies, he stopped for a while, sitting on a bench with Bernard next to him. Then he was on his way again, head down, focused, back to the beach to continue the walk on the sands to Hemsby; another four miles or so.

When he was walking along the beach from Caister-on-Sea to Hemsby, mile after mile of sand with the sun on his back, he started, ever so slowly at first, to have this feeling, which grew into utter certainty, that Adam was behind him. Ian was out front. Bernard to his left, two steps behind. Adam to his right, alongside Bernard.

Ian felt that if he kept going at this slow and steady pace, Adam would stay with him. And if Ian were quiet, could control his breathing and the swish-swish-swish of his shoes in the sand as he walked along, he could hear Adam's soft and gentle breaths and the pit-pat of his sandals. That skippety-hop walk he did when he was really happy.

But Ian knew that if he turned around to try and see Adam's face, so full of determination, his arms and legs moving along like a little soldier, he would not be there. He would vanish in that instant. The only way Ian and Adam and Bernard could stay together would be if Ian just kept going; on and on.

And so he did. Up along the beach, by Hemsby and West Somerton, and on towards Horsey and Waxham and Sea Palling. Mile after mile. Step after step. Ian just kept his head down. One foot after the other. Hour after hour. With his dog and his little boy behind him. And you know what? It made him happy. It gave him a sense of peace and contentment.

It was just extraordinary. This feeling that Adam was there. The comfort. The joy of it. And Ian could hear him so clearly, Adam. All three of them walking in time, their breaths in and out.

Ian knew that if he was distracted by passers-by, by nods and smiles and conversations, or if he stopped to take a drink, even a mouthful of water, or just to check the lump, that the spell would be broken, and he and Bernard would be on their own again.

Somewhere on the beach between Horsey and Waxham, after hours of walking into the failing light and darkening skies, Ian stumbled – collapsed – and lay with his face in the sand and his rucksack pressing hard into the sweat of his back.

And he heard breaths and steps approaching and opened his eyes to see Bernard, his ever-faithful Bernard, coming up to him and sitting down in his stiff-backed way. And Ian lifted his head and looked beyond Bernard and there was nothing – nobody – there.

Ian lay down for ever such a long time. Until it was cold and dark and the sweat on his clothes had dried and stuck to his back and under his arms and between his legs. Then, he sat up and reached wearily into his rucksack, taking out food and drink for himself and Bernard. After that, at last, he was on his way again.

And now, hours later, somewhere this side or that side of Sea Palling, he really did not care where he was. He was walking next to Bernard on a path through the woods, and he could feel a presence behind him. Not Adam though. A malign one.

And he turned, repeatedly, but there was nothing there but the dark and the shadows and the crackle of sudden movement in the bushes behind the trees. So, he shouted in a husky voice at whatever it was and cursed and worried to himself who or what it might be.

Until finally, at the end of the day, he picked up Bernard and ran as best he could, stumbling and falling and getting up again, until he was out of the woods and into fields. He went into the middle of one where he could see all around and just sat there, sweating and cowering, until at long last he collapsed into an uneasy, troubled sleep. As he did, he thought it had not, after all, been a good day. Indeed, he wondered if he would ever have a good day again.

10
SEA PALLING TO MUNDESLEY

SATURDAY 9th JULY

(12.9 MILES, 4 HOURS 14 MINUTES)

Ian, with Bernard just behind him, stood outside a pharmacy later the next morning. They were somewhere between Sea Palling and Mundesley. Maybe halfway and inland a bit. Ian was not sure where exactly and could not care less. He had more important things to worry about.

There were three elderly ladies already queueing inside the pharmacy. One more stood outside, just in front of Ian and Bernard.

The man in the queue behind Ian was huffing and puffing and sighing and generally making it plain that he wasn't happy waiting here. Passive-aggressive. No, not that. Anyway, Ian knew, could sense, that something really bad was about to happen.

Ian and Bernard had risen early and set off from the wooded area outside of Sea Palling just after 7.00, heading north up the coast. It was one of those bright and sunny days that you just knew was going to be hot, hot, hot. When you looked out from the beach towards the horizon, there was a hazy mist where the sky met the sea.

Ian wanted to get another 12 to 15 miles done today. He knew he'd have to pace himself, and Bernard, carefully.

He hoped to get the bulk of the miles out of the way by midday before it got too hot to walk comfortably. They'd rest up somewhere till about 16.00, start walking again, and keep going until they arrived at Mundesley.

As they walked, Ian noted a village was a mile or two off the coastal path and he decided that it was well worth a short detour. He wanted to get some pills and potions for his aching back and feet from a pharmacy, and to stock up on supplies if there was a village store. He had a fancy for a pizza and bread pudding and hoped he might find them there. And maybe some dog treats and another toy for Bernard; the last bone thing having vanished already. All being well, they would arrive just before noon.

As Ian and Bernard had walked up to the pharmacy, a white van had gone by them, then stopped, and started to reverse to go into the disabled parking space behind them. Ian had scooped up Bernard and, as he walked by the white van, he turned and gave a disdainful, down his nose, look at the driver. Ian wished he hadn't as it was this driver that now stood behind Ian and was cursing, "Like I've nothing effing better to do than stand here."

It had, up to this point, been rather a pleasant morning as Ian had tried to put his troubled thoughts behind him. They had set off on the coastal path when it was still quiet. Ian had seen rabbits time and again and watched as Bernard dashed off like a young pup into the undergrowth towards them. There was one occasion when Ian had seen half-a-dozen or more rabbits together, all scattering as he approached, where he thought Bernard must surely come back with at least one poor bunny hanging from his jaws. But he never did, although he looked hot and happy after each escapade.

And Ian stopped every so often to listen as he heard different bird sounds. There were, he thought, three that he heard most. A peep-peep. A chirping. A whoopy-whoop. Possibly a whoopy-dee-whoop. Each time he heard such a noise he looked around, although he never saw any of the birds. He could not help but assume they had flown off when they heard Bernard lumping about in the undergrowth.

On they went, out of the wooded parts and on to open plains and the sounds of the woods, the scurrying of creatures, the odd hoot of an owl, changed to those of the seaside. The calls of seagulls and, further out to sea, the odd toot-toot of a boat. They made good time although, as they approached the turning for the village, they started to flag – what with their aching feet and paws and the heat of the day.

The man behind him suddenly marched by Ian and the elderly lady up to the pharmacy door, which he then peered through. "It says five people at a time… there's only three in there."

"I'm happy waiting here," the old lady said.

"I'm effing not," the man replied, marching back.

He stood behind Ian again and muttered and swore and shuffled about and Ian hoped the old lady moved inside before something bad happened.

Ian felt nervous. He could feel the impatience and anger in the man behind him. A palpable presence. Young, tall, strong. A workman. Someone who did something physical. Lifting things. Digging with a shovel. Shifting things. Someone who would be largely inarticulate in an argument but quick to throw the first punch.

He felt he should say something placatory or lightly amusing, partly to defend the old lady and also to soothe the situation. But he could not think of what to say, and he worried he may stammer or stumble over his words and look foolish. So, he stood there silently, hoping the queue would start moving and nothing else would happen. He thought of his own, long-gone nan, and how she would feel if she had been spoken to like that. And he felt rather ashamed of himself standing here doing nothing when he knew trouble was brewing.

Of course, the man's anger was illogical. If five people were

121

allowed in the pharmacy at one time and there were three in there already, it meant that the old woman and Ian, by implication, should go inside the pharmacy, leaving the man at the front of the queue outside. Ian felt he should point out that wherever they stood, inside or out, there would still be six in the queue and that the man would still be in sixth place. But he suspected that the man would not understand such logic and any comments would just make things ten times worse.

And so it happened. The man swore, "For eff's sake!" loud enough for Ian and the elderly lady to hear, then turned to storm off.

Bernard was standing in his way. Ian swung round as he heard the thud and the yelp from Bernard and saw Bernard kicked over onto his side. The man was already climbing into his van.

"Get your dog out the effing way," the man bellowed. "Or I'll run it over." Ian made a grab for Bernard and pulled him close as the van revved up and roared off.

Ian was stunned by this sudden outburst of violence. It unsettled him. He turned to the elderly lady to say something, but she had seen what had happened and just tut-tutted while she walked into the pharmacy, leaving Ian and Bernard outside on their own. Bernard got up and stood there panting and staring into the distance. Ian put his arms around his dog and pushed his face into the fur behind the dog's neck. He needed to gather his breath.

It had all happened so quickly, and left Ian shaken. He knew now, after the event, that it could all have been avoided if he had just spoken to the old lady early on and maybe chivvied her inside. Or stepped back and let the angry man go in front "If you're in a hurry". But he also thought that both of those things – these doings – were cowardly and he did not like to think of himself like that. He thought perhaps he was a coward, deep down inside, and he did not feel good about it.

Ian also thought he should have confronted the man when

he kicked Bernard. That he should have remonstrated with him, maybe even kicked him back on the shin. But it was all so fast. And Ian needed to help Bernard, move him out of the way of the van and comfort the dog. If he had gone for the angry man in some way, verbally or physically, it might have been even worse. Ian might have ended up sprawled on the ground with a bloodied or broken nose. And Bernard kicked again.

But there was something else, something more important than any of that.

Ian suddenly remembered the vet's words. The growth could burst and cause unbearable pain as it bled out.

And Ian feared that the man's kick had done that, burst the growth, and Bernard was about to die.

**

It was the fear that Ian remembered most afterwards. Fear that Bernard would die in agony in his arms as he ran to and fro for help.

He would also remember the panic as he rushed into the pharmacy asking where the nearest vets was, and everybody had just ignored him as though he were a madman. The old pharmacist even turned away.

And the embarrassment as he ran helplessly up and down the road asking people to tell him where he could find a vet. Hurry, please!

An elderly man in his 80s, pushing a trolley, half for support, half for shopping, was the first to stop and listen to Ian as he explained Bernard had been kicked and needed to be seen by a vet as a matter of urgency. The man sucked his clacky-old false teeth and thought for a minute as Ian stood there screaming in frustration inside. The elderly man then reached out to stroke Bernard on the head and said he'd had a terrier as a boy and started telling a story about it.

Like I bloody care, thought Ian, as he turned and walked

on quickly, asking a group of teenage girls where the vet's was. They giggled and laughed, partly because they were that type of age but also, Ian was sure, because he looked so wild-eyed and desperate. (He'd somehow left the old lady's mirror behind in the carrier bag and had not checked his appearance for ages.) One girl, coolly flicking her hair back as though she were a catwalk model, said, in the broadest Norfolk accent ever, that there weren't none round here, aa-rr, aa-rr, but there were one, aa-rr, aa-rr, somewhere or other which was 15 minutes away by, aa-rr, aa-rr car.

It was at this point that Ian had just about had enough and decided that he was going to run down the street, turn left at the top the way they had come in and head back over to the fields to find a tree where he'd lie down with Bernard ready to die. But then this big and brassy woman in her 50s with badly dyed ginger hair and a white streak down the middle – possibly her natural hair colour rather than an affectation – stepped forward and told him what he needed to know.

"There ain't no vet here, my love," she said, touching his arm which calmed him for a moment.

"But there's Barbara up there." She pointed to a side street slightly along and on the left. "At number 14. She does all the dogs round here."

Then she turned and looked at Bernard and went to walk on. "But he looks alright to me," she added. Like that was some sort of expert bloody medical analysis.

And Ian was then banging the knocker on the door of the old Victorian end-of-terrace house, and there were sudden and explosive sounds of dogs barking and running inside the house and out the back. Ian waited with Bernard in his arms, expecting the door to be opened, but there was nothing other than the endless noise of the dogs. He knocked again, his fist on the door, all sense of good manners gone as he feared for Bernard's life.

He held Bernard tight, tucked in between his right arm

and his chest and, despairing, wrapped his left arm around Bernard's neck and pulled him closer in. Ian thought that Bernard was going to die now. And Ian was not ready for that. Not yet. He had not really prepared himself, assuming that it, the end he could not think about, was still some way off. But it was not. It was going to happen here on this doorstep with these dogs snapping and snarling in the background.

Unexpectedly, almost beautifully, thought Ian, he heard a woman's voice inside, with a strong Yorkshire accent, "Alright, alright," and the door was opened, and he saw an elderly, whippet-thin, white-haired woman pulling her jeans up, saying, "Give me a minute. I was on the lav." And she batted and cursed at the dogs, shoo-ing them away. And, at last, she looked at Ian's face and Bernard in his arms and pulled the door fully open, saying, "This way," as she hurried back down the hallway.

Ian followed, pushing by the dogs leaping up as he and Bernard rushed by them. He could barely breathe, filled with the sense that it was all just too late.

They moved to a kitchen, full of open cupboards and jars and packets and half-full saucepans simmering on the stove and a jumble of overspilling carrier bags on the floor. And just mess everywhere. Opened cartons and packets. Bin bags. Some old bag lady, this.

The old whippet-thin woman swept everything off the Formica table – a newspaper, pens, a pad, some sketch she was doing of a cross-eyed dog – and shouted at her dogs to go on and get out of it and invited Ian to put Bernard on the table. Ian held back a sob, knowing it was all over for his old pal. That he was going to die. Right here and now. And there was absolutely nothing that Ian could do about it.

***

Sea Palling to Mundesley was, Ian reckoned, no more than 12 or 13 miles and should have taken, give or take, about four and a half hours to walk at a steady pace. The first half of the walk this morning took maybe two hours or so. The second half just seemed to go on forever. From early afternoon until dusk. Not surprising really. By the time he got here, he was almost on his knees, both physically and mentally.

Ian now sat on the beach at Mundesley and thought it was a sorry-looking place; bleak and empty and windy, as most of the walk from here to Hunstanton was likely to be. It struck him suddenly that he had not gone to the Pleasure Beach at Great Yarmouth. Too late now. Who cared anyway? It made no difference. He sighed. He'd go inland a little later, before it got properly dark, along lanes and into fields by a river, to find somewhere to sleep. Think about all the different types of rides at the Pleasure Beach, to check his memory was still functioning properly.

He took out the baby booklet and a pen, flicking through the pages, looking at the little stick figure he had drawn on the bottom right of each page the other night. He wished he had his reading glasses. He flicked fast so that the stick man seemed to run. Then more slowly so the stick man slowed to a stroll. Then he stopped flicking. And the stick man just stood there.

"What's wrong with him?" the Yorkshire woman had said urgently, looking down at Bernard on the table.

"He's got a growth on his liver," Ian had replied, almost shouting, "and someone's just kicked him. If it's burst, he'll bleed to death."

The Yorkshire woman leaned in, running her hands up and down the dog's body, checking his eyes, his anus, all over really.

Ian gazed out to sea. The vast bleakness of it. The sky was dull and darkening. The sea a huge expanse of grey. He wondered what it must be like to walk out into the sea and just keep going. Walking. Swimming. Drowning. A while ago he had read a story online about a teenage girl who had stood on an empty beach like this one, taken off all her clothes, folded them neatly into a pile, and left them there. And then walked into the sea.

Someone, a passer-by, had spotted the pile of clothes and rang 999. Ian could not remember exactly what happened next, whether a boat went out or a helicopter or maybe both. Either way, the young girl, somewhere out at sea, had been saved. If she had not left a neat pile of clothes to be found, had gone in fully clothed, no one would have known what she was doing and, most likely, she would have been lost at sea. Ian did not like to think about that. The water. The breathing it in through the nose and mouth. The knowing you were about to die. Because of Adam.

He did wonder whether this girl's actions were more of a cry for help than an attempt at taking her own life. He would keep his clothes on. Partly for warmth but mostly because, when he got so far out, his waterlogged clothes would weigh and pull him down. And, if he were rescued, he would not want to be naked with everything down there lolling about this way and that as they hauled him over the side and rolled him onto his back. He would at least keep his pants on to keep everything in place and tickety-boo.

The Yorkshire woman had felt gently around Bernard's stomach, pressing here and there as quickly as she could. She nodded to herself. This grim-faced woman about to announce his imminent death.

Then she opened Bernard's mouth and looked inside. She nodded again and made a noise, almost a grunt of satisfaction. As if to say, "thought so".

Next, she put on a rubber glove, reached for her mobile phone on the side and switched on the torchlight. Ian had instinctively looked away. He had known what was coming. What the verdict would be.

Ian looked down at the baby booklet again and remembered that they had bought something like it when Adam was born, in a fancy knick-knack shop in Bury St Edmunds. They'd been filling in time between seeing a film at the independent cinema and having afternoon tea at the hotel down by the Abbey Gardens. Kate had spotted it in the window and shown it to him, and they had agreed it was something they should buy; to record the landmark moments of the baby's life. First smile, first tooth, etc. They had done something similar with the older children so many years earlier.

And Ian had memories of writing in the pages in a blue fountain pen that Beth had bought him one Father's Day. *Love You Dad, From Your Favourite Daughter xxx* engraved on the side. He had written in his best handwriting, thinking before he wrote and writing it out carefully word by word.

He did not know where that booklet was now. Had forgotten about it in the aftermath of Adam's death, and not really recalled it until this moment. But he knew he had not seen it for ages. Not since Hunstanton. And he wondered if Kate had tucked it away somewhere, opening it now and again and reading Ian's careful notes and little smiley faces and thumbs-up drawings. Or maybe she could not bear to see it at all and had thrown it away.

"He's alright," the Yorkshire woman had said finally. "All's well. There's a growth. Benign or malignant. Hard to say. Depends how fast it grows. Let me show you where." He had felt where she showed him to put his fingers before turning away and sobbing quietly whilst she busied about. Then he thanked her and offered money and she said no, but he could buy a bag of her home-made dog treats, which he did. He left after shaking her hand and then carried Bernard all the way to Mundesley.

And he now looked down at Bernard sleeping by his side. His old pal. And ran his hands along the dog's ribs and stomach. He thought he could see the lump but might be imagining it. He looked away, not really wanting to see it nor think about it.

He then sat and drew on each of the pages of the baby booklet, next to the stick man, a little running stick dog. Flicked through and watched them running faster and

128

faster. And he smiled and laughed so loud that Bernard sat up with a startled look on his face.

"Time for bed, old friend," Ian said, "time for bed." And he got up and, checking everything was where it should be, started to head inland to find a place to sleep. And test his memory. To refresh himself. Bernard looked at him as though he were mad – "What's wrong with here, I'm very comfortable" – but, slowly, reluctantly, got up too and followed Ian for a mile or so across fields and woods to Sleepyville.

**

It was the child's piercing scream that alerted Ian to what was happening. The terrible danger.

He had just shot five cans over five times at the "Shoot 'Em Up" stall at the Pleasure Beach and was walking away with the prize under his arm; the biggest, pinkest, fluffiest teddy bear anyone had ever seen.

He looked up to see the Ferris wheel had stopped, tilted to one side. The little girl was in the top passenger car, hanging on to the rail for dear life.

Ian put the teddy bear on the ground next to Bernard. "Look after this," he instructed a young teenage couple nearby.

"Until I come back," he added as he pushed his way through the watching crowd, by the tall, gormless-looking man who was in charge of starting and stopping the wheel, and on to the passenger car at the bottom of the wheel.

"Hold on!" he shouted up at the little girl. "I'm on my way."

He climbed from one passenger car to the next, working steadily upwards towards the child. He felt the Ferris wheel creaking and groaning as if it were about to tilt completely off its axis.

In the distance, he could hear the sound of sirens. Police cars, ambulances, fire engines. By the time they got here, it would be too late. The little girl would have fallen to her death.

Only Ian could get to her and save her life.

He glanced down, hoping someone in the crowd would have the sense to fetch a blanket or a tarpaulin. Something, anything.

Half a dozen of the strongest fairground workers could hold it out wide so that Ian could drop the little girl onto it safely.

But they all just stood there, mouths wide open and gaping, their faces full of horror, watching him climb up.

He was high now, on the Ferris wheel that was tilting ever more dangerously to one side. If it toppled over, everyone in the crowd below would be crushed to death. He could see the newspaper headlines now. *Britain's Worst-Ever Fairground Tragedy*. And the sub-headline, *Hero Dies in Vain Trying to Save Little Girl*.

He climbed on, one passenger car after another, until the little girl was in sight. She was hanging half in, half out of the top car, holding onto the rail with her left hand, her body dangling in the air, a small cuddly toy of some kind in her right hand. She was crying out, but Ian could not hear what she was saying.

The wind was stronger here, coming in from the sea, so fierce that her cries and his calm and measured replies were blown away in a moment. He felt alone now, just him and her, with the sounds of the crowd below, even the sounds of emergency vehicles, all silenced by the wind.

Hand over hand, step by step, he clawed his way up from one passenger car to another. Almost within touching distance of her now.

Suddenly, with a terrified sob, the little girl's fingers slipped from the handrail, and she fell.

Ian instinctively put out his left arm, catching her around her waist and somehow managing to swing her in towards his chest. He held her tight. He could hear the little girl sobbing, her head on his shoulder. He had saved her life.

Down below, he could hear the screaming of the crowd changing to a stunned silence as the little girl fell and again into cheers as he caught her. Loud, never-ending cheers. He knew by now that the fire engine and the ambulance would have arrived and that the firemen and the paramedics would be standing there open-mouthed.

Although he had saved the little girl, he knew that it was not over yet. Ian now had to climb back down, with his left arm around her, using just his right arm and feet to manoeuvre from one passenger car tipped on its side to another; all without being able to see where to put his feet.

"What's your name, sweetheart?" Ian asked gently.

"Ella," she answered between sobs.

He added, "And what's your dolly called?"

"Bunny," she replied.

"I want you to wrap your arms around my neck, Ella, hold Bunny very tight, and shut your eyes."

Ian pulled and pushed her into position as best he could. Checked she was holding on tight. Had Bunny. Was keeping her eyes shut. Then, he started climbing back down from one passenger car to another. He stopped for a moment in each one to check she was safe and well. Then he climbed down to the next one.

The wind grew ever stronger, and he could hear and feel the creaking and grinding of the passenger cars and the Ferris wheel itself as if it was all about to tilt and crash to the ground at any moment. The crowd heard the noises too and he could hear their shouts and cries and sensed they were all backing away.

It was up to Ian now, no one else was coming, nobody down there was going to help. He worked his way on, five cars, stop and check. Four. Stop and check. Three. Stop and check. Two. Stop and check. And into the last passenger car and he turned, as he saw the little girl's parents running forward and he put her into their arms.

"Wait!" he said to them, bending down and picking up the cuddly toy that she had dropped on the ground.

"Here's Bunny," he added, wiping dust from it before

handing it over to the grateful parents.

And, with that, Ian – the hero – slipped into the crowd that rushed forward and disappeared into the night. Bernard trotted after him.

11
ANOTHER FAMILY GET-TOGETHER

(15.00 ONWARDS)

The three children – Alex, Beth and Joe – sat in the orangery at The Cape, facing a journalist and a photographer from the local newspaper. Alex answered all of the basic who-what-when-where-why questions one after the other. Ian's age, what he did, all of that. Beth sat on the edge of her chair. Joe did not really know quite what to do. He just sat upright.

It was Beth who had arranged this, badgering and bothering away through texts and WhatsApp until everyone went along with it to keep the peace. Neither Alex nor Joe had had any success finding Ian and Bernard. "Needle in a haystack," Alex had muttered to Joe as they arrived.

Kate had decided not to take part; thinking it might be best if she left it to the children to make the appeal. She bustled about the kitchen and went back and forth providing cups of tea and glasses of squash and the last tin of biscuits in the cupboard left over from Christmas. Hannah was round at her family's house. Glenn was fitting a ceiling hoist on the coast somewhere down in Essex. A place he'd never been to before. Yasmin was doing a fitness class – twerking, more like – at the leisure centre.

"And how do you feel, the three of you, knowing your Dad has just vanished like this?"

133

"Do you have a message for him?"

"What would you say if he were here now?"

"Well," Alex said, thinking how to answer. The other two looked at him, waiting to see what he said. In his head, Alex had the answers almost immediately. "We're angry that he's been so stupid, to worry Mum and all of us like this." And "Come home, you idiot." And "What the hell were you thinking?" But he did not think that was what he should say either to this journalist or to Dad when he eventually turned up with a muddy face and one shoe and Bernard limping in behind him. In fact, Alex wasn't sure, at this exact moment, if this interview was a good idea at all. Too late now though.

He cleared his throat, deciding to speak before Beth started ranting and raving and they'd all come across as a mad family, and who could blame Ian for going on the run? "We're all very worried about our dad and where he's gone and what he's doing. Obviously. And our message to him would be to get in touch and let us know you're okay. Please. And, um…" At this, Alex stopped. He was going to say, to give his third answer, as "Welcome home" but realised this sounded rather, well, twee.

And Alex looked up at the journalist, his young and eager face, waiting to scribble down the answer in his old-fashioned notepad. And then across to the photographer, an equally youthful and keen-looking woman, barely out of her teens, ready to take photographs once Alex had finished talking. And he knew suddenly, as clear as day, what it was he was meant to say. What needed to be put in the article. The headline really. *Come home, Dad. We love you.* So, Alex said that quickly and then dipped his head down. Joe nodded his head vigorously and looked away.

"Yes, we do," said Beth, and Alex and Joe both expected her to add "Me most of all". But she did not. She just sat there blinking.

There was a moment or two's silence as the young journalist checked over his notes, flicking to and fro between the pages.

He read out loud what he'd written down, the main points of it anyway, to double-check with the three children that he'd got everything just so. He had interviewed a local author the other week and had made a note of her new, self-published book title correctly but had missed out the subtitle which was, apparently, so important, so utterly vital, that its absence had triggered a letter of complaint to the Independent Press Standards Organisation.

"Ian Wilkerson... 54... six feet tall... long salt and pepper hair... bald patch... (the children glanced at each other with worried looks knowing Ian would not want this printed but, not being sure what to say, they kept quiet)... don't know what he was wearing... Bernard... 12-year-old Jack Russell... white and tan... last seen at Felixstowe Ferry... late afternoon... Monday the fourth of July... gone for a walk, possibly up or down the coast... a breakdown... I won't put that," he added quickly, seeing their worried faces.

The young journalist then paused and asked if he could see the note that Alex had mentioned Ian had left for them; maybe take a photograph of it? Alex had anticipated this and, having been handed the note by Kate just before the journalist and the photographer had arrived, he had been able to fold over and carefully tear off and throw away the PS line. He just knew that the PS would trigger a whole new set of questions and dog-mess-related answers he did not want to give. Nor did he want a headline like *Dad Has Breakdown After Treading in Dog Mess.*

So, he handed the cut-down note over to the photographer and she fiddled and faddled about, taking shots of it as though she were entering it for The Pulitzer Prize for Photography.

And the journalist asked if Kate would join them for a group photograph (and the children were all relieved Yasmin was not there poking her tongue out and striking inappropriate poses).

Finally, he asked for a photograph, a recent photograph, of Ian and one of Bernard and, ideally, the two of them together. And the three children all looked at each other and pulled "aarrgghh" faces.

***

Alex went and got the box of unsorted family photographs from the top of the wardrobe in the spare room. None of them were particularly new; it was all mobile phone photos these days and no one ever bothered to print them off. He returned and put the box on the coffee table between the children and the newspaper team. They all sat there for a second or two looking at it.

Of course, the issue of choosing a photograph of Ian (and probably Bernard) for the newspaper article was a tricky one. Alex, Beth and Joe, despite the potential seriousness of the situation, would normally choose one where Ian looked the most awful; perhaps that one where he had a long blob of stripey toothpaste on his chin without realising it.

The photographer and the journalist would have a different idea, wanting a good clear shot of Ian and the dog. Hopefully, Ian might look a little sad and vulnerable to make readers go "aah". And the dog should look a friendly sort: the kind that everyone would like to have; that wouldn't drag its bottom across the carpet at random times (as Bernard often did).

Alex gestured to the journalist to have a rummage. The journalist hesitated, feeling that really, no, it was their choice.

He said that it would be good if it, the one they chose, was a picture of, er, Dad and dog looking at the camera. The photographer looked dubiously at the jumble in the box but said nothing.

Alex, Beth and Joe all leaned forward and started going through the photographs.

Joe pulled out one and showed it to Alex and Beth. Ian was laid flat out and fast asleep on a towel on a sunny beach somewhere. Head back. Mouth wide open. It looked as though he might well have been snoring and dribbling too. Beth and

Joe were either side of Ian, heads close to their father's, doing thumbs-up signs. A family favourite for sure, and it made Joe smile to remember the day, but Alex slightly inclined his head as if to say no, no way, don't show them that.

Beth found an absolute corker of a photograph of the back of Ian's head, taken somewhere or other on a day out years ago. His sweaty bald spot shone and glistened in the sun and Beth suddenly remembered how, on one holiday, with a photograph much like this, they had cut round Dad's head with scissors and stuck the piece on the middle of the dartboard in the garage. They got a "50" every time they hit the bald spot with a dart. This suddenly made Beth feel unbearably sad. The thought that she might not see her stupid old dad again.

Alex then came across the photograph of Ian where he looked like Jabba the Hutt from *Star Wars*. He was sitting back on a sofa one Christmas with a huge tub of cheesy footballs resting on his stomach (which, by an amazing coincidence, did itself bear a striking resemblance to a football). His head seemed to gloop into his shoulders, missing his neck out completely. His left eyelid was drooping. He had crumbs and goodness knows what in his white, stubbly beard. Alex hesitated, the idea of this glorious, hideous photo on the front page of the newspaper in his mind, but then decided, after a titanic struggle between good and evil that no, best not.

"Do any of you have anything on your phones we could use?" the journalist asked, glancing at his watch.

"Anything really with Mr Wilkerson and Bernard," added the photographer. "Just the two of them together?"

"If we can get a good headline and a really nice photograph, it will help... people will see it and watch out for your dad," the journalist summed it up.

So, Alex and Beth and Joe sat there scrolling through their phones, screen after screen of photographs, with lots of themselves and their partners, some of places they'd been, holidays, of course, and one or two from family get-togethers at Christmas. Slowly, as they scrolled down and back and forth, each of them noticed, one after the other, that lately, the past year or two, there were hardly any photographs of their dad, at least none that made them laugh or smile or feel happy.

The only photographs of Ian were in group shots of the family, and he seemed to be on the edges of these, standing there, as he always did, with one eye half open and the other shut, not quite looking at the camera and generally seeming awkward. And, Alex thought first, as if he didn't really want to be there. That stung Alex because he hadn't really noticed or realised this before. His dad had always just been there, joking and always saying the wrong things and offending people who didn't know him. Just being Dad. And now he wasn't there. And for the first time Alex was worried; properly worried.

He looked up at Kate as she came through and Beth asked her if she might have a photograph of Dad and Bernard on her phone. Kate thought for little more than a second or two and said no, she hadn't taken any photographs of Ian for years. It was at this point, when Kate, Alex, Beth and Joe all stood or sat there with their phones in their hands, that a sense of something terribly negative – fear, worry, alarm – seemed to settle on them and they all looked at each other with feelings moving close to despair.

Alex dipped his hand into the box, moved photographs to one side, and took out a photo of Ian that looked much like he did today.

Then, a flick through here and there, to a photograph of Bernard sitting up on the lawn, his paw raised, waiting to be given a treat.

And he passed these to the journalist and went to say something like "these are best we can do of our Dad and Bernard". But, for some reason, he could not bring himself to speak at all.

***

138

And so, finally, they came to the group photograph in the back garden with the photographer looking everywhere before deciding that here, yes, just here, with the magnolia tree behind them, was the perfect place to be.

Alex. Beth. Joe. Kate hung back, had shaken her head *no* when the photographer suggested she join in and again, more firmly, when it was suggested again. Kate, frankly, did not want to be photographed crying. So, she stood by the journalist and watched.

The photographer lined the children up, with Alex and Joe to either side of Beth who was a little shorter than the two boys. She gave Beth the two photographs, one of Ian, the other of Bernard, to hold up, one in each hand.

Alex did not really know how to stand and look. He remembered how, whenever they were on a day out in London as a family, they always seemed to come across a demonstration and Ian would stride up to the front, put his hands on his hips, stare heroically into the distance, and demand one of them take a photograph. Usually, Ian got away with this but at one demonstration, about endometriosis and the lack of NHS support, he was berated by other demonstrators and had to slink away. Alex thought that if he struck such a pose and his dad saw it, then it might send a message to him. So he did something similar, hands on hips, chin up, gazing outwards.

Beth held the two photographs up in front of herself, feeling rather foolish, and wondered whether anyone who read the article in the newspaper in a day or two's time would actually be able to see the photograph of her dad and Bernard the dog. She thought not. But she stood there and looked suitably sad at the camera. Then glanced at Alex, looked him up and down, and said, under her breath, "You look like you need a poo." Alex smiled and then quickly blanked his face, not feeling sure that a smile was appropriate in the circumstances. He put his arms down by his side.

Joe stood to the other side of Beth with his hands in his pockets, just looking calmly at the camera. He recalled, years ago, one birthday, his he thought, when Ian had lined the three of them up, just like this, against the garage wall. Had them standing there, chins up, backs to the wall, like they were prisoners about to be shot. Ian had taken photographs with his new mobile camera and, a few days later, *Wanted* posters appeared all round the house. *Wanted... For Not Cleaning His Bedroom. Wanted... For Not Emptying The Washing Machine* and *Wanted... For Farting Gratuitously*. This felt like that, but sadder.

And the photographer asked them all to smile... to act cheerful... to look straight at the camera. This way, that way, never seeming satisfied.

Then to put the photographs of Ian and Bernard to one side and get in close together. Maybe the boys' arms around Beth's shoulders. She pulled a face. But yes, that's perfect (the pose, not the face).

One more gesture to Kate to come on, come across, and suddenly, unexpectedly, she strode over and stood in the middle next to Beth and Joe on the other side. And the whole this way, that way nonsense started again.

Kate looked straight at the camera, Beth and Joe's arms around her waist, Alex's hand on her shoulder, and just wondered if this were the most stupid thing to be doing. To make the whole shebang public. To hold up Ian's breakdown, for that must be what this was, and their marriage and their family to everyone in Felixstowe and Suffolk and East Anglia. To read over. To speculate. To gossip about with each other. The sympathetic looks at work, the hushed voices, the utter insincerity of nosey people who just wanted to know what was going on.

And she felt, with the young photographer snapping away, that she should just put up her hand and say "Stop! Enough. No more." That she had changed her mind and did not want all of this... this focus on them. But she stayed put as Alex and Beth and even Joe made encouraging comments and smiled and put her hand here and her arm there and let the photographer finish what she was doing. And at the end, Beth said, with such force and certainty, that "Dad will read this, and he will come straight home," and Kate, really, did not then know what to think or say or do.

So, she thanked the photographer and the journalist – just being so damn polite; too polite maybe. And Alex and Beth and Joe swarmed round and seemed so positive and grateful and excited, especially Beth, that Kate thought maybe, if it brought Ian home and they could fudge around what happened, it might all be worth it. And the journalist said they'd run the story as soon as they could and it would go all across East Anglia, in sister papers too, and he and the photographer seemed so enthusiastic that Kate felt ever so slightly guilty about her doubts.

"Well," said Kate, coming back into the orangery after showing the journalist and the photographer out of the front door, "let's see if that works... fingers crossed."

Beth, as you'd expect, had it all planned out. "If it doesn't, and he doesn't come home in the next few days, we'll have to call in the police."

Kate just went, "Um..." to that and felt that, maybe, they should have gone to the police first, before the newspaper. Done this all more discreetly. Still, too late now.

Alex and Joe just looked at each other and nodded. Whilst Kate was showing the journalist out, they'd decided that they'd head up to Hunstanton tomorrow and put up some more home-made posters (this time featuring that legendary Jabba the Hutt photograph).

12
MUNDESLEY TO WEYBOURNE

SUNDAY 10th JULY

(14.3 MILES, 4 HOURS 43 MINUTES)

It was today, Sunday boring Sunday, that the gloom really set in with Ian. The melancholy. The fed-up-ness of it all. The "I wish I hadn't started all of this" kind of thoughts swirling round his mind. Back to how he had been feeling at home but somehow worse. It was more, what was it… desperate. And it lasted all day. And didn't stop then.

For now? Mundesley. Trimingham. Overstrand. Cromer. East Runton. West Runton. Sheringham. Weybourne. A list of little-known places, mostly. From another time. Pre-World War I. Another world. He had jotted them down at the back of the baby booklet, after reading a sign along the pathway. He reckoned it was 14 miles in all to Weybourne. Whatever that was like. He had no idea. Bleak, most likely. Most of it was on this coast.

Ian hit a wall of sorts at about the halfway point. Like a marathon runner, he thought. He felt exhausted physically, as ever, but this was more of a mental thing. He just wanted to lie down and put his face in the grass. And so he did. Bernard sat patiently by his head.

The day had begun much the same as ever. They'd slept by the edge of a field somewhere in Mundesley and woke feeling refreshed by the cool dryness of the already sunny day. They had eaten cold pork pies and pasties just beyond their sell-by dates from the rucksack and Ian squirted some water from a bottle into Bernard's mouth. Then, after doing what they needed to do ablutions-wise, they were up and on their way just after 7.00.

They went this way and that for a while (Ian still lacking any sense of direction) and, finally, after speaking to a stooped old man with a flat-cap and a black Labrador (which Bernard studiously ignored), they went along some back streets to a main-ish road. Then by some cliffs and after that they saw a giant golf ball way over there (an RAF air defence radar thing, probably).

Muddy paths and hedges and fields led them after a few miles to Trimingham and a church. St John's. It was still lovely and sunny, and there were trees that looked like they'd been standing for centuries. It was peaceful. But there were also lines of sad-looking, faded headstones at different angles that went straight into the grass. And it was at this point − seeing those sorry headstones − that Ian had felt the first real swoop of despondency. He had intended to look inside the church but, what with Bernard possibly doing the dragging the bottom thing and a vicar maybe wanting to talk about God and Jesus, he decided to press straight on towards Overstrand.

At home, whenever he felt low, as he did more and more, Ian would go to a spare bedroom, Joe's old bedroom, and lie there with his face in a rug, a fluffy, greenish... no, turquoise... no, whatever the colour was. Teal. That was it. The colour. He would lie there as long as it took for his mood to brighten. Or until Kate shouted up the stairs to do the potatoes or put a paper bag of doo-dahs into the recycling bin, or whatever dreary task she wanted him to do. "Vacuum the loft stairs and do the corners!"

Here, he had thought the grass would feel much the same as the rug; soft and inviting and, somehow, um, peaceful. But he could feel his nose in dirt and worried that if he fell asleep a worm might wriggle up and into his brain and get stuck somewhere, so he turned his face to the side and lay on his cheek. Bernard fidgeted and gave him one of his sidelong, long-suffering looks.

The walk from Trimingham to Overstrand could only have been two to three miles but its undulating, hither and thither path and Ian's endlessly falling mood meant that it had seemed longer. So much longer. They had taken a main road out of Trimingham and through a pretty little woodland that would normally have revived Ian's spirits. But Bernard went and rolled in something which Ian spent ages wiping off with spit on an old piece of grubby kitchen roll in his jacket pocket. He put the folded-over piece of kitchen roll back in his pocket as he could not find a bin. It made him feel dirty and smelly. He could not bring himself to sniff his fingers.

The next part of the walk went by fields and cliffs, where he saw some birds flying high and swooping down as if on air currents. Ian wished he knew what these brown and white birds were. He felt so ignorant at times. He thought they were swallows but as the only birds he could 100 per cent identify were robins and magpies and crows (possibly ravens) and pigeons (wood and ordinary) and seagulls and flamingos (pink, one-legged) they could, so far as he was concerned, be just about anything. The name "mudlarks" came to mind, but he did not think that was correct.

And next they went by a farm and along a sloping road and a big concrete wall and promenade to a car park. He hated concrete on a seafront. The big, cold slabbiness of it. He used to walk Bernard with Joe and Adam to Cobbolds Point in Felixstowe and back by the groynes and the wooden fency things to the steps at Jacob's Ladder and up and back home. But they had concreted it all a few years ago, so the bin lorries could go up and down, and it was all so bloody awful. The ugliness of it.

It was no use. This laying down in the grass. There was no way he was going to be able to fall asleep and let that rally his mood when he awoke.

And he knew that, if he lay like this for long enough, someone would walk by and stop and assume he had collapsed and he had a terrible image of a big hairy farmer rolling him over and very forcibly giving him mouth-to-mouth resuscitation and him spluttering and choking as their tongues touched.

He rolled over and lay on his back and gagged on his own saliva and he coughed and caught his breath and sat up.

Overstrand to Cromer had been another two to three mile walk. There was a café and toilets at Overstrand, but he was so fed-up with everything by this point that, other than stopping to let Bernard drink from a dog bowl left outside, they just carried on walking. He was not in the mood to chat or banter with anyone in the café. He could, he thought, walk along the cliffs to Cromer or by the beach. He chose the clifftop. It was not a good idea.

As he walked by a golf course close to the clifftop, he felt light-headed and dizzy and, for one extraordinary moment, he had a sudden urge to walk to the edge of the clifftop and look down. More than that, if he were honest, he had an almost overwhelming desire to run to the edge and throw himself off. He imagined himself soaring like a bird out over the cliffs and above the sand and the shoreline and down towards the sea where he would gently skim the surface and eventually disappear beneath the waves never to be seen again.

He had grabbed Bernard, who was trotting along a few steps ahead minding his own business, and held him tight, pressing his nose into the thick fur behind the dog's neck. He ignored the smell from where Bernard had been rolling in something earlier that morning. After a moment or two, they walked on, Ian counting from one to 100 in his head to distract himself from anything but walking in time with the numbers. Missing the odd number now and then that was hard to recall, and going on to the next.

Ages later, they finally saw Cromer Pier and he recalled the joke that he had been repeating every time Cromer had been mentioned since they'd last visited 30 years or so ago. That he had once caught crabs at Cromer. He suddenly realised it wasn't very funny. Young people never got the joke at all.

Sitting up, Ian looked around. He was just beyond Cromer where he could not bring himself to stop. A grassy path leading back to clifftops on the way to East Runton.

He had to keep going, walk off this low mood. The despair. The misery.

Before starting off again, Bernard just behind, Ian decided he was going to blank his mind and walk and walk and walk.

***

Ian was already regretting leaving Cromer by the time he had walked up the gentle path away from the promenade and back on to the cliffs.

Along a main road for a little while and by a caravan park and on his way to East Runton. He should have stopped for longer at Cromer, he thought, tried harder to cheer himself up there. Too late now.

He saw surfers walking by on their way to the beach at East Runton but decided to just keep on walking. He was a mile or so out of Cromer by now; the same distance again to West Runton.

Ian could not keep his mind blank. Instead, he kept his thoughts in the here and now. He did this by looking at what was around him and spotting something and thinking about it until he exhausted those thoughts, and then looked for something else to think about. Really inconsequential. Harmless. Easy on the mind. The first thing that caught his eye was an old rice pudding can. He did not stop and pick it up, knowing he would instinctively pull back the lid and find something horrible in there. A used condom most likely. Or human excrement. And that wasn't what he wanted to see in a rice pudding can. It would put him off rice pudding. Not that he had eaten rice pudding since he was a child.

He had not eaten rice pudding for so long because he had read somewhere or other about a plane crash in the Andes where the survivors of the crash, to stay alive until help came, ate each other. Or at least they had eaten one of the survivors. Whether he volunteered or was killed or simply died belatedly and the rest then scoffed his remains, Ian was not sure.

Anyway, asked later, one of the survivors had said in an interview that brains tasted a little like rice pudding. Ian had always thought that this was unlikely given that one must have, in some way, a meaty taste, whilst the other was mostly milk and cream and, well, rice. But the first time he had eaten rice pudding after reading the Andes story, he had felt the rice oozing over his tongue and between his teeth and gums and it made him feel sick and so he had never eaten it again. But then he suddenly remembered feeding it to Adam in his highchair. Rice pudding from a little jar. He had forgotten that and it made him feel sad, so he moved on to think about something else.

East Runton to West Runton was not far to walk. Not much more than a mile really. Maybe a mile and a half. It was more roadside walking than, what was it, walking in nature (which he much preferred).

But there was a wildflower meadow. And a caravan park. And more cliffs. And he followed Bernard and kept away from the edges.

And they came to a beach with rock pools where they lingered for quite a while. Just to get their breath back. It could only be a few miles out of Cromer, but it felt longer in his melancholy mood.

Ian saw a small crab in the corner of the rock pool and put his finger in close to it to see what the crab would do. It did nothing. Ian thought that maybe crabs had their eyes to the side of their body things. Shells, that was it. So, he moved his finger to one side and waited for the crab to do something, but it didn't. Not a bloody thing.

Ian then had a sudden image of all of them at a rock pool many years ago. Him. Kate. The four children. He thought it was at Hunstanton but was not sure. They all stood there looking in, and Alex suddenly reached down and pretended to pick up a crab. Beth had screamed and run away, and Alex had chased her with the imaginary crab until she had fallen over and landed on her face in wet, sandy mud. And she then chased Alex and punched him, and it was all rather traumatic by the end of it. But recalled with affection later. And Ian could hear Adam's laughter in his head, and it made him feel sadder still.

Ian put his hand into the water, arched as though it were a crab, and he marched it up and down to see what the crab would do. But it just sat there, the crab, and Ian wondered if it were dead. And so he pushed at it with his thumb and the crab lurched lopsidedly towards him. And Ian jumped back. Then he walked on again and Bernard followed at a slower pace.

Ian had had a cup of tea at a café by the beach at West Runton. "The Gap", as he thought the waitress called it. A cheese and pickle sandwich. A sausage roll and a bowlful of water for Bernard.

He had a chat with the waitress who topped up Ian's empty water bottles from a tap. Then they were on their way again.

A long, flat and grassy path by fields and caravan parks to what he thought the waitress had called "Beeston Bump". A big hill. More clifftops followed by some steps down and on towards the wide promenade at Sheringham.

And Ian still thought about something as he walked along. Not just anything. But something specific he had seen close to them. It had to be neither here nor there really. So he could distract himself and just keep going without feeling even further downhearted. He watched a lone seagull that soared high above as if following them like a whatsit in the desert. A bloody thing. Not a parrot. A big thing. Not a hyena, but like that in a way. The seagull looked as though it were being held aloft by the breeze.

It called out as it suddenly swooped and fell, a strange squawking noise. It sounded angry, aggressive even. And Ian remembered all of them being on a beach somewhere, perhaps Looe in Cornwall, when Adam was little, and a seagull had swooped down and snatched a sandwich clean out of Adam's hand. Just a slice of tomato left fallen onto his knee. They had all laughed.

Adam. Always Adam. No matter what, Ian's thoughts would always come back to him. He wanted, at these moments, to give up and, if there were a bus stop or train station anywhere nearby, he thought he would do so. But he kept going. There were times when he did not know how he did. This long nightmare of a walk.

And so Ian and Bernard came to the last few miles of the day and their walk from Sheringham To Weybourne where they'd rest up, find something to eat and search for somewhere to sleep overnight.

It seemed the longest walk moving slowly upwards on an endless flat track towards their destination. Ian had no idea what they'd find on their arrival.

He felt as though they were in another world. A prehistoric age of endless cliffs and tides and fossils and flints beneath their feet. On and on they went, back in time, until they reached Weybourne.

They did not stop at Weybourne. Just kept going. Had they stopped there a while, maybe had something to eat and sat out on a bench by the main road, they may have seen Alex and Joe driving by in Alex's old car. Or perhaps Alex or Joe would have spotted them. And Ian and Bernard would have surely got into the car and gone home, and things would have sorted themselves out. Not gone the way they were going to go.

Alex and Joe had been in Hunstanton that morning and

put their posters up down and around the pier where Ian, they thought, would surely go at some point. And they had driven around, hoping that, somehow, they might see him wandering along in that absent-minded, stumbling way of his with Bernard trotting along a few paces behind.

One of them, Joe most likely, came up with the idea that, instead of driving straight home, they should go through places where Dad might be. So they went here and there, to places where Ian and Bernard had never been, and to one or two places, including Weybourne, that were on or close to the route. And in Weybourne, Alex and Joe missed Ian and Bernard by no more than 10 minutes. It was that close. But then it may as well have been 10 hours.

***

Another night, another field, thought Ian. Same old, same old. He was getting used to this tiring and uncomfortable life now, but he wished in a way that he wasn't.

They had eaten their fill of sausages and chips and drunk their water and were ready to go to sleep. Bernard was already laid out flat, sleepy and silent.

Ian sat up knowing he would get indigestion if he lay down straight away. He reached for the pen in his jacket. And the booklet. Peered at it. Checked his lump out of habit (still the same). Then he flicked through the pages to watch the stick man and the stick dog do their chippety-chop run from front to back. And looked at the family tree he'd drawn the other night. Then turned the page over.

When I Was a Child was the heading. "When I was a child, Pudding," thought Ian, "my life was an utter misery." My always angry father. My beaten-up mother. And me alone, cowering in the corner of the room, whilst my father did what he did to my mother in front of me. She left, eventually, and took her own life somewhere out there when I was a young teenager. My life did not start, and become happy, until I went to university, met Kate and never looked back. "But I do not want you to know any of that, Pudding," Ian thought. "I just want you to know joy and love and happiness in your life."

Ian sat there thinking what he would write; what he wanted Pudding to read when he was what, five, six, or seven? It had to be something nice and simple. Sweet. Things that would make the boy happy to know. He could not bring himself to write of his father; neither to name him nor put anything down about him. He wanted to write about his mother, to acknowledge her, to talk of his guilt, but did not know how to do that without opening it all up. This deep and wide scar with its tissue-thin skin over it.

He sighed and, after more thoughts, started writing. *When I Was a Child... I wanted to have a lovely mummy and daddy just like you have. A daddy who talks to me and listens to me and plays with me and picks me up when I fall down. And hugs me. Always lots of hugs. And a sweet mummy who sings to me in the bath and washes my hair and blows bubbles and reads to me as I fall asleep and kisses me on the forehead and is there when I wake up in the morning and when I go to sleep at night. A mummy and daddy who say, "I love you" all the time.*

Ian wanted to add something else more, about love, pure and absolute love, but he had run out of space.

So, he just drew the outline of a little heart and shaded it in carefully up to the edges.

Then he turned the page and sat there feeling shaky and emotional, although he was not sure why.

He thought, "I wasn't a very good daddy, Pudding, not to your daddy or to your Auntie Beth or Uncle Joe." He hesitated a while, thinking about how he had always been a practical type of father – making sure they had enough money, were taken to school and picked up on time, had MOTs on their cars – all of those things. But he had never told them he loved them or even hugged them and wondered if that meant, all in all, he was a failure. And he was unsure whether he should add "And Adam" and if a small child, Pudding, should be told about another small child dying, in case it upset them.

It was all too much to think about. When he was young, none of these things, these messy and painful emotions and feelings, were ever mentioned let alone talked over. His grandpa had skin cancer on his head and had a piece of skin taken from his thigh and put on the back of his head. When Ian noticed Grandpa's baboon-bottom head as a child and asked about it, he was told he'd bumped his head putting his shoes away in the cupboard under the stairs. And no one ever mentioned what happened to Uncle Robert, his mother's brother, who had simply vanished without further mention when Ian was about five. It was 10 to 12 years later that Ian learned he had taken his own life too.

He took the pen and amended the heading, so it read *When Your daddy Was Young.* Feeling emotional and writing quickly before he changed his mind, he put, *He was loved just as much as you are. He was kind and thoughtful and was nice to his sister and brother and shared his toys. And his mummy and daddy thought the world of him. As your mummy and daddy think the world of you.*

There were more pages. *What I Wish I Had Known When I Was A Child* was next and, pages on, *My Wishes For You Are* was the last.

He would do those later. Another time. When he felt happier. Tonight, he just felt sad and wasn't really sure why.

He put the booklet and pen away and lay down and made himself as comfortable as he could. Pulled Bernard closer. It would be some time before he fell asleep.

13
WEYBOURNE TO WELLS,
WELLS-NEXT-THE-SEA

MONDAY 11th JULY

(13.5 MILES, 4 HOURS 26 MINUTES)

There had been days, thought Ian, as he sat, Bernard by his feet, on a wooden bench in Weybourne early the next morning, when he felt like doing touristy things.

The rowing boats at Thorpeness. The lighthouse at Southwold. The rollercoaster at Great Yarmouth. Even yesterday, in a way, poking a finger into the rockpools on that beach outside Cromer.

Other days, he wanted to crack on. As he did today, with the possibility of reaching Hunstanton by tomorrow evening. Besides, touristy things made him feel sad. It reminded him of his family. And Adam.

He was going to walk to Wells-next-the-Sea today, a pretty seaside resort some 14 miles away.

Through Blakeney – about half way – which they should get to by lunchtime. They'd rest there a while.

Then on to Wells-next-the-Sea after that to arrive by teatime. Well placed to get to Hunstanton the evening after.

Sometimes, he would walk on main roads – he remembered that horrible A12 – and other times in the countryside, by fields and heaths and the cliffs and beaches and the sea as well. These seemed never-ending at times, but he much preferred nature-walks to urban walking. He felt happier then.

He liked the peace and quiet of it, although he wished he was more in tune with nature and knew the names of trees and bushes, the birds in the trees and above the cliffs.

The only words he could think of to do with the sky were "aurora borealis" and "Donner und Blitzen" which his German teacher at school had told him was a sweary German expression. Neither seemed of much use on the North Norfolk coast.

Ian finished off one of the white rolls he had just bought from the village store; he'd always enjoyed eating bread when it was still fresh.

He tipped his head back and emptied a bottle of water into his mouth. Then tucked the bottle back into his rucksack with the others. He'd refill it when he could later.

He made sure Bernard had eaten his sachet of food and drunk some of his water from his paper bowl. Then thought of the day ahead with something close to despair, his mood still in his boots.

What he needed to do today, he thought, other than walking at a steady pace and getting to Wells-next-the-Sea by teatime, was to not think about anything that made him feel sad. Kate. The children. Their partners. Adam. Pudding. They were all off limits. He had to blot them out somehow.

And his health. Not the physical stuff – the aching feet, legs, arms and back, the endless sweatiness of his armpits and between his legs. Not even the lump which seemed to be much the same as ever. But the other stuff. The mental side of things. He must not think of his fraying and unravelling mind. The brain tubes that were failing and made him forget names and places and... you know, stuff.

He just needed to focus on putting one step in front of the other. Counting from one up to as far as he could get. Until he could switch off for a while. Walk along as if in a trance. With the sun and the wind on his face. Smiling and nodding and keeping going whenever he saw anyone. Until he got somewhere. Blakeney, at lunchtime.

Ian got up and packed his bits and bobs away. Then, he looked around what was a rather delightful village. He had noticed a tearoom last night but, what with one thing and another, chose not to visit this morning.

He whistled to Bernard who, in an oh-so-slowly and why-are-we-still-doing-this type of way, got up ready to walk. He looked at Ian, who thought the dog seemed as downhearted as he was.

They trudged on. One, two, three, four, five, six, seven, and more. It was going to be a long day. A tiring day. A make-or-break day in a way. Ian was exhausted and, quite frankly, ready to give up. He thought there might even be a moment, if things went really badly, when he could just lay down out of sight somewhere and die.

***

They walked all morning, Ian and Bernard, from Weybourne to Blakeney. By trees and fields. It was never-ending, and they were getting slower and slower.

It seemed to take forever. He had intended to walk for half an hour and stop for 15 minutes. And again. And again.

By the time they arrived, they had been walking for 15 minutes and stopping, sitting down, laying down even, for half an hour. Two hours or so had become more than four.

Ian had managed to keep going by counting his steps. Up to 500, hit-and-miss, and starting again. Then counting trees. And birds. And trying to name the trees and birds (which he could not really do). Then he tried to remember lists of things. The cars he had owned. The names of the children's friends when they were small. Players from Ipswich Town Football Club. The ones who won the FA Cup. And the best starting 11 he could think of from the players he had seen. Some of it he remembered, most of it he didn't. And he could not figure what would be normal to remember and what wouldn't.

He should surely be able to remember the cars he had owned even though he wasn't really that sort of man, cars and pubs and so-called manly stuff. He could recall all of them except the white one. The box-like one. From years ago. He could see it in his mind's eye but could not name it. And the only registration plate he could remember was the car his mother used to drive – a Morris Minor, DPC 76B. Or 760B maybe.

He could not recall the name of Beth's best friend at school, when she first started school. A little blonde girl, with a fringe and her hair tied up in bunches. A pretty girl. He could recall the mother's name, Karen, but did not know why that had stuck in his mind. The family had moved out of the area after two or three years and Beth had sobbed for ages about it.

Ian and Bernard wandered around Blakeney. By a pub and a coffee house and a fish and chip shop and a convenience store where Ian filled up the rucksack with food and drink as usual.

Then they sat down on a bench for their rough and ready lunch. A pasty and a can of fizz for Ian. Another sachet of meat and a bowl of water for Bernard.

Nice place, Blakeney, thought Ian. A bleak, flinty landscape. A seal out there in the sea. And the sound of seagulls breaking the eerie silence.

His mind, all the way from Weybourne to here, had been on David, his old swimming buddy. Or at least it kept coming back to David between his lists and counting to 500. He remembered how, when David was in hospital, the focus had been on getting him better physically; or at least to make him more comfortable.

No one had given much thought to his mental health. It seemed to Ian that David, having been diagnosed with fast-spreading, not-long-to-live cancer, had had some sort of mental breakdown and had turned in on himself, ready to die. Or maybe they had given him such strong medication that it befuddled him. It haunted Ian, that encounter with

David in a wheelchair up the town. It was as though David had, quite simply, lost his mind.

And that was what frightened Ian most of all – at least, losing his memory. Not just the odd thing – forgetting the name of Barry, the man that also swum with them from time to time or the name of the Ipswich Town Football Club manager after Roy Keane and before the other fellow. You know. That one. Thingy. Chubby Chops. But having his mind washed out so that most of what had happened in his life – was still around him – just did not exist any more.

Ian got up off the bench. Tidied things away into his rucksack or the bin a few steps away.

Another village. Bench. Bin. Another long walk ahead of him. It was all too much really.

He got up and gestured to Bernard, come on, damn you! Bernard sat there ignoring him. Ian picked Bernard up and sighed. It was going to be an up and down walk.

***

"Happenstance" was the word that came to mind as Ian stood looking into the thick, tangled mass of bushes and brambles by the side of the path.

Ian did not, as a rule, believe in miracles. Coincidences, yes. Miracles, no. He thought there was a word, "happenstance", that described a big coincidental event.

And if that was the case, he thought, staring at the rusty old bits of metal hidden in the depths of those bushes and brambles, then this was a happenstance moment.

It was at lunchtime when things started to go badly wrong; just as the sun was hot and relentless, high in the sky. Bernard was ahead and putting one slow but steady paw in front of the other. Ian was lagging behind. Not so much because of the usual aches and pains but because he felt dizzy. Really dizzy. Bernard then stopped and sat down and simply refused to move a step further. Ian lifted Bernard up and held him in his arms. It worried Ian, this stopping and sitting down. He had not seen Bernard do it so much before.

Ian thought that it might be more than just feeling tired – that it might be something to do with the cancer growing and twisting and turning inside of Bernard. That he might be in pain. Ian gently moved his fingers so that they were on Bernard's belly, close to the growth. He ever so gently pushed the tips of his fingers into the fleshy parts whilst watching Bernard's face. He did not seem to be in pain, just stared into space, then turned his head away as if to suggest that this wasn't a very nice thing to do. Prodding someone's stomach uninvited.

Ian soon felt dizzy again, a mixture of the sun and his tiredness and the weight of Bernard in his arms. Bernard had always been a sturdy dog and something of an unyielding mass at the best of times. Now, in the heat, his great big lumpiness was something of a tipping point. Ian looked around to see where they could lie down. It was, in some ways, something of an oasis, not an oasis, a desert, in that all he could see were fields, stretching out to the horizon. No trees. No bushes. No ditches. Nowhere to tuck yourself away out of sight, hidden, for a snooze. And so he made do, carrying Bernard off the path into the fields and he was asleep, passed out really, almost as soon as his head touched the ground.

Ian was woken up by someone shaking his shoulder and shouting, "Are you alive?... are you alive?" in his face.

He came round to the smell of onions and the sight of an angry-looking, shaven-headed man with a red face six inches from his.

"I thought you were dead, you drunk old bastard," the man shouted, before backing off and re-joining a group of hikers on the path, heading back towards Blakeney. Rugby sorts by the look of them.

Ian had sat up bleary-eyed and looked around to see Bernard sitting a few yards away, watching him with that weary look he gave Ian from time to time. As if Ian had somehow embarrassed him. This dog that rubbed his bottom on carpets. Bernard then looked away as if he had concluded that this incident was the ultimate humiliation. Ian puffed out his cheeks, angry that his rest had been disturbed in such a peremptory manner. That a man and his dog on a hot and sunny afternoon could not have a lie down and mind their own bloody business without being interrupted by some hoi polloi passer-by.

He looked down and saw he had been sick on his T-shirt and that, somehow, his trousers were all stained in different places and his well-worn shoes, one half off his foot, looked as though they should really be thrown away. He sighed and ran his fingers through his bedraggled hair and over his cheeks and chin where some crumbs from the morning's bread roll seemed to have stuck in his stubble. He wished he had not lost that old lady's mirror. He wondered how awful he must appear.

Ian stood and dusted himself down and realised he must look like an old drunken hobo, and he did not quite know if he was angry or sad about what had just happened. He whistled to Bernard to walk on, to resume their journey towards Wells-next-the-Sea (which just seemed to be miles and miles away right now) and set off on his wearied way. He turned after a dozen or so steps to say something and looked back to see Bernard still sitting by the tree, staring into space, avoiding Ian's gaze.

Ian whistled. Bernard ignored him. He whistled again. Bernard seemed to be pretending he could not hear. Then he did the special "let's go NOW" whistle. Short whistle. Short whistle. Long whistle. But the blasted dog just sat there staring into the distance. It was something of a stand-off. Ian gestured at Bernard to hurry up. He waited. He waved goodbye. Walked on a few steps. Looked back. Waved his fist at the dog and shouted at him to get a move on why don't you, Stubby Stumps? Then, finally, marched to the dog and picked him up and the two of them, one angry, the other aloof, staggered off along the coastal path. And then that happenstance moment occurred when Ian spotted an old Silver Cross pushchair – 50 years old or more – in a mass of brambles and bushes.

He dragged it out. Pushed and pulled at it. Put Bernard in the seat. Walked on. A hobo pushing his faithful old companion.

And all they saw the rest of the way was an elderly couple in matching fleecy red jackets and brown knee-length shorts. As they approached him on the path, the old man stopped and rummaged in his pocket, "Here's £5, get yourself a hot drink and something to eat." And Ian did not know what to say or do, so he took it and mumbled his thanks.

***

Ian walked all the way from Blakeney to Wells-next-the-Sea pushing Bernard in the battered old pushchair. Bernard sat up, unmoving and staring towards the horizon like Nelson at the Battle of Thingamy. Bat bollocks. Agincourt. No, not that either. Anyway, it was more of the same – fields and trees, on and on and on. He was close to utter despair.

It seemed to take ages again. The pushchair, despite his kicks and constant fiddling with the wheels, was like a supermarket trolley; always pulling the wrong way. Passers-by seemed to think he was a jolly fine fellow pushing his old dog along like this. But Ian soon grew to hate every smile and smirk and silly comment, well-meant though they were. "Drop dead, Rat Face!" or "Eff off, Lard Arse!" he shouted in his head each time, and that helped lift his mood a little.

When they finally arrived in Wells-next-the-Sea at teatime, Ian was pretty much flat out exhausted. He felt every day of his 54 years. And his mood, which had bumped and clattered along the ground all day long, was now trodden down deep into the dirt. He'd simply had enough.

The David thing, that he had been thinking about all morning but was not going to think about all afternoon as it was just too depressing, filled his mind as he walked to Wells-next-the-Sea. David had been worse than he had first thought. Not knowing who Ian was. That was nothing really. Hardly anything.

Ian had bumped into David's daughter and son, Mia and Liam, up the town just before David had passed away. Mia, who worked in finance for a big corporation in London, had "come home for a visit" so she said, although the way she put it, not meeting his eyes, and her body language, all turned away, suggested the end was nigh. And Liam, who worked in shipping admin at the docks, had taken "a few days off". So, David's passing was imminent.

From their conversation, Ian wondered if David's mind had now gone completely. Ian asked them to pass on his best wishes and they smiled and pulled polite faces and said non-committal things that made Ian realise that, whether they passed on his comments or not, David would not really take it in. And it hit Ian hard that, perhaps, David did not even know who they were any more.

Wells-next-the-Sea was another old-fashioned, 1950s-type holiday resort. A bucket-and-spade world. Lots of places to eat. Plenty of fish and chips although he was getting to the stage where he was sick of the sight of them. And the smell. And everything about them really.

It was so busy. And everyone seemed to glare at him pushing Bernard along. And tut-tutting when he got in their way. And he just could not be doing with it any more.

So, he abandoned the pushchair in a side road out of sight behind a block of toilets, and went to a convenience store to top up the rucksack. And to a fish and chip shop. Bernard waiting patiently outside each time. Then they were on their way.

The David thing – going from a big, strong, striding-along man to a brain-dead vegetable in a wheelchair and finally dying – had preyed on Ian's mind the whole afternoon. What worried Ian was that he would go the same way soon. That, one way or the other, he would end up spending 20 to 30 years just sitting in a wheelchair staring out of a window with his washed-away mind and dried-out urine and excrement all down his legs. That they'd have to peel his stuck-to-the-skin underwear off him.

Ian feared that this was his future. That the general forgetfulness he was now experiencing – the stumbling over words he should know and the stop-right-there moments when his brain just point-blank jammed – would roll into something worse.

That he would forget their names first – Pudding and Adam and Yasmin and Glenn and Hannah and Alex and Beth and Joe and even Kate. Then who he was and what he did, and what he liked and what he did not like; him, his personality, his being, would ebb away. He would sit there and feel a sense of bafflement and anger about what was going on around him.

Grunting angrily at these people, the old woman with the still pretty face, the spikey-haired man with the tattoos, the gormless-looking dollop, the shouty woman, and the pretty one with the elfin ears and the cute baby, wondering why they were all standing around trying to smile rather than crying.

A mile or two out of town, in a wooded area near the beach, Ian and Bernard settled down out of sight. To eat. To do their business. To patch themselves up. To recover for the next day.

And it was here, as day turned to night, with an unexpected chill in the air, that Ian decided that he did not want to become old and ill and stupid and useless.

He would rather bow out of life before he lost his mind. As he started to nod off, he decided he would think more about it on the way to Hunstanton tomorrow. What he should do exactly. To end it all.

***

It was Ian who saw the boy out there in the mud.
Some distance away. Sinking into the ooze.

164

In that marshy part, that no-man's land, close to where the river moved slowly to the sea.

There were other people around. Nearby, on the riverbank. A family group. Mum. Dad. Three children. Boy. Girl. Boy. They were to the left. Talking amongst themselves. Distracted. Three or four men. Late teens, maybe early twenties. Fit and strong. They were to the right, taking no notice. Drinking and laughing.

None of them saw the boy. Out there. Struggling silently. At first, up to his knees. Swaying from side to side. As though it was funny, or a game to be played. His arms flailing around. Like a windmill, some might say, laughing if they had seen it and turning away to get on with whatever they were doing. Whilst the boy continued thrashing, his legs slowly sinking into the mud.

Ian knew in a split second that this, the boy in the mud, was not a game. Not a piece of fun. Not funny at all. That it was going to end badly. In tragedy, even, if someone did not act now. Did not wait until the boy sank further down, and was sucked in. His arms no longer flailing about but gripping and grasping at non-existent edges as he was pulled down into the mud. And Ian was up and running.

The boy stopped thrashing for a second or two, no more than that.

He saw Ian get up onto his feet and start running towards him. Stuck there in the mud.

He smiled at Ian. Thank you. Thank you so much for coming to rescue me.

Ian realised that he, and he alone, could get out there in the mud to save the boy. That, by the time he had called to the family, and they had turned and seen and reacted, he would already have gone by them, running as hard and as fast as he could.

Same with the men. They would be stronger and fitter than Ian but, again, he would have been up to them and beyond and

165

off the riverbank and into the mud before they would have had the chance to respond to his shouts for assistance.

And there was no time, none at all, to shout to the yachts out there in the distance. To call to someone on the riverbank to press 999 on their mobile phone, to bring in the coastguard boat and helicopter. By the time they arrived, it would all be too late.

The boy was up to his waist now, and no longer waving his arms.

Instead, he had his hands down, on top of the mud, trying to push himself up and out of it.

He glanced at Ian, his face full of hope that Ian would reach him and save him in the nick of time.

Ian was running, so hard and so fast, but it seemed to take an age. It was as though the distance between him on the riverbank and the boy out there in the mud was further than he anticipated. He kept going, his heart pumping and legs and arms a blur, but he did not seem to be getting any closer.

He shouted, screamed really, at the family over towards his left. But they did not turn and look. They did not seem to hear him. He did the same to the group of men on his right. Really yelled, felt the spittle from his mouth over his face. But all they did was tip their heads back and drink more beer from their cans. Laugh as though nothing was happening. And nothing mattered.

Suddenly, above, from out of nowhere, he heard and saw a helicopter coming in fast from behind and over his head. Ian shouted at it, partly to attract its attention but mostly out of complete and utter joy. That it would circle and come down closer, a paramedic hanging from a rope ladder to pluck the boy out and to safety. But it did not. It simply carried on its way out to sea.

The boy was stuck fast now, arms by his side as if glued in place, and he was up towards his shoulders in the mud.

He looked at Ian, such a look, but he did not yell or scream or beg or plead.

Just stayed there ever so still, almost peaceful, with that look on his face as he watched Ian running towards him.

And Ian was there, at the edge of the riverbank, where the marsh turned into mud, just as the boy slipped below the surface. Ian lunged for the boy's head, pushing his hands down as far as he could into the thick, almost sticky, mud where he thought the boy might be. He felt then as though his own arms were stuck tight, as if in hardening cement. It needed all his strength, pulling his hands out, almost in slow motion.

Frantic now, the boy below and choking on the mud, Ian tried again and again to find the boy's head or shoulders or arms; anything he could get hold of. In and out. In and out. In and out. His hands fast to go in. Slow to come out. The mud reluctant to loosen its grip on him. He was sobbing now, Ian, knowing it was too late. That the boy had somehow slipped down and down to lie at the bottom of the riverbank.

On his fifth or sixth, final attempt, Ian had him, the boy, by the shoulders, straining to reach in further to get hold of him under his arms. So that he could pull and twist and pull and twist and pull and twist him to the surface. Up he came, the boy, with great long tugs and pauses and shouts of agony from Ian, pulling him up through the gloop and onto the surface.

And he rolled the boy over onto his back. Wiped the mud from his face, his nostrils, his mouth, his ears.

But the boy was dead. Had been from the moment he went under, and the mud forced its way into him. His eyes. His nose. His throat.

And it was Adam, of course. And Ian cradled his little boy in his arms and wished he were dead too.

PART THREE:
A B&B IN HUNSTANTON

14
A BREAKFAST, A NEWSPAPER
& A WALK TO THE CLIFF
EDGE

Ian sat on a wooden picnic table outside the café at the top of the cliffs at Old Hunstanton, Bernard by his feet. They'd walked too far today, Ian thought. All the way from Wells-next-the-Sea. Heads down. Unthinking. Wanting to die. Both of them now utterly exhausted. Bernard lay there panting endlessly. That wasn't good to see.

Ian had wanted to press on, to get here by late afternoon. To walk about in sunshine. To retrace footsteps. But Bernard was slowing and needed to be carried time and again, which slowed them even more, and it was gone 20.00 by the time they arrived. About an hour to sunset. Not enough time to do anything really, other than eat and find somewhere quiet to sleep for the night.

It was almost empty now, the adjacent car park, and just Ian and Bernard were at the café. At a table round the side. Facing the cliffs. The sun going down. Ian hoped the café shut at nine and not eight and that they'd make him something hot to eat.

The waitress stopped as she came towards him, her pad open, and pen ready for the order. She stood there looking at him as though she knew him. Or maybe she had been on her feet all day and had simply had enough. Or perhaps she was angry at their late, last-minute arrival. Time for her to go home soon, most likely, once he and his old pal had left.

Ian glanced away, unsettled by her stare. He wondered if she might be a friend of Beth, Hannah or Yasmin. But this one was too old. With her tied-back hair and plastic apron and sensible shoes, she was in her 40s, maybe older. Perhaps she knew Kate, although that somehow seemed unlikely.

He went to ask her for a menu but the thought of her sighing loudly and going off and coming back and slapping it down on the table troubled him. So, he just requested an all-day breakfast and a cup (not mug) of tea, and a glass of water. He hoped she would take the order and that there would be more than one sausage. He did not like to ask, to get involved in a discussion about the price of an extra sausage. If there were two sausages, Bernard could have one of them. If not, they'd share it.

It was here, at this café, that they'd got the ice creams all those years ago. Kate not really wanting one but agreeing to share a 99 with Beth, who then promptly changed her mind and said she'd rather have one to herself.

The three boys, Alex, Joe and Adam, all wanted a 99 with not one but two flakes. If they could? Please? Squabbling boisterously. Noisily. Happily, although Ian did not realise how happy they were at the time.

He and Kate said they'd share a 99 but then, somehow or other, they'd got six ice creams anyway. He paid, not sure if he were paying for five or six. But the children were off and away, heading towards the path to the beach and he did not have a chance to check his change as he hurried after them.

He looked up again as the waitress returned with his cup of tea and a knife and fork and serviette in one hand, and a bowl of water in the other. She had guessed why he had asked for a cup, not a mug. She put the bowl down next to Bernard who sat up and drank noisily from it. "Thank you," Ian said simply, and asked if she had sweetener, or sugar if not, he added, in case sweetener might be unheard of so far up here on the Norfolk coast.

She rummaged in her apron pocket and took out four packets of sweetener, putting them on the table next to the cup of tea. He looked at them glumly, the thought that she assumed

172

he had such a sweet tooth bothering him. That he must look fat, and unable to resist the equivalent of four teaspoons of sugar in a cup.

He looked at her once more, standing there, not moving, not going to get his all-day breakfast. And she smiled at him. He thought perhaps it was meant to be a nice warm smile, but she had something green, maybe cabbage, stuck between her front teeth and so he looked away. After a pause, when he thought she was going to say something but didn't, she went off.

The café, thought Ian, was much the same as when they had last been here. Rather rough and ready. Windswept. A nice, down-to-earth place. They'd sat at this bench and the one next to it most days, for breakfast, ice creams or tea.

And the big open clifftop field where they used to park the huge old Espace he could never quite get to grips with. The field looked just as he remembered it, with its bare patches in the grass all around the edges and the potholes at the entrance and exit that everyone drove carefully around.

And the toilets over there. Where he used to take Adam to have a wee, his little boy bubbling over with excitement so close to the cliff and the pathway and down to the dunes and the sea. If he shut his eyes now, he could almost hear Adam babbling away happily.

The waitress returned, plonking his all-day breakfast in front of him. Bernard edged forward, his head resting on Ian's thigh, his eyes plaintive, ready to eat.

Two slices of bacon. Two sausages. Two eggs. A slice of fried bread. Beans. Mushrooms. Tomatoes. Ian sat there looking at it. Goodness, so much of it. This was what he used to have here before, he remembered. He suddenly wished he had not ordered it or anything like it. In fact, he did not know why he was sitting here at all.

"I thought you might like to see this," the waitress said, putting the folded-over regional newspaper down on the table. She paused, waiting for him to say thank you, to open it, to look and start a conversation. But he just nodded his thanks, and after a long moment, she was gone.

Ian sat there looking out towards the cliff. You could not just go up right to the edge, he thought, like you might do at Beachy Head. At least not from here.

You would have to climb over a metal fence, fight your way through bushes and then, maybe, you'd be at the edge and looking down.

But it could just as easily open out by a pathway, the one that zig-zagged its way down the side of the cliff, taking day-trippers and holidaymakers to the shingly beach and back. Not much point throwing yourself onto a pathway, then limping away with a sprained ankle.

He took his knife and fork and cut the two sausages into pieces. Ten in all. Then fed them one at a time to Bernard who snatched at them, swallowing the pieces whole one after another.

Then the bacon, cutting it into smaller pieces and making Bernard sit and wait for them. Again, the dog gobbled down each piece the moment it was offered. This troubled Ian a little, the wolfing down of food. He wondered why Bernard did not sit and chew and savour the taste.

He pushed his fork into one fried egg followed by the other, the yolks bursting and running across the albumen. He went to cut the fried bread to dip into the yolks and eat but suddenly stopped. He had no appetite at all.

He knew sitting here, at this café, at this table, ordering what he used to eat before, was a terrible mistake. That this, coming here to Hunstanton, was wrong. All these memories now closing in, tormenting him. Bringing his mood down into the depths.

He had wanted to, in some way, pay tribute to Adam, to remember him at his happiest. To somehow wipe the slate clean of all that had happened. Or at least come to terms with it. So that he could go back home and start afresh.

But he realised he could not simply revisit where they had

been, relive what they had done, and somehow make peace with it. That this would simply torture him, drive him to the cliff edge rather than to the beach. And all he had really intended was to walk along the beach where they used to wander.

Ian got up, took a £10 note and a handful of coins from his pocket and tucked them under the saucer of the teacup. He whistled to Bernard to follow him as he left the café and walked away.

He did not notice the newspaper on the table, nor its headline. *Please come home – Family's plea to missing dad.* Nor did he see the photo of himself. The one he didn't like. The one when he was at his heaviest and it looked as though he did not have a neck.

***

The waitress stood inside the café looking out, watching the man and his Jack Russell walking away.

She waited to see which way they went. Left, towards the clifftop. Or right, to the pathway down to the beach.

She then made her way out to the picnic bench to clear away the plate and crockery and the dog bowl. She sat down and opened the newspaper, re-reading the front-page story.

The family of a missing 54-year-old father of three has appealed for him to come home, one week after he left his home in Felixstowe, Suffolk.

Ian Wilkerson was last seen walking Bernard, his Jack Russell Terrier, by the Dip at Felixstowe at around 17.00 on Monday the fourth of July. His family has not heard from him since. He is considered to be high risk.

She wondered why he would have left home, what would have driven a man to get up and go like that.

And why he had been described as "high risk". What was it about him that made him so?

Depression, she thought, instinctively touching the long-faded scars on her left wrist.

His eldest son Alex said none of the family had heard from him since and that they were "heartbroken" not knowing where he is.

Appealing for news, Alex added "Someone must know where he is. This is completely out of character."

"Dad has a lovely wife, three loving children and is to become a grandfather later in the year."

She studied the photograph of the man in the newspaper and the one of his dog alongside of it. It was definitely them she had just met. He looked down-hearted and dirty and homeless now and the dog seemed to be on its last legs. But it was them.

There was another photograph, a family group, and she checked the faces of each of the members in turn − the older woman, who would have been beautiful when she was younger; still was, really. Two sturdy young men and a young woman in between them holding up two photographs she could not see clearly: presumably, the same as the ones in the article.

Nice people, she decided. Although this was a posed shot, they all looked, pushed up close with their arms resting on each other, a close and loving family. Only the photograph of the man worried her. There was something about him that was alarming. As though he were crying out for someone to talk to him.

"As a family, we don't know what to do. All we can do is to keep saying 'Come Home, Dad, We Love You' and that somehow this message will get through to Dad."

Ian is described as white and six-foot tall with long salt and pepper hair, balding at the back, and with short white stubble. The family has not had any contact from him for the past seven days and want to stay positive.

Anyone who has seen Ian or who has information about where he may be should contact Suffolk Police on 101.

The waitress looked again at the photo of the missing man at the top of the page. He had an odd-looking face, slightly lopsided, and a funny smile. That might, she thought, have been because he was looking into the sun. But there was kindness there, inside him. She felt sure of that.

She sat at the picnic bench for a minute or two, thinking.

Then she got up and went back into the café and took off her apron and hung it on a hook, shouting over her shoulder to the café owner that she was leaving now, and she would see him in the morning. She put on her jacket, picked up her handbag and hurried out, the newspaper still in her hand.

She had thought that the missing man would go to the right, down to the path that led to the sand dunes, the beach and the sea. But he had turned left, to follow the path along the top towards Hunstanton itself. The clifftops. It was the sudden thought of the cliff and the words "high risk" from the newspaper that made her walk much faster than she normally did.

***

Ian stood on the clifftop, beyond the bushes and the wire fences. Four steps from the edge.

He held Bernard in his arms, looking down towards the beach. The tide was out.

Dusk was falling fast, and it would be dark soon. Ian wondered if he could stand here waiting without anyone really noticing him. Until it was properly dark.

It was strange that, looking back at the holiday, all he could remember was Adam.

The sweet things he did. His smile. The expressions on his face. The funny things he said.

The way he used to run along, holding up his little Thomas the Tank Engine train in his right hand, way above his head.

Ian could still see people on the beach, mostly walking back towards Hunstanton.

Families with young children skipping here, there and everywhere. Ahead. Behind. Then holding hands.

Ian could not remember when he last held hands with Kate. Nor with his children. With Adam, most probably, on this beach down below.

Adam loved that little Thomas the Tank engine.

Wrapped his podgy little hand around it. Making choo-choo noises. Trying to whistle.

They prised it out of his hand at bedtime. He slept with it under his pillow.

Ian did not know how far the drop was from the clifftop to the beach. He was never very good at lengths or distances. And everyone seemed to think in metres these days, as he did although his judgement was hit-and-miss.

The beach was a mix of rocks and shingly sand. As he took a step towards the cliff edge, he wondered if it made any difference. Landing on rocks or on sand.

Whether one might kill them both outright, the other leaving him paralysed from the neck down as Bernard ran away chasing a dog in the distance.

On the last day of the holiday, the day it happened, they had gone into the old-fashioned toy shop in Hunstanton.

So Adam could choose another toy, a going-home present. Percy, Thomas' best friend. Or Rosie, Thomas' girlfriend.

He chose Rosie, stomping back with Thomas in one fist and Rosie in the other. Alex and Joe teased him about picking Rosie all the way to the café.

Looking down again, as Bernard grew restless in his arms, Ian could still see one or two groups, families of four, walking in the shadows. Below where they would fall if they went straight down.

He turned to Bernard who twisted around and looked out towards the sea. Lifting his head up, the wind in his face, sniffing the air. "Ozone", Ian remembered Kate saying on that holiday as they walked along the nearby pavement. "Breathe in the ozone." As if they could somehow suck the goodness into their lungs.

Ian looked back, away from the cliff edge towards the pavement that went from Old Hunstanton to Hunstanton, and there were still people walking there, taking no notice of him and Bernard. It was getting so dark now. It would get darker. Then it would be time. He put Bernard on the ground for a moment.

When they had recovered the body – Adam's body – from the sea, Ian had asked whether they had found Thomas or Rosie.

A stupid, senseless question. He knew that as the words left his lips. They had looked at him, these boatmen, bewildered, as if he were talking nonsense. He knew he was. He was on the brink of madness.

At some point when the tide had come back in and out again, he had walked that beach to see if he could find Thomas or Rosie. He did not.

And now, at last, it was properly dark. The moon was shielded by clouds. And the streetlights were far from where he stood. There were no longer any passers-by. No one to watch him or see what he was going to do. Ian picked Bernard up again and held him close. His old, dying pal.

He gazed down for ever such a long time. He could not now see the beach. But he did not believe that anyone would be down there beneath him.

He held Bernard tighter in his arms and kissed the dog on the head. Then stepped forward. One step, two. Stood there. Waiting. Decided to count down from 60. Stumbled over the order when he got into the mid-40s. And again, in the 20s. Stopped counting. Stepped forward one more time instead. His toes now right at the edge. He could count down from 10 easily enough. That's all he'd need.

15
THE CURVE IN THE ROAD, LIFE OR DEATH & A HANDFUL OF CHANGE

The waitress had seen the missing man, "Ian", as she now thought of him, turn left as he walked away from the café. She had expected him to walk back towards the car park. It occurred to her suddenly that he was on foot and had walked all the way from Felixstowe this past week.

Had he turned right, towards the path and beach, she would not have gone hurrying after him. Maybe just rang 101 and left a message that would somehow work its way through so that his family would know where he was. At least, where he had been. And that he was safe. Alive.

Turning left offered more possibilities than turning right where she would have expected him to walk his dog down along the beach towards Hunstanton. Left and he could walk away from Hunstanton. Just go straight out of town towards Burnham and Wells. Or he could turn and go along the cliffs. And that was what worried her. The cliffs.

There had, over the years, been suicides from the cliffs between Old Hunstanton and Hunstanton itself.

Young people mostly. Troubled souls. Their lives summed up and tidied away in a few paragraphs in the local newspaper.

She had once stood there too, willing herself to step out and over the edge. Not so very long ago.

She hurried to the top of the road and along Lighthouse Close to Cliff Parade and the pavement which ran parallel to the clifftop. It was dark now. There were some half a dozen people here and there in the distance. By this pavement and further away on the other side of the road. She stopped now and again, peering at them. No sign of the man and his dog.

She decided that the man would be five minutes or so ahead of her; maybe a quarter of a mile. She knew the distance from the café to the pier at Hunstanton was about a mile and a half and that she could walk it not much more than half an hour. She would walk that far now to see if she could find him. If he planned to walk to Hunstanton, with his dog sniffing and leaving its mark every few metres, she might catch up with him in 20 minutes.

She knew the place where he could throw himself to his death. He could push through bushes, weeds and brambles and scramble over the wire fences to get to the edge. Just beyond the Samaritans' sign, Talk To Us – If things are getting to you – Call 116 123. She swallowed. And walked faster. She knew how it felt. To be "high risk". A phrase that covered so much. Anxiety. Depression. Suicidal thoughts. She knew exactly what it was like.

To choose between a fiancé and elderly disabled parents. To spend the best part of your life as a carer as the world sailed on by. Getting married. Having children. Living lives. Being happy.

To be left, at 39, with a run-down bungalow sold for a small flat, few savings and part-time jobs, cleaning and waitressing, to make ends meet. No one to share her life with.

She kept walking as fast as she could without running. There was no one about now, as she got towards halfway along the clifftop pavement. She had hoped there would be people. Maybe a gang of teenagers who she could approach for help. Who would run ahead for her.

But there was nobody at all; it was down to her. She did not know what it was about this missing man that had her chasing him along the clifftop. Whether it was the newspaper article and the words of the man's son. The talk of love. Or if it was meeting him at the café and seeing that last, haunted look on his face.

She took off her shoes and tucked them into her handbag and ran as best she could. The clifftop pavement curved just ahead of her. And beyond, the last place where he could throw himself off. As she approached the curve, she braced herself for what she expected to see.

Nothing. And what she must then do. Although she realised it would be too late.

Look over the cliff to see if she could spot the man and dog on the beach below. Then dig into her handbag for her mobile phone and press 999.

She suddenly thought she would have been the last person he spoke to and who saw him alive. And she would probably have to meet his family to tell them all about it. And how she did not run fast enough to save him.

***

Ian wondered, as he stood gazing downwards, his toes on the edge, how long it would take to fall from the clifftop and hit the sand below. A few seconds, he guessed.

And whether, when someone fell to their death, their life flashed before their eyes like people said it did at the end.

And, when a man and a dog went over together, if they would hit the sand at the same moment or whether the man, being that much heavier, would land first.

Ian knew, from experience, that time had a bendy quality to it. He recalled a minor car accident once on the A14 where he had taken his eye off the road when edging forward in a traffic queue and looked up just before ploughing into the back of a lorry. That could have been no more than a few seconds but the time between seeing the lorry and hitting it seemed longer.

He did not think that a whole life, more than 50 years of it in his case, could re-run through someone's mind in only a few seconds. He thought it was more likely that it would just be edited highlights at best. Or perhaps his final memory would be of the last full and proper look he had of Adam's face as he held that 99 ice cream in one hand, the two trains in the other.

He wondered what happened after death. He recalled Kate's uncle, Tony, talking just after his first heart attack. As he laid there on the pavement outside the bookies, slipping in and out of consciousness, waiting for the ambulance to arrive, he had expected to see a bright light as he was called towards heaven. Instead, he reported later, all he could see in his mind was what he called a "wet blackness"; "like a big dark puddle of oily water," he'd added, trying to explain it.

The light, thought Ian, was what he would see as he landed on the beach.

He'd look up to see the moonlight through the clouds.

And the moon would be obscured by Bernard hurtling towards him.

He stepped back from the edge. Put Bernard down by his feet. Shook himself. Realised suddenly that he had been sweating profusely. That his clothes were sticking to him even though the night air was chilly.

He did not think, when he got to the edge and stood there, that he could have gone over. That butterfly mind of his, coming up with thoughts and reasons not to. The image of Adam in his head was what stopped him for sure. And the thought, not far behind, of Kate and his family and what it would do to them. And another image in his head of Beth, his glorious, irrepressible daughter, screaming in pain.

He reached out his hand and patted Bernard on the head. The dog sat there waiting patiently for his instructions. Sit, stay, walk on – Bernard was a good dog really. Maybe that too was why Ian did not jump. He could not bring himself to take his pal over with him. Nor leave him behind to his fate on the streets.

Ian stood there for an age, back outside the bushes and wire fences.

Decided, finally, enough was enough. That it was time to find somewhere to sleep for the night.

In the morning, he would start the long walk home to see what awaited him.

***

Ian turned and stepped to the side as he heard footsteps and heavy breathing behind him, half expecting someone to come running up to push him over the edge.

The waitress from the café stopped a few feet away. Her eyes were wild and unfocused. Her face was flushed. She looked as though she had been running.

He thought to ask her flippantly, to make light of things, if she had brought his change. £1.50 or so he made it. But he thought better of it and just said, "Hello."

She lurched forward, her head down, hands on her knees, bag on the ground, as she fought to gather her breath. He waited, not sure what else to say. He thought maybe he should step forward and pat her on the back. A kind gesture. But that might look as though he thought she was choking. And he knew that she was not. That something was terribly wrong.

He wondered whether she had seen him standing on the cliff edge with Bernard. Decided that was the most likely reason. She was strolling home after work, spotted him, and had started running when she thought he was going to go over. She was trying to get to him before he did, but had not noticed, in her panic, that he had already stepped away.

He was touched. That someone, a complete stranger, would run to try and save his life. It made him feel emotional. He wanted to thank her, but was not sure how. He had never been very good at this. Emotions. Especially when it was all right there in front of him, all sobs and gasps, and he had to address it, to deal with it, there and then.

"Are you alright?" Ian said as neutrally as he could.

She was still gulping in air, trying to steady herself.

"I'd have been happy for you to keep the change," he said, adding, more cheerfully, "you didn't have to run all this way after me with it."

A long silence. Broken only by her jagged breaths. Ian thought he had misjudged the moment. But felt some form of jollity was best. Safest. To keep the emotion at arm's length.

"I... I thought..." she stammered, her voice then tailing off. She gestured towards the cliff edge; "... you know."

He nodded, unsure whether to make another joke of it or to tell her the truth. That it had crossed his mind. More than that. He had come close. Then changed his mind at the last moment. He thought she probably deserved his honesty.

"Ah, well," he answered finally, leaning forward to stroke Bernard's head. After a long pause, as he thought about what he was going to say, he went on, in hesitant sentences. As if to absolve himself. And her too.

"I've walked here all the way from Felixstowe down in Suffolk. This past week or so. With my dog. Rough camping... we've never done anything like it before." He paused a while, thinking. "It's been a... a holiday, I suppose. In a way. For the two of us. We're..." he stopped again, searching for the right words, "... not too well, us old boys, what with one thing and another. Something of a last hurrah I suppose..."

She did not seem to know what to say, so she just stood up and looked awkward, glancing at him and away, out towards the sea.

He noticed a newspaper and her shoes sticking out of her handbag on the ground.

He thought maybe he should comment on the shoes but could not find the right words. Instead, he went on, stumbling again through his sentences.

"I came here years ago. With my family. I... we lost our youngest. Adam. Down on the beach there. In the sea... I...

I thought it was time I came back." He stopped again for the longest time. Until he thought she was going to reach out and put her hand on his arm.

He was waiting until he could speak without choking. "Pay… my… respects." He got the words out. Just about. Then made a spluttery noise as he drew in his breath and coughed out at the same instant. He fell silent.

They stood there, the two of them, Bernard between their feet, looking out at the black sea, both lost in their own thoughts for a while.

"Walk me home?" she asked suddenly, abruptly, as though the idea had just occurred to her, and she needed to express it quickly before she had second thoughts and changed her mind.

He turned to her and smiled and did not quite know what to say, whether he wanted to or not, nor what she was really asking, whether it was for her benefit or his or whether he was just over-thinking things as per usual.

"Yes, okay," he said quietly. Then, surprising himself, more loudly, "Thank you."

And she smiled back and bent to put on her shoes, tidied her bag, and turned, looked left and right, and started crossing the road.

All matter of fact. And Ian followed her with Bernard trotting by his feet. He wondered what the evening held in store. A mix of awkwardness and embarrassment, most probably.

16
INNARDS, ENTRAILS & MATTERS OF THE HEART (& TROUSERS)

They sat, eating quietly, opposite each other at a small Formica table by the window of the kitchenette of her two-bed flat in a backstreet in Hunstanton. "Clean enough," thought Ian, "but grotty... poor as a church mouse" as Kate would have put it. He suddenly wondered what Kate would think about him being here now, like this. She'd probably find it unlikely; and funny.

The Victorian house, divided up into six separate flats, looked out over the street, cars filling every available space to either side. The sea was somewhere to the left, he believed, and you could probably see it if you leaned out of the window far enough. Not that he would try; knowing him, he'd topple over.

They picked slowly at their plates of spaghetti bolognese, sipping now and again at their glasses of red wine from the half-empty, screw-topped bottle between them. They were largely silent and, Ian knew, the longer they stayed like this the more awkward it would become. But he could not think of something to say that was, what was it, small talk. He had never been very good at that. He thought perhaps he should maybe just finish eating and make an excuse to leave.

It had started off well enough. As they walked to the flat, she'd turned and said, "I'm Sarah by the way." She smiled and he noted the green stuff in her teeth had gone. She looked nicer than he first thought. A rather solid woman for sure, no nonsense, and you'd never win a wrestling match with her. But she had a pleasant, open face. She had pretty eyes.

"Ian," he had replied, "and this is Bernard," he added, "my dog." "Well, d'uh," he thought to himself, but did not say aloud.

He had thought perhaps he should walk beside her, but realised he'd have to keep hopping on and off the narrow pavement. And Bernard would get in the way. Best not, he decided. He might stumble and sprawl by her feet.

"More bolognese… or spaghetti?" she asked, smiling at him from the other side of the Formica table. She reached out towards the two bowls between them. Ian wondered if this was how they did it in posh restaurants. Separate bowls. Kate had always just mixed it all up and slopped it out onto his plate. In his lap once, when he'd suggested he did not like spaghetti all that much and would rather have had home-made beefburgers and those thin crispy frieshe really liked.

Truth be told, Ian wasn't the biggest fan of bolognese. It made him think of innards. And this bowlful of it seemed to be full of tinned tomatoes and they looked to him like bloodied livers and kidneys and hearts and other bits and pieces. What was it? Entrails. Even the word made his stomach churn.

He shook his head and said he was fine, thank you, but then, catching the expression on her face and noting the large amounts of bolognese and spaghetti still left in the bowls, he changed his mind and said yes please, and she seemed quite relieved about it. He hoped he would not gag on the tomatoes.

"The flat's just up here," she had said, turning left into a side street as Ian and Bernard followed her from the seafront. "I bought it last summer."

"I looked after my disabled parents… Mum died… then Dad the year before last… so I sold the family bungalow in Heacham… and moved here. It was a fresh start for me."

He had nodded, not sure what to say. Wondered whether she was just making conversation or actually saying to him, in a roundabout way, "I live alone … why don't you come on in?"

She served two great dollops, first of bolognese, then of

spaghetti, onto his plate, the spaghetti laying there, hanging half on and half off the side. He tried to think of something light and amusing to say, but nothing came into his mind other than tapeworms, which did not seem appropriate. And then she was filling her own plate and the two bowls sat there empty in the middle between them.

Ian looked at his plate – what amounted to a full and complete second helping with three big red tomatoey-gutsy lumps in the middle – and wondered how he was going to choke all this down.

He started mixing the spaghetti and bolognese together, cutting and pushing small portions of the mixture into his mouth. He suddenly had a terrible fear he may gag on it, especially when it came to the tomatoes. And he wondered if he shouted, "It's delicious!" if or when he did gag, whether that might fool her. As if the food was so wonderful that he could not shovel it in fast enough.

When they had got to the big old Victorian house over on the right side of the street, she had pointed and said that her flat was on the top floor. Then, without hesitation, she added, nonchalantly, take it or leave it, up to you kind of thing, that she had a spare room if he wanted somewhere to sleep for the night. "Bernard can sleep in there with you… by the radiator," she added, for clarity.

And he had said yes and thank you. And he did not quite know how he felt as he followed her up the narrow staircase to her flat, Bernard close behind.

She asked if he'd like to use the bathroom and he did, recoiling in horror at the sight of his grimy face and sticky-up hair in the mirror. He knew he really needed a shower but there was only a bath with a shower-head attachment above it. And he could not bring himself to have a bath. So, he washed his face and hands and ran wet fingers through his hair, drying them on the edge of a bath towel. Then wondered if his breath smelled. He had cleaned his teeth with her toothpaste, rubbing it over each tooth with the side of a forefinger. Then swished with mouthwash from a bottle on top of a cabinet.

He sat and waited at the table whilst she busied around, taking tubs of this and that from the fridge, filling a saucepan, boiling a kettle, and getting a bottle of wine from a box under the sink and generally fussing about, until they started eating.

**

It was the small lamp over in the living area beside the television unit that broke the silence and eased the awkwardness between Ian and Sarah.

A glowing thing with a black base that didn't really give off much light, thought Ian.

And it wasn't particularly nice to look at, really. Like a large, craggy lump of earwax.

"What's that?" he asked, adding "that lamp thing?" as he saw her puzzled look.

"Oh, that," she replied when she saw what he was pointing at. "That's a Himalayan salt lamp... they're very popular. It was a Christmas present from... my... ex... friend."

"It's... orange plastic?"

She shook her head. "It's carved from pink Himalayan salt... millions of years old... it has lots of health benefits."

"Oh, yes?" He tried to keep his voice as neutral as possible. Then swallowed some more spaghetti bolognese.

She put her fork down, then raised her fist front of her and stuck the thumb out. "One, they clean the air. Two, they ease allergies. Three, they raise your mood. Four, they help you sleep." She raised her little finger. "There's a fifth benefit but I can't remember what it is."

"Bring you wealth?" he said as blandly as he could.

"Mmm, maybe..." she laughed, looking around. "That one's not worked for me."

Ian leaned forward to look more closely at the lamp. "So that glow inside is, what... Himalayan energy?"

"No, it's a 40-watt lightbulb."

"Doesn't the heat from it melt the plastic... the salt?"

"No, I don't think so."

"Ah, I see," Ian said.

They glanced at each other at the same moment. Both laughed out loud. Ian wondered whether they were thinking the same thing. Probably not, he decided.

Even so, it made things easier between them as they carried on eating and drinking, more cheerfully now.

***

"You're on your own, then?" Ian asked after chatting for a while; the weather at this time of year (mixed), Hunstanton Pier (noisy), and her Peugeot car (old, unreliable). He thought, a second or two later, that he could have phrased it better, more, what was the word, diplomatically. Yes, that was it.

It struck him suddenly that he had always been like this. The thoughts in his head blurting out of his mouth before he could phrase them properly. Even now, when he could feel his brain slowing and stumbling at times, he still seemed to speak first and think second.

"Yes," she answered simply. "He was, ah... my boss at work... at the café. He's just..." She hesitated for several seconds. "He was separated from his wife. He went back to her before Christmas... for the children. So he said."

She stopped and her mouth twisted in a strange way for a second or two. He was not sure what to say to that. To commiserate. To say how hard it must be to continue working with the man at the café. Or to ask something. About being alone and probably being on her own for the rest of her life. How lonely it must be.

But then he thought he might not say anything. He heard Kate in his head for a moment or two, saying to him quite clearly and in her slightly raised voice, "Don't speak. At all! You'll only say something stupid and make things ten times worse."

He felt sad for her. Sad that she had no partner, no children, had nothing very much really.

This rundown flat. Her job at the café during the summer. He guessed she did something else in the winter. Cleaning, most likely. Offices and such.

Not that women necessarily wanted marriage and children these days. He knew that was a horribly old-fashioned view and he should keep it to himself and, better still, not even think it. But he thought perhaps that she did anyway.

"I was engaged once," she went on, brightly enough, and as if reading his thoughts, "after my A-Levels… I didn't go to university. I met Stephen… on the pier. And…" her voice suddenly sounded wistful and faded slowly as she added, "We were together for two or three years. Well, two years, nine months and …"

She glanced at him as if knowing the exact length of time was somehow rather desperate. He smiled at her, still not really knowing what to say. His default mode was flippant, but he realised this wasn't the time or place. That she had years and years of emptiness and sadness behind her. Ahead too, most likely.

"What happened?" he replied, sensing that she wanted to talk, "If you don't mind me asking."

She leaned back in her chair and swallowed the last mouthful of her wine. Then she spoke, as if she had said it so many times to so many different people.

"My mum and dad needed looking after," she said quietly. "Mum had fibromyalgia and… all sorts. Dad had mobility issues and… dementia eventually. They couldn't have managed on their own… if I had left… abandoned them."

"Stephen wanted us to move away. To London. He was offered a job in the city. Get married and have children and…" she waved her hand, "… all of those things."

"I had a choice. Them or him and... everything." She stopped and suddenly did not seem to know what to say. She looked around, ever-so-slightly teary-eyed, and raised her hands as if to say, "So here I am... Little Miss... Missed Out".

Ian wondered if, at this point, he was meant to get up and go round the side of the table and hug her to, in some way, console her. It seemed, for a moment, as if she were being ever-so-slightly theatrical about it and he thought that was maybe what he was expected to do.

And he did not mind doing that, although what might happen next worried him. And, of course, he might have got it terribly wrong, and she might look appalled and recoil in horror if he suddenly launched himself at her.

So, he mumbled yes and oh dear, and stuck his fork into a big, bloody-looking tomato that burst and made him feel sick. And they settled back into another slightly awkward silence where Ian felt maybe he should have done or at least said something. Then they were finishing off their food and she picked up the bottle of wine and tipped the rest into each of their glasses. Half and half.

"Do you want to go through to the living room?" she asked, lifting the two glasses and passing them to him, "whilst I..." She got up and turned away and he didn't catch what it was she said. Another sentence for sure.

This was the difficult part, he thought, as he turned towards the living area. What came next. He did not know quite what he thought about that. He felt himself stirring in the downstairs department and wasn't sure about that either.

"The beast is rising" Kate would have said, followed by, in an ever louder voice, "Lordy, Lordy..." (or something like that), "beware of... THE BEAST!" He couldn't help but think Kate would be revelling in his awkwardness right now.

17
WAR OF THE WORLDS, WINE & A FEW WORDS AT THE BEDROOM DOOR

Ian walked into the living area, holding the two half-full glasses of wine. He guessed what came next – the sitting by each other on the sofa, the opening of the second bottle of wine, the more intimate talk between them – could be tricky. Very. Very. Tricky. He wondered whether he had made a terrible mistake coming here.

It occurred to him that he could just put the glasses down now and slip on his shoes by the front door and go. Hurry away into the night. But Bernard would probably sit there by the radiator looking at him dolefully and refusing to move. "I'm settled here now, Baldy, what do you want to leave for?" And he thought of her face and how she had been looking at him. What was the word? "Desperate" was far too strong. As was "needy". "Vulnerable" was probably the word he wanted. Near enough. And "kind" too, he thought, and "caring". A good person. She deserved better.

He could not bear the thought of her watching him from the kitchen window as he scurried away with Bernard held like a hostage in his arms. And her maybe thinking he had stolen something from her. He imagined her rushing to check her handbag. The shame of it. That she might think so badly of him.

Ian looked around the living area again. A beaten-up, brown striped sofa and two matching armchairs. A TV and a DVD player on an old pine TV unit, a handful of DVDs below. That silly lamp. A matching pine sideboard and coffee table that had seen better days. As it all had. This mismatch of hand-me-downs and charity shop buys.

It struck him that when they sat down together, he was wearing the same clothes, other than the T-shirt, that he had worn all week.

And he had not really rinsed his pants and things that much, if at all actually, what with one thing and another. His clothes must smell by now. Of sweat and mustiness. Body odour of some sort. He'd had a whiff of a fruity smell, like a rotting banana, once or twice already that evening when getting up and down and thought the wafts must be from him.

He whistled to Bernard to bring him to his feet in the hope that any unfortunate odours might be attributed to the dog rather than to him. Bernard would almost certainly break wind at some point anyway and that would be enough to cover just about everything and anything. The dog moved slowly and reluctantly, almost grudgingly, towards him, thought Ian. He imagined he could hear a loud sigh.

He put the glasses of wine down on the coffee table, jigging Hunstanton Pier coasters about so it was all just so. Then, as he waited for her return, he went over and looked at the DVDs at the bottom of the TV unit. A dozen there in all, split about equally between romantic and violent films. An odd mix.

He wondered how the "what comes next" would work out. He thought he would keep things light and amusing as best he could. He could hear Kate in his head, "Just be normal. Don't be you. And whatever else you do... don't try to be funny. At all."

He worried what he would do, how he would react, if she rested her head on his shoulder at some point or maybe put her hand gently on his leg.

Thought he would be flustered by it. Would struggle to say and do the right thing. Not least because he knew, deep down, that the gesture, the hand on his thigh, would excite him. That he would be torn. And would not know how to respond.

She came through into the living room with another bottle of wine in one hand and a corkscrew in the other which she waved her other hand above her head, saying, "Ta-da!"

And she was brisk and jolly, perhaps covering her embarrassment, uncorking the bottle and making a popping noise with her mouth and pouring the wine into the two glasses.

She sat in one of the armchairs almost opposite the sofa and raised her glass and said, "Cheers!" and smiled at him in a friendly, but not over-friendly, way. Just cheerful. And he felt relieved by that.

"You have an eclectic…" Ian paused for a moment, sipping from his glass and wondering if that were the right word. He started over, waving his hand towards the TV. "Your DVDs are… um… different."

She laughed. "Yes, some are mine, the others are… were… ah, his. Andy's." She stopped and he wondered if she would elaborate or if he should ask about the man from the cafe.

"Did you want to put one on?" she asked. "Let me guess which one you'd choose," she added, before he could answer. She went down on her knees and shuffled across to the TV unit and rummaged through the DVDs.

"This one?" she said, holding up a copy of *The Shawshank Redemption*.

"Yours or his?" Ian replied.

"His… but I like it too. Do you want to watch this one?"

"It's quite long," he said, "and it's been a tiring day what with one thing and …"

"Do you want to go to bed?" she interrupted, looking at him.

He looked back at her and her dead straight face and was not sure how to take the question. Quite what she meant. Whether she was teasing him or not. She continued looking at him and he flushed and glanced away before speaking.

"How about that one?" he said, pointing to the DVD on top of the pile.

"*War of The Worlds?*" she said, a little sceptically, he thought. Almost scornful. "H.G. Wells," she added. He expected her to go on, "Because we're eight-year olds."

But she did not, although he thought she made some huffety-puffety noise as she bent down to load the DVD player. She pressed buttons on this remote control and that and sat back down opposite him.

And they started watching the 1950s film, with its simple storyline and primitive effects, and he remembered how he had seen it many years before on television one Sunday afternoon when the children were small. And he wondered suddenly what the hell he was doing here. What madness had driven him to this. To be sitting in a flat with a stranger so far from home, his wife, and family, not knowing where he was.

He bent over and patted Bernard by his feet, in case she looked across and saw the emotion in his face.

He wished he could get up and go. Just leave. Be done with it all, and go back home to where he belonged.

But he composed himself and glanced over at Sarah. She looked back and smiled at him, so he soldiered on.

They sat there sipping their wine. She topped his glass up and then her own. And they watched the television. In what might be described as a companionable silence. He felt this should be pleasant, something nice and relaxing. But he felt uncomfortable when he thought of Kate and the family. And guilty too, in a way, that he was maybe leading this Sarah on, encouraging her.

She suddenly reached for one of the remote controls on the armrest next to her and pressed a button to freeze the DVD. Then got up and handed the remote control to him.

"Here," she said, "men have to be in charge of these. It's a primeval thing." And she turned and went out of the room.

And he saw that the bottle of wine was nearly empty and wondered if she had gone to get a third. Or if she had gone into her bedroom to change and what she would be wearing when she came back out. And whether she was ever so slightly drunk.

She came back out with another bottle of red wine and a large box of chocolates, Milk Tray. Then, she picked up her half-full glass of wine and gestured to him to start the DVD again.

She sat herself down next to him on the sofa with the box of chocolates between them. And he knew the time was approaching. The moment of truth.

When he either went one way, or the other. Stayed here, at least for a while, or went home.

And he did not, in all honesty, with those pretty eyes and her being so close and smelling so nice, know which way he would go when she leaned in close against him and that moment arrived.

***

She pressed buttons on the remote control and *The War of The Worlds* DVD came back on. Ian had pretty much lost interest in it by now. If it wasn't for the situation he was in, the predicament he had got himself into, he'd have nodded off ages ago, he was so tired. Bernard was already snoring gently in fits and starts by his feet.

She opened the box of chocolates and rummaged through, picking and choosing three before handing the box to him.

"I prefer hard chocolates," she said, "I don't like soft ones." She looked at him and he did not know what to say.

He wondered if she was now drunk or had maybe taken some medication when she was out of the room. She seemed different somehow.

What was the word he was looking for? Aggressive wasn't quite right. Not flirty either. Not exactly. Assertive might be better.

He took one of the chocolates, biting into it; it was rock solid.

"That's a hard one," she said. "toffee. You'll have to keep

sucking until it goes soft. That's what I do."

He glanced at her again, just in case, but she was back to the box once more. "Here," she said, "try this one, the one with dimply bits … it's a strawberry one, better for your teeth." Then she laughed.

He swallowed the half-chewed toffee down with a mouthful of wine. Then ate the strawberry chocolate in two quick bites.

They both sat back, watching the DVD. The film rolling along in the background to its inevitable ending. Ian thought it was a nice little film.

Sipping wine. Taking it in turns to choose a chocolate from the box. Ian was coming close to falling asleep.

He could not remember the exact ending of the film and that bothered him. He thought the Martians caught a cold or flu or something from the human race and that killed them off. But he was not sure. It would be Covid these days, of course.

He was aware of her getting up and turning off one or two lights and putting on a lamp and disappearing and coming back in her pyjamas and that – the change of clothes – was enough for him to sit up straight. She had a newspaper in her hand.

"Did you read the newspaper?" she asked, holding it towards him. It was the one she'd put next to him on the bench at the café.

"Yes, thank you," he said. He could not be less interested in reading the local newspaper right now.

"Okay," she answered slowly, doubtfully, putting it by the side of the sofa and sitting back down. "I wasn't sure you had done …" She nodded to herself, thinking. "Okay."

He noticed some of the buttons on her top were undone and he could see the shape of her breasts through the material of her pyjamas.

There was also a red mark, maybe a smear of jam, just below the pocket. He thought perhaps he could see it better from this angle than she could, what with her breasts being in the way.

"So…" she said and he could sense she was thinking

something over and choosing her words carefully. "You've walked all the way from Felixstowe?"

"Pretty much," he said. He stuck his feet out in front of him – battered old shoes, no socks – and put them back down on the carpet.

"Feet seem to be holding up okay… as is everything else… just about. We're pacing ourselves."

She nodded, thinking again. He thought that having told him something about her life, she was expecting him to reciprocate, telling her about himself and his family and what he was doing here.

"I've taken early retirement… redundancy really," he sighed. "I worked in marketing… writing business stuff. Um, I've also had one or two health issues… and my dog's got a growth… a lump on his liver… and so I thought, you know, I'd… we'd do something different."

She leaned forward and ran her hand over Bernard who lifted his head lazily before going back to sleep. She kept her hand on the dog's tummy for a while, as if waiting for Ian to go on, to explain, to open up to her.

He decided that he did not want to talk about Bernard's lump or Kate or the family and especially not Adam. Nor anything about standing on the clifftop. All this doom and gloom. He just wanted to sit here for a while and be himself. To not be someone's husband or father or the man who was going to take his own life.

"I'm…" he laughed suddenly, surprising himself. "Ah, 54 and I have a family and a house and a dog… all the usual things… and I'm going to be a grandpa later this year… and I'm…" he laughed again, "…probably just having a mid-life crisis."

She turned to him and smiled, and he was not sure whether she was going to lean forward and kiss him.

He sat there, not moving, and smiled back at her. Watched as different expressions crossed her face. As though she were making a decision.

Then she took his glass and hers and placed them on the coffee table in front of them. Put the box of chocolates between them on the table too.

She slid across the sofa and, half nudging, half turning him back towards the television, she put her arm through his and rested her head on his shoulder. That, he decided, was nice enough. Settling back to watch the end of the film.

And he felt that this, sitting here, was going to be just fine. At least for now.

***

Ian woke when he felt Sarah stirring beside him. If she had not, he thought, he'd have just slept right through. (And probably all the better for it.)

They both seemed to sit there for a minute or two, gathering their thoughts, as the end credits for the film came up on the television.

Then she was up and away, brisk and efficient, saying she would make his bed. He reached for the remote control and jabbed away at it until the DVD player was turned off.

Ian wondered, as he sat on the sofa waiting, if he should make a pass at her. Just gently, to be polite. Whether she might be offended if he did not make a gesture of sorts. Or if she might be more offended if he did. Women could be tricky like that, he thought. Not that he really knew either way.

And he had never been sure what a pass was exactly. He thought maybe it might be something subtle like a nod or a wink, but probably not both, at the bedroom door. He was not very good at that sort of thing. He did not have much experience.

Ian did not really know women that well. Had only ever had two girlfriends before Kate and that was at college when he was doing his A-Levels. One in the first year, the other in the second. Neither of them could be said to have been long relationships.

He had gone out with the first one, Jayne, for three or four months and they had, you know, done this and that, and on three occasions, the other (albeit not that successfully). But, at the Sixth Form disco at Christmas, he had danced with her, rather too boisterously, and knocked her flat on her back in front of everyone and she had got up, the heel on her left shoe at a right angle, and limped off. It wasn't the end of the relationship, it had gone on a few weeks more, but it was certainly the beginning of the end.

The second one, Janice, started towards the end of the second year; in the Upper Sixth as it used to be called. They had met as part of a group that hung out together and went to bars and cinemas. He had circled her for weeks and eventually plucked up the courage to ask her out. They were together for a couple of months, maybe three, and were intimate but not as often (or as successfully) as Ian would have liked. She disappeared for the summer without a word and did not return his calls and she went to university somewhere far away in the autumn and that, sadly, was that.

Then there was Kate, who he fell in love with deeply and forever on first sight; or so he always claimed whenever anyone asked him. And it was, near enough, true to all intents and purposes. He had fancied her like hell, and was amazed she was interested in him. And that they had similar thoughts and hopes and plans. They just seemed to fit together so well. "Like peaches and cream," he'd sometimes say. "Like a sack and horse muck," she'd reply. And that was his love life. More horse muck than peaches and cream these past few years.

"All done," Sarah said cheerfully, standing in the doorway of the living area and smiling at him. He thought she suddenly seemed rather jolly again. Perhaps too jolly. Whether she had somehow just had another drink or was over-compensating for her embarrassment, he did not know. He was, he thought, a rotten judge of people really. Women anyway. And he had no idea what to say or do next.

Ian looked again at her pyjamas, cream-coloured with teddy bears imprinted on them. She looked clean and fresh; her face stripped of makeup. There was something in her plainness, her simplicity, that suddenly appealed to him. The uncomplicated nature of her life. He wondered what it might be like to start over anew.

"Thank you," he said, getting up and glancing towards Bernard, who seemed to be asleep by the coffee table. He had hoped he could make a fuss of Bernard, to distract himself from the situation. But Bernard just lay there snoring ever so slightly. Ian nudged him with his foot. And so, finally, he moved towards her, expecting her to step back from the doorway. But she did not.

"I…" he laughed, as he stopped close to her. "Um… thank you for saving my life." He felt he should be jovial. Light-hearted. Frivolous even.

She laughed too, "You're welcome." She looked at him and smiled and he did not know how to respond to that. He was not sure what type of smile it was.

He could feel his body responding again. "Down below", as Kate might have put it, gently mocking him. 'Down below' was an all-purpose phrase covering everything both physical and medical, from sex to haemorrhoids. The moment – the pause – seemed to go on and on.

"Does your dog need to pee?" she said, looking down at Bernard who had followed and now stood beside Ian.

"Um," Ian laughed, wondering whether he had just completely misjudged the moment, in fact the whole bloody evening. "No, he'll be fine. He'll wake me if he needs to go."

"What… he whispers in your ear, I, ruff, ruff, need a pee?"

"No," he laughed again, realising that maybe the whole evening had been somehow spoiled what with him being on edge all the time. "He'll just pace up and down and that wakes me."

"Rather you than me," she answered and added, stepping

back, "I'm done so the bathroom's all yours, and the bedroom's second left."

"Okay." He suddenly saw her for who she was. Just a nice, kind person. Lonely too. "Thank you for everything."

"I need to be up early. 7.00. Breakfast 7.30. Out at 8.00?" She looked at him as if to say, "Is this alright with you, leaving here at 8.00?"

And he nodded. As he went to walk by her, she put her hand on his arm and reached out to kiss him on the cheek and they both said good night to each other.

And so he went to bed with Bernard following in his footsteps.

18
THE PERFECT BREAKAST,
THE MOBILE PHONE
& 007 - LICENCE TO CALL

Ian slept right through to what must have been gone 7.00. He was woken by the sounds of Sarah moving about. He wondered if she were being louder than usual to wake him. So she did not have to knock and put her head round the door and risk seeing him lying there fast asleep and sprawled out naked flat on his back with all his gubbins on display. Not that he was. But she did not know that, of course.

He got up, put his jacket and trousers on over his T-shirt and pants and shook Bernard gently awake. Shoes on, they both ambled out of the room and the flat and down through the building and outdoors so Bernard could do his business. He cocked his leg against a tree over by the pavement in a half-hearted way and looked at Ian as if to say, "We didn't really need to bother, did we?"

After he and Bernard came back, he said hello to Sarah in the kitchen and went to the bathroom, before coming out and sitting down at the table for breakfast. And, unexpectedly, given the moments of awkwardness last night, he thought it was all going to be very pleasant. He wished he had felt like this, that it had been this way, the night before. He had the strangest but loveliest feeling of happiness. He did not know why.

It was, thought Ian, quite simply the nicest breakfast he had ever had in his life.

Not just the spread across the table – toast and cereals and yoghurts and a pot of tea and a cafetiere of coffee and a carton of orange juice.

But the atmosphere, the mood, the feeling between them; they were totally at ease, like old friends.

They talked on and off as they ate and drank as though they were catching up on each other's news. She spoke about her job. He told her how he filled his days. She said she was starting an evening class in the autumn, an arts thing, something she had always wanted to do. He said he had been doing some writing lately, thinking of the baby booklet, but did not elaborate more than that. They were just finding common ground really.

Almost all of what they said was, Ian thought, neither here nor there. Trivia and doo-dah. But it shaded in, coloured in, the backgrounds of their lives. Gave them a better understanding of each other and how much they seemed to have in common. In terms of their likes and dislikes, anyway. There seemed to be such a lot.

And in between their conversations and eating of this and drinking of that, there were, what was the word, silences, but not tricky or strained silences. These were not silences that he needed to fill, to think of something to say and to blurt out, just to ease the awkwardness. They were companionable, that was the word. Or amiable. That was not quite right, but it was close.

It felt as though they had known each other forever and could just be completely relaxed.

As they finished eating and drinking ("no, no more for me thank you"), Ian wished that this moment, this utterly peaceful and idyllic moment, could last forever.

So, he sat there smiling and at ease – so happy – for the first time in as long as he could remember.

Suddenly, she glanced (almost theatrically for him to see) at the clock on the wall. He saw it was a few minutes before 8.00 and decided it was time to go.

"Well," he said, as he got to his feet reluctantly and whistled for Bernard. "That was lovely. Thank you for that. And the

210

bed. And last night. And, you know… everything."

He was not sure if he should step forward to kiss her, but she just sat there, although she was smiley-faced enough. She took a last sip of her tea and looked at him full in the face and beamed a lovely smile. And he did not know quite know what to make of it all. He felt fluttery somewhere deep down inside.

***

"I've got a list of jobs as long as your arm… you could do them… if you like," she said casually, smiling as she handed a paper carrier bag to Ian as he and Bernard stood by the front door ready to go. "A dripping tap… some grouting… to keep yourself busy. It's on the side of the fridge. The list."

She said it in a jokey way and did not look at him, reaching down instead to pat Bernard on the head. He knew what she was really asking him. There was a moment when he felt she was holding her breath.

As he was doing. And had she looked at him when she made these comments, and their eyes had met and they had both seen what the other was thinking for sure, he thought maybe he would have done. At least for a while. To see how things went.

But she looked straight down and made a fuss of Bernard in her sudden embarrassment. And the dog stood up and rested his paws on her thighs and she turned and went towards the kitchen to fetch him something from the fridge. And the moment was gone. Lost, you might say.

He wondered, as she came back through holding a piece of chicken in her hand, whether he should suggest he would stay. For a day or two. To tidy the place up, he could add. You know, earn my keep.

But he was not sure if he had misjudged things. She seemed flustered one moment, calm and sensible the next. And he did not know whether he really wanted to stay or not. He thought he probably did. But he knew the longer he stayed here, the harder it would be to go home. It was difficult enough now.

And then she was giving the little piece of chicken breast to Bernard, who snatched hungrily at it, and she was patting and stroking the dog in a fussy way as if to say, "Goodbye, I don't expect I'll ever see you again." And Ian just dithered and delayed and did not really know what to do or say. It was as if he were waiting to be told.

Finally, given the lengthening silence, he glanced down into the paper bag and saw what looked like foil-wrapped sandwiches, a carton of juice, an orange and a tube of yoghurt which he could squeeze into his mouth. A perfect packed lunch.

"Thank you," he said, jiggling the bag slightly. He hoped that the sandwiches would not be just cheese on its own and he knew he would not eat the orange. He remembered, when he was small, that his mother said he could not eat oranges as they upset his stomach. He had never really put that to the test as an adult as he did not like the whole peeling, pips and sticky fingers routine.

"Oh," she said suddenly, all brisk and busy now, "I just remembered."

And she was gone, back into the kitchen and out again with an old-fashioned mobile phone in one hand and a pen and a magnetic fridge notepad in her other hand.

"Here," she said, handing him the phone, "in case you need it. It's… long story… an old one I had in the drawer… it's fully charged… and there's a SIM card in it with… enough if you have to text anyone or call the police… or me if you like, you know, if you are about to fall over a cliff. *Before* you fall over, ideally. I'll come and save you."

They looked at each other at that point and both smiled.

And he thought maybe he'd like to stay.

But that it was too late as she was already saying goodbye.

"And… I've put it in the contacts list… but just in case," she added, writing something down on the top sheet of the pad and tearing it off and giving it to him. "My mobile number… in case you want it… if you need to talk any time… on your way back… or when you've got home."

He took the sheet of paper, glanced at it, folded it in four, and put it in his back pocket. Then hesitated as she stood there with the pen and notepad stuck out in front of her as if willing him to take them.

He took them. "Let me give you my mobile phone number for after I've got home… if you need me, you know, any time, just let me know. This phone or that. I'll come and save you too," he replied, jotting down his number, *07956 106 007*. "007… your licence to call."

She did not seem to know what he meant as she took the pad and pen back from him. Perhaps she wasn't listening.

She paused for a second or two. Then took a newspaper from under her arm and went to push it into the side of the paper bag. Then she stopped and changed her mind, as if something he had said had confused her.

"It doesn't matter," she said, shaking her head. She then reached up and kissed him on the cheek. He thought she was going to say something else – "bye-bye", maybe – or some words of affection.

But she was already turning away and towards the kitchen. Her back to him. A funny, stiff-backed walk.

He stood there for a moment, expecting her to come back out again. To say a proper goodbye. He wondered if he might kiss her. Properly this time.

But she did not return, and he felt sad about that. Making a clicking noise to Bernard, he gripped the paper bag tightly, opened the door and left.

***

Sarah watched Ian from the living room window, looking down as he walked up the driveway to the pavement and turned left, the Jack Russell trotting by his feet.

She liked that little dog, Bernard. Could imagine herself with him on the sofa next to her in the evenings. His head on her lap, her stroking his tummy. Fetching him a treat when she made her 22.00 hot chocolate.

She liked the man as well. There was sadness in him. Kindness, too. She would love to snuggle up to him in bed at night, his body wrapped around hers. Spooning, they called it. She wanted him to stay. Not to do the silly household jobs.

Just to be there. When she left for work. When she came home. At night.

Maybe she should have said, "I would like you to stay," but she did not want to sound sad or desperate, as though he were her last chance of happiness. Even though she thought, most likely, he probably was.

She should have been more forceful about it. She felt he might have stayed, given some encouragement.

Ian stopped just outside the stone pillars at the top of the driveway. She could just see his head. He was looking down at something and she wondered if it was the mobile phone she'd just given him.

She took her phone out of her pocket. Held it in her right hand and stared at the screen, willing it to ring.

She waited patiently with her gaze fixed on her phone. Then glanced up and he had gone. She could see the back of his head through the trees as he walked away up the street.

She thought for a moment that she should go after him. That it was not too late, even now. She looked around quickly to see if he had left anything behind. But there was nothing there, not that he really had anything anyway. His clothes. The rucksack on his back.

She wondered suddenly if she should run after him and give him the newspaper. But she hesitated as she guessed at what he would say. "How long have you had this?" and "Why didn't you show it to me before?"

And they would both know the answer to the second

question, and she could imagine him walking off all angry and indignant. And that would be the end of that.

But then he was gone anyway, beyond the line of trees by the side of the street. And she wondered which way he would go and whether he intended to walk back the same way he came. She never asked.

And she also wondered if he might use his phone to call her tonight just to say he was safe and camped out in the woods, or wherever it was he might be sleeping.

And she thought maybe, if he did not, she might just send him a text to ask if he was well.

If not, she felt certain that this was it. That she would never see or hear from him again.

And she did not want it to end like this. Two inarticulate, unhappy people missing out on something that might be really rather wonderful.

PART FOUR:
THE JOURNEY SOUTH

19
HUNSTANTON TO SANDRINGHAM

WEDNESDAY 13th JULY

(8.5 MILES, 2 HOURS 48 MINUTES)

Ian stood, Bernard by his side, at the top of the road, looking out across the green towards the cliffs.

Hunstanton and the pier some way to the left. Old Hunstanton and the café along to the right.

Ian hesitated, dithering endlessly, deciding which way to go; what to do really.

He wished, he thought, he still needed, more than anything, to pay tribute to Adam in some way before he left Hunstanton. But he wanted to do it so that it felt uplifting; that it would celebrate Adam's life, short though it was, rather than focusing on all that was lost. All the years that Adam and the family never had together.

And he felt good at this moment. Happy, even. Last night and this morning showing him that he had the capacity within himself to find pleasure in his life. To turn things around. To restore his life to what it used to be, or something close to it. With Kate and the children and their partners. And this baby on the way. Pudding.

He knew, instinctively, without having to run through it in his mind, what he did not want to do. To go on Hunstanton Pier. Or the beach below the cliffs. Nor the café in Old Hunstanton. To retrace their footsteps and to relive what happened. Scratching and tearing at the big, still gaping, wound. It was time to leave it be and start letting it heal. At long last.

He decided what he was going to do. He would walk along the road beside the cliffs towards the pier at Hunstanton.

Then veer off to the left towards the town centre where he'd go and see if that old toy shop were still there.

He'd buy a Thomas the Tank engine figure as a tribute to his beautiful boy. He knew what he was going to do with it.

As he walked along, Bernard a step or two behind, he worked out the plan and elaborated upon it, in his head. Played it out. He was going to buy a Thomas and, if he could, a Rosie as well. He'd keep them in their packaging. Just hold them, one in each hand, as he walked back towards the pier. He did not intend to go on the pier itself. Nor the beach. Too many bittersweet memories to deal with if he did.

But he would walk along the prom. Maybe sit a while on a bench. The sun on his face. The breeze in his hair. His pal by his side. And he'd just be in the moment and cherish it. And that, he thought, would be his simple but perfect, tribute to his youngest son. To Adam. Sitting there with Thomas and Rosie and just being happy.

He was not sure what he would do with Thomas and Rosie after that. He liked the idea of seeing a small boy and a little girl – a brother and sister, maybe six and four, walking along hand-in-hand – and giving the two trains to them and watching the look of delight on their faces.

But he knew, deep down, that was probably not a good idea. Mum or Mum and Dad would look him up and down, with his straggly hair and stubbly beard, his dishevelled clothes, his old dog, and wonder who the heck he was and what the hell did he think he was doing? So, he thought maybe he'd just leave Thomas and Rosie on the bench, propped up, for someone to find and take home to be loved.

When he got to the town centre, he went straight to where he thought the toy shop was; but the premises were now a coffee shop.

And so, in case it had moved, he walked up this road and down that one and went by all the shops in the little criss-cross of roads. All over. Everywhere. The toy shop was not there.

He realised then that it was still early; not even half past eight. So, he got a coffee and a little something from the coffee shop and sat outside at one of the tables.

This, he thought, this instant, would be his tribute to Adam. It was, in all respects, a topsy-turvy moment. Comings and goings in and out of the coffee shop. Cars roaring by. A cyclist whizzing about on a bicycle. Women clippety-clopping on their heels on their way to work in the shops and the theatre and the hotel and the pier.

He put sweetener in his coffee – his latte. Ian had not had one of these for ages. He stirred the cup, drinking the coffee slowly, savouring each mouthful. It was nice and milky and not too strong. It was, what was the word? No, he could not think of it, and did not want to strain for it. Not now. Not at this moment. It was a nice word though. Not lovely or wonderful. But something like it. Not frothy. Flappy flops.

He looked at the little something on the plate in front of him. A round, soft piece of shortbread with a smiley marshmallow face on it. Just the thing that Adam would have chosen. And Ian pulled the sticky marshmallow face off the biscuit and put it to one side. As Adam would have done. Then he licked his fingers. Just like Adam. Broke the shortbread into four. As would Adam. Ate each piece slowly, one after the other, savouring them. As Adam always did with biscuits and cakes and any little treats.

Ian was crying now, not weeping or sobbing, just crying gently, almost in a happy way. Normally, he would put his head down so nobody could see him. Now, in this moment, he did not. He sat there with his head held high. And, when he had eaten the fourth piece of shortbread and with his face all wet from tears, he took the marshmallow face, folded it over, and pushed the whole damn thing into his mouth. Just like Adam used to do. And so he sat there, crying and swallowing and choking (mostly choking actually), paying his tribute to his youngest son.

After that, and once he had wiped the snot from his nose and the red drool from the mallow face on his chin and he had click-clicked his tongue for Bernard, he was on his way.

He wanted to do one more thing in Hunstanton before he left and headed home, and so he set off back to the shops.

He had spotted a charity shop, not far from where the toy shop used to be. And he wanted to get a second-hand book to read on his journey. A Sherlock Holmes maybe, or something like it.

He decided that the journey south was going to be joyous and not sad, as so much of the journey up here had been. He was going to look forward, not simply retracing his footsteps back along the coast down through Cromer and Great Yarmouth and Aldeburgh until he stood, his mood in his boots, waiting for the ferry to take him across from Bawdsey Manor to Felixstowe Ferry. Back home defeated.

He was going to walk inland, head up high, straight down south, through Norfolk and Suffolk – by Sandringham and through Thetford Forest – and would pick up a map from a newsagents before he left town so he could spot and stop off at any sights on the way. He toyed with the idea of saying goodbye to Sarah at the Old Hunstanton café before he left or instead maybe leaving a little "Thank you" on the doorstep of her flat, a pot plant rather than flowers. But he decided not to do either. He'd find it difficult to walk away.

Onwards and upwards then. A new journey home through sunlit glades and dappled woods. He was going to focus on the future and what he needed to do to put things right with Kate and the children and to prepare for a new life with Pudding. He was going to try very hard not to let any negative thoughts seep into his mind and make him unhappy. He was going to arrive home triumphant.

Within a few minutes, he was standing outside the charity shop, Bernard by his side, and saw an old and battered ventriloquist's dummy in the window. *Mr Parlanchin −£50!* on the sign. He was not sure it was a proper Mr Parlanchin, not at that price. But still, it was just what he wanted. A big, overgrown schoolboy really.

He remembered, when they were here in Hunstanton, they had seen a show on the pier. With a ventriloquist and his dummy. Just like this. And Adam laughed and laughed and laughed. Ian had meant to buy a dummy when he got home but had forgotten about it what with work and everything. And so, like so many other things he'd always intended to do, he did not and never thought about it again. Until now.

Ian looked at the dummy and down at Bernard who gazed back with one of his long-suffering "Jeez, now what?" looks. "Charlie. We'll call him Charlie," Ian said as he counted out five £10 notes and pushed open the charity shop door which went clang-clang-clang.

***

Ian, with Bernard by his side and Charlie sitting upright in the rucksack with his head facing backwards, left Hunstanton some 40 minutes later. After picking up a map and some bits and pieces from a supermarket, and having a last look around, he finally turned away from the pier and headed out of town.

He went southwards along the Kings Lynn Road instead of northwards along Cromer Road up and back and round the way they came. He knew if he went near to the café at Old Hunstanton, he'd find it hard not to stop, especially if he saw Sarah by the outside tables. Then what might happen? So, he walked the opposite way. Briskly. To put as much distance between them as soon as possible. Just in case he changed his flippety-flop mind.

Had Ian gone along the pier itself or even to the theatre

opposite or the bar along the way, he might well have seen the A4 posters that Alex and Joe had put up not so long ago. But he did not. No matter. Not really. Ian was on his way home anyway. And happy too. At least for now.

The first part of the walk, along pavements and roads, was pleasant enough in the sunshine with Bernard trotting behind and Charlie keeping watch.

Ian saw a sign for Heacham, where Sarah used to live, after about half an hour. He decided not to detour as he did not know where her family bungalow was. Instead, he wanted to press on, as he knew that thinking about Sarah at this time was not a good idea. Maybe later, when he was closer to home and would not turn back.

After about three quarters of an hour he looked over to his left and saw fields of lavender and he sat down close by and took a break. Charlie one side, Bernard, ignoring Charlie, the other.

When Ian had got Charlie from the charity shop, he had fiddled about with the dummy, his hand here, his fingers there, whilst the little old lady made encouraging noises. Like some stooge in the audience. Fact is, he would rather have got to grips with the dummy, the great slab mouth either shut or hanging open like some gormless halfwit, without being watched and chivvied-on by the well-meaning but oh-so-fussy old dear with her nods and mumblings.

He played along and she said how clever he was to get the hang of operating it so quickly. And he felt that he could work things well enough and could imagine himself with Charlie on his knee and Pudding, and perhaps other grandchildren in time, Lump and Chump and Tiddly-Thump, in a row in front of him laughing at the little playlet he'd made up and performed for them.

And now, sitting here, with Charlie by his side, Ian felt he needed to start practising what he was going to say, as Charlie, to make children laugh, and how he was going to speak without his lips moving. And in a child's voice. And loud enough to be heard. He'd practise as he walked along the way.

The second part of the walk, from the lavender fields to Snettisham, was another two or three miles and a further 45 minutes or so. Maybe more. Much more. Ian was not good at times and things. He made a note of distances and times each day but suspected they were all rather hit-and-miss. Way off, probably.

As he went, he practised saying, without moving his lips, a word that began with A and one with B and another with C. Arse and Ollocks and Cack. Egg and Faff and Goys and Girls. And so on. Some were easy to say, others almost impossible. Sometimes he'd forget where he got to and had to start over.

So engrossed was he when he got to saying, "Hello, boys and girls!" in a loud childlike voice that he was unaware of strangers' wary looks, the mother who right-turned and wheeled her baby in a buggy across the road or the cyclist who shouted something beginning with "F" that was lost to the wind as he cycled by.

By the time they approached the outskirts of Snettisham, and Ian and Bernard were tiring, and Charlie's head was slumped at an alarming angle as though it were about to drop off and roll away, Ian had the makings of an act. A formulative one anyway.

He had Charlie's voice – a high-pitched schoolboy voice to match his appearance. He had the rudiments of a series of childlike jokes repeated one after the other. "Knock, knock," he'd say. "Who's there?" Charlie would reply. "Doctor," he'd answer. "Doctor who?" Charlie would ask. "Yes," he'd conclude. "I am."

Ian sighed, realising that the act itself, with its lame jokes and him forgetting the punch lines (or saying them first) and doing Charlie's voice as his own, and vice versa, and generally stumbling over his words, was not really going to get any laughs. Even from small children and half-asleep toddlers. It needed some serious work. Jokes from a children's joke book.

And, probably, Charlie needed to be telling the jokes. Not him. He had to be the, um, well, the dummy in the act.

The last part of the morning's walk into Snettisham took him up to a roundabout, where he dillied and dallied, and got tooted several times by an angry car driver, before going straight across.

Pavements and roads and concrete and cars and just so much, what was it, hustle and bustle. Blather and bother.

Ian could not face this, this busy bollocks, all the way home. He wondered whether he should turn west towards the coast, and double back along to Hunstanton and beyond; back to the way he had come from. But then he was in Snettisham, and he wandered around for a while, Bernard trailing by his feet. He went by a pub and along the wrong road away from the centre and down to a vets and back again, by a war memorial and on to a Co-op food store. All in all, it seemed a nice enough place to stop a while and take a breather.

He found himself a bench to sit on – a black, circular bench, wrapped around what was the site of an old chestnut tree but was now a brick thingy – a whatsit, actually, if you must know – with a wooden post and a Snettisham sign at the top.

And he decided he would have the lunch that Sarah had made for him, sharing the sandwich with Bernard and drinking the carton of juice and the yoghurt and putting the orange on one side. And he would check the mobile phone in case Sarah had texted him. And so he took his rucksack off and put it at his feet and went to open it, reaching inside, when he suddenly realised Charlie's head had fallen off somewhere back down the road and he had never even noticed.

***

Ian sat on the bench, Bernard by his feet, and he could feel his mind racing. Just flitting from this thought to that.

It did this sometimes, when he felt really stressed. As he was now, because he had lost Charlie's head. Headless Charlie's

226

head.

And he knew his mind would just go here and there, getting more and more agitated, unless he was able to steady it. He needed to do something practical to focus his thoughts.

He took the packed lunch from the rucksack and put it on the ground in front of him. He then placed the foil-wrapped sandwiches to the left. The carton of juice next to that. Then the orange. And the squeezy-tubey yoghurt thing on the far right. He tidied them, lining them up better, although he knew that he had to be careful not to get too focused on this, this calming thing, in case he became obsessed, and it became a habit.

There was an old boy he knew, not so long ago, who lived near them. Ian would sometimes see him on a dog walk and pass the time of day. Other times, he would walk on by if – when – the man was doing his OCD routine. The man would stand there and remove his coat and wave it about, shaking off imaginary dust. Then put it back on and brush down the left sleeve and the right, then the front and back and the shoulders. And he'd take the coat off and wave it about again. Sometimes, if Ian were walking Bernard, he'd see the man doing this on the way out and, half an hour later, on the way back.

Ian looked at the lunch items and picked them up in turn, just concentrating on studying them. He unwrapped the sandwiches, chicken and lettuce and mayonnaise, nicely made with a sprinkle of pepper, and looked at them, describing the ingredients to himself in his head. He read the back of the carton of juice and the yoghurt tube to see the more detailed ingredients. He thought about the big fat orange and whether he could throw it from here to the bin over the way. But he held on to it for now.

As his thoughts steadied, he retraced his journey in his mind, from Hunstanton to Snettisham. Maybe four or five miles, that's all. Two hours or so, he'd guess.

Charlie – all of him – was definitely there at the lavender

fields. He remembered putting him in the rucksack when he got up to go.

Charlie's head must have come off somewhere between there and here. It must have been when that car toot-toot-tooted him. That was a while back.

And so, Ian ate the lunch that Sarah had made for him. The sandwiches. The carton of drink. The yoghurt. He reached into the rucksack and got a sachet of food for Bernard and squeezed it out on the ground by his feet. Then, he took out a bottle of water and a new papery-plasticky bowl he had bought at the Hunstanton supermarket. He poured some water for Bernard.

Ian thought about Sarah and the time he had spent with her. She was a nice person, he felt, and kind as well. To feed and spend the evening with him. To put him up for the night. And give him breakfast and this packed lunch made with such care. He did not know, he could not tell because of his inexperience with women and his discomfort with people generally, whether she might have been receptive to his advances. And he was not sure if he wanted to make them. Kate was always there, standing just behind him with a look of disbelief – horror, really – on her face. He felt confused.

He watched as Bernard ate some of the food on the ground, not all of it, and lapped at the water loudly and quickly. And he wondered whether the growth inside Bernard was now growing and maybe pressing on his stomach so that he did not want to eat as much. But he needed to drink, the growth somehow making him so thirsty. Or maybe it was just the heat and the walking. Or perhaps he was simply having an off day, and Ian was thinking too much.

And now all that was left was that big fat orange. He did not want to eat it, knowing his fingers and hands would get all sticky if he tore it apart and ate the fleshy, stringy pieces.

It struck him that, as he wanted to become a proper, throw-your-voice ventriloquist, he could somehow use it as a head for the now Headless Charlie. Or whether a thing, a yellow thing, a melon, that was it, may be better. Or a watermelon maybe. The fruit (or was it the vegetable?) equivalent of Ian's big head.

But the thought of sitting there with Charlie on his knee with an orange for a head whilst he did his "Knock, knock, Doctor Who" routine — and passers-by seeing him — was enough for him to decide no, best not.

Ian packed away the leftover bits and pieces into the carrier bag that Sarah had put them in. As he did so, he noticed a neatly torn-out and folded-over page from a small notebook at the bottom of the bag. He did not know, rummaging about, how he had not noticed it before. He took it out and opened it, not sure what he was expecting to see.

Sarah had written, in block capitals at the top of the page, her name (as if for emphasis). Then below that the phone number that she had put into the mobile phone's contacts list and had already given to him on a piece of paper. There seemed to be lots of sevens in the number. She had drawn a line carefully through each of them so he would not mistake them for ones. Below that there was an x — he was not sure if that was just the way she signed off or was, more specifically, a kiss for him.

He turned the paper over and back again as if there might be something else on it — something more, not obvious, that wasn't quite the right word, something more definite. Like *Call Me!* But the x, if it were a kiss and not a sign-off that she did for everything, was probably clear enough. He took out the mobile phone she had given him from his jacket pocket. He had kept it switched on in case she called or texted him. He checked it. No calls, no messages.

Ian tidied everything away. Put the rubbish and that big fat orange in the nearby bin. Whistled to Bernard. Checked Headless Charlie was in the rucksack before swinging it over his arm and onto his back.

His mind, all over the place at lunch, was now focused on Sarah and the mobile phone and whether he should call or text her; and, if so, what he should write.

He'd give it some thought as he walked along, Bernard by his side, Headless Charlie on his back, all the way from Snettisham to Sandringham. He pondered, his mind wandering again, whether, when they got there, they might see, you know, any of the Royal Family. And what he might say and do. "Your Majesty…" followed by a curtsy. No, not a curtsy. A bowel. No, not that either. A… you know. A thing.

***

The walk from Snettisham to Sandringham – whether Ian was going to the big house or, more likely, the surrounding woodlands – was, or should have been, an easy enough journey.

Pretty much due south, about four to five miles walking time, excluding stop-offs for eating and drinking, weeing behind trees and general wandering about whenever anything caught his eye (or he went the wrong way), of about an hour and a half. Maybe two hours.

The distance and the journey time were based on going down Lynn Road as they left Snettisham. Not School Road – an easy mistake to make – which added a mile or two and the best part of an extra hour's walking.

As he ambled along School Road heading south (so he thought, it was actually more south-east), his mind was on Sarah. And how a telephone conversation might go if he called her later on today, this evening. He felt, sensed, that she would not call him; that giving him a phone, her number three times and putting that *x*, was enough of an invitation. More than enough. That she would not go further. And he knew how a conversation might unfold.

"Hello, Sarah, it's Ian. Thought I'd let you know I've arrived safe and well in Sandringham… yes, Bernard's fine… not bad, thank you… quite a nice walk." Then he might ask about her. "How was the café today? … oh yes? … It's been warm here too…" Whatever was said would be superficial, about their respective days and the weather and what they were having to eat for tea or dinner, whatever she called it. And, once they had got the politeness out of the way, there'd be this long silence with an unspoken voice between them, thinking, "Well?" as in "Well, what do you really want?" He would not know what to say.

He thought, maybe, it would be better to text her. He could put something straightforward but cheerful. *Lovely packed lunch. Thank you. Picked up sausages and chips* (whatever) *for tea. Now bedded down for the night in woodlands near Sandringham.* And he could add a larky *Bernard sends his love.* Maybe. And sign off *Ian* or even *Ian x.* Then sit back and see what she put in reply.

School Road went by, not unexpectedly, the local primary school, and came to a left or right where Ian, and it was a complete fluke because he wasn't even thinking at the time, turned right – the best way to go – down Manor Lane.

This then led into Bircham Road and that just went on and on (and on plenty more) for ever such an age; not that Ian noticed, what with him thinking about Sarah and saying this and texting that.

After a while, he got to a crossroads and stopped and had a sudden "Where the heck am I?" moment, and he thought he'd gone the wrong way. He could now go sharp left to Fring, straight on to Great Bircham, or right, doubling back towards Sherborne which, looking at the sun, he thought was the correct way. And it was.

Sarah would text back, he was sure of it. And quite quickly if he timed it right – if he texted later in the evening when she would be sitting down by that silly old earwax lamp and watching television. He imagined her there now in those pyjamas. And he thought a little more about those pyjamas and this and that and the other. And that, the other, made him think about Kate and the expression she would have on her face. He said "What?" to her in his mind, as if he had not actually been thinking about what she knew he was thinking about. And she would give him one of her looks.

How are you? Sarah would text in reply, and he would say that he was *fine and how are you?* And she would state how she was *well, thank you.* and ask about Bernard. And Ian would chatter – so far as you can chatter away in a text – about Bernard. And they would go back and forth, much as they would in a phone conversation, being… careful… and guarded.

Then, one of them would put something like, *All for now! Catch up tomorrow?* And the other would reply *Yes! See you soon!* And they would end it there. Both of them re-reading and re-living the conversation for the rest of the evening and, most likely, through to the next exchange of texts the following night. And that, he thought, would carry on every time until one of them, what was the best way to put it, one of them broke cover and said what they were really thinking.

Ian and Bernard stopped at Sherborne and rested on the verge of the road, leaning against a stone wall by a pretty little church. That, and some cottages, were about all there was to see hereabouts.

They drank and ate from what they had in the rucksack, Headless Charlie resting by Ian's side. A tractor, loaded up with some grassy stuff, went slowly by and the farmer waved cheerfully at Ian. Then pointed at the headless dummy and laughed, "Murderer!"

Ian called back, asking how best to get to Sandringham… which way, please? "Follow this road," the farmer answered, still laughing, pointing down the way, "until you get to Dersingham, then turn left and you'll be there." Then he was on his way. And Ian, Bernard and Headless Charlie, after a little snooze, were as well.

Ian thought about Sarah again, knowing that, at some stage during their texting, whether it was tonight or somewhere down the line, one of them would have to put something to indicate where they wanted to go with this. He thought it would begin by being polite… mannered… formal. Then one would add an extra *x* or two and the other would respond; perhaps with a smiley-faced emoji (if they had them on this old phone), and so on.

And the thing was, to be utterly honest, Ian did not really know where he wanted to go. He liked the idea of being in touch with her but was not sure why. It might, he thought, simply be because he was lonely deep down inside. Kate and the children were always so busy. They never seemed to have any time for him, nor much interest in him. Their eyes glazed over whenever he started talking. He could talk to Sarah. She would be receptive. And they could be friends. He did not, now that David had passed away, have anyone to talk to about his personal thoughts and feelings.

But he was not sure whether Sarah would be happy with that; maybe she would want more. He thought perhaps he could flirt with her a little to see if she responded and took it further. But he had never been good at flirting in real life; the wink of the eye, the nudge of the elbow, the double-entendre. And he had no idea how to do it subtly in a text. He sighed; it was all a bit too much for him. Really, it was.

Dersingham was a much busier place than he'd expected – well, busy compared to the church and houses of Sherborne where the passing of an old tractor was the only thing that ever seemed to happen there, the highlight of the day.

He walked by a village hall and a pub and another pub and on to a fish and chip shop where he bought a medium cod and chips and two battered sausages (for Bernard) for their tea. He put the wrapped-in-newspaper fish, sausages and chips in the rucksack and set off towards Sandringham Estate and Country Park.

After a while, and he did a fair bit of walking as he did not want to be on Crown land where he might be shot as a spy or a terrorist, he slipped off the road into dense woodland. And, although it was still early and light, he thought this would be a good place to rest overnight.

***

Ian, Bernard and Headless Charlie sat together side by side against a tree in a dip in the woods somewhere in Sandringham.

It was dark now, had been for a while, and Ian had sat there all this time, tense and nervous, waiting for something to happen. What with it being so close to Sandringham and, you know, Royalty.

He had expected to hear a helicopter above, flying low and shining a beam of light down on them. "You there! Stand up. Hands above your head!" Or police. Or army. Or dogs. On the ground, coming through these woods at regular intervals, sweeping for the thingies… the bombs. But it was quiet and still and peaceful.

It was almost as though the woods had been stripped of all its wildlife, rabbits and birds and owls. And Ian could not hear a single sound anywhere, not a crackle, a shuffle, not even a sniff. And so, eventually, he relaxed, and he held Sarah's old phone in his hand, deciding what to put.

Hello, Sarah seemed formal. So, he deleted that and put *Hi, Sarah*. Then he thought that people did not bother with greetings like that these days. They just got on with it. *Ian here!* He put. Then added *And Bernard!* But that just sounded a bit, what was it, naff? Especially the exclamation marks. Like he was an eight-year-old. So he deleted that too.

The packed lunch was lovely - thank you. He thought that was a good beginning. So, he sat and looked at that for a while, wondering what to put next.

He thought of telling her about Charlie… and losing his head… maybe using the orange as a replacement. But that sounded, well, just plain bonkers.

He then deleted the "packed lunch" line because he had thanked her for it when he had left. Several times possibly. So he did not want to repeat himself again. He knew, with his mind fading, he repeated himself more than he should.

I'm waiting in the woods. Near Sandringham House. I've got my homemade bomb. Am hiding from the police. That made him laugh. He thought it might make Sarah laugh too. But then he thought if he were stopped by the police, and they looked at the phone, he'd have a lot of explaining to do. So, he deleted that as well. And sighed. And sat there a while longer.

Hi, he wrote again, and thought that was okay. He thought he should start with a greeting.

How are you? He added, as that seemed polite, and should also encourage her to reply in kind.

I am well. Bernard is too. He thought that was just the easiest thing to write.

I've got as far as Sandringham. He added so she'd know he'd walked a fair distance.

Ian. He hesitated and put an *x* after his name.

He read it back. Ummed and aahed. Pressed send before he could change his mind (again). There, that's that − let's see what Sarah has to say, he thought. He then reached into the rucksack and took out and unwrapped the cod and chips and sausages which he tore into pieces for Bernard to eat. He spread everything out across the flattened-out newspaper, and had a bottle of water too, and that little papery-plastic bowl for a squirt or two of water for Bernard.

He checked his phone repeatedly as he picked at his chips and medium-sized piece of cod. Obsessively, even. Expecting to hear from Sarah almost immediately. Ready to answer her with friendlier, more open responses. He checked maybe 10, 11, 12 times (if not more) over the 15 or so minutes he spent picking at his food and what Bernard had left. He then screwed up the newspaper and shoved it angrily into the bottom of his rucksack.

He ran water over his face, went behind a tree for a wee and a whatsit and came back and put together a makeshift bed from his jacket and bracken and leaves and lay down waiting for sleep

235

to come; whilst constantly checking his phone. It was a shame that he was so angry – not angry really, maybe disappointed was a better word. Had he been calmer, he might have read through the newspaper wrappings and seen the family's appeal to him. What's more, in a calmer frame of mind, he might have noted that Bernard had again not eaten much. And worked out what that might mean.

20
THE POLICE VISIT

WEDNESDAY 13th JULY

(19.50 ONWARDS)

Six of them sat in the living room at The Cape – Kate in Ian's stripey old armchair to the left of the fire (where no one else wanted to sit), Alex, Hannah and Joe, all just arrived, on the new-ish sofa, Beth and Glenn somehow squeezed onto the other striped armchair to the right (where Bernard would sometimes sit when Kate was not around to shoo him off). Yasmin was on her way but running late – waiting for the cakes to come out of the oven or some such.

They – well, Beth really – had contacted the local police online to report Ian (and Bernard) missing and, after a flurry of emails and texts between Beth and the local community policing officer, or whatever her title was, "Call me Lisa" was coming round to talk to them. Sometime between 19.30 and 20.00, hopefully.

And so they all gathered, as Kate did not want to do this alone. She asked Alex and therefore Hannah to be there. "Not to eat – just a cup of tea." And Alex told Joe who mentioned it to Yasmin, who said she'd make some toffee and ginger cupcakes to go with the cups of tea. And Beth just had to be there, of course. And Glenn sat there quietly half on, half off the armrest (Beth having hogged as much of the chair as she felt she needed).

"You've not heard anything I assume?" Kate asked in a

routine rather than an expectant way, just looking around.

"D'uh, no!" Beth replied. "That's why I called the police."

Alex and Joe exchanged glances as if to say, "let's not mention the posters we put up from Aldeburgh to Hunstanton".

Alex leaned forwards and reached into his back pocket, taking out a folded-in-half postcard. The pier at Great Yarmouth on the front. On the back, *Alex and Hannah*, and the address in *Brightwell Close, Felixstowe, Suffolk*, and a second-class stamp with a blurry postmark on the right.

That message on the left. *I am sorry* on the first line. *I hope your pregnancy and Pudding and everything go well for you.* on the second, third and into the fourth. And a little shaded-in heart underneath that.

"It came this morning, Mum," Alex said, handing the postcard over to Kate. "A postcard from Dad in Great Yarmouth," he added, so the others would know. "An apology for being rude at the gender reveal."

And Beth was up there, standing right next to Kate and leaning in sharing the same breathing space, so she could read what Ian had written.

"That's not his writing," Beth said loudly. "I can read it. I can't normally. Someone else wrote it."

"So, what is it then?" Joe said savagely as he sat, confused, on the sofa. "A ransom note? Pay up or we'll send you his dick in a jiffy bag?"

Kate looked sharply at Joe and, after their eyes met, Joe was suddenly quiet. He dipped his head down as Kate read out Ian's words in a measured voice, so everyone knew what was what. "I am sorry. I hope your pregnancy and Pudding and everything go well for you." She then turned the card over and looked at the front of it.

Alex watched her closely, wondering whether she would incline the card in the light, maybe seeing the imprint of the little stick figure on top of the theatre on the pier. The one that Alex had seen straight away when he had picked up the postcard on the doormat earlier this evening. Had realised it was just the old man being daft as usual, but knowing that others, Beth inevitably, would see it as an announcement of his imminent suicide. As if he were going to climb onto the roof of the theatre on the pier and throw himself off. So Alex had licked his right thumb and gently wiped away the ink so no one, hopefully, would see it.

Kate did not, or at least did not say anything. She looked up at everyone sitting there watching her. "It's Dad's writing, his best handwriting so that Hannah could read it." She smiled at Hannah who smiled back. "You can't usually... I can't read the postmark though... Saturday maybe ... second-class stamp anyway." She thought a while and added, "We had some happy times on that pier, didn't we?"

And Alex and Joe murmured their agreement, both commenting on the Chuckle Brothers' shows and how they'd queue up for photographs and autographs afterwards. How Joe still had one of those photos stuck up under a magnet on their fridge.

Alex said how he used to love the picnics on the beach most... oh, and seeing those Disney films at the cinema... even driving back in the dark through country lanes. Scary when we were young!

Beth, of course, cut right through the cheerfulness and said in a strangely subdued voice, that Dad had definitely taken his own life. Then she started crying.

Nobody quite knew what to do at that. Beth was one for shouting really, even when there was next to nothing to shout about, her foghorn voice echoing around the house about this, that and the other. Or screaming. Yelling sometimes. Or bellowing. And variations thereof. She never did or said anything quietly. Until now. Glenn shifted uncomfortably on his armrest. Alex and Joe both looked at each other, as if to say, "You comfort her, she might punch me."

Kate got up out of the armchair, and quite unexpectedly,

Hannah rose from the sofa. They headed towards Beth who struggled up, pushing Glenn out of the way whilst sniffing and snuffling, perhaps rather too theatrically. The three of them embraced. And Kate consoled Beth saying that, no, really, Dad would not take his own life and would certainly not declare it through a postcard of the pier at Great Yarmouth. "I just thought…" said Beth, and Kate said "No," and that, this rather awkward moment, was that.

And the doorbell ting-a-ling-a-linged and they all fell back into their places, Beth looking angrily at Glenn as he took up the armrest and half of the armchair cushion too, leaving her squashed in somewhat. And Kate and Alex looked at each other and Alex said, "I'll get it," adding vaguely to everyone, but mainly Beth, "I don't think we should mention the postcard, not now, as the police are less likely to look for him if they think he's holidaying in a bed and breakfast off Great Yarmouth seafront," as he headed for the door before anyone could reply.

***

Kate made way for Call Me Lisa – who looked about 15 – so that she could sit in the armchair to the left of the fire.

Kate sat down by the sofa, next to Alex, her back against the side of the armrest.

The young policewoman checked her mobile phone, scrolled up and down, back and forth. Kate thought she looked nervous. And she was; this was her first missing person case.

"I've got most of the details from… online and my conversations with… Bethany. I just wanted to check one or two things and I meant to ask first, I see Mr Wilkerson, Ian, has been featured in the local newspaper. Have you had any response to that?" She looked at Kate first who thought about the hushed questions from a handful of colleagues at work, none of whom she really knew and were just being nosey, and her brusque, walking-away responses. She shook her head, no, nothing. Beth, who had experienced similar situations at her primary school, shook her head as well.

Alex and Joe both said "No," at the same moment. Quite a few people Alex had tattooed these past few days had, in fact, asked about his Dad and seemed genuinely concerned. Alex had smiled and grimaced and just said his Dad was having a "turn" or a "funny five minutes" or something like it. "He'll be back soon enough." There were moments of quiet sympathy or maybe empathy, whichever it was, or perhaps a bit of both.

Joe had found it harder at the docks with one or two workers asking if his Dad had turned gay and run off with his lover. And he had told them to eff off. Not that there was anything wrong with that at all, but Joe couldn't imagine his Dad doing anything like that. He had a terrible image in his head of his Dad's big white arse in the changing rooms when they used to go swimming on Saturday mornings and he had not been able to shake that image off for ages. And now it was back in his head again. Possibly forever. Glenn and Hannah had not heard anything at all (which was probably for the best).

"And other than the note that he left… that you texted me," Call Me Lisa asked, "You've not heard anything from… Ian… since… no one has been in touch?"

"No," Alex replied, leaning forward and going on without stopping before anyone else could speak, "we've not heard anything."

There were glances between the family, and everyone hoped Beth would not blurt out about the postcard… and suicide… or anything like that. Somehow, and it must surely have been a titanic internal struggle, she didn't.

"I…" Call Me Lisa hesitated, gathering her thoughts. "I, we, need to assess how far Ian is at risk. Low risk means there is no apparent threat to Ian or the public." She looked around and smiled and nodded as they listened. "Medium is where he might be in danger to himself or… sorry… a threat to the public." Everyone sat quietly except Beth, who laughed. "High

241

risk, I don't think this applies, but it's where there is a real or immediate danger to, ah, anyone."

There was a babble of noise as everyone – well, Alex mainly – said Ian wasn't a danger to anyone ever. That Ian was soft as butter. Wouldn't hurt a fly. Couldn't even bear to put traps out when the sea had burst its banks the other year and mice and rats and goodness knows what had come up into the garden. How he had to call someone in with a van and tubes and traps and things to sort it all out whilst he locked himself inside the house with the doors and windows, even upstairs, shut.

And Beth remembered the time when she had played tennis at the local club and was in a final against another little girl. And the girl's father had shouted and jeered at Beth to put her off her play. No one did anything to stop him. Just watched. Middle class folk, see. All nice and polite. Even when they should know better. And how Beth came home in floods of tears having lost and Ian went straight round there and shouted at the father in front of everyone who secretly hoped Ian would punch his lights out. But he didn't. "My Dad would never hit anyone... hurt anyone," Beth said firmly as if shutting down the subject.

"So, we just need to decide what level of risk he is to himself," Call Me Lisa said and added, "is he on medication or having treatment for anything, physical or otherwise?"

And they all looked at Kate who suddenly remembered an unopened NHS letter to Ian on the shelf in the hall. And that set her wondering. But she did not want to go and open it now in front of them all, so she just said, "No."

"Does he have any financial, employment or..." the young policewoman hesitated, "ah, relationship issues that you know of? I'm sorry. I have to ask." They all waited for Kate to speak. She thought for a while.

"No, not really. I mean... he's been made redundant from his job, but he never liked it much anyway... and he's maybe been a bit... well, he's made himself useful around the home and he

242

walks the dog, and he swims... or did swim. I think he might have stopped, I'm not certain." Something, she wasn't sure what, struck her quite forcefully. As if she were missing something really important, she should have known. "Financially, things are okay. I think with what I earn, at the hospital, I work with diabetes patients, and his redundancy package. I... think he'll get a part-time job, probably. Somewhere. I don't know where."

She sighed, and carried on speaking as if talking to herself, unaware that everyone was listening to what she was saying. "We're fine, Ian and I. We've been together for... years and years. And yes, we're fine now. Definitely." And it occurred to her suddenly that maybe they weren't. Or at least Ian wasn't. "He's been a bit... I don't know... distant lately. Forgetful. Withdrawn I suppose." Then she just stopped. Point blank. A growing realisation maybe. And it was ages before she finished what she was saying.

"I think... I think he's just having a mid-life crisis that's all and has gone off for a while to pootle about with his dog. He'll come back when he's ready. He's not... he doesn't... this is so out of character. He can be rude, or people think he's rude when he's just trying to be funny, and he gets on people's nerves at times, quite a lot really, but he always apologises and puts things right and so no, no he doesn't." She stopped and found that she was crying softly to herself.

Alex then spoke up. "We had a little brother, me, Beth and Joe. Adam. He passed away in July... a long time ago now... but Dad still... suffers at this time of year. Goes a bit wobbly."

And Joe spoke too, "We think he may have gone to where it happened... Hunstanton." He hesitated as he saw Call Me Lisa note it down, and looked at Alex to see if they should mention the posters, but Alex did not nod or smile so Joe left it there.

Beth, listening to all this, burst at last, "I think he's gone back to Hunstanton ... (deep breath)... to kill himself." Everyone turned and could see what Call Me Lisa was thinking – "high risk".

It was towards the end, after everything had been talked over, back and forth, when Call Me Lisa casually asked if she could look around and that alarmed the family.

She had handed Kate a missing persons advice leaflet and talked about something called the Herbert Protocol and what the police would be doing. And everyone seemed pleased with that. It was all just fine. Done and dusted.

But then Call Me Lisa said, "Do you mind if I take a quick look around?"

Kate laughed. "Do you think he's hiding in the attic?" But the young policewoman did not smile back, and Kate suddenly thought she had a rather hard face.

"Be my guest," Kate said, gesturing towards the door. "Feel free." Then they all sat there looking at each other, pulling faces and shrugging and, well, being rather bewildered, as the policewoman went out of the living room and into the other downstairs rooms.

"She thinks we've killed him," said Beth.

"It's just routine." Kate answered, flicking through the leaflet. "... Search the home or place last seen in case they are hiding or may have fallen or been injured... children can climb in very small spaces... she's just doing her job."

"I think we'd know if Dad were hiding somewhere... all the biscuits and chocolates would have vanished into thin air long ago," Alex laughed.

"And we'd have heard the screams if he had fallen and hurt himself – remember that time he twisted his ankle?" Joe added.

"He couldn't get into a very small space," Beth stated.

"Not with his head," Alex replied.

"Or his arse," Joe added, that awful image in his head again.

They could hear her now, above their heads, going from one room to the other. Through the bedrooms and on to the landing. They held their breath as they waited to hear Call Me Lisa pulling down the ladder for the loft. She did. And they looked at each other as if to say "seriously?" "Don't worry," said Kate, laughing in an "I can't quite believe this is happening" way. "He's not in the water tank … or under the floorboards. He'd not fit."

Call Me Lisa then came back into the room a good while later and smiled, although Kate thought it was more of a professional smile than a genuine one.

"I'm sorry. I have to check," she said to Kate. "You know how it is. Checklists. Boxes to tick. Forms to fill in." Kate nodded.

"Ah, I just need to take a look around outside now if I may?"

They all stood on the patio looking out across the garden as Lisa walked down to the magnolia tree near the bottom and looked back at the house. And it suddenly struck Alex, gazing around, how utterly hopeless at DIY his dad was. A compendium of disaster. The patio all lumpy and uneven and sinking over there to the left where he hadn't put enough soil, or whatever it was meant to be, rubble perhaps, underneath.

Then there was the garden shed that Ian had got the man with the van and the tubes and the traps to move in case there were rats nesting under it. There wasn't a nest, but the man had left Ian to move the shed back into place because Ian said – boasted, more like – that he could do it easily. And Ian had dug a bigger hole and mixed some concrete and poured it in and it was too runny or didn't dry properly or something and the shed was still off-centre but now leaned at an angle. Like the Leaning Tower of Pisa.

As a gardener, Ian was no better. He had part-dug fresh flowerbeds where he was going to have rows and rows of beautiful, prize-winning red roses. But he lost interest in that halfway through. Then there was the allotment – the "Garden of Delights" he called it – towards the back where he was going to plant potatoes and carrots and they were going to be self-sufficient in vegetables. "In case of nuclear war or alien invasion." That never came to anything either. And there was the pond... the water feature... the cascading waterfall of lights; all came to nothing.

And another thought then struck Alex as he looked across this no-man's land of a garden.

All we need now is for Beth to say that we'd had a postcard from Great Yarmouth, and it wasn't in Ian's handwriting – but someone else's – and the policewoman would put two and two together and think we've murdered the silly old fool. And put him under the patio. Or beneath the shed. Or the flower beds. And they'd be back with dozens of police and sniffer dogs; all of that. There would be photos of them all, grim-faced after being arrested and marched down the drive, in the local papers.

At that moment, as if Alex had just had a terrible premonition, Beth stepped off the patio and spoke loudly (even for her) so that everyone could hear, "There's something I've got to say!"

And Alex said, "Effing hell," or something much like it quietly under his breath.

21
SANDRINGHAM TO
SWAFFHAM

THURSDAY 14th JULY

(15.8 MILES, 5 HOURS 11 MINUTES)

Ian came slowly out of sleep the next morning. He had been in a dream, something close to a nightmare really, where he was being chased. He was not sure what was chasing him but knew he had to get away. That his life was in danger. Bernard's too.

As he awoke, he heard dogs, a snarling pack of dogs, somewhere in the distance – but coming ever closer. And he remembered his fears from the night before; that he was trespassing on Crown land and might be discovered by the army or the police and arrested as an international terrorist. That would need some explaining to Kate and the children.

Ian got to his feet, accidentally treading on Bernard who jumped up yelping. Ian shoved Headless Charlie's body in the rucksack. A half-empty bottle of water too. He scooped up Bernard under his left arm, his rucksack on his back.

And he ran. Just as hard and as fast as he could. Eastwards. Towards where he thought the sun was rising. Out of the woodland. To the road where he would be safe. Just walking, he'd say, if he was then stopped by the army or police, towards, you know, the place. Where I'm walking to. Grimsdale. Mr Grimsdale. No, not Mr Grimsdale. Mr Grimston. No, Grimston. On the map he still had in his back pocket. He'd point to it. There. We are walking there, he'd say, and hope they did not ask why.

Ian could hear the dogs, so many of them, pulling on leads and snapping and barking, desperate to be let loose. They were behind him now, not so very far, and coming closer. Being held back until he was in sight and the handlers would then unleash the dogs who would come bounding towards him, bringing him down, as he cowered with Bernard beneath him, protecting his old pal's life.

There was nothing but trees in front and all around as he ran as fast as he could across the ground. He had no sense of where he was going, not really, although the lightening sky in front of him suggested that was where he wanted to go. He tried to stay in a straight line but stumbled once or twice on the uneven ground and almost fell over, sinking to his knees and kissing Bernard's head, before getting up and keeping going as fast as possible.

They'd be there now, the dogs, in that little dippy copse where they'd slept last night, rushing here and there, picking up his smell and the scent of Bernard. And he wondered, as he ran, gasping for air, if this was where the handlers would let the dogs loose. "Go!" they'd yell, "go!" and the dogs would pick up Ian and Bernard's trail through the woods and be on them, snarling and biting, in no more than a minute or two.

He could see now, over there, ahead of him, the place where the trees ended and started again a little further across.

The road in between. A country lane. Whatever. Wherever. Somewhere he could slow to a walk and put Bernard down.

And stroll on as if not doing much at all, just minding their own business.

Ian kept going on the point of exhaustion, his hair and face hot and his clothes wet with sweat. Walking normally now, Bernard down by his feet. As though he had just come off the road to wee and was now wandering back on. Then he stopped suddenly, listening. It struck him that he could not hear the dogs. They were not barking. He wondered if they were now through the trees behind him and were there, all in a line, the handlers to their side, waiting for whoever was in charge to lift a tannoy to their lips.

"You there! Man with dog. What the hell do you think you're doing? This is Crown property. You're trespassing. Down on your knees, sir. Down on your knees." A gunshot, a warning shot just over his head, forcing him to the ground, his arm around Bernard.

Ian turned. There was no one there. No dogs. No handlers. No man with a tannoy and a gun. And he cocked his head to one side and listened for the sounds of dogs in the distance, perhaps going another way, chasing someone or something else, whatever it was. And all he could hear were the sounds of the woods coming alive. And he wondered, not for the first time on this journey, nor the last, whether he was now going stark, raving mad.

***

It was an hour or so later, when they had come out of the woods and had eaten a makeshift breakfast from various packets and bottles in the rucksack and Ian had checked the phone (no reply from Sarah), that they walked along a way and reached the lost-in-time village of Newton. And it was here that Ian had the most wonderful stroke of luck.

It was a ladies' bicycle, quite old-fashioned with a leathery old saddle. And a biggish wicker basket and a dring-dring bell upfront. It was leaning against a garden gate. A clumsily-written *For Sale – £60* sign propped up in the basket.

Ten minutes later, having pressed six £10 notes into a middle-aged man's hand – "My wife's just had a particularly nasty hysterectomy and won't be cycling again, not with that saddle" – Ian was off, peddling away southwards down the B1440 towards somewhere or other. He was not sure where exactly although Swaffham, where he planned to sleep tonight, was along that road, he thought. Maybe 15 miles or so away.

He'd put Bernard in the wicker basket in front and the dog sat up gazing ahead, his ears flapping up and down in the breeze. Charlie, Headless Charlie, was tucked away in the rucksack on Ian's back. Ian had intended to have Charlie sitting up with his shoulders and arms poking out of the rucksack. But he felt that, from a distance, this might be mistaken for a headless whatsit. A Snow-White thing. You know. A Dopey. A Grumpy. Bloody hell, a Snotty whatsit.

He did not want any issues with some half-witted Norfolk resident calling the police and reporting him as a serial killer of dwarfs. That was it. Snow White and the Seven Dwarfs. And it was Sneezy. Not Snotty. And so Ian put his head down and peddled along, the sun on his head and back, the wind in his hair. He really hoped that he might come to a hill where he could peddle up and freewheel all the way down.

But he knew Norfolk was flat. As flat as a witch's thing. From Snow White. Not a red apple.

Ian diverted down the way to his left after a while (eastwards most likely) towards a water tower at Appleton. A big old Victorian structure. He thought he'd have a look.

He did and decided it was much like The House in the Clouds at Thorpeness; and most likely a holiday-let, too, for Londoners up for the weekend. Paying silly prices the locals could not afford or would not be daft enough to pay.

Ian then somehow managed to get confused by the position of the sun and went the wrong way, trying to cut the corner off his journey without success. He eventually doubled back on himself to the B1440 an hour or so later.

As he cycled along – in this perfect moment of bliss – he thought he would think happy thoughts about his family. Of Alex, to start with. Snapshots of moments in his life. He remembered when Alex was born, and the midwife held him up and he was all crumpled and bloody. And Ian had said, instinctively, "Oh my God, he's so-oo ugly." He recalled the look that Kate had given him – her Medusa "Turn to Stone" look (although they laughed about it later).

Alex flying a kite in the park round the corner. Wobbling on a bike with stabilisers. Running into hospital with a Batman car held high to see Kate and new baby Beth. Alex and Beth running into hospital together hand in hand to see Kate and new baby Joe. And Ian on the bed with Kate holding Adam with Alex, Beth and Joe all standing around the bed, excited. All of them so happy .

An older Alex playing Sunday morning football. Holding exam certificates above his head. Doing karate in that smelly old school gym. Passing his driving test. Taking his first, old-banger-of-a-car for a drive. Getting his university offer for Nottingham. Up to then, the first 18 years of his life, it had all gone wonderfully, beautifully well.

Ian got terribly confused again as the road he was on, the B1440, reached another, the larger A148, and he was not sure which way he was meant to go. Left or right. To get to Swaffham.

So, he got off his bicycle and leaned it against an old brick wall and walked Bernard up and down on a verge for a while to do his business. He checked the map in his back pocket but that was not detailed enough for him to tell so he spoke to an elderly lady wearing yellow rubber gloves and washing the front windows of her stony cottage. She said go that way down towards – and he did not quite catch the word – Hilton or Hington maybe; and turn down the B1153.

So Ian was on his way again and, ten minutes or so later, he was heading along the right road as happy as Harry or Barry or whoever it was. Celery. No, not that at all. And he thought about Alex once more.

How they'd seen him off to university on the train. Then texted and emailed and phoned him regularly, each of them, and all seemed well. They saw him regularly at weekends. Ian remembered those meals. He was happy doing his arty course. Slowly he'd started ducking out of get-togethers and they saw him less and less. Ian recalled the disappointments. But they did not worry, just assuming he was busy and getting on with life and being happy.

They'd got a text from a young woman one night some time later revealing Alex had collapsed and been taken to hospital. Depressed and anorexic. His head wasn't straight. And he was taking drugs. Medical and recreational. So he spent a while in hospital. Followed by months in the Priory. Ian did not want to think too much about these times. There was no happiness to be found in them, only endless horror. He cycled on; head down and peddling furiously for ever such a while.

But he'd come back from that, Alex. Lived at home. Picked up with old friends. Became an apprentice at a tattoo studio in the town. Had girlfriends. Got better, physically and mentally, putting on a little weight and just becoming the old, jolly Alex again. Then he met Hannah when she came in to have a small flower, a sweet William, tattooed on her ankle. Happy days were here again.

This is the life, thought Ian. A warm, sunny day, cycling along a country road, lane really, fields as far as he could see either side.

Not a car in sight. Bernard sitting up, comfortable and happy and not a care in the world. Headless Charlie asleep in the rucksack.

And Ian felt such a sense of peace. He was living in the moment. No thoughts or cares other than just cycling along. Bliss. Utter bliss.

Ian was proud of Alex and how he had turned his life around these past few years. He became a full-time tattooist, producing all sorts of tattoos from Disney rabbits to wild-eyed madmen with chainsaws. Ian tried to remember as many as he could, teasing Alex about the cute ones and the more savage ones and everything in between.

Alex just seemed so, what was it, balanced these days, encouraging Joe with his work and placating Beth in her madder moments and just getting along so well with Yasmin and Glenn. A nice man. A lovely man. A family man.

And this, all of this Hannah business, getting a house together and both of them working and Hannah becoming pregnant and... so much love between them, you could see that just looking at them... and now the baby coming soon. It was all a perfect ending for Alex. And Ian was so pleased. More than that. Utterly delighted.

Ian cycled into Grimston where he planned to stop for a stretch and a yawn and an early lunch and a sit down and possibly even a snooze on a bench in the sunshine.

It was another one of those places that time had long forgotten. The kind of village where all the young boys would have lined up with pitchforks and broom handles ready to march off to war all those years ago. Where the sun always shone through an endless summer.

There was a clock. A signpost. And a post office and a store. A pub. He checked the clock. And the signpost. Visited the stores. And went to the pub. With hindsight – some time off yet – Ian would not have stopped at the pub. He should have cycled on by.

***

Ian was not a drinker, never had been really, and had been known to lose control of his senses fairly quickly when drinking alcohol. One pint and he would make jovial but personal comments to anyone in earshot; jovial to him, possibly over-personal and offensive to them. That, the one pint, was the strict cut-off point whenever Kate was around.

Two pints was into "anything can happen" territory. Two tankards of scrumpy on the way back from a holiday in the West Country once and Ian had had to lie down on a bench on a village green for two hours. It would have been longer if Kate had not lost patience and drove them all home with Ian slumped against the window on the back seat. Anything above two pints was unknown territory. Until now.

It was sunny and hot and, although he was not a pubgoer per se, he had built up a terrific thirst and thought that a pint of the local cider, whatever that was, would go down a treat. So, he ordered a pint and a slice of pizza with salad and some crisps and water and a bowl for Bernard and made his way into the garden where they allowed him to lean his bicycle against the wooden fence where he could see it, just in case. And he sat there, waiting for his lunch to be served on the table in front of him. Bernard, as ever, sat by his feet.

"Alright?" Ian said to the only other person in the pub garden, a man of about his own age, mid-50s, but dressed in old-fashioned clothes, like a farmer, flat cap, and boots even in this warm weather.

The farmer nodded back, agreeably enough, and supped carefully at his half-drunk pint.

And so they sat there, these two old fellows, side by side near enough, at adjacent tables, all quite companionably.

"Sunny," Ian said emphatically. He was never very good at starting conversations. But he felt he needed to say something. They could not just sit here in silence.

"Uumph," the farmer replied.

"A nice breeze," Ian added, raising his voice at the end of his sentence, half statement, half question.

"Uuhhh," the farmer responded.

And that, thought Ian, was that. He could not immediately think of anything else to say other than "Do you come here often?" or "Do you live round here?" And both of those sounded rather odd. Especially together – they sounded almost like a proposition. And he did not want to create that sort of impression.

So, he sat there and watched the farmer out of the corner of his eye. The farmer lifted his pint, all stiff and mannered, to his lips. As though it were an awfully dangerous thing to do, or the liquid was incredibly precious. That he might somehow spill it (even though the glass was only half full).

And suddenly the barmaid was there, putting Ian's pint and pizza and salad on the table.

The crisps too although, and Ian did not say, these were for Bernard to eat.

And she was gone and back again, putting a bowl of water by Ian's feet. Bernard went straight across, lapping thirstily at the water.

"I had a dog like that once," the farmer said after the barmaid had left.

"Bernard," said Ian, opening the crisps.

"Ernie?" asked the farmer and Ian looked over at him and noticed suddenly that his right side, the closest to Ian, was stiff.

"Bernard," Ian repeated, tipping the crisps on the ground.

"Bernard," the farmer nodded.

A moment or two's silence. Except for Bernard snatching and clacking over the crisps.

And the farmer laughed, a rumbling-up, coughing sort of laugh, and his glass shook, and he put it down hard on the table. "Stupid name for a dog," the farmer stated.

"Well, yes, I suppose so. I'm told that when he was a puppy, he looked like a Saint…"

"My dog was called Parson Jack. I called him Parson," the farmer interrupted and went on as if talking out loud to himself, "when I was a boy. I used to take him ratting… and rabbiting… all across the fields, all over."

The farmer talked away, reminiscing over the dog, the best dog he'd ever had, and what it did and when and how it had always slept curled up by his feet at the end of his bed every night. He sipped his pint for a good while, and then said that the dog had lived until it was 17, no, 18, and died in its sleep, and that was the best way to go.

He talked on about other dogs, and how they were all good dogs in their way, the Labrador, a mixed breed mongrel, and a Retriever who was slow and lazy and so on and so on. But none quite as good… as memorable… as beautiful… as treasured… as Parson Jack… when he was a boy and young and strong and all the world lay before him.

Ian sat back and drank and ate and nodded at the right moments and asked and paid for another pint when a solid sort of man, the landlord, came out to check all was well. And Ian had offered the farmer a pint and he'd huffed and sighed and said he was happy with the one he had, thanks all the same.

And the farmer went on, still talking about the blessed Parson and their adventures and sounded wistful, perhaps even emotional. Ian drank his second pint there in the sunshine with Bernard stretched out in the shade and suddenly felt, what was it, very something or other towards this poor old boy.

His lunchtime pint. Then the limping back home to his empty cottage. Alone, all alone. Looking out of a window, and watching the world go by. Hour after hour. Day after day.

The world passing him by. This sad old chap. Ian felt very, oh bloody hell, what was it. Maternal? No, but like it. Brotherly? Fraternal, that was it. He felt he should help in some way. Cheer him up.

The farmer finished his pint and Ian called the landlord over and ordered and started on his third pint and then decided, quite suddenly, that he would stand up and say something to the farmer. Something… magnificent. Epic. Unforgettable. So, he stood up and wobbled back and forth for the best part of a minute, but then sat back down again without having said anything at all. The farmer made that old rumbling laughing noise from his throat. Ian just sat there and smiled beatifically.

Ian might, he thought, have nodded off for a minute or two – passed out possibly – as he turned to see the farmer getting slowly to his feet. The farmer nodded at him, said something he couldn't quite catch, and moved towards the young man standing in the pub doorway holding a toddler – a pretty little girl – in his arms. The girl leaned forward and put her arms around the farmer's head and kissed his face, "Bampa!" And then they were going.

Ian suddenly noticed, and it made him jump and shout "aaahhh" quite loudly, a young woman standing by him, holding a baby in her arms. Boy or girl, he could not say. "I'm sorry if he was bothering you, my Dad," she said to Ian, who slowly shook his head. "He's got, you know… in the brain. It's inoperable," she added. "He loves his lunchtime pint and a chat, so we drop him off and he comes back and sits with us for the afternoon and tells us all about it. You've got to make the most of every day, haven't you?" She smiled and waved at him as she was leaving.

And Ian went to stand up. To be polite and say it was all fine and thank you too and goodbye.

But by the time he got to his feet, she had gone, and he wondered if he should go after her or at least shout something over the fence. Then he decided he would sit back down and finish his pint. He had a good third of it left.

But, he somehow missed his seat and sprawled on the ground next to Bernard who just sat there ignoring him. And he thought, at this point, that it was all really just a bit too much. All of this. Whatever it was. Just too bloody much.

***

It was fortunate for Ian that the pub, the Old Bell, was on the B1153, the road that would take him to where he wanted to go – Swaffham.

As he stood there at the front of the pub, holding his bicycle – holding on to his bicycle for dear life some might say – he could either turn right and go back the way he came or turn left towards Swaffham. A 50/50 choice.

He thought about it for a while, to be sure, to be clear in his

257

head, and turned left – luck or judgement it was hard to say – and started walking, pushing, and wobbling his bicycle along. Bernard was by his side as ever. Headless Charlie was still in the rucksack on his back.

And it occurred to Ian, as he walked, concentrating on putting one foot in front of the other and keeping the wheel of the wretched bicycle away from his feet, that he felt hot and sick and sweaty and really needed to lie down somewhere. Just to shut his eyes and let these feelings pass. But he did not want to do that in public. He did not wish to lie down opposite these houses or by this deli or in front of that old lady over there just standing and looking at him as he passed by.

He thought he would say hello to her and wave in a jovial manner so that she would not think there was anything out of the ordinary about him. Nothing to see here! Walk on by please. Go on Granny, clear off out of it! So he thought some more about saying hello and waving and which he should do first. The hello. Or the wave. Or both together. But then she was gone. The old lady. Too bloody fast for him!

And now there was a group of teenage girls going by. And they seemed to be laughing and waving at him. So, he smiled and waved back, and the bicycle wobbled in front of him. He stumbled over the front wheel, but just about managed to stay on his feet and keep going. And he did not think the girls (or anyone for that matter) had noticed. Not really. And all of a sudden, or so it seemed to him, he was out towards fields and there was a bright light above him and it seemed to be following him and he thought, with great certainty, that he was about to be abducted by aliens. Ian knew he had to hide just as fast as he could.

As he awoke, what must have been two hours or more later, laid out flat on his back behind a hedge in a field, he wondered why a cow was licking his face.

He eventually sat up, his head full of pain and his front full of sick, to see Bernard sitting close by looking at him with a bored expression. His rucksack was beside him. The bicycle over by the hedge.

He got slowly to his feet. Squirted water on his face and into his mouth from a bottle in his rucksack. Then took off his T-shirt. Wiped it on the hedge. Squirted some water on it. Put it back on. Said a stream of arsy-effing-bollocks swear words all rolled into one. And was then oh-so-reluctantly on his way.

As he cycled along, slowly and warily, with Bernard in the basket and Headless Charlie in the rucksack on his back, he decided to keep thinking happy thoughts (even though his head was now splitting). He thought about Joe. And he wanted to think about Joe's life from his birth up to today, picking out the best, the loveliest bits, in snapshots. But all he could think about, and it made him laugh out loud and wobble unsteadily on his bicycle, was the carboard box football games.

Joe had told him, not so long ago, that when it was quiet down at the docks, they would pass the time by setting up makeshift goals at either end of the warehouse and kicking empty cardboard boxes up and down. Not just one but as many as they could at the same time. And the scores would sometimes be 54-53 or 93-91 or 67-63, and the way Joe talked about it made it seem like these were epic World Cup Final battles.

And much as he loved Joe, all he could see in his mind was Joe's intense face – the same one he had when he sat on a potty when he was young – as he hoofed a cardboard box from one end of the warehouse to the other and charged after it. And he could imagine Joe dribbling this huge, falling-apart cardboard box around big, thick-set dock labourers. And taking corners. And headers. And scoring the winning goal with an overhead bicycle kick. Ian had to stop thinking about this, after a while, as he was chortling so much that he came close, several times, to falling off the bicycle.

This really was the back of beyond, this part of Norfolk, thought Ian once he had emptied his mind of Joe's antics. From starting to cycle back near the sign for St Botolph's Church, it was field after field, both sides, just as far as the eye could see. It was all flat although Ian felt as though he were peddling uphill all the way.

He got muddled, hopelessly muddled, when the B1153 crossed the B1145 – who wouldn't? – and went back and forth in his confusion. He checked his back pocket but the map, such as it was (too general, not detailed enough), was not there. It must have fallen out in the field, or bloody somewhere.

He stopped by St Nicholas' Church just along the B1145 to get his breath and he asked an elderly gentleman gardening there how to get to Swaffham. The man looked at him, put his big fork thing in the ground, and told him which way to go. And Ian was on the road again, still feeling it was all uphill.

Joe was a good lad, thought Ian, and when his mind had settled and was free of the alcohol, he could do that snapshot thing he had done with Alex. He remembered holding Joe in his arms just after he was born and Ian did not say anything about him being so ugly, as he had learned by then that babies tend to come out all squished and misshapen. And yet with this one, Ian thought he was rather beautiful, with his dusting of hair and snub nose and delicate fingers.

All his life, his early life anyway, Joe was an accident waiting to happen. Tripping over. Falling down. Stumbling about. "Here he comes again!" the nurses at the local cottage hospital would say as Ian or Kate brought him in. And they'd patch him up with bandages and splints and plasters for a twisted this and a torn that and off they'd go back home until the next time. Joe would always smile through everything. Each trip and every fall would be met with a chuckle or outright laughter.

And he swore lustily from an early age. From about five. When he started school. "Well, that effing hurt!" he would shout after he had fallen down a step. "Eff me, I've broken my leg!" he'd yell after clattering down the stairs (even though he hadn't). Everyone would look at Ian as if Joe had picked up these choice phrases from him. It wasn't Ian and nobody ever quite knew who it was (possibly another child at school). And Ian then stopped thinking about Joe, anything really, for a time.

Ian felt that this part of the journey – endless fields punctuated few and far between by signs for Gayton, Gayton Thorpe, East Walton and Narford – was the longest, the hardest and the most horrible distance that he had endured since he set off all that time ago.

The fact is, he did not feel well. His head, of course, was hot and clammy and felt full and thick inside. A headful of heavy porridge. His neck and his back ached. His legs and his feet as well.

And he smelled. Of sick. And it was in his hair. He touched his hair and it felt as though it were spiked up with gel. And there was dried stuff – more sick – in the lines and creases of his neck. And his T-shirt was all, well, it was just too awful for words.

Ian stopped cycling near woodland outside of Swaffham, in a lay-by just before the road reached the busy A47. He got off the bicycle, lifted Bernard out of the basket and leaning the bicycle against a tree out of sight from the road, Ian and Bernard (and Headless Charlie in the rucksack) made their way into the shaded copse.

Here, he made sure Bernard was fed and watered and he took off his T-shirt and rinsed it through with water from a bottle in the rucksack, before hanging it over a bush to dry. He washed his hair and face and hands and rubbed water on his neck and his white lump (still the same size) before sitting against a tree and shutting his eyes. There, that's better. A little anyway – not as much as he would have liked.

It was later, sometime towards 18.00, that he awoke and decided that they'd have some cobbled-together tea from whatever was left in the rucksack. They'd then, as they were comfortable enough here – and hidden away and private – settle down for the evening.

He'd check the mobile phone to see if there was a message

from Sarah. And he thought what she might have written and what he would reply. And, if she had not messaged him, whether he might message her anyway. And later he'd get that baby booklet out and write something nice in it. Have a good night's sleep and start over afresh the next morning. A clean slate as it were. Perfect.

***

Ian lay on his back in the woods. Bernard on his left. Headless Charlie over there, sitting up next to the rucksack by the nearest tree. Ian put the mobile phone (still no reply) to one side. He held the baby booklet up above his head wishing, as ever, that he had his reading glasses with him.

Squinting at it in the moonlight, angling it this way and that, turning the pages slowly, looking at the different headings. He went back and forth but kept returning to one particular page.

What I Wish I Had Known When I Was A Child was the heading on that page. With a big empty space below for his words. And it just made him feel terribly sad. And he knew why.

"I wish I had known love, Pudding. That's what I wish. That I had a mother and a father who loved me. That I had had a happy childhood. That Mum hadn't... died. That I'd been allowed to live with my nan and grandpa rather than my father and... her." He said this aloud, but quietly, in the sing-song voice of Headless Charlie. As if he were talking to Charlie. As though Headless Charlie were Pudding. His grandson-to-be. Madness, he knew, all of this. These moments of insanity. His mind unravelling. He sat and thought a while and carried on talking but in his head this time. And in his own voice.

"The first time in my life that anyone told me they loved me was on my 18th birthday. It was my nan, my mum's mum. She and my grandpa had sent me a card and a cheque for one hundred pounds, a lot of money in those days. My father could not stand my grandparents, they were too soft and sentimental for him, so I called them from a telephone box at the end of the road. I thanked my nan and she said, her voice breaking, 'We love you, Ian.' And I did not know how to reply, so I said, 'Thank you very much,' politely, and then, 'Goodbye Nan,' and I put the phone down carefully.

"My childhood (and really it was this that made him feel painfully sad) made me what I am today. It ruined me. When I was little, I had to keep all my feelings in, just bottle them up. Excitement, thrills, happiness – showing them would mean they would be knocked out of me. I had to be quiet. Respectful. Be seen but not heard. Not really be seen, ideally. And I could never show fear or anger or temper at all. They'd all have been bludgeoned away by my father. And that's why, Pudding, I can't talk about things, hug anyone, tell them how I feel about them. I can hide behind a silly, jovial mask at times. Burst out. Shout a bit. But down inside, I am still that fearful little boy keeping it all in."

Ian rolled onto his front, reaching for his jacket in the rucksack. Pulled it out. Rummaged. Took out his pen.

He then folded the baby booklet open to the page where he wanted to write and flattened it, making sure he had a nice, level surface.

He knew, in his head, what he wanted to say to Pudding. And he began writing, carefully, until he had it all just so.

You can be happy. He considered putting *you have a lovely mummy and daddy* but remembered he had written something like it before. And he thought about stating *you have a lovely home* but did not think that the size of a home, the niceness of it, was what it was all about. A loving home, maybe, but that was too much like saying a lovely mummy and daddy. *Always be happy,* he thought about adding, *That's what it's all about - being happy.* But that seemed very repetitive, and he thought he should really just be writing, *It's all about love.* So, he just added a little heart and shaded it in.

You can do anything. Ian had wanted to be a novelist when

263

he was young, to write adventure stories. He had tentatively mentioned this when his father was grilling him in readiness for an 11-plus exam to get him into grammar school. But his father, who was a bank manager, had a client who was a novelist and sneered that the man was so poor he had to earn a "proper living" as a window cleaner. And his wife took in clothes to iron (as though that was the most shameful thing ever). So, Ian (who passed the 11-plus) ended up doing a degree in business management and spending his whole life on marketing budgets and profits and losses and endless press releases and crap.

You can be whoever you want to be. He knew he was not what he wanted to be – neither inside, as a human being, nor outside, having spent – having wasted – all his working life on numbers and charts and nonsense. And that made him sad and angry. And he wanted more for Pudding. *Shoot for the moon*, he wrote, then wished he hadn't as it sounded a bit, well, a bit of a cliché. He added *Be an astronaut! Or a footballer! A ballet dancer! Whatever makes you happy!*

Ian looked back over what he had written. And he felt good about it. He had used the right words, mostly. Expressed what he wanted to say, near enough.

He shut the booklet and put it and the pen back into the rucksack. He looked at Headless Charlie and decided to leave him out for the night. Stroked Bernard's head and back. They shuffled closer to each other.

Then Ian turned on his side, with one last check of the mobile phone (still no reply) before rolling his jacket up into a pillow. And he was asleep within moments.

22
SWAFFHAM TO THETFORD FOREST

FRIDAY 15th JULY

(10.5 MILES, 3 HOURS 23 MINUTES)

Ian and Bernard and Headless Charlie awoke to rain, a shimmering, spitting-gently-through-the-trees kind of rain. The first rain they'd had on their journey going there and coming back. It took Ian by surprise. Although he had not given it any thought at all; if asked, he would have said he had presumed it would simply be sunny every day.

He sat up straight, wiped his face with the palm of his left hand, and put his jacket over his head and shoulders. He shuffled on his bottom towards the tree that Headless Charlie was leaning against.

He called to Bernard and the blasted dog just lifted his head, looked wearily across (as if even that were too much effort), and carried on laying where he was. In the rain and wet. The stupid dog. Ian reached into the rucksack for a sausage roll and a bottle of water and Bernard, slowly, reluctantly, came over. As if it were the last thing in the world he wanted to do. Like he was doing Ian a massive favour.

First things first, thought Ian, we're going to cycle to Swaffham (which he reckoned was a mile or two down the road) and have a proper stock up on supplies at a supermarket; enough to see us through.

Then they'd cycle south, Bernard up front, Headless Charlie on the back, the 10 miles or so (he estimated) to Thetford Forest.

Spending the day there, just relaxing. Watching for squirrels and rabbits and listening for owls and the birds in the trees and just drawing breath for the final few days ahead.

And they sat there, by this tree, big and solid and tall and proud, as the rain turned from a drizzle to something closer to a proper heavy shower. They were sheltered here, under the tree, and could watch the rain falling. And Ian suddenly felt terribly low. That his life had come to this. Sitting with his old dog amongst trees in the middle of nowhere eating a stale sausage roll from a packet and drinking lukewarm water from a plastic bottle that crackled every time you put the thing, the thingamabob, the blessed tit thing, in your mouth and sucked on it. He needed to get busy.

So Ian emptied his jacket and his rucksack and put everything on a dry-ish patch of ground in front of them – including folded-over money, the baby booklet and pen and Sarah's old mobile phone. Why he'd never bought spare T-shirts or pants or socks or trousers or anything like that amazed him really. And he did not have a mirror to check his appearance or scissors to trim his hair or his beard or to cut his nails. He wondered why this was and thought perhaps there was something wrong with him. That all of this, by and large, had never occurred to him. As though there were great big holes in his mind.

He looked down at his hands and shoes and his jacket and his T-shirt and trousers and just thought he was, what was the word, the exact word he wanted to use. Dirty. Shabby. Dishy. No, not bloody dishy. Dish worthy. Something. No, it was gone. He looked a mess. He sniffed at his clothes, pushing the fabric of his T-shirt and then his jacket up to his nostrils. And he smelt sweat and dirt and damp and sick and he could not understand why or how he had got into such a state. And he just felt even lower.

Ian heard a rummaging and a rustling noise amongst the

trees, close to where they came through last night. He sat up straight watching and listening.

A rabbit. A fox, maybe. Perhaps even a deer. He had once seen a muntjac deer in woodland close to where he lived. It was a magical moment as the deer stood and looked at him for what seemed an age before turning and disappearing silently back into the trees. Like some mythical creature from Narnia.

There were more rummaging and rustling and other swishing noises as it, whatever it was, whatever they were, a mother and a baby muntjac, moved off into the distance. Back to safety. Away from Ian and Bernard, who did not even bother to raise his head to see what was going on.

Ian sat back against the tree, thoroughly fed-up again. The rain was slowing now, easing off, and he knew he would soon have to get up and go. And the thought of that, another day's cycling along unfamiliar roads to places he had never heard of (nor wanted to visit), made him feel even more, what was it… depressed was too strong a word; but he felt he was heading down that road. Misery Road.

He looked at what was in front of him on the ground, ready to be packed away, and decided suddenly that he was going to text Sarah again. In case his first text had gone astray. He thought a while. Then decided what he would put. *Hi Sarah. It's Ian. (And Bernard). We are about one third of the way home. Near Swaffham.* He could leave it at that. Just a cheerful statement. Or he could add *How are you?* which would be polite and encourage her to text back. Should she wish to do so. He did not know how to end it. *Ian… Love Ian… Luv Ian… Ian xx*

Ian ummed and aahed as he reached for the phone to turn it on. He wondered whether there might be a message from her. He pressed the phone on one side and the other and finally both sides at the same time. It was a full three minutes before he realised the mobile phone was now stone cold dead. Whether she had replied or not, he'd not now know. He hurled the phone as hard and as far as he could into some bracken way, way over there.

At last, as the rain stopped, he got up (reluctantly) and put everything back into the rucksack, Headless Charlie on top. And he tucked the baby booklet and the pen into his jacket pocket.

He spent five minutes, maybe more, searching, ever more irritated, through bracken and grass and twigs and leaves and some mushroom-type stuff (which he put his knee into and had to wipe off clumsily on grass) before he found the mobile phone. He put that in his jacket pocket. He'd charge it up when he got home. Start over.

And he click-clicked his tongue at Bernard, and they walked out of where they had slept and went this way and, doubling back, that way and another and one more way to be sure until finally Ian had to admit that – the bicycle that he'd left by the trees just off the lay-by in the road was gone.

**

Ian walked to Swaffham, holding Bernard all the way, in an absolute fury. Two miles or so, down the Westacre Road, by the A47, and into town in about three quarters of an hour. He kept watch for the bicycle, either abandoned by the side of the road or with someone on it, as he went. Had he seen someone on it he would have run at them hard and fast and pushed them right off and got on the bicycle, put Bernard in the basket, shouted, "Up yours!" and peddled off quickly. But he didn't.

In town, he asked two or three silly old beggars where the nearest superstore was. One was half-deaf, cocking an ear at Ian, the next clacked his false teeth round his mouth like they were marbles and the third rubbed his chin and said, "Let me see now…" and Ian just about stopped himself throwing back his head and screaming.

More by luck than anything else, he found a Tesco superstore, asked a security guard smoking a cigarette outside to keep an eye on Bernard, and went in and bought enough food and drink to fill the rucksack. Came out to check Bernard was okay. Then back in again for T-shirts, pants, a pair of shorts, socks, and floppety-flop shoe things too. Not trainers. Or flip-flops. You know. Things. Ian checked Bernard was alright. Finally, he went and changed in the toilets, washed his grubby face and filthy hands, collected Bernard, and they were on their way again.

Leaving town, still edgy but not raging, he saw two old biddies – Laurel and Hardy lookalikes, one skinny, one stout – by a bus stop. He asked them for directions to Thetford Forest and after squawking and squabbling for a while, they agreed that there were two ways to go.

Left, down London Road, was the quickest. Mrs Laurel said. You can walk all the way. Right, you can go right, too? Mrs Hardy countered. Right down, oh, you know, where Jean lived before she died, and it will take you there. But it's longer, a mile or two more and you'd need to turn down the A-something-or-other before you get there, added Mrs Laurel as if to say, "Don't take any notice of Mrs Hardy, she doesn't know what she's talking about." Mrs Hardy had a little grumble and groan and eventually agreed that, yes, well, left might be the better way.

As he walked by the golf course with Bernard close behind, he remembered the last thing that Mrs Hardy (who had to have the final word) had said. "If you go by a golf course you know you've gone the wrong way." Ian struggled again with his mood at this point. Not so much because he'd gone the long way – however much longer that might be – but because there was a fellow in the car park, wheeling some wheely thing full of, oh, bloody, um, bloody clubs who looked like David from a distance. It made him feel sad that David was dead. And he had no one to talk to any more. He thought about David as he walked along.

When David had died, his family was overcome with grief,

maybe even by madness. The son, Liam, had turned up on his doorstep and announced, like he was reading a shopping list, that his father had died two days earlier and they were now taking it in turns going round door-to-door to tell everyone, because everybody knew David and loved him. Whether that was every door in Felixstowe or just those doors belonging to people who knew David, Ian could not tell.

And Ian, not sure what to say when confronted with this emotional, face-to-face scenario, came close to suggesting that they might want to put up a statue for David or at least a plaque, because he knew that would make David laugh. But he looked at the young man's tormented face and said instead that he was very sorry to hear the news. He did not invite him in – Ian had never been very good at anything like that – and there was a moment when they just stood there silently looking at each other.

And Liam then took out and unfolded a sheet of paper headed *Dad's Swimming Friends* under which he had listed various names from swimming – *Jack, Martin, Eddie* – along with descriptions of other swimmers there that, presumably, David might have known. He handed it to Ian who said, not to worry, but he could tell everyone at swimming for them. But the son said that no, that was not his place to do so (not in an unkindly way) and that he wanted to do it. Face-to-face. They would want to know (even though, thought Ian, a good third of them would have no idea who David was, and another third could not care less).

So, they spent an agonising five to 10 minutes where Liam asked for the surnames of Jack and Martin and Eddie and Ian did not know any of them. (He had never heard of an Eddie full stop.) And Liam asked, quite insistently now, where they lived as if Ian must know. He said he had no idea other than Martin who lived "somewhere round here", and he waved his arms vaguely which seemed to anger the son even more.

They went through the descriptions of the other swimmers –

blond and tall and thin man and *heavy woman with a red swimsuit* – and so on. And Ian wondered who had provided these descriptions and who the heck these people were. And Ian said he did not know any of them other than one that "might be Ruth?" but that triggered another round of questioning about her surname and where she lived and more suppressed anger.

And the son stalked off, obviously out of sorts and furious with Ian who had not been able to provide any help at all. Ian then had this image of the son banging door-to-door to announce to people who had never heard of David that he had died and them looking dumb-faced at the son. And this idea made him laugh – and would have made David laugh loudly too – although he felt rather mean about it. Ian then kept on walking, feeling more and more tired.

It did not help his mood that Ian was carrying Bernard again who just seemed to walk a few yards every time he was put down and then stopped and stared into space as if to say, "nope, that's it for me, matey". Then, as he had done so many times, Ian would walk on and go back and shout at him and wave his fist and cajole and even beg the wretched animal to walk. Just for a while. Please! But he did not and so he was carried aloft, Mr High and Mighty, by Ian.

And it was at Cockley Cley, when Ian had just had a good moan at Bernard (who simply ignored him and stared ahead) that they went the wrong way. Just the other side of Cocky Clacker, Cocker Leeky or whatever the stupid place was called, the road forked into two, left or right. Had he been focusing on what he was doing, concentrating, or even giving it a moment or two's thought, he would have turned left which, later on, would have veered left again and got them back on to that shorter route the old ladies had mentioned.

But no, he went right, although to be fair it was more a sort of straight-on, ambling-slowly-to-the-right kind of road rather than a sharp right turn. And on they went. And on. By a sign for Gooderstone to their left. On again. Further on still. And a sign for Oxborough on their right. And it was another hour and a half, maybe even more, by this time.

There was nobody or nothing – not a single thing – on this road. It was as if Ian and Bernard had somehow slipped through a crack in time and it was now the 1960s or 1940s or 1920s and they were utterly alone. They stopped at regular intervals. Ate something. Drank some water. Carried on. Stopped again. Ate something. Drank some water. Carried on. And it was, to be frank, all becoming a terrible slog. Ian spent his time cursing, using every swear word he knew, all rolled up together into long mother-fudders of made-up words. Not that it made him feel any better. Not really.

They reached the A134, after all this endless stop-start-stop, "I hate the bastard who stole my bicycle" nonsense, and they had to turn left and do the whole bloody thing again all the way to Thetford Forest. And Ian just thought "Arse Balls" and walked – stomped – off the road, into a field of long grass, just to take a breather. A lunchtime break, because it must be that by now, surely. Ian put Bernard down and took off his rucksack and lay it next to the dog. As he got back up – down, up, down-up, way too quickly – he suddenly felt very dizzy. Almost overcome. As he stood there, crouched over, almost at a right angle, he felt a terrible pain in his head and sharp, almost needle-like pains in his arms and legs.

He thought for one awful instant that he must be having a stroke, and this frightened him very much. Not least because he did not want to lie here, all twitches and spasms, before becoming paralysed, out of sight, hidden away, never to be found until after Bernard had eaten him and only a skeleton with gnawed bones was left. And so, he stood up straight as if to fight back, to say no, I won't give in to this. Damn you to hell. As he thought the words, his mind swirled, and he fell back heavily and lay flat out on the grass.

***

Not to put too fine a point on it, but Ian was sure he had just had a stroke. And that he was going to die here. Stiff from the neck down. Hidden from view. In the long grass. In a field. By the A134. Bernard sitting there watching him. Waiting.

His head was all mushy. His mouth bone-dry. His tongue a huge gagging lump. He had twanging pains in his arms and legs even if he moved, twitched, ever so slightly. He wondered, trying to bring the right words together to formulate thoughts in his mind, whether he was about to have a second stroke that would render him unconscious. Or if he would lie here like this, washed out and ebbing away, hour after hour, getting slowly weaker until he died. Or Bernard bit – too soon – into his fleshy thigh. He hoped he'd be gone and beyond reviving by then.

He wished suddenly, more than anything, that he had a whatsit. A thing. Not a firework. Nor a Catherine wheel. Not a rocket. For God's sake. A flare. That was it. Or a kite. No, not a kite. That was just stupid. What he really wanted, what he'd wished he'd brought, what he needed most, was his own mobile phone. So he could call Kate and speak to her before he passed away.

"I love you, Kate," he said in a whisper, his voice high-pitched and strangulated as though he were speaking in Headless Charlie's voice (although he had not intended to do so).

He struggled in his mind to think what it was he wanted to say next. After a while, he spoke again; still in something close to Charlie's sing-song voice.

"I have always loved you, Kate. And… the children." He stopped and named them in turn in case Kate thought he could not remember. "Alex. Beth. Joe."

He hesitated, his mind bringing random thoughts together. He knew Kate was not there, not really, but it somehow felt as though she were close by. Her presence comforted him.

"And Adam. I loved Adam… We all did. We all loved Adam." And he stopped again. And his mind wandered and roamed and, for a moment or two, his thoughts became clear

273

and lucid. And he wanted to tell Kate how he felt that first time he had seen her sheltering from the rain at that bus stop near the university. How he had adored her all these years but could never quite bring himself to say so. How proud he was of the children and their partners. And how honoured he was to be their husband and father. And how he wished it had not all gone so wrong and for so long. Because of Adam. Not because of Adam. Because of him. How he, Ian, had been since Adam.

"I'm sorry," he said, still in that schoolboy's squeaky voice. "I've made such a mess of things. Please forgive me."

He thought suddenly that this was all too maudlin, too melancholy. And that Kate would laugh out loud at his sudden and nonsensical sentimentality. He had never spoken like this before. But he meant what he said. Because he was dying. And he thought she would understand it.

"I love you, Kate," he said, sensing that she, or at least her presence, was about to leave.

He swallowed and his voice seemed to lower, moving away from Headless Charlie's squeak. "I love you so much, Kate," he said again, these last words comforting him as he drifted away.

So much time had passed that it was dark as he came round. He could feel, somehow, that Bernard, his dear old pal, was still with him and was not going to eat him. Not alive anyway. And that, wherever they were going, they would go together. And that somehow felt right. And proper. And how it should be. And he recalled what Kate's uncle Tony had said had happened that time he had almost died. He had seen "blackness", as he called it. It was like that now, near enough, thought Ian, blackness all around.

And he saw in the distance, or could at least sense, a light. It was like looking down a long railway tunnel and seeing a strong and steady beam at the other end. He had thought, from what people had said, that he would be drawn towards it, and perhaps even see those who he had loved and who had gone before. Mum. Nan. Grandpa. But this light now seemed to be coming towards him. And it was wobbling about as if it wasn't sure it wanted to come for him or not.

Ian worried what this meant. That maybe, somehow, the light would flicker and dim and suddenly be snuffed out. And he wouldn't be going where he thought he was going. He had never really believed in an "up there" and a "down there" but if the light for up there went out that meant there was only one place left for him: down there. He did not like the thought of that. He watched as the light came closer, ever faster, first this side and then that, until it was so close and so bright that it blinded him. And he heard a deep and sonorous God-like voice. "Look at the state of you... pissed as a fart."

***

The huge and hairy man, all angry face and bushy beard, hauled, literally hauled, Ian up from the ground and onto his feet. And Ian stood there all wobbly with his splitting headache and his aches and pains and feeling sick. But he was not dead. And he had not had a stroke. He was alive and okay. Well, okay-ish.

The man, who had a gun and a bag and things – fur things and tail things... like rats hanging from here and there – just seemed furious. "Go on, you old drunk," the man shouted in his face so close that Ian could smell whisky and tobacco on his breath. "Get out of here! You and your stupid dog."

Ian feared that the man might kick Bernard (who was just sitting there quietly minding his own business), like that other angry man had done when they were queueing for the pharmacy all those days ago. And that the man might kick Bernard so hard on his growth that it would burst, and he would bleed to death out here in the middle of nowhere. And so Ian grabbed Bernard and, as the nasty, horrible man shouted, "Go on, get out of here!" He ran, walked, staggered back up on to the A134, turning left towards Thetford Forest. He stopped for a while, when he felt calmer, catching his breath and gathering his thoughts. And then he started walking again.

This time, after his mind had settled, he replayed — or re-lived as much as he could remember of — David's funeral in his head as he walked this straight and never-ending road. It was, in its own way, a joyous occasion. A celebration. But sad too. Poignant, that was the word he was looking for.

Ian drove to the crematorium on his own, parking somewhere near the back of the car park. He did not know anyone there other than David's wife and son and his daughter who had put the invitation through his door a week before. He walked in behind the other mourners but before the family followed with the coffin.

The service was something of a blur and Ian tried to unpick it in his mind as he walked, so he could think it over in its correct order. It began with a speech by a professional celebrant full of carefully rehearsed platitudes, hushed tones, and politically correct nonsense. "Bollocks to that," David would have said.

A speech by his best friend — best man at his wedding — seemed to go on and on with the man recounting every so-called adventure they'd had together. How they had run out of petrol somewhere once late at night and they had to walk home. How David had once worn a wig at a fancy dress party, and it had fallen off. How one of them, neither ever admitted to it, had once put two teabags in the same mug by mistake. How David had once said something terribly funny — "au revoir" — when meeting a Frenchman somewhere or other. On and on. This endless dirge.

And there was music. Some football song from the 1960s, a tune by Kylie Minogue, and a classical song sung by someone who Ian had never heard of. The daughter and son rested their heads on either side of their mother's shoulders during that.

Speeches by his wife, daughter, and son — high-pitched, breathless, racing — were hard to sit through; more so for David's brothers and sisters and cousins on the front row who were in floods of tears. Ian bowed his head two or three times.

Then everyone was filing out to the strains of some football song or other – David being a season ticket holder at Ipswich Town Football Club - and there was a long queue as the 50 or so mourners lined up to say something to the wife and son and daughter standing at the end of the pathway by the floral arrangements. Ian had no idea what to say and wondered if they would notice if he slipped off to the toilets to the right and simply disappeared. He thought it might look bad though if someone spotted him hurrying across the car park to his car.

Then he was there, right in front of the wife, and they leaned one way and the other as he went to shake her hand and to pat her arm and, finally, into an awkward embrace. Ian said he was so sorry for their loss. The son came up and shook his hand. And the daughter went to hug him, and Ian instinctively leaned back, and it was all rather embarrassing. Ian was pleased when he could walk on.

As the mourners all stood there looking at the flowers, a man – a stranger – said something to Ian about it being a nice service and how David would have been so pleased. And Ian, looking at the burly fellow who must have worked with David at the docks, said that "David wanted to be put in a bin bag and taken down the dump." This was true and was meant to be jovial but seemed to cause offence, with the man turning and looking at the writing on a card on a wreath rather too intently before walking off.

So Ian stood there on his own and the wife and the son and the daughter came all the way round to speak to everyone again. And the wife said she was sorry Ian was not being invited back to the house, but it was for only close friends and family. And Ian answered that it was okay, he understood and, yes, for sure, that was fine (even though it wasn't, not really, and David would have wanted him there).

As he had walked back to the car, he was suddenly overwhelmed by the funeral and the speeches and the songs and all of it really. But most of all, how many friends David had, how everyone was so upset and how much love there was for his old swimming buddy. And Ian wondered what his own funeral would be like – a million miles from this one.

Ian, carrying Bernard as he had done for the past hour and a half, came at last to the edge of Thetford Forest. He was sticky and hot and felt exhausted and full of aches and pains. All he wanted to do was to go into the forest just beyond the first line of trees. Take off his jacket and roll it up as a pillow. Kick bracken into place as a rough and ready mattress. Check all around and go to sleep. Until dawn and beyond. Whenever he felt better.

As he stopped by the trees, and put Bernard down, he reached over his shoulder to take off his rucksack. And he realised that he had left it behind. Back where the angry man had chased him and Bernard away. And that almost everything they had, their food and drink, Headless Charlie, their bits and pieces, their money, all that money, had now gone. And he did not know how he could have been so stupid that he had walked this past hour and a half or so without realising the rucksack had not been on his back. Exhaustion, he supposed.

Ian found a dip – a ditch by the side of the trees – where they could sleep for the night. He pushed bracken and leaves and other debris about for their makeshift bed. Then took off his jacket and lay down with his head on it, with Bernard by his feet. That's all they had left now, he thought, what was in his jacket. The baby booklet. A pen. Sarah's dead mobile phone. A handful of notes and coins. And 50 miles from home. Maybe three days of walking. He worried how they would do that as he fell into a long and uneasy sleep.

23
THETFORD FOREST
TO IXWORTH

SATURDAY 16th JULY

(11.6 MILES, 3 HOURS, 50 MINUTES)

Ian stood, alone and silent, behind a tree, in the middle of the woods, in the dark of night.

Every part of his mind and body screamed at him to run just as fast and as hard as he could.

He was not alone in the woods. Someone or something was close by, hunting him down. To kill him.

His instinct was to run, but he did not know which way to go. There were trees, tall trees, rising to the sky all around, in all directions. For miles and miles. And it was a moonless night and so dark that he realised, if he ran, he would make so much noise that the thing, whatever it was, would hear and be on him in seconds. And, with the undergrowth so thick and dense, he would stumble and trip and fall to the ground. And he would roll over onto his back. And the thing – this monstrous being – would be at his throat, tearing at it.

So, he stood there, to the side of the tree, and just waited. Hoping that, somehow, the thing would not see him and just go on by. And Ian could wait there for five, maybe 10, minutes, before breaking cover and heading off in the opposite direction. To safety. Wherever that might be. But he could hear himself breathing so loudly, great big shuddering breaths, full of fear and panic. And, with each terrible breath, in and out, in and out, his body shook, not just trembled, but really shuddered and the branches and bracken beneath his feet cracked and crackled so sharp and so loud in the silence.

He smelled, his natural body odour so strong and pungent, triggered by the terror in his mind and in his heart. All of him – his hair, his face, his body, his clothes, his shoes – smelled; an overpowering scent that made this chase… this hunting… so much easier for whatever it was that was pursuing him. Had been pursuing him so long and so relentlessly, never pausing, never giving up. The thing would go on until Ian was caught and killed.

It was already following his scent, had done for ages, and was now closing in, getting ever closer and closer.

Ian just stood there, too scared to stay, too terrified to move. Knowing the thing was almost upon him. He could hear it now – this monstrous being – as it shuffled and crept and slithered through the undergrowth towards him.

In the distance, Ian heard the barking of a dog. His dog. Bernard. His old pal. Bernard never barked. But he was barking now, loud and strong, calling for Ian. Demanding to know where he was. And he could hear Bernard moving, running, like a young, tough dog, here and there, and calling, barking, over and over again. Where are you? Where are you? Where are you?

But Ian did not call back "I'm here, I'm here" because the thing was so close. The other side of the tree now. It had tracked Ian down by his scent, crept up towards the tree, ready to attack. And was about to do so when it heard Bernard's barking. Now, it had stopped and was listening, deciding what to do. Ian could hear it, just there, only a metre or two away. And he did not know what it was going to do.

And Bernard was barking again and getting closer, coming this way, and barking some more. "I'm coming. I'm coming. I'm coming." But the thing did not turn and run away as Ian had hoped. He heard it move to face where Bernard was coming from. It was going to attack Bernard as he broke through the trees. And so Ian stepped out from behind the tree so that he was one side of the thing and Bernard would be the other. They would fight together.

As Ian woke and sat up beside the tree, in the middle of the woods, as dawn was breaking, he saw the fox by the edge of the clearing. The most beautiful red fox with its big, bushy tail.

And he watched Bernard with his back arched, mouth snarling and snapping, watching the fox, protecting Ian.

With one long last look at them, the fox slipped away into the undergrowth and disappeared amongst the trees. And Ian leaned forward and hugged Bernard long and hard.

***

The next part of the journey, from Thetford Forest to Ixworth, was always going to be difficult, if not hellish. Ian had now lost, in relatively quick succession, the bicycle and the rucksack with their food and drink and money – pretty much all their money – and Headless Charlie. His mood was so low. And it would get lower during the day.

All he had left was what he was wearing, plus that pen and baby booklet and Sarah's dead phone . He counted out £7.62 in loose change. And Bernard of course, although Ian rather took his dawdling presence as a negative; the delay something of a nuisance. (Later, Ian would look back and regret that feeling at times.)

As he set off, realising it was going to be a hot day, he really wished, in no particular order, that he had something, anything, to eat, plus a bottle of cold water and a clean pair of pants and socks (the current ones now having that "dried sweat feeling" about them).

And he thought, as he had done with Alex and Joe, that he would think happy thoughts, picturing snapshots of Beth and her life, as he went along. To keep his sagging spirits up. He remembered when she was born, late one cold and wintery night in November all those years ago. After a labour that just seemed to go on and on for hours, Kate decided to have a bath. Once she was in, it all happened so fast. Ian, instead of pulling the emergency cord, turned off the lights in the bathroom. And could not find the cord to turn them on again. So, Kate somehow lifted herself up – the baby's head dangling – and did it. The midwives came running. Ian got in the way. Then fell over. And shouted that the baby would drown in the bath water.

The baby was born, lifted swiftly and professionally out of the water by one of three midwives there, tweaked, and handed to Kate to hold. And the midwife had asked, since neither Kate nor Ian had looked, if they wanted to know the baby's sex. And Ian, having seen – "quite clearly actually" – the baby's penis on the last scan and having told everyone about it and even painted the bedroom blue, said "No!" and laughed, and the three midwives all stared at him in such a strange way. And Kate had a little peek and said, "It's a girl," and gave Ian one of those looks of hers before saying, "We'll call her Bethany."

Ian slipped out before the afterbirth turned up and went back in later and looked at the baby in a plastic, wheeling-about-thing, like a trolley, and said she was just perfect. He had not looked closely as, being a little early, she was a shade of yellow. Kate and Beth had to spend a week together in hospital. Ian took charge at home and gave Alex Coca Cola and crisps for breakfast, wore dirty clothes for a week and Kate came back to find a huge pile of washing next to a broken ironing board. Still, it was a happy memory all in all.

Ian assumed, as he trudged slowly down that A134, Bernard close by his side, that he would soon arrive in the town centre of Thetford where he could get something to eat and drink. And maybe find a public toilet to wash his face and hands and the back of his neck.

£7.62 and three, maybe four, days to walk home. What a

sludge. Not sludge. Trudge. Whatever. What a slog it would be. He wondered if they could manage, food- and drink-wise, on what was it, no, his mind wouldn't let him do the precise maths. It would be £2.50 a day, give or take. Less than £2, if it took four days.

After some time, he arrived in what was Mundford, where he bought water and a pack of two out-of-date sausage rolls (one each) for £2.76 from a village store. He was dismayed to be told by the woman behind the counter that Thetford, the town itself, was still about eight miles away down the A134 that took him through the rest of the Forest, north to south. And so, fed and watered, he set off again. Feeling even lower. Bernard lagging behind. He thought again of Beth to keep his mood up, his mind flitting over so many memories.

The first children's tea party she went to when he bought her just the prettiest party dress and she pulled faces and just… what was it, gurned… when he tried to take a photograph.

She had a soft, floppy dolly – a rag doll kind of thing – and, when she settled down to sleep, she would pull the hair, the woollen strands, from it and push them up her nostrils.

His mind was all over the place and he knew it was tiredness causing it. But he kept going, back and forth, with his memories of Beth over the years.

Dropping her at school and watching her running in so fast and so happy that her straw hat would blow away and she would not notice. Ian would have to follow her, picking it up, and taking it to her.

And so many friends, Lucy and Alice and Freya and, just an endless expanding list, coming to tea and staying over and hiding here, there and everywhere when it was time for them to go home.

And still Ian walked along, Bernard in his arms, down that long and never-ending A134, the forest stretching out to either side. The sun was so high and hot in the sky. And he ached. All of him. From the top of his head to the tip of his toes. And his

T-shirt stuck to his back. That was the worst thing, he thought. Of so many things. His sticky-stucky back.

He wondered, as cars went by ignoring him as ever, whether he might thumb a lift. He'd never done it before, but he had to do something. Before he gave up. He thought a little more as he walked along and decided he looked too, what was it, bedraggled, for anyone to stop voluntarily. He considered slumping to the ground. As if that might encourage someone to stop and give him a lift. But, most likely, they'd just manoeuvre around him shouting, "Get up, you piss artist."

He sighed and went on (and then on some more), going through blink-and-you-miss-it Lynford, ignoring the signs for Grimes Graves and Thetford Forest Park and some bloody picnic site and the power station and Two-Mile Bottom, and thinking the forest would never end. That perhaps he really had died, and this was the hell he'd gone and got himself into. Like an episode of *The Twilight Zone* where someone was killed and, not realising, relived their last moments over and over on an endless loop.

He thought of Beth as she grew up. All the GCSEs. The A grades. All the A-Levels. More A grades. Durham University. A 2:1. Then back home to train as primary school teacher. The trainee teacher of the year for East Anglia. Head hunted by someone on the panel to join their school. Success after success.

Idiot boyfriend after idiot boyfriend. An endless stream of half-witted simpletons trailing in her wake. Jake, who had to be air-lifted to safety when, after a drinking spree with the lads in Cornwall, had found himself stranded on a rock somewhere out at sea. The posh one who broke into French or Italian without a moment's notice, quoted Shakespeare at every opportunity and answered every question with "Yah, Yah". And, finally, the one who said he wanted to be an accountant and Ian had replied to be careful, because accountancy might be too exciting for him.

And Beth was just so popular. To the family she was simply "The Foghorn", loud and irrepressible, prone to excited highs and yelling lows. And yet everyone – school, teachers, parents, small children and more – just seemed to love her. And, of course, the family did too, it was just that they knew her better and saw all sides of her.

It was at the point where Ian was going to just lie down in the road and give up (whether the car behind stopped, went round or even over him) that the A143 came – trundling rather than racing – out of the Forest. At long last.

And as he staggered on, stop-start, stop-start, stop-start, he crossed a roundabout on the A11 and came into the built-up area on the outskirts of the town centre of Thetford. Civilisation, or something close to it.

And that, the car showrooms, the business park, the recycling centre – never was Ian so pleased to see a council tip – seemed to help him rally. And by the time he went by the railway station he was, if not exactly running, at least putting one foot in front of the other without stumbling. He had a sense of hope.

***

Ian stood in the Co-op corner store, somewhere or other on the outskirts of Thetford, looking at the foodbank near the door with its piles of brown paper bags, like a no-frills lucky dip.

Feeling the coins in his pocket; £4.86. And thinking about the number of days left. Today to Ixworth. Tomorrow to Needham Market. The day after to Ipswich. And home the next. So, four days, most likely. Not much more than one pound a day for food and drink for the two of them. Not enough.

He knew, if he had to, he could get a taxi home although goodness knows what it would cost from here… or Needham Market… or Ipswich even. But if Kate was not at home (and she would not be during the day), and he could not find cash or a card, there would be hell to pay with the driver. And besides, he wanted to walk up that drive, head held high, Bernard by his side.

Ian did not know the rules for foodbanks. He assumed you just took a bag if you needed it. He could pick up one on the way out as he left. Then, sit on a bench up the road and go through it.

He wondered what would be in the brown paper bag. Maybe just food; dried and tinned stuff, most probably. Or fresh fruit and veg? He'd need some water, and something for Bernard too.

He thought you might be able to pick and choose – that the bags may have different contents – but was not sure. So, he stepped back, and pretended to look at what was on the shelves in front of him. But keeping an eye on the foodbank as well.

After standing there a while, moving back and forth, "Sorry," "Excuse me," and glancing towards the door where Bernard sat patiently outside, a solid, middle-aged man in a suit came up behind him and said something quietly. Ian jumped, surprised, and apologised and asked the man to repeat what he had said. "Do you have your voucher?" he repeated, perfectly politely. And Ian looked at him, baffled. And asked what he meant. "You should have a voucher," the man said, nodding towards the foodbank.

And Ian, suddenly feeling hot and embarrassed and wanting to leave straightway, asked where he got a voucher from. The man, despite his rather burly presence, was surprisingly sympathetic and said you, i.e. Ian, could get one from a GP or a social worker or the Citizens Advice Bureau, although that wasn't open until Monday. Then you brought it in and exchanged it for a food parcel.

Ian wanted to say "So, you can't just take one… if you're hungry… and have less than £5 to last you and your dog for four days," but he felt awkward and shamefaced. And just wanted to go. But he needed to get something to eat for them for this afternoon and evening and wanted more water without buying another bottle. So, he just said, "Ah okay. I just need to get one or two bits then," and he held out a handful of coins to show he had some money. And that, the holding out of the money, made him feel more humiliated than anything else.

The man stepped back and went away. Ian walked up and down the aisles looking for the cheapest things he could find to eat.

There were tins, but he had nothing to open them with. And packets of dried meals that needed to be brought to life with hot water he did not have. And fresh bread, but he wanted something to share with his old pal.

And he thought, "I've got one pound, what can I get for one pound?" He could not really see anything at all.

He found himself following, although that was not quite the right word, a young woman with a child in a pushchair, up one aisle and down the next. He could not see how old she was or if the child was a girl or a boy – not that it really mattered – but he noticed she had a list on a piece of paper. It was a short list and it had numbers, prices, next to it, added up and totalled. So, she knew what she was getting and how much it would cost.

And Ian watched, from a way back, so as not to alarm her, and he saw her going from one shelf to the next, taking items off and looking at them, checking prices, and putting one back and another into the basket resting on top of the hood of the pushchair. At one point, he must have got too close without thinking and she turned, and he thought she might smile and laugh, and he could stop and speak to her and pass the time of day and say something nice about her child. But she just looked, what was the word, frightened, as if he were about to say something to her or even touch her. So, he said he was sorry and moved back.

He thought, probably, that this was what it must be like to live for so many people these days; a world of benefits and foodbanks and choosing this tin or that and no treats for your child dressed in charity shop clothes. And he was just a stupid old man, privileged in a way, feeling sorry for himself because he had only a handful of coins in his pocket even though he could get a taxi – an effing taxi – all the way home whenever he wanted. And he felt ashamed. He turned to the freezer section thing next to him, took a cheap packet of out-of-date scotch eggs and queued up to pay and leave.

As he was leaving, he saw the man in the suit – clearly a security guard or a store detective, whatever – moving across the shop towards him. Making a beeline as it were.

He did not know why. Not for sure anyway. He had a horrible feeling the man was going to press a £5 note into his hand and say "Here, get yourself a hot drink" or, worse, "Get yourself a mirror and a comb or some toothpaste, mate." He would take the money, he thought, and give it to the young woman.

But he was not sure how he would do this nor what she would say. She might think him patronising or, worse, that he wanted something from her in return. He could not see her anyway. And the man was coming closer, so Ian slipped out of the shop, click-clicked to Bernard and hurried away.

**

Had Ian somehow managed to look at a map before he left Thetford, asked someone for directions or done anything other than assume that "going south" was the best route home, he would have learned that there were three ways to get to Ixworth.

He could go to the left along the A1066, a distance of 11.5 miles. Or, go down the A1088, which was the straightest and shortest route at 9.5 miles. He could instead go to the right and follow that A1344 again and, if he could, more by luck than anything else as per, make a sharp left turn halfway along by RAF Honington, that would get him to Ixworth in 10.7 miles.

Ian being Ian, he just went straight down south on the A1088, figuring that at some stage he'd see signs for Ixworth and, in due course, probably tomorrow, signs for Ipswich and Felixstowe and home at the Ferry. And, by a complete and utter fluke, he was correct.

He knew, having thought about Alex and Joe and Beth at various times as he walked along, that at some stage before this walk ended, he would need to think more about Adam.

He trawled his memory. And there were happy times to remember on the holiday. He tried to focus on these, from the day of their arrival, when Adam chose pick-and-mix sweets from a supermarket, through to that last evening, when he had eaten beans on toast and had pushed them up his nose to make the others laugh. And they had.

But always – always – his mind kept coming back to that last fateful day. Those final moments. And the aftermath, which even now seemed a blur of pain and agony. He walked on, trying to blank his mind.

As Norfork gave way to Suffolk, Ian thought after a while that this was a rather pretty part of the journey. But still, it was hard going. Pavements. Concrete. Roads. On and on. With villages few and far between in this bleak landscape. It was exhausting.

Euston – now back in Suffolk – was a pleasant village. And they sat on a verge. Gathered their breath. Shared a scotch egg. And water; Ian squirting the last from the bottle into Bernard's mouth. And then they were on their way again.

They stopped, some way further down the road, at Fakenham Magna. Another village. One more village sign. Another village church. Shared the second scotch egg. No more water though. A longer stop this time. Then up and away again. This endless journey.

When Adam was a baby, Ian would hold him high above his head with his strong left hand, lifting Adam up and down. And Adam would laugh and splutter and the drool from his mouth would ooze out and land on Ian's face. He'd shout "Aarrgghh!" and they'd both laugh.

They went to see a film at Cineworld in Ipswich one summer afternoon. That last summer. Just the two of them. He could not recall the film, but they entered the cinema late and it was pitch black and Ian somehow got his thigh stuck between a seat at the end of a row and the wall. Adam had gone and sat on someone else's lap. They both laughed about that.

They'd camped in the garden that summer too. Ian and Joe and Adam and Bernard. The three of them filling the tent side by side by side. Bernard, at the other end, crawling his way up and resting his head first next to Ian who pushed him away (dog's breath), and to Joe who did the same (dog farts), and to Adam who hugged him tight and said, "I love you, Bernie."

Ian and Bernard stopped for a fair old while, mid-afternoon, at the village of Honington, which was stuck in the 1940s. They wandered around and saw a primary school that seemed vaguely familiar. A graveyard full of bumps and slopes and angled headstones. Someone shouted "Hi-De-Hi!" at him as if to say "Cheer up!" and he smiled vaguely at the man.

A top up of the water bottle from a tap outside the church and the cheapest chocolate bar from a corner shop to eat later and they were on their way again. Their slog – for that is what it now was – broken only by the sound of jet fighters taking off and coming into land at the nearby air base.

And, with Ian carrying Bernard for the umpteenth time, they eventually came into Ixworth Thorpe. One of another hard-to-distinguish-from-each-other villages where you could swap one village sign for another and walk around by the stores and the church and the school and the sense of lost-in-time stillness and not know which village was which. They went over to the far side of the green, out of sight, and had a rest and a snooze (quite a long one actually), before setting off once more.

It struck Ian, as he walked along thinking about Adam, that he – Adam – was always saying, "I love you." I love you, Daddy. I love you, Mummy. I love you, Alex. I love you, Bethy. I love you, Joe-Joe. I love you, Bernie.

Ian had forgotten that. The I love yous. And he was pleased that he remembered. He did not know how Adam had learned it or why he said it so much. It was not said in a, what was it, a needy way. Just as a simple expression. And Ian remembered that he would always say it back to Adam. He had forgotten that too.

And Ian walked on and on and every snapshot he had in his head, each scene he replayed in his mind from then on had Adam saying, "I love you." And somehow, and Ian was not sure how or why, that seemed to make him feel a little happier.

By the time they got into Ixworth and had a look around, it was already getting dark. Ian did not know where the hours had gone today. He had tried to pace themselves as best he could, knowing both he and Bernard were getting close to the end of what they could do. They were old men finishing their incredible journey sometime soon.

He bought a plain sausage from the fish and chip shop and the man behind the counter, all grumpy face and surly manner, topped up his water bottle for him. They sat on a bench and ate and drank and Ian looked at Bernard, really looked at him, and saw what he should have seen for a while now. A dog that had really had enough of all this palaver.

Ian stroked Bernard and made a fuss of him. Then carried him up and down and round and about looking for somewhere to sleep for the night. He had hoped to find woodland or a field or somewhere away from people where they could bed down nice and safely. But it was all shops and houses and bus stops and cars and to-ing and fro-ing. And so, eventually, he made his way to the village hall and thought that behind this building was as good a place as any.

***

Ian leaned against the wall behind the village hall, Bernard by his side. There was, frankly, nowhere else to go at this time of night in this type of place. This built-up area. It was a ramshackle hidey-hole with grass and mud and brambles all around, but there were no footprints here or trodden-on cans or screwed-up crisp packets or anything like that or worse. So, he thought they'd be safe here for the night.

But he still felt wide awake, and so he reached into his jacket pocket and there he was, a moment or two later, ready to write another page in the baby booklet. He thought the booklet, to be honest, was now a right old mess. Half-completed entries. Scribbled notes. Scribbled-out notes. That jerky stickman. His wibble-wobble stick dog. Thumb marks. A smear of blood from goodness knows when. A brown smear that looked rather unpleasant. He'd have to somehow tidy it up when he got back home. Maybe even try and buy another one from somewhere and fill it all in again neatly.

Ian turned to the headings towards the back of the booklet, just before the notes section where, as someone looking at it for the first time might think, he seemed to have drawn a large penis and written "Anus" next to it. (They'd have to go, for sure.) He looked at the last heading that he was expected to fill in. *My Wishes for You Are*. He thought a while and simply wrote a list, in no particular order, of the main things that came to mind.

My wishes for you, my darling grandson, are that:
You are so very, very loved. Mummy and Daddy are always happy.
You can shout and sing and dance with joy.
You can press your face against a window so your nose is squashed flat. and you can see right up your nostrils.
You can talk to Mummy and Daddy about anything whenever you want.
You can put your pants on your head and socks on your hands and run around pretending to be a monster.
You will hug all the time.
You will always say how much you love each other.

Ian stopped to have another think and decided there were other things he wanted to write. Things that were important to him and that he wanted Pudding to know.

About himself. And Pudding. Grandpa and grandson.

And he thought, he knew, he'd probably never be able to say these things out loud. Being him. The way he was. So, if he wrote them down, they would always be there for Pudding. And Pudding would forever know how his grandpa felt about him.

And my wishes for us, from your loving grandpa, are that:
You know how much I love you with all my heart.
We will see each other as much as we can.
I will always be here for you.
We will play Doctor Who and the Daleks and we will run through the woods together to get to the Tardis and fly away.
I will carry you on my shoulders. And hold you in my arms. And kiss you. And tell you I love you every time I see you.
We will make home-made cakes together and eat as many as we want. We will have lots of milkshakes too.
You will be the best grandson I could ever wish for.
I will be the best grandpa I could possibly be.
I love you.

He sat there for a while, re-reading what he had written, with Bernard's head resting on his leg. And he wondered if it was all rather, what was the correct word for it? Schmaltzy? Was there such a word? He thought there was and that it was an apt description. It was all just too… sentimental. And he wondered whether Kate would raise her eyebrows when she read it. And if the children would laugh at their silly old man. And Hannah, he thought, in particular, might not like it at all. He did not think, what with one thing and another, that Hannah liked him very much. If at all. She was just being polite. And that made him terribly sad.

So, he lifted the page and put his fingers on the edge of it, ready to rip it out and tear it into little pieces. And he got as far as tugging at it, and it ripped a bit, and then he stopped. And read again what he had put. And he thought about it.

And he decided that this was what was in his heart, daft and sentimental though it may well be, and he wanted Pudding, his grandson, to know it.

He then went back and, as if to emphasise everything, drew a little heart next to each of the comments and shaded those hearts in. Then he read it again and decided that this was now all too sickly sweet and sentimental, so he went back to one line, *You can put your pants on your head and socks on your hands and run around pretending to be a monster* and changed it to *bottom monster* and drew a big plump bottom next to it. And that, he concluded, was that, and it was time to get some sleep.

24
ANOTHER POLICE VISIT

Everyone – Alex and Hannah, Beth and Glenn, Joe and Yasmin – was due round at The Cape at 20.00 for something to eat. An Indian takeaway – the usual set meal for six plus one or two veggie extras – collected by Alex and Hannah on the way over. Cakes by Yasmin. Drinks and an update from Kate.

At 19.20, as Kate was putting on her makeup – going through what Ian called her 101-point checklist – there was a knocking on the front door. Assuming this was Beth, come early for a worry and some reassurance, Kate went to answer it.

And there was Call Me Lisa standing on the doorstep and, from her face, looking like she had something important to say. Just Lisa though, on her own, not with a colleague, thank goodness. So, Kate knew this was not going to be that "please sit down" news. That Ian had been found dead.

Kate pulled her dressing gown around her, apologised for her appearance (although she looked just fine) and invited Call Me Lisa inside. They made their way through to the living room where they had talked the other day. And Kate sat in the stripey armchair to the left of the fireplace – Ian's chair – and Call Me Lisa sat in the one to the right (Bernard's chair as and when he could).

They exchanged the courtesies of greetings and Call Me Lisa asked, in a polite and relaxed way, when it was that Ian had left home. And Kate replied that it was on Monday the fourth of July, sometime in the afternoon. Call Me Lisa took out her phone and pressed buttons and scrolled down, back and forth, to the point where Kate wanted to shout, "So what's the news... what's happened to Ian... what do you have to tell me?" And Call Me Lisa asked if Kate, or anyone, had heard from Ian since, you know. And Kate answered, "No," and was relieved by the question as it meant for sure that Ian was still alive.

And Call Me Lisa started talking, quite carefully, as though she had rehearsed what she was going to say and how she was going to say it, in a bland and neutral voice. And it was this, the rehearsed nature of the opening words, that suddenly alarmed Kate. She was about to just say, right now, point-blank, "Is Ian dead?" but she hesitated and listened to what Call Me Lisa said right through to the end.

"Um. As part of our enquiries into a missing person who might perhaps be vulnerable... at risk... possibly a danger to themselves... we do a number of things... checks, really. Background and other checks."

Kate could have screamed at this point. The mannered sentences. The carefulness of it all.

"As part of that, our colleagues in Norfolk have been making enquiries in Hunstanton... where I think your son and daughter said he might go... and he, your husband, has been there."

Kate nodded, as if to say – to cry out – go on, tell me more.

"So, Ian left here on Monday the fourth of July, and it seems he walked, with his dog... Bernard... all the way to Hunstanton. He arrived there on Tuesday, the 12th, in the evening, and... he... spent the night there... and set off home on the 13th, Wednesday just gone, the next morning. So, if he keeps up the same pace, he should be back home on... Wednesday or Thursday this coming week."

Kate sat back in the stripey armchair, absorbing these words, making sense of them. Something in those sentences stuck out in her mind. The way it had been said.

"He's been reported as being fit and well... the walk along

the coast in all that lovely sunshine must have done him good...
and he's on his way back. So that's a positive."

"Where did he spend the night?" Kate cut in, with an equally
calm and balanced voice and just as forced and unnatural.

Call Me Lisa shrugged and made a puffing noise with her
mouth and said, "I don't know." Although she clearly did – and
was not saying all that she knew.

"A B&B? A hotel? Somewhere else?"

"I'm not sure. A private residence I think."

"You think? You don't know?"

"A private residence. Someone he met there, um, put him up
for the night, I believe."

"A woman? He stayed the night with a woman."

"I couldn't say."

"Can't or won't say?"

"I don't know. I've just been told he walked to Hunstanton,
stayed the night, and is coming home ... and he's okay. Safe
and well and happy."

"I bet he's happy," thought Kate.

There was an uneasy silence. Kate realised that Call Me Lisa
surely knew more than she was letting on – who the Norfolk
Police had spoken to and where and what Ian had done and
where he had been and with whom – but was not going to say.
Data protection. Privacy. All of these things.

"I can tell you," Call Me Lisa went on, "that there have been
posters of your husband put up all over Hunstanton seafront
and we think he may have seen those and headed on home. So
well done to whoever put those everywhere."

Kate nodded, distracted for a moment, realising that would
be Alex and Joe. Her good boys. Maybe Glenn too, going up
and down the coast in his van, fitting stairlifts and ceiling hoists.
Maybe he'd been up there one day. Bless him.

After a little more conversation – the police weren't going to
search any more but do let me know when Ian returns and blah
de blah – Call Me Lisa was up out of the armchair as if she

were late for something else. Kate showed her to the front door.

Call Me Lisa stood in the doorway and turned to look at Kate, and Kate thought, you know, you jolly well know my husband spent the night with another woman. But you're not going to tell me.

Call Me Lisa put out her hand and Kate shook it and turned away. And Kate went back indoors and shut the front door behind her. Possibly a little louder than she would normally do.

***

Alex and Hannah, with Alex driving and Hannah holding the Indian takeaway in a big box between her feet, were the first to arrive at The Cape.

Just at the moment that Call Me Lisa was driving out in the police car. Alex pulled his car to the side to let her through and went to open his window to speak to her. But she nodded and smiled as they came alongside each other and kept going.

"Please yourself," Alex said, before turning to Hannah; "she's in a hurry," he added.

"Good news," Hannah said and Alex was not sure if she were telling him or asking him.

"I guess so," Alex replied. "Yes, for sure. Has to be," he went on, sounding more cheerful, she'd have stopped otherwise, surely? To have warned him that his mum would be distressed.

Alex remembered the terrible moment a few nights before when Call Me Lisa was looking around the garden and he was seeing it through her eyes. All the possible burial places for his stupid old Dad; the sunken patio, the wonky shed and bed after bed full of turned-over weeds. Alex was only grateful that the old man had not built the underground shelter he had talked about – "in case of nuclear attack or aliens" – which would have probably seen the whole of the garden give way into the sea; to Call me Lisa, a sunken mausoleum full of irritating old people they'd killed, culminating in Dad. The most irritating old person of all.

And Beth had piped up – "There's something I've got to say!" – and he thought she was going to tell Call Me Lisa about the postcard from Great Yarmouth written not by Dad but by someone pretending to be him. And she'd have stood there like Hercule Poirot at the end of some film where she'd look accusingly at each of them in turn. And pointing too, most likely. Then Call Me Lisa would demand to see the postcard and he'd hand it over all shame-faced and embarrassed. The next thing they knew she'd have called in dogs and forensics and goodness knows what to turn the house upside down and dig out the garden.

But Beth had said, in a voice cracking with emotion that they... the family... when they went to Hunstanton... with Adam... used to go to the Pier... in Hunstanton... and the beach at Old Hunstanton... and that Dad... my lovely dad... would have done that this time... on his own... and walked from one to the other... alone with Bernard... along the clifftop. Her voice tailed away... and stopped... and finally started again... "He's going to throw himself off the cliffs."

Alex let themselves in with the key he still had on his keyring. Took the big box from Hannah and went through to the kitchen, Hannah a few steps behind. "Hello-oo-oo," he called out in a cheery voice.

Kate was there, busying around taking out plates and bowls and knives and forks and spoons and glasses and bottles of Coke Zero and lemonade and orange juice (smooth, no bits, for Glenn). She was putting them on trays ready for the children, their partners, whoever, to take through to the big table in the orangery.

Alex went up and kissed Kate on the cheek. Hannah held back. Kate then slipped her arms around Alex, quite unexpectedly, and pulled him close, her head on his shoulder. This alarmed Alex and he thought for one horrifying moment that she was going to sob out the words, "Your dad has been found dead at the bottom of the cliffs." It was the best part of a minute – a lifetime for Alex – before she spoke.

"Your dad's alright," she said quietly, stepping back and patting Alex on his shoulders with her hands.

Alex studied her face, her blank mask of a face and thought she would have been more delighted. "Is he safe? I mean, what's been happening? Is Bernard okay?"

Kate turned away, taking trays out from the side of this cabinet and that, and one kept under the sink in case there were drips from the pipe that Ian had fixed (or not fixed properly) not so long ago.

"He's, ah, walked to Hunstanton… like we thought… took him a week… the police have spoken to people who saw him… met him there… and now he's walking home… he should be back on Wednesday or Thursday. Bernard's fine."

Kate spoke in a calm and balanced voice in between taking a carton of Indian food out and putting it on a tray followed by another and so on. "Here," she said, holding a tray out towards Hannah. "Take this through please."

As Hannah left, Alex stepped forward towards Kate. "And that's it? He's walked there, and walked back, simple as that. There's more to it than that surely? Has he had a breakdown? What did the policewoman say?"

Kate filled up more trays with cartons of Indian food, turning this way and that, first to a drawer, then to the sink, and back to the Indian food and the trays.

"She didn't say much… she just had some notes… The Norfolk Police went up and down Hunstanton… showing his photo I imagine… and he was recognised… and he must have talked to someone… I don't know who, she did not say… and he is fit and well and coming home."

"So that's good news, Mum. Isn't it. Good news?"

And she turned and smiled at him, and she was about to say something else, to answer, to fill things out, but then everyone – Beth and Joe and Glenn and Yasmin – was piling in through the front door and shouting and laughing and joking and commenting on Hannah's swelling tummy. Kate pushed a tray of Indian foil cartons at Alex and sent him into the orangery.

There were whoops and cheers and all sorts of noises from the hallway as Alex stopped off en route to the orangery to share the good news. Dad's walked to Hunstanton. He has NOT thrown himself off the cliff – a huge cheer for that – and he is now walking home. He should be back for Wednesday or Thursday. Another big cheer. And Bernard's fine too. One more huge cheer.

And Beth came bounding into the kitchen, quickly followed by Joe, and threw, literally threw, herself into Kate's arms and hugged her and sobbed and Joe, not normally outwardly affectionate, put his arms round both of them and hugged them hard. And he picked up a tray of plates and glasses and was gone in case anyone saw he was crying as well.

After they had all been back and forward to the kitchen a time or two and gabbled excitedly to each other and hugged a bit more and Yasmin did a twerky bottom dance thing, they all sat around the table, with their plates and side plates and knives and glasses and started eating and drinking; helping themselves to whatever they wanted.

It was quite like old times with everyone chatting away and talking over each other and sharing stories and making fun of each other. Asking how Hannah was getting along. And they all said that Kate must tell them "the moment" Ian arrived home (with Bernard), and they'd all come round that night. And Alex said he'd hug Dad. Joe replied that Dad didn't like huggy stuff. And Beth just said, straight out, that she'd punch the stupid old man but then tell him she loved him.

Finally, as the evening neared the end, they all turned more and more often, instinctively, towards Dad's chair at the head of the table. There was that big old box on it, and they shoved all the empty and half-empty cartons and dirty serviettes and leftover stuff into it. Later, Kate would pull off the cheap tablecloth she'd bought from Tesco and use that to squash everything down into the box before taking it to the grey bin out the back.

Alex raised his glass – well, the can of cider he'd found at the back of the fridge – and said, in a careful voice. "To Dad, may we see you soon," and, in a louder voice, "you silly old sod!"

They all raised whatever was closest to hand – a glass, a bottle of water, a piece of naan bread in Joe's case – and toasted Ian as loud as they could. "YOU SILLY OLD SOD!"

Then they were up and packing away and saying goodbye and they all – even stiff-backed Glenn – kissed and hugged Kate goodbye. And nobody seemed to notice, and Alex seemed to have forgotten, that Kate was a heck of a lot quieter than they might have expected her to be.

***

Kate sat at the dressing table in the bedroom looking at herself in the mirror as she brushed her hair. There was a time, she thought, when I did not need to wear makeup and looked just fine without it. So many years ago.

Now, only the smeary and ever-thickening lens of her glasses – and a slightly dimmed light – stopped her from seeing how she really looked.

Old, crumbling and falling to pieces, she thought. Each line, every wrinkle, a battle scar from being married for 30-odd years to that ridiculous man.

It had been a love match, for sure, when they'd met at university all those years ago. Still was, in a baggy old cardigan kind of way. They were an odd couple even then; him instinct and emotions and her organised and practical. But they hung out together and seemed to laugh a lot and then one thing led to another and there they were married with a house by the sea and a mortgage and jobs and children.

He was, of course, autistic, or at least somewhere on the

spectrum. Not that anyone had ever said. And he would have responded, loudly and with indignation, if it had ever been suggested. It was that – the autism that was so much part of him – that she had loved. His enthusiasms, his over-reactions, the childlike sense of wonder at times. And his inability to stop his thoughts coming straight down and out of his mouth; for good or bad. Bad mostly.

And they had had their children. Alex, who Ian had said was ugly within seconds of her giving birth. Beth, who was so like him, and who he adored, and called his "favourite daughter". Joe, who seemed to sometimes get a little lost in the mix. And Adam as well. Their little and late surprise – their "surprise and delight", Ian called him – who lost his life in Hunstanton and that, the death, had come close to destroying Ian with his overwhelming guilt. All of them in their own ways, really.

Kate took off her glasses and put them to one side. Her face looked better like that, she felt, without glasses; blurrier and harder to see.

She opened and dabbed a finger into a pot, rubbing the cream wherever she thought the lines on her face were worst. Everywhere, really. She should slap it on thick like a face mask. *The Phantom of the Opera.*

She put more on her neck. You could date me, she felt, by the lines on my neck. Much like the rings on a tree. "Goosy-Goosy" neck, he called it, whatever that meant. The stupid man.

Kate was going to leave him once. Ian. When he was at his worst. And there had been many bad times over recent years as Ian struggled to come to terms with what had happened. Shutting everyone out. Being so angry. Turning in on himself, the guilt eating away at him.

She took a little key from the back of her jewellery box and unlocked the bottom drawer to the left of the dressing table. Took out an envelope tucked away inside. Looked through what was there – a letter, a card, a dried flower that had almost fallen apart, and a string of photos from a photobooth. Then put them back.

She had met someone at work. Just an ordinary fellow. A widower with two grown-up children. A porter. They'd literally bumped into each other – she had walked into a trolley he was pushing as she came round a corner of a corridor – and it went from there. For a while. He'd wanted her to leave Ian. But she couldn't. Ian. Their children. The home. She wouldn't know where to start. So, she finished it. And was never sure whether she regretted it or not. The affair. Or the ending of it.

And she was reaching for what he called her strappy-band thing that she wrapped around her hair at night. Her ears if he started droning on when she was trying to sleep.

She peered – that was exactly the right word – at herself one more time in the mirror. Sucked in her cheeks. Turned her head from side to side.

"You look like a skeleton," she said out loud, her voice sounding strange in the emptiness. And no wonder, she thought in her head. You haven't eaten properly since the silly old fool left.

And now he had gone. Just vanished with Bernard. That ridiculous note. Those horrible flip-flops that she had thrown one after the other into the garage for him to clean up when he got back. As she knew he would. She did not know when. She had assumed he would have got as far as Rendlesham Forest. Stayed the night. Spooked himself. Then come home the next day, having fallen into mud, or down a riverbank, or into the sea. Half-dressed and stumbling. The old dog just behind.

She found it hard to believe he had made it all the way to Hunstanton. And on foot, presumably. All without mishap. That, somehow or other, after a week or so of walking – inevitably without washing properly, having a shave, changing his clothes – he could spend the night with a woman. She laughed out loud suddenly. Almost raucously. The thought of it. She laughed again, not so loudly this time. She was not sure how she felt about that. The whole damn thing of it.

And so, he was on the way home. And she could imagine him arriving, limping up the drive as if he had just staggered away from a head-on car crash. And he would nod and grunt and push by her − she'd recoil in horror at the sight and smell − and he'd say he needed the toilet *now!* Then she'd wait for Bernard as if it were the ending of *The Incredible Journey* when the family thought their two dogs and a cat had got lost and died in the mountains. Suddenly, they had all appeared over a hill, and everyone screamed and shouted with joy and lived happily ever after.

She wondered if Ian would tell her about this woman. And whether she would tell him about Richard, the porter from the hospital. Who was still at the hospital, although she usually only smiled at him when passing in a corridor. And, when he stopped her the other day to ask how she was − because he must have seen the newspaper article − she had cut the conversation short, albeit as nicely as she could.

Kate opened another little pot on the dressing table. Dabbed a finger in and rubbed the cream into an elbow. Then again with a finger on the other hand onto the other elbow.

Then rubbed some cream into both hands, mostly on top, where her hands seemed to have acquired liver spots and bulgy veins. "Wear gloves," the daft old man had said when he first spotted them.

And so, finally, Kate got into bed. She could sleep on her usual side, the left. Or his side, the right, nearest the door (so that, as he had once said, he could tackle any madman who broke in and save her). Or the middle. She went across the middle. The whole bed. And lay there thinking all sorts of thoughts.

25
IXWORTH TO NEEDHAM MARKET

SUNDAY 17th JULY

(14.8 MILES, 4 HOURS 53 MINUTES)

As they slipped out of their hidey-hole behind the village hall at Ixworth not long after sunrise, Ian wondered just how much longer they could keep going on this endless journey. Not long, he thought, and that's a fact.

He reckoned it was close to 20 miles to Needham Market. They had walked that distance in a day before, into Great Yarmouth, but it was a slog then and it was somehow worse now with little food and water and hardly any money. After that, it was at least another day or two to go towards Ipswich and on to Felixstowe and, finally, the Ferry. He did not know how they would do it.

Thing is, they were both exhausted. Physically and mentally. And he could not help but feel that Bernard was coming close to suffering. As he now was. One way or the other, he thought, this would be the last day. He hoped he would not end up in hospital. Or have to take Bernard to the vets.

They walked, slow and steady, in sunshine and growing warmth, down the A1088 heading south, maybe south-east. More trees and fields and, what was it, nothingness really. They trundled along.

Then crossed the A143, which would take them west or east.

Ian dithered for a moment, guided by the sun still low in the sky. They carried straight on. As they were.

By Grimstone End to the west and by Stowlangtoft to the east; magical-sounding places he'd never heard of. Just shimmering out there in the distance. They trudged onwards.

Ian blanked his mind as he walked along, focusing on putting one foot in front of the other. The slip-on shoe things he'd bought at the Tesco superstore were cheap and ill-fitting and downright uncomfortable. His sweat-soaked socks made his feet damp and blistery and he had to ignore all the discomfort, the pain, and just keep going.

And he smelled again, a sweet and sickly, almost decomposing, stink. It was as though his body had sweated out everything it could into his clothes. That sweat had then dried. And turned to moisture again as he walked. Then dried overnight once more. And was now turning to moisture again. The stench seemed to come from all over his body. And his clothes. Even his jacket that he had wrapped around his shoulders.

He ran his hands over his head and face. His hair was all flat and even though he ran his hands through to lift it up, it just sat there, stuck to his scalp. And he could feel his bald patch now. With his fingers. And he knew he should stop bothering it as it would just make it worse, as Kate would say, but he had to keep checking it. And his face was all red and sweaty, he thought, and felt all rough and lined with a white – pure-white – moustache and beard; if he pushed his lips out, he could see it. And it made him feel so, what was it, fed-up. No, stronger than that. Desperate.

And they reached a village called Norton which seemed to be one long road really.

A village hall. A primary school. A pub. A petrol station (where he refilled the bottle of water and bought an out-of-date packet of crisps to share with Bernard).

And they walked on and stopped for a while by a Salvation Army place. Just to catch their breath and recharge themselves.

It was here, on this grass verge in the middle of nowhere, that Ian really looked at Bernard properly, as if for the first time, on this long walk. He had been eating one crisp, putting the next on the ground in front of Bernard, eating another, one for him, the other for Bernard, and so on. Then he looked down to see a pile of crisps, uneaten and untouched, and Bernard stretched out, looking uncomfortable, on the grass.

And there was, what was it, how could he describe it… a thinness about his old pal. Not exactly emaciated, somehow the word came to him easily, but a boniness. Ian could see ribs that had never been noticeable before. And… he simply did not look like the solid, rather stocky, dog he had always been. This deterioration had happened in front of Ian's eyes. Over the past, well, however long it was they had been walking. The combination of walking so much and for so long and eating less and less, and stupid, processed food really, reducing Bernard to this.

Ian ran his fingers along Bernard's stomach, gently pushing and prodding here and there. And Bernard lifted his head and gazed at Ian, not looking as if he were saying, as he normally would, "Excuse me? Do you mind?" It was more a look that said, "Yes, I'm not feeling so good any more." And Ian found the growth with his fingers, and it was bigger than he thought. And that made him feel sad. And he vowed he would carry Bernard from now on.

He carried Bernard as carefully as he could for the next part of their journey towards Needham Market. He felt so hot and sticky. And it just seemed to go on and on forever.

Southwards, maybe south-east, down that A1088. It got busier in places and, at one point, came within touching distance of the roaring A14.

He moved on to another road, eastwards, to get away from the busier road, to Wetherden, and then on down towards Haughley and on still along a never-ending road by the side of the A14.

Ian knew that, for Bernard, the growth was now going to grow bigger and bigger, that much quicker, pressing on his stomach and his other organs, making him less hungry and getting thinner and thinner. The process had already begun and was now progressing quickly. The growth, which Ian had never been able to feel immediately before, was now easy to find with his fingers. And Bernard was not eating what he used to do. And Ian worried whether that was because he had not been giving him proper dog food lately; but sausage rolls and scotch eggs and nonsense.

He jiggled Bernard in his arms and the dog seemed comfortable enough with the careful repositioning. And Ian thought that next, the growth would press harder on his stomach, and he would be less likely to eat and Ian would have to feed him slivers of chicken and peas and soft-boiled rice. And, ever bigger, it would eventually press so hard that Bernard would wet and soil himself. And Ian thought that this, just before this really, had to be the time when it would be kinder to take him to the vets.

They stopped more and more often, to give Ian a breather, and he watched as Bernard, rather than settling down to rest and snooze, just stood there awkwardly. And he was not sure if this was because Bernard expected to be on the move again shortly or whether sitting down, laying down, was painful for him. Before lifting Bernard up again, Ian ran his fingers along and onto the growth, pressing it gently. Ian and Bernard looked at each other and Ian wished that Bernard could talk and tell him what to do.

There was a road, Tot Hill, that ran alongside the A14 and all the way to Needham Market.

Ian, carrying Bernard, walked along it, crossing the A14 towards Stowmarket and onwards.

He then just put his head down and walked and walked and walked to Needham Market.

***

It was the sign for – the teasing promise of – free tea and cake that made Ian divert towards the village hall at Needham Market and the Women's Institute meeting starting shortly at 14.30.

And his aching feet. His painful back. The shining sun on the back of his sweaty neck. His dry throat. The fact that he was carrying Bernard; the dog's tongue lolling out as if he, and not Ian, were doing all the hard work.

It had nothing to do with the obligatory talk on mental health. He'd happily listen to that or something on flower-arranging or weeding the garden if he could just sit down and have a nice cup of tea and a slice of Victoria Sponge. And gather his breath for half an hour.

"I'm sorry I'm late," he said as cheerfully as he could as he limped towards the two old dears standing by the door. They looked like they were about to close it. "I hope you're not waiting for me," he added jovially, putting Bernard down and reaching into his pockets for some change for the admission.

The old dears made various clicking and clucking sounds as if to say, "Leave it… we're in a hurry," and waved away the last few coins he held out in his hand. "We're all ready to start," one of them said. "If you'll come inside, please."

They stepped back to let Ian and Bernard walk through (hobble in, more like), and the roomful of mostly elderly women turned to look at them almost automatically as one, and then broke into a light round of applause as Ian and Bernard stumbled forwards.

Ian smiled and waved his left hand towards them and wondered whether they thought he might have an illness that made him walk like this. Or an artificial leg. And whether, if he played it up a wee bit, someone might fetch him a slice of cake.

"Keep going! Keep going!" one of the two old dears behind him said. Although he was not sure where he was meant to go. The other lady came up alongside of him and took him by the

311

elbow.

This made Ian feel awkward, the fussing around, the twitching, the flapping about. He had been in a wheelchair once, for a while, years ago, after he had broken an ankle falling off the promenade onto the beach. People talked over him to Kate. As if he were half-witted. This felt like that.

The room was almost full – standing room only – with rows of cheap wooden chairs in a semi-circle around a desk, and a couple of chairs to either side. And, behind it, an old-fashioned screen like his grandpa used to have for showing holiday slides. He went to sit at the back but there were no chairs to spare there. The old dears fiddled and faddled some more and moved him on. He limped forward as best he could.

To the front then, although he and Bernard would want to slip quickly to the back at the end where tea urns and plates of cakes were laid out across a trestle table. Even from near the front, he reckoned he could get to first place in the queue for cake before any of the elderly ladies.

He went to sit in the front row, but there were no seats there. It was all becoming something of a pantomime with the audience following his every move, oohing and aahing and laughing as he did a double-take and a stagger each time and had to carry on towards the front. Like a swot at school, he thought.

"Here," one of the old dears said, pointing to a chair next to the table. He sat down, going to turn the chair around towards the screen so he could see the slides as they came up. The other old dear stopped him.

So, Ian sat looking out towards the row upon row of faces watching him. And he pulled Bernard across towards him so they both sat together. He wished he had never come in and made a spectacle of himself. Now, he had to listen to some dreary old talk about loneliness and grief and mental well-being, when all he really wanted was that cup of tea and that slice of cake and a quick wee before he went on his way.

As the other old dear started talking about the importance of good mental health, and the audience turned towards her, he thought he'd sit back, shut his eyes for a while and let her sing-song soothing voice help him to relax. A semi-snooze followed by a big slab of cake washed down with hot, sugary tea. Lovely.

The old dear stopped talking. There was a ripple of polite applause. And a silence. He sat bolt upright wondering whether he had nodded off and snored or even worse.

They were all looking at him. Everyone. The old dears. The audience. The two old ladies at the back by the urns and plates and stuff. With bated breath as it were.

The old dear repeated what she had just said. "So please welcome today's speaker who is going to talk to us about his mental health journey," and she smiled at Ian as if to say "over to you".

Ian did not normally swear out loud or under his breath or even in his head. But he did on this occasion. "Arse bollocks," is what he thought as he rose reluctantly to his feet (although he did not say it out loud).

He knew, of course, and should have realised much earlier, that this was all a dreadful mistake, a confusion. That whoever was meant to be giving this talk had not turned up. The old dears at the door had assumed he was the speaker running late and, well, here he now was in front of everyone.

"Oh dear," Ian said, a more polite phrase than the one that had almost been on his lips. He paused for such a while that the audience became restless.

"I'm going to tell you about… my journey. I've just walked from Felixstowe to Hunstanton and am now coming back. I…" He laughed, a little nervously, and added, "But that's not what you want me to talk about." Everyone was looking at him and seemed to be unsettled in some way. As if he said the wrong thing.

"I, um, don't have any slides. I did stand on the cliffs at Hunstanton… but I didn't take any photos. And, er…" He stalled as his throat dried, and he looked around and saw a bottle of water and a glass on the table.

"That's better," he said, his hand shaking as he put the glass back down next to the half-empty bottle. He thought a while longer and, as the audience started to become ever-so-slightly restless again, he shut his eyes and began talking as slowly and as calmly as he could.

"I have everything. Had, anyway. I've been with my wife for... so many years. I have three children and they are happy. And that's what it's all about, isn't it really? Being happy." There was a ripple of noise, mumblings of agreement, and it somehow gave him the strength to go on.

"And they... our children... all have partners. We have to call them that these days, don't we? And they are... very nice... people. I'd be proud to be their dad." He stopped for a moment. To say the next sentence in his head. To see if he could say the words out loud without crumbling. "And I am going to be a grandfather... a grandpa... later this year." There were more sounds of approval and one or two of the elderly ladies clapped and then a few more and, before he knew it, everyone seemed to be clapping.

He opened his eyes, and they were looking at him and seemed happy, waiting on what he had to say next. He liked the clapping. It made him feel good.

"I've known heartbreak," he said, looking round and nodding. "We all have, haven't we, one way or the other? We've all had our share of rotten times... we've all lost a loved one, I'm sure."

The audience responded with sad faces and nods and comments, and he felt, in some unexpected way, filled with positive emotion.

"We lost our little boy, Adam, some years ago... at Hunstanton." He raised his hand at the reaction, with some of the ladies calling out to him. "It's okay. No, it's okay. I'm okay."

"All these years, I've bottled it up and suffered and shut myself off from everyone who... mattered."

314

He gulped. He should have said "who loves me" but knew that he would choke on the words.

"I had some sort of breakdown, I think... recently. And I walked to Hunstanton to... to, well, I was thinking about taking my own life."

And he felt the audience, as one, draw its breath as he pressed on.

"But... I didn't... obviously... I'm here."

He laughed nervously, then carried on before they could react.

"I'm alright. I'm not going to... not now... because of what I've discovered. What I've learned from my journey... about mental health... is... it's hard dealing with bad stuff, really horrible stuff, and it somehow feels easier to suppress it. I have for years, and it's rotted me away inside. My heart. And the longer you bottle it up the harder it is to let it go. You have to talk about things, I think."

He glanced at the elderly ladies in the audience. They were quiet and still and listening to him and their faces were full of concern. He hurried on before he flushed and became embarrassed and lost his nerve.

"And because of that, suppressing it all, I haven't been there for my wife and children, not for such a long time. I mean... I remember anniversaries and birthdays and... if the children need money, or their car breaks down, whatever, I'm there... I am. But I am not there in a way... emotionally. I've never told them how I feel about them."

He noticed one of the elderly ladies on the front row had her head down whilst another a few rows back dabbed at her eyes with a handkerchief and he wondered, suddenly, if this were all too bleak and miserable.

"But my journey... to Hunstanton and back... I've had all sorts of little adventures and people have been very kind and generous towards me... and there are good people and nice things and kindness out there and you have to go and find it

315

and embrace it."

He didn't know where he was going with this or quite what he was trying to say in his rambling, meandering, roundabout way. But then he looked up at the click of the door and a man, an earnest-looking man with horn-rimmed glasses, all hot and bothered, stood there watching him.

"And so, I'm going to go home today... end my long journey... and I am going to tell my wife and my children that I love them. And I am going to talk to people, professional people, about my thoughts and feelings. And I am going to kiss my wife and hug my children. And I am going to try to be the best husband, the best father... the best grandpa in the whole wide world."

There was a moment's silence. Ian was not sure if they were going to clap or if they were expecting him to go on with a fuller talk with various top tips and to do checklists.

So, in his awkwardness, he waved the man at the back forward.

Some of the elderly ladies began clapping. Others turned to see who he was gesturing towards. There was a chaotic minute or two of confusion when no one, except possibly Ian, knew what was going on.

Then, as the man approached Ian, they shook hands and the man said he was sorry he was late, and Ian replied that it was okay, and turned to the audience and bumbled through a few words saying how he was the warm-up act and now here he is ... the real speaker!

The proper speaker introduced himself and there was a round of applause for him as he opened his battered old leather satchel and took out a laptop and a USB stick and turned it all on and got everything together and just so in an organised manner. He looked up at the audience and smiled and introduced himself.

"My name is Martin Harris, and I am a counsellor working with families and young children. I also work for the Samaritans.

I'd like to talk to you today about mental health."

"I'm sorry I'm late… satnavs, eh… and I'd like to thank… my, er, predecessor, for standing in so admirably for me…"

He looked around to gesture for a round of applause. Just in time to see Ian grab a piece of cake from the trestle table and slip out the door with Bernard trotting close behind him.

***

As he strolled along the high street at Needham Market in the sunshine, Bernard in his arms, Ian took a long, last look around him. The pretty little church, the independent shops, some vibrant, others run down, and the pub at the far end of the high street.

And Ian guessed it must be a good 20 miles, some seven hours walking or more, much more really, to get back to Felixstowe Ferry. The quickest way would be to head up to the A14 bypass and walk along it with all the lorries thundering by to Felixstowe docks. And he'd arrive home, shattered and half-deaf and fed-up, somewhere between 23.00 and midnight. Maybe even later.

He did not want to get home in the early hours, waking Kate, having to explain himself, talk things over, all of that, and get washed and changed and ready for bed with Kate shouting "Pooh pooh. You smell!" at him. And it would all get tense and frazzled, and he'd end up sleeping on the sofa in the living room.

Ian sat on a bench near the pub. He lifted Bernard up from the pavement and put the dog by his side. Bernard stretched out, almost carefully, before resting his head on Ian's thigh.

And Ian stroked Bernard's head and felt, what was the word, ah no, he could not think of it. He sat for a while searching his mind. Wistful. Melancholic maybe. Something like that for sure.

He ran his hand along Bernard's back and then, as the dog

tipped backwards for a tummy rub, further along searching for the growth. And he found it again, so easily now, and realised that time was running out.

They'd had a good old go. Him and Bernard. When he had set off, he had no real plan. Other than to walk to Hunstanton and pay tribute to his beloved Adam. And it had been a long journey there for the two of them. But he felt it had done them good, physically and mentally. And it was nice to be together in the open air in their... thing... their doo-dah... their adventure. Yes, that was it. Their *Boys' Own* adventure.

Standing on the cliff – going too close to the edge – and meeting Sarah had been the turning points. He liked her. Felt sorry for her. Admired her in a way too. She had sacrificed her own life for her parents. He thought, when he got home, he would charge up the phone she had given him and text her a message to say he'd arrived safely. Maybe to stay in touch. Updating news to each other.

Things had been better after that. Paying tribute in his own way to Adam. Coming back with Charlie and the bicycle. It had started off so well. But things had gone wrong – losing the bicycle and the rucksack and Headless Charlie followed by the long trudge back with his mood up one minute and down in his boots the next. And so he had got here, dragged himself here, to Needham Market, and the talk at the Women's Institute thing, such as it was, had cleared his mind. He thought he had spoken quite... not elegantly... that was not it... but quite... no, it doesn't matter. He had spoken his thoughts aloud, and got his head straight at last.

Ian got up, lifting Bernard into his arms, and carrying him as much for the cuddle as anything else. And Ian turned round and about on the high street, not sure which way to go.

It was at this moment, when he was weighing up his various choices, that he had what he thought was just the most amazing stroke of luck he'd ever had. Some might say that, given all the posters that had been put up, the newspaper stories and the police having been made aware of him, the moment was inevitable at some stage on his journey. But the timing of it was certainly happenstance.

A police car being driven along the other side of the road slowed, crawled along and came across, pulling alongside him. A young policewoman opened the window and leaned out and laughed and said something like, "I think I should be asking for a selfie or your autograph." Ian did not quite catch what she said – or at least could not make any sense of the nonsense – and so he went in closer. "Ian. Ian Wilkerson?" she said cheerfully. "Jump in. We're taking you and Bernard home to Felixstowe Ferry."

There were two of them in front, two young policewomen, and they seemed tickled pink, pleased as punch, over the moon – just plain happy – that they had Ian and Bernard in the back of the police car. And they took it in turns to tell him about the story in the newspaper and pretty much repeated his children's comments word for word. And how his two boys had been up and down the coast looking for him and putting up posters. And how he'd been reported as missing to the police by his daughter and everyone was on the lookout for him. And how they – his family – must love him very, very much. Those were the exact words – "very, very much".

It was then, as they were coming up towards the Copdock Services, some 15 minutes away from home, that Ian bowed his head and wept.

And Bernard, who was by nature a stoic sort of fellow, put his head on Ian's lap as if to say "there, there, old chap".

They stayed like that until the police car pulled up outside The Cape, and one of the young policewomen got out and opened his door and said, with a flourish, "You're home, Ian, you're home at last."

And so he was.

PART FIVE:
HAPPY EVER AFTER

26
LIDL JESUS! OH
LIDLE JESUS!

Ian sat at the desk in what he now called his office – Joe's old bedroom – with Bernard stretched out by his feet. He had spent the last 20 minutes looking impassively at what he'd written on the computer screen. He was really waiting for his mobile phone to beep-beep-beep with an incoming call.

He gazed out of the window towards the sea. So rough and choppy. He'd always liked this time of year just after the clocks had gone back and Halloween and Bonfire Night still lay ahead.

And this was his favourite time of day. Just as it was getting dark. And it was cold and windy outside and snug and warm indoors. He and Bernard on their own. Ian waiting for this call. His mind wandering, as ever, all over the place.

The walk – that epic adventure – now seemed so long ago. And he wondered whether it, any of it, had made any real difference. With Kate. And Alex and Beth and Joe and Hannah and Glenn and Yasmin.

When he'd got home, Kate had been out, a swimming exercise class at the leisure centre. When she returned mid-evening, they sat and shared half a bottle of wine, and he told her about his journey. She asked one or two vague questions about Hunstanton and what he did there. They went to bed, and she brushed him off with a "not tonight", and he lay back looking at the ceiling for ages, wondering why he'd bothered coming home at all.

It was much the same with the children, after an initial flurry of interest and some anger from Beth at the next family get-together. It all just settled back into the way it was. Life went on. As if he'd never been away.

Ian had got himself a job though, working from home as an online editor for a local news service, putting out daily updates and weekly summaries of what was happening in and around Felixstowe Ferry. He had seen the ad when scrolling aimlessly through Facebook pages with nothing better to do. Applied for it, not expecting to be interviewed, let alone be offered the post.

He suspected that there were relatively few replies – an always-on-call job with no prospects and a low salary – although his years living in the area and having worked for the council and supposedly knowing everyone and everything hereabouts was in his favour. He had started at the beginning of September, and it was on-off work, a flurry of press releases to wade through and calls to make and calls to be returned with long periods of quiet in between when he wrote up the news and posted it online on a website and on Facebook and on Twitter.

The news was a mix of dreary information and stuff and nonsense. Tide charts, the opening times of local post offices and supermarkets and petrol stations. Badly written press releases to be put out verbatim from local sponsors. And so many endless interviews – a child (with smug-looking parents) who had grown pots of water cress for charity, a man (with mad, staring eyes) who could recount all the numbers of Pi from memory, and so on. Ian enjoyed it.

Ian's mind, to his surprise, seemed to be working better; at least for now. He had his checklists and notes and did his memory and other exercises regularly. He still flip-flopped over odd words and phrases that wouldn't come quickly enough but had learned to slow his speech and look for other words when that happened. The lump on his shoulder was a fatty mass that subsided with antibiotics. He was, as the GP's letter that he'd left on the side so long ago revealed, in the early stages of Type 2 diabetes. He now took tablets for that and walked more and ate better and was losing weight, which helped with his blood-sugar numbers.

Bernard – beloved Bernard – was thinner and did not want to walk as much. But he still seemed happy and had more good days than bad ones when he did not want to eat or was sick when he did. Ian fed him by hand three times a day; thin-cut pieces of chicken and peas and mouthfuls of rice. And he lay down by Ian's feet or in the basket over by the radiator for most of the time. Ian let Bernard walk around the garden whenever he wanted to go outside. Now and then, they would venture a little further, just down to the jetty where Bernard would stand at the end and gaze out beyond the boats to the horizon. As if remembering Hunstanton.

Ian and Sarah had become good friends, "mobile phone pen pals", if that were the right description, over the past few months. He had texted her to say he had arrived home safe and well. And she had replied the next day with a jolly text about being so busy at work and how she was going to go on holiday to Edinburgh for a week soon to see the sights. And they'd texted, once or twice a week, ever since. Chit-chat. They'd both kept it just so; warm and friendly, with an occasional *x* and a heart at appropriate moments. It was nice to have a friend like that, thought Ian.

And then Ian's mobile phone went beep-beep, and he picked it up to see if it were a call or a text message (having set the same sound for both, well, for everything really). And it was a text message from the man he had spoken to earlier that morning who had said he would call back once Ian had spoken to his regional editor. *So, what will you pay for an interview and a photograph?* Ian sighed, recalling that the regional editor had confirmed that, as a free local online news service, they could not pay for anything at all.

Happy to do an interview and run the photograph but cannot pay; sorry. And then the abrupt reply, *I will take it to the nationals!* Ian texted back *OK.* A long wait. And Ian wondered what the next comment would be from this man who claimed to have seen the face of Jesus in a bag of King Edward potatoes from Lidl.

Sunday Sport will pay good money for a vegetable like this came the response. Ian thought, "Only if it is shaped like a penis or a vagina." But he just put *Best of luck* and turned his phone off for a coffee break. He click-clicked to Bernard who stood up slowly and Ian lifted him carefully and carried him downstairs, smiling and chuckling to himself as he went. Lidl Jesus. He was, he thought, happier, all in all, than he had been for a while; he just had to sort things out with Kate and the family but that would all fall into place once Pudding was born. Not long now. Just a week to go.

***

That evening, they had another family get-together in the orangery at The Cape. Ian and Kate. Alex and Hannah. Beth and Glenn. Joe and Yasmin. They all knew this would be the last before Pudding arrived. That it would – should – be a joyous occasion.

Some bright spark – Alex, most likely – had suggested they had a curry, a really hot one. What with Hannah being seven days away from her due date. It might trigger something, Kate had added. Not at the table hopefully, Ian had replied, and pulled a face at the thought of Hannah's afterbirth laying there like a big bloody blancmange on the wooden floor, Bernard circling it warily.

And they all came back and forth into the orangery and fiddled about with plates and food and drinks and everything; other than Hannah, who sat at the top of the table. And they all petted and made a fuss of Bernard who lay on the armchair in the far corner, taking in the last few rays of sunshine. Then they got stuck in.

All the talk through the starters was about Hannah… and Alex… and the baby. And how ready they were for the birth.

Hannah had packed a bag. That was in the hallway ready to go. Just as soon as her waters broke. Or she felt, not spasms or convulsions… contractions. And Alex had a mostly empty diary for tattoo appointments these next two weeks; and, when it came to it, he'd text a colleague, the one that looked like Charles Manson, to get those re-booked.

Hannah said how her dad had got the smaller bedroom ready for the baby and had built shelves and a cupboard in a recess – Kate and Beth both said at the same time that it was a good job Ian hadn't done anything – and how he'd painted the walls… and Mum had made the curtains… on and on and on and bloody on.

And the dad had put down new carpet for them all round the house as a present. And he'd sorted the garden, ready for the spring, so the baby could sit on the lawn and put up a shed too for good measure. And built a third runway for Heathrow most probably, thought Ian, although he did not say.

The sainted mum had made curtains – lovely stripes here, a wonderful shade of something or other there – for every room in the house. And cleaned the oven… and baked cakes… and made knitted baby clothes… and crocheted soft toys. And would probably deliver the baby as well if she could. And all of this… this hoo-hah… infuriated Ian but he was not sure why.

Through the main courses, Hannah spoke a little about how she was feeling as all of them, well, Kate, Beth and Yasmin, seemed to want to know the details.

And she talked about how she had to sleep on her side at night and, lowering her voice, how her boobs were like something or other (Ian could not quite hear but it was something "massive") and, leaning forward to Kate, how her, you know… and Ian (thankfully) did not hear anything of the rest of that conversation at all.

Ian then changed the subject and asked if they had settled on a name yet. He wondered, but did not say, whether they might name the child after Hannah's father, Kevin (which would be the last straw; really it would).

Alex said that, yes, they had chosen Pudding's name and they wanted to tell everyone after the birth, when they would text everyone with the baby's name and weight and the time of birth. If that was okay. It was just their sweet little secret right now. And Beth asked whether, if she had a guess and got it right, they would confirm the name. And Alex said no, because you'd all want a guess and that would be six guesses in all! And Hannah added that if anyone was close, they'd want a second guess and, before you knew it, there would be six... 12... 18... 24 guesses!

Kate asked if the baby would be a Cartwright, after Hannah, or a Wilkerson, after Alex. They glanced at each other, and Hannah said Wilkerson... because... we'll get married sometime. And there was whooping and whistling and, after all sorts of questions, Alex said, quite firmly, "We'll marry when we're ready... now... change of subject!"

Yasmin asked Hannah what she would do after the baby was born and whether she'd go back to work... or teacher training... whatever.

And Hannah had replied that she wouldn't be able to go back to the teacher training as it was full-time. But that she would be looking to get a part-time job – something arty if she could – at some point, "to help out".

And that, and Ian almost groaned aloud at this moment, her mum and dad were going to look after the baby when she was at work. Of course, they bloody well will! But Ian did not say this.

As they came towards the end of the meal, and it was time to pack everything away, Hannah suddenly said, looking at Ian for the first time that evening, that she'd be happy to tell everyone what Pudding's middle name would be. And they all looked at each other and back at Hannah as if to say, "Yes please! If you're sure?"

And she said, in a surprisingly emotional voice, "Our baby," and she reached out and took Alex's hand "… will be called, Uh, Uh, Uh, three syllables… and then Charles, his middle name… and then Wilkerson." This simply stunned Ian because Charles was his middle name… and Joe's … and his uncle's who had died … and his grandpa's… and his great-grandpa's… and it was the family name, really.

Everyone said that was nice… and lovely… and just right. And then, not long after, they finished the meal – Hannah's nether regions all still stretched but intact – and packed away all the leftovers and empty plates and Glenn popped to the toilet… and Yasmin did too… then Beth, just in case, and finally Ian and Kate were standing by the front door seeing them all out. Ian patted Hannah on the shoulder as she was leaving and said thank you, ever so quietly. And she smiled back at him and kissed him on the cheek. And Ian and Kate were left standing there, in the hallway on their own, and they turned and faced each other and for the first time in ages, they embraced and kissed (a proper kiss, not a dainty peck on the cheek).

***

Ian sat up in bed, his arms folded across his chest, watching Kate sitting at the dressing table.

Going through her beauty regime. Eleven, you know, whatsit things, to do in all. Before she came to bed.

Halfway through now. It just seemed to take ages. So much longer every night.

"That went well," Ian said, before adding, "the meal… they're all happy, aren't they? All of them. Together." Half question, half statement.

Kate turned and looked at him, nodding agreement. "Yes, they are. Three lovely couples." She took off her glasses and started brushing her hair.

"Joe and Yasmin are a good match. You wouldn't think it, but they are. He's got a good one there, Joe," Ian said.

"And Beth and Glenn... I hope they can have a baby next. That would make them so happy." Kate smiled and went to say something, but Ian ploughed on.

"Alex and Hannah and Uh Uh Uh. What sort of name is that? Uh Uh Uh?"

Kate laughed as she began rubbing cream into her forehead and cheeks and round her lips and on her chin. "Apollo... Zachary... Uriah?"

"I think I'd prefer Uh Uh Uh," he replied, then added, "hurry up!"

She smiled, putting cream on her neck, and wiping her hands before doing that tying-up thing with her hair. "Dominic... Nicholas... Benjamin... so many possibilities."

"Don't feel you have to list them all... hundreds of them probably... not now... just come to bed."

Kate laughed as she rubbed cream from a little pot into her hands and elbows. The last (rather hurried) thing. "Nathaniel... Orlando... Finnegan..."

She stood up and turned round and used her thumbs to lift the straps of her negligee up and off her shoulders. The negligee fell to her feet, and she stepped over it. "Finnegan... begin again?" she asked Ian.

He laughed and threw back the duvet. "I'll have a bloody good try," he thought, as he pulled her gently towards him.

27
BERNARD, DEAR
BERNARD

Ian had taken to noting down each evening, on the back of a postcard kept folded over in his back pocket, how Bernard had been that day.

Good, Bad or *50/50.*

Depending on whether Bernard had got through a whole day eating normally, without being sick and still wanting to walk; or not.

The young, pudgy-faced vet had told him at the last check-up a month or so ago that the growth was benign but growing steadily and Ian would know "when it was time" – time to bring Bernard in to be put to sleep, he had assumed. But Ian did not understand how he would know. As if by some instinct. Or perhaps Bernard would look long and meaningfully at him with his big brown eyes to indicate, "Yes, I'm ready now."

He did not think he could judge the moment. Did not want to do it too early when Bernard was still mostly well and happy. Nor leave it too late when Bernard might be suffering, on and on, without Ian noticing.

Ian knew how it would happen – it was on his mind so much. The growth would simply get larger and larger, pushing against and then pressing ever harder on Bernard's organs. Until he would not want to eat, would become listless; may even start urinating or defecating involuntarily.

But Ian did not want to wait that long. He wanted Bernard's last days to be happy-ish ones. So, he started keeping a daily record of how things were going.

He decided that when there were clearly more bad days than good, or there was a run of bad days, this would be the time to do it.

The vet had shown him, guided his hands and fingers into place so that he could feel the growth. "There," the vet had said. "Can you feel it?" and he had nodded politely, as he knew where it was anyway, having checked it now and then ever since the Yorkshire woman showed him where it was.

He had tried, when he had got home with Bernard, and regularly afterwards, to feel to see if the growth were any bigger than before. But he could never be sure. He thought maybe it was growing inwards, away from and out of reach of his fingers. And Bernard always gave him one of those long-suffering looks and he half-expected the dog to sigh and roll his eyes. So, after a while, he stopped and did not try again.

But he thought the growth must be getting bigger. The vet had said it might grow quickly or slowly. Could possibly stop for a while. A week. A month. Maybe longer. Or grow ever so fast. Even super-fast. As if, really, the vet did not know very much at all. Was most likely guessing. The only certainty being that it would eventually kill Bernard from the inside. And that Ian would somehow magically know before it got to that point.

Ian sat down in the chair by the window in the orangery. Just before he followed Kate upstairs to bed. He turned on the lamp next to him, fished the postcard out of his pocket, and reached for a stubby old pencil on the window ledge.

He licked the tip of the pencil and turned the postcard over. Then he wrote the day's date – Hannah's due date funnily enough – and added *Bad* next to it. He then glanced at Bernard over in his basket by the radiator. Bernard sat there looking back. He had watched Bernard for ages now. How he walked. The vet had said that, as the growth started pressing harder, Ian would notice it. He had assumed the vet meant the way in which Bernard walked or possibly sat down.

When he was a young child, he remembered staying with

his nan and grandpa one weekend; it must have been before his mother died as he did not see them much after that, and certainly not to stay over. He went to church on the Sunday with his grandpa, who played the organ there. They had walked up a steep hill. Then, afterwards, they had walked back down. Grandpa would stride ahead as though on a march and Ian struggled to keep up.

Then, at some time, his grandpa had an operation and, when Ian stayed again after that, he noticed Grandpa's walk was completely different. He no longer strode ahead but ambled along with a rolling gait. His nan had said it was Grandpa's cowboy walk. On reflection, Ian now suspected his truss was too tight. Anyway, Bernard still walked as he had always walked. Stiff-legged at the back. And not using his right back leg whenever he went up or down the stairs. And he seemed to have no problem sitting or lying down.

The changes were slower and more subtle than that. When he was well, he would always eat his food in the morning and the evening. Not necessarily immediately, but the bowls would be emptied by the end of the day. Then he'd sometimes leave one or the other. And Ian tried changing the food. Now and then, Bernard would leave his food altogether that day.

And he'd be sick. Every so often. As if something disagreed with him. And Ian kept feeding him chicken and rice and other plain foods that would not upset his stomach. But it was not often, just enough for it to be noticed. It could be something. Equally, it might be nothing.

And then he had sometimes stopped wanting to walk. Going out the front gate and hesitating after a few steps. Standing there, staring into the distance. Ian would say, "Come on, old boy!" but the dog would just not want to move at all. So, they would go back inside.

And these changes would happen at different times, occasionally they would take place together.

Often, they would come and go. Sometimes they would last

longer and then disappear. It was a blur really.

Ian looked down at the postcard and the notes for the past seven days – *Good, 50/50, Bad, 50/50, Bad, Bad, Bad*. And he realised what this now meant. He started crying and could not stop for ever such a long time.

***

Ian decided that he would give Bernard another day or two to see if he might have a sudden run of good days. But, as he sat at his desk the next morning with Bernard by his side, he noted that Bernard did not move, did not want to eat, and just lay there with his head on the edge of the basket looking at Ian. And Ian knew then that it was time.

He had telephoned the vets later that afternoon just before the surgery shut for the day and said he needed to bring in Bernard. To put him to, you know. He hesitated and choked on the word "sleep". The assistant, and he did not recognise her voice, did not seem to understand what he was saying so he blurted it all out in fits and starts and they agreed he would bring Bernard in at 8.40 the next day before the vets opened properly at 9.00. Ian paid in advance with a card as he knew he would struggle to do it, and make polite chit-chat, on the day.

That night – counting down the hours – was agony. Ian and Kate watched some historical programmes Kate liked on the television, Bernard in a basket by their feet. When they got up to go to bed, Kate lifted Bernard gently and, with Ian carrying the basket, they laid him at the end of their bed.

Not that Ian slept. Kate did, after a while; she had to, as she had a busy day at work tomorrow. They talked a little about Bernard before she went to sleep, and she kissed Ian on the cheek goodnight and said it would be too much for her to come to the vets in the morning. She was sorry.

And now he was here in the surgery on his own. Bernard by his feet. One last time. Ian stroked Bernard's silky ears.

He had been shown to a chair in the waiting room by a brisk, new assistant, the one he had spoken with on the telephone. She then disappeared behind the scenes.

And he watched the clock turn towards 8:40 and hoped nobody else would come in and want to talk, to pass the time of day.

Ian could hear a commotion behind the door of the vet's room. A man and a woman talking. Things being moved. Clanging. The door about to open.

He had not looked up on the internet exactly what putting a dog to sleep involved. Assumed an injection and then a fading away. He thought Bernard would need to lay on his side and was not sure if he would be agreeable to that. Even now he could be a stubborn little fellow.

Ian lifted Bernard up in his arms and held him there, his nose against the dog's soft ear. They sat there waiting.

And then the door was opened and the bald vet, the one Ian liked but had not seen for ages as he had been off sick, came out and waved Ian and Bernard through into the room. The brisk attendant was there, and he could see from her face that she was not as unemotional about it as he would have expected.

And Ian put Bernard on the examination table and the vet started talking, gently explaining what he was going to do, and inviting Ian to stroke Bernard one last time.

Ian stroked Bernard and wanted to say something to him, really rather meaningful, about the time they had spent together and what Bernard meant to him, his best pal. How much he loved him.

Instead, all he could think of to say out loud was "good boy", and he knew that if he tried to say even that he would break down in tears and he would be lost.

So, he just stroked Bernard's head and ears and down along his back and even his two front paws, where two black nails poked out from between the fur on his left one. And Ian wondered how he had never noticed them before.

Bernard sat up, as if to attention, waiting to be told what to do, and it was all Ian could do to hold himself together.

And then there was some banging and stomping outside in the waiting area and the door swung open, and Ian turned. Alex and Joe stood there, hot and sweaty from running to be there in time. Ian lowered his head as they went to either side of him with their hands on his shoulders. He found their presence unbearably moving.

It happened so fast. The vet injected Bernard and, as the little dog started to fall, the assistant wrapped a towel around him and laid him on his side on the examination table. The vet stepped forward and closed Bernard's eyes and then the vet and the assistant were gone through a side door leaving Ian, Alex and Joe with Bernard. Ian bent and kissed Bernard on his head. Alex stroked Bernard's side. Joe his leg and stubby tail. And none of them said – could say – anything as they stood there for the longest time.

Ian eventually moved again towards Bernard, kissing him on his head and then turned, opening the door and walking out, waving at the vet and the assistant in reception. And he was by the car, Alex and Joe coming up close behind. He fiddled with his keys. And dropped them. Then picked them up and clackety-clacked trying to get the key into the lock. Alex put his hand on Ian's shoulder and Joe reached to take the key. Ian stopped and turned and the three of them suddenly embraced. And then, finally, Alex pulled away and said, tearfully, "Got to go, Dad, drop Joe back at work," then he paused and laughed, "and take Hannah to hospital... Her waters have broken."

28
THE ARRIVAL OF
UH UH UH

With the benefit of hindsight – so easy to look back and see the ifs, buts and might-have-beens – there was a moment, an incident, where everything changed for Ian, although he would not have realised it at the time. It happened two days later, after Bernard was put to sleep in the morning and Pudding, now officially Joshua Charles Cartwright, Wilkerson to be, was born in the evening. At 21.52, to be precise. And weighing seven pounds, six ounces.

Over breakfast, Kate and Ian were talking about going round to Alex and Hannah's later that evening to meet Joshua for the first time. They'd meet outside at 18.00 and go in together, and then come home and have a fish and chip supper. They were talking in the orangery before Kate set off for work and Ian went upstairs to work at the desk in Joe's old bedroom. They were having a cup of tea and a warmed-through croissant each. And things were getting better between them. As they talked and reminisced and consoled each other about Bernard. Things weren't completely sorted, of course. But better. There was still a way to go; lots to do.

Ian's mobile phone beep-beeped, and he saw a message from Sarah. It began with the word *Help,* and he went to scroll on through it, but Kate was talking, and he felt he needed to be seen to be listening to what she was saying. But he knew this help message was a quietly serious one, as Sarah had never texted *Help* before. So, he quickly texted back a thumbs up and a heart to be encouraging.

"When we get there, don't say Joshua's ugly," Kate said.

"Well, I …"

"You did with Alex."

"Yes, but his face was all…"

"He'd just been born."

"And don't say he has a big forehead… or his ears stick out."

Kate paused and then went on. "Hannah will be very sensitive about the baby… all new mothers are… and she'll pick up on anything you say that's less than 100 per cent positive… even if you think you're being funny."

He sighed. "As if…"

Kate continued with her spoken-out-loud thoughts. "So don't call Joshua… Slabhead… or Pinocchio… or a fat lump… most babies are chubby… or Ratfink."

He said, "I'll just smile vaguely."

Kate looked at him. "Don't do that, you'll frighten Hannah. Just try to… don't go over the top… or be all quiet like you're sulking because no one's paying enough attention to you… just try to be somewhere in the middle. Be friendly with everyone. Try to be normal. As normal as you can be."

Ian nodded in agreement, distracted by the thought of the *Help* message from Sarah on his phone. He fiddled with his phone ready to read the full message. But he hesitated a moment as Kate finished eating and drinking. To be polite.

Then, as she went to get up to pick up her mug and plate, and get ready for work, the doorbell ting-a-ling-a-linged. Ian, without thinking, went to answer it, leaving his empty cup and half-eaten croissant on a plate and his mobile phone on the armrest.

The postman was at the door. With a parcel that he could not leave on the doorstep, as it needed to be signed for. And the postman did not have a pen… blah, blah, blah… as he had offered it to someone at the last house he had visited and that person… blah, blah, blah… had used it and it had run out of ink. And Ian smiled and grimaced and laughed and nodded at approximately the right moments. And then went into the kitchen for a pen where he expected to see Kate hurrying to leave for work, but didn't, and found a pen in a pot on the windowsill and signed the postman's card and gave him the pen to keep. Yes, no, really. And then, finally, he went back into the orangery.

Kate had gone, was busying about upstairs getting ready for work, and she had taken his cup and his half-eaten croissant and plate away. And his phone had slipped off the armrest and was down by the side of the cushion. He picked it up and saw the message from Sarah was already there, waiting to be read. *Help. My birthday party. The Café. 21.00. Saturday next week. Stay the night? Love Sarah xx.*

He sat there, thinking about this, and that his thumbs up and heart were a sufficient reply, when he heard the front door being opened and then shut with a bang; the wind having caught it. He walked to the front door to wave and shout a goodbye to Kate. But, by the time he got there, she was already driving away.

***

Ian sat in his car, alongside a long brick wall in a road just off Brightwell Close, where Alex and Hannah and Baby Joshua lived in their end-of-terrace home. He was full of emotions – happy, excited and, more than anything else, nervous – that he would say or do something wrong. It was strange – he did not feel like a grandfather... he knew he could not say that out loud to anyone... but felt sure that when he saw and held Joshua in his arms all those feelings would come rushing in.

He checked the clock on the car's dashboard again. 18.21. Kate must be running late. He would sit and watch in case Hannah's parents turned up; he was not sure what he would do if they did. He knew he and Kate would have to go in and be polite in the face of their smothering attentiveness, but he hoped they could meet Joshua for the first time on their own.

He had texted and called Kate several times during the day to see who was bringing what, but her mobile phone was switched off or dead; whatever. So, on the seat next to him, just in case, he had a bunch of mixed flowers for Hannah, a bottle of Jack Daniels for Alex, and a recently bought online and re-written baby booklet for Joshua. He thought about looking through it whilst he waited but knew that if he did, the openness of his emotions would worry him, and he might decide to leave it behind.

And then Kate was there in her car, pulling up in front of him. She was out of the car straight away, opening the boot and taking out all sorts of goodies; flowers and balloons and brightly coloured bags and a box and, you know, things you could put up on the walls; banners and stuff.

Ian left the flowers and the bottle of Jack Daniels on the seat. They looked rather lame – last-minute-visit-to-the-supermarket lame – next to Kate's extravaganza of gifts. He hesitated, his hand on the baby booklet, not sure whether to take that in or not.

Kate was already away and crossing the road and up the path to the house. So much excitement! Ian grabbed the baby booklet, got out of the car and ran after her. As he came up close to her on the path, to put his arm around her, Alex opened the front door and welcomed them in.

Hannah was sitting there on the sofa in the living room, tired and exhausted and beaming with pride, in a fluffy pink dressing gown and white fluffy slippers. She looked beautiful, thought Ian. And she was holding Joshua, wearing a white little thing, a matching top and bottom whatsit. There was a small towel by his head. "That was well-timed," Hannah said, smiling at them. "I've just finished feeding him." And she lifted the baby up and he promptly drooled milk all over her shoulder.

Ian and Kate just stood there, side by side, enthralled, neither of them knowing quite what to say. And then Alex, who had nipped into the kitchen, came back with a tray with cans of drinks and glasses and cupcakes and biscuits. He put it on the battered old coffee table and went to hug Kate. There was a moment or two's shimmy-shammying as Kate went to give him the gifts and he moved this way and that and put them on the sofa next to Hannah. Then came back for a proper hug with Kate and the usual pat-punch on the shoulder for Ian.

And Ian and Kate sat in the two armchairs either side of the sofa and watched as Alex and Hannah and Joshua oohed and aahed over the card and gifts (well, Alex and Hannah really). Alex put the card on the mantelpiece above the fireplace along with half a dozen others already there. Then he dashed into the kitchen and rummaged about in a drawer and came back with a lump of blu-tack which he used to put up the *Welcome Baby* banner on the wall. And Hannah opened the gaily-covered box full of cardigans and bootees and bibs, an almost endless stream of all sorts of lovely things.

Hannah passed Joshua to Kate to hold and there was a lot of have you got him and are you comfortable… and is Joshua comfortable? And Ian piped up to say, "support his head," and Kate gave him such a look as if to answer, "I know!" that he sat there quietly in the chair opposite and just watched, trying to see the baby's face.

They stayed like that for ages, all oohing and cooing over the baby, and feeling happy and contented just being in the moment. And Hannah and Alex talked about the birth. How it seemed to take forever – hours and hours – between the waters breaking and going into the delivery room. And how Hannah screamed and screamed said Alex – don't say it like that, replied Hannah, I wasn't that bad – and how the baby suddenly plopped out and looked kind of surprised. And, as they twittered on (and on), Ian thought he would ask if he could hold the baby. He suddenly wanted to do that very much.

But the doorbell rang as he was thinking what to say, and Alex went to the door and opened it. Ian turned, expecting to

341

see Hannah's ghastly family barging through to take charge, but in came Beth and Glenn and Joe and Yasmin, all laughing and joking (quietly, the baby is asleep!) with cards and presents galore. And they all sat around on the carpet, each of them getting as close to Kate and the baby as they could (the baby really) whilst Hannah and Alex opened the presents and it was all just, well, really rather wonderful.

All too soon, with Hannah looking tired and the baby needing to sleep, Alex was gently getting them all up and ready to say goodbye and we'll come and see you all in the coming days. And so it seemed to Ian, everyone had held or touched Joshua, even matter-of-fact Glenn, and big gruff Joe. Ian was the only one who hadn't had a chance to do either. He watched as Alex put Joshua carefully into his buggy over by the radiator, pulling a little knitted blanket over him.

With everyone leaving, Hannah and Kate had slipped into the kitchen and so Ian, before he went, popped his head around the door and said to Kate, "I'll go ahead and get fish and chips, see you at home." But Kate seemed to be in deep conversation with Hannah – motherly talk about breast-feeding and... front bottom stuff most probably – so she barely glanced up at him. "See you later!" he said.

And then, with Alex at the door seeing everyone off, Ian was alone in the living room with Joshua in his buggy. Ian went across and looked down at the sleeping baby boy. His grandson. Their first grandchild. Joshua Charles. And he ran his little finger gently along Joshua's cheek, marvelling at his, what was it, not booty... or bottom... beauty, yes, that was it. He took the baby booklet and tucked it by the side of the baby. Then leaned in close and whispered, "I love you, baby Joshua. Your old grandpa loves you."

And that's how it ended.

Or should have ended.

With everyone living happily ever after.

Ian went back and forth from the kitchen to the orangery, laying out placemats and crockery and knives and forks and glasses and a jug of water and bread and butter and a hefty squirt of tomato ketchup into a, you know, a white ceramic thing.

Brought the fish and chips – regular cod and chips twice – out and onto the plates. He kept them in their newspaper wrappings so they'd stay warm until Kate arrived back any minute.

He switched all the lights on and off and then one or two of the lamps back on again. So it looked just so. Then went to the kitchen and checked all around in case he had missed anything. Sat down at the table in the orangery and waited.

Ian decided, straight away, that he should have a bottle of wine ready. He went into the kitchen, found and opened a bottle of something-or-other rosé, picked up two wine glasses, and went back to the orangery.

Ian checked his watch. He did not know what time he had left Alex and Hannah's. But it must be more than 45 minutes. And Kate was just saying bye-bye to Hannah as he left. He assumed she'd be 10 or 20 minutes, back before him most likely.

And then he glanced and saw on the table in front of him, propped up by the artificial flower arrangement of roses and whatnots, a small, rectangular white envelope with *Ian* on the front of it in Kate's neat and careful handwriting.

There have been times when life – everything – you – has been hell.
I could have left you once. I met a man at work. He wanted us to start a new life together.
I stayed with you all these years, especially after Adam, because I loved you and all we had together – our children, our home, our life.
I know what happened with that woman in Hunstanton and I forgave you for it. I have, after all, done the same to you.

I thought we had, since you came back, put everything behind us and things might be getting back to how they used to be.

I saw your mobile phone message to that woman this morning. So many messages since you came home. You have not finished with her. You are only just beginning.

How could you?

Ian sat and read the letter two, three, four times. He turned the letter over as if expecting to see something else written on the back. Maybe *Lol* or *April Fool's!* even though that was still five months away.

He tried to make sense of what she had written. That she had met someone at work. Had had an affair. Thought about leaving him. He could not believe it was true.

And that she had scrolled and read his messages, so many of them with their kisses and their hearts and that final message from Sarah ending *Stay the night?* And his instinctive thumbs up and heart reply.

He stood and walked upstairs to the landing where he could see out of the big arched window and to the long road between the greens of the golf course and on to Felixstowe and beyond.

And he wondered when − if − he would see the front lights of her car appear, bobbing and weaving in and out of sight along the road as she came back home, or whether he should leave the house now and walk away, imagining his old pal Bernard by his side.

THE END

ABOUT THE AUTHOR

Iain Maitland is the author of the mental health memoirs *Dear Michael, Love Dad* and *Out of The Madhouse* (co-written with Michael Maitland). These are available on audio, too, read by Michael Simkins and Iain and Michael Maitland respectively.

He is also an Ambassador for the teenage mental health charity Stem 4, at stem4.org.uk. He regularly shares the family's story at conferences, talks and on webinars.

Iain has written two crime thrillers, *The Scribbler* and *The Wickham Market Murder*, and is currently writing a series of psych thrillers, including *The Girl Downstairs* and the Amazon Best-Seller *The Perfect Husband*.

You can find out more about Iain Maitland at his website, IainMaitland.net and via Twitter at twitter.com/iainmaitland Please feel free to get in touch.

AUTHOR NOTES

I've been a full-time novelist since 2016 and always write a few words at the end of each novel – to thank you for reading it and to answer the questions I think you might have. First things first, the obvious questions for this semi-autobiographical story.

Am I, Iain, and the Ian in the novel, one and the same?

Is my old pal Bernard (2004-2018) the Bernard in the novel?

Let me tell you a little about my background so you can decide for yourself.

Back in 2015, when I was a year or two younger than Ian, I'd spent 30 years as a freelance journalist, writing about business and finance and property. By that point, I'd had enough of forward contracts and exchange rates and decided I'd become a full-time author instead. So I did.

I've been with my wife Tracey since schooldays back in the late 1970s. We live in a nice home near the sea in Felixstowe in Suffolk and have three children, Michael, Sophie and Adam and, in 2015, Bernard the dog too. So, by and large, much like Ian.

Back in 2007, Michael went to university and experienced anxiety and depression and, eventually, anorexia before spending five months in The Priory. He then, a while later, came home and we thought we'd lose him – that he would take his own life. Desperate times for Michael – for all of us really.

So, the first two books I wrote were therapeutic in many

ways. *Dear Michael, Love Dad* told the family story and *Out of The Madhouse* (written with Michael) looked at what happened from Michael's viewpoint. The memoirs were picked up and featured across the national media; allowing us to share the story with many parents and children who might be where we were all those years ago.

Michael and I were especially proud to be asked to be Ambassadors for the teenage mental health charity, Stem4, going into schools and colleges to talk about mental health issues. We are still so proud to be Ambassadors to this day. It's a wonderful charity. Please have a Google and check it out.

I am most proud of Michael – the proudest dad in the world. I recall receiving a text telling me he had been taken to hospital. We expected him to die that night. I remember going to see him in hospital, slumped in a wheelchair, utterly broken. And then a visit to The Priory; face to face with real-life horror. And, of course, there was that night he came home to die.

Yet here he is today, strong, well and healthy; physically and mentally. Married to Georgia. A beautiful son, Jonah. Michael works as a tattooist in Felixstowe. He has turned his life around. If you or someone you know is in the depths of despair, try to get through today. Then tomorrow. And so on, one day at a time. There will be happier times ahead if you can just hang on in there.

After the two memoirs, I moved on, thinking that was that. I've been writing thrillers ever since, including *Mr Todd's Reckoning* which was to be a six-part TV series until, tragically, our lead, the lovely Paul Ritter, passed away and no one could face taking it forwards. And, more recently, *The Perfect Husband*, which was an Amazon Best-Seller; what a thrill that was.

Dear Michael, Love Dad and *Out of The Madhouse* never really went away though. There was an audio of *Dear Michael, Love Dad* read by the brilliant actor, Michael Simkins. Michael (Maitland) and I were asked to record the audio of *Out of The Madhouse*. And we still do talks for Stem4. And I'm always being asked about them whenever I am interviewed in the media. I suspect they will always be around one way or another. And I'm delighted with that.

Lots and lots of people have asked what happened afterwards – how are Michael and I and the family these days? So, I'd been thinking about coming back to it all for a while even though the answer is not much really; we've just been rolling along happily. I really wanted to write about Bernard. And Tracey and I had a day out in Hunstanton a summer or two ago and I stood on the clifftops there and so many thoughts swirled around my head.

And so, I decided to write this semi-autobiographical novel which was first called *Pudding* and then *The Walker* and, finally, *The Old Man, His Dog & Their Longest Journey*. It could kind of be the last book in a trilogy of mental health memoirs or, if this is well received, it could be the first of a new trilogy – I certainly have a couple more stories inside me good to go.

I wanted the underlying cause of the journey to be something shattering in the way that Michael's troubles had ripped through our own family. But I did not want to re-hash Michael's story, partly because some people, with little or no knowledge of mental health, could not understand what triggered Michael's downfall. There had to be trauma or abuse or some terrible something, surely? There wasn't. Michael is the first to say he had the happiest childhood. Stuff just happens sometimes.

So, I made the cause the death of his youngest son. I have not lost a son – an almost unimaginable horror – but I drew on my experiences with Michael and traumas and tragedies amongst our wider family. For example, my nan and grandpa lost their son, Roger, at a young age and I have clear memories of how that unfolded throughout their lives. Even 30 years on from his death, my grandpa would still call me "Roger" without thinking now and then. Although this thread is fiction, I have tried to write with sensitivity.

So, going back to answer those initial questions for you.

Iain/Ian? Kind of – I'd say it's probably about 50/50. Maybe more. I had not realised until after I had finished the novel that Ian had his breakdown at the same sort of age that I threw everything up to become a full-time author. Perhaps there is more of me in Ian than I first thought.

Bernard/Bernard – much closer, although the real Bernard was mad about tennis balls. I did not want Ian to take a ball with him on the walk or write a story about a man throwing a ball for his dog 1,000 times. The tennis balls had to be left behind.

And finally, which members of my real family are in the novel? Kate and Yasmin are completely fictitious characters. Alex, Beth and Joe are, ah, "inspired" by Michael, Sophie and Adam. Bethany is most like the incomparable Sophie when she was younger. Glenn and Hannah are a little like Glyn and Georgia; just a touch… or maybe more. What they do have in common is that my family are just as marvellous as they are in the novel.

Thank you for reading *The Old Man, His Dog & Their Longest Journey* – do get in touch if you'd like to do so.

Iain
Iain Maitland
April 2023

ACKNOWLEDGEMENTS

Bringing a novel from my mind to your Kindle or paperback involves a lot of teamwork in between.

I'd like to thank all at Vellum Publishing especially; Jack, for reading the MS and spotting its potential; Alex, for giving it the green-light; Isobel, for line-editing; Sophie, for doing the marketing; and Louise, for co-ordinating all of us. It's been a joy.

Outside of Vellum Publishing, I'd like to thank Amy Pennington for a fabulous cover and Georgia (Maitland) for her wonderful sketches both on the cover and throughout the book. You took it to a higher level. And Michael (Maitland) for the two cartoons of me.

Michael Simkins and Charlie Mortimer were generous both to read the MS and to offer kind words for us to put on the cover. Thank you both so much.

I'd also like to thank my family for inspiring me to write this novel; my wife, Tracey, my three children, Michael, Sophie, and Adam, and their partners, Georgia, Glyn, and Sophie. And my gorgeous grandchildren, Jonah and Halley.

Finally, to everyone who has supported me along the way – former publishers, literary agents, those who have bought my novels, left positive reviews on social media, or just said a nice word or two somewhere down the line – thank you very much.

And a PS. Thanks to Bernard (2004-2018) too, of course. My best pal.

BV - #0049 - 250523 - C0 - 198/129/21 - PB - 9781915608079 - Matt Lamination